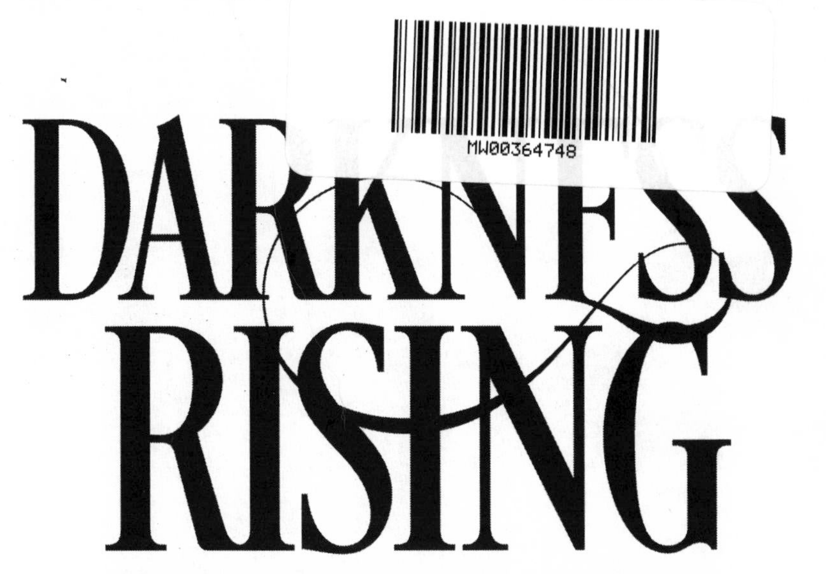

DARKNESS RISING

DISCIPLES OF THE HORNED ONE TRILOGY VOLUME ONE

JAMES E. WISHER

James E. Wisher

The Disciples of the Horned One Trilogy:

Darkness Rising

Raging Sea and Trembling Earth

Harvest of Souls

Edited by: Janie Linn Dullard

Cover Art by: Fiona Jayde

Sand Hill Publishing 713161.1

ISBN 13: 978-1-945763-01-4

Book One

The Family Disappointment

Chapter 1

The sun shone down through a cloudless sky, bathing the training yard in warmth. Damien St. Cloud wanted to turn his face up to the light and let the sun warm him, but that would be a breach of protocol and the last thing he needed was to get yelled at for something so simple. There were plenty of other things for the masters to yell at him about.

He took a deep breath, enjoying the sweet scent of spring blossoms blowing in over the wall. He stood at the end of a line of thirty-six other boys and girls, all thirteen years old and third-year students at The Citadel, the kingdom's training school for warlords.

Whoosh crack!

Damien managed not to wince when the master brought a wooden training sword down on the collar of the first boy in line. The Master of Fitness was a great bear of a man with huge muscles made even more massive by the infusion of soul force. He wore a blue tunic trimmed in silver with matching pants, the same as all the students, the only difference a silver shield pinned on his broad chest that marked him as a master of The Citadel.

The sword snapped in half, the broken-off chunk flying across the yard, kicking up dust when it hit the dry dirt of the yard. The student never flinched or cried out; he'd mastered his soul force enough to make his bones as hard as steel and his skin tougher than leather. Strengthening the body was one of the most basic skills a warlord learned during his training at The Citadel. All the third years could do it—all except Damien.

Whoosh crack!

The next student in line, a fit girl named Tenna, took the blow as stoically as the first. She had short blond hair and a mean streak. Tenna liked to punch Damien whenever she got close to him, which was as seldom as he could manage. Tougher than most of the boys, she could take on anyone and usually win.

Back when they were first years, before anyone had use of their soul force, Damien had been the best student in his class. He could take anyone, hell any two of his fellow students, in a fight, barehanded or with practice weapons. But now, everyone else had mastered the basics of using their soul force except Damien, leaving him the weakest student in the class. He'd only made it through his second-year graduation tests because of his exceptional skills and the fact that none of the tests required him to use soul force to complete them. Not this year. This year he had to demonstrate the ability to toughen his body enough to take a blow on the collar without getting hurt.

Whoosh crack!

Another student, a giant idiot of a boy named Stan, who wouldn't know decent technique if Damien drove it through his stomach, took the blow without batting an eye. Stan might be an idiot, but he was better than anyone at strengthening his body.

Damien turned his focus inward, to the great, seething mass of power in his core. For as long as he could remember everyone had told him he had the greatest soul force in his generation; fat lot of good that did him. He tried to coax the power out and run it along his bones, wrapping them in a matrix of power that would make them unbreakable. The masters all said this was the simplest technique and any third year and most second years should be able to do it with no trouble.

Damien focused all his mental energy on moving the power through his body. He'd spent countless hours studying and meditating, trying to get the power to obey his commands.

Nothing.

His power just sat there, mocking him. So much power he should be able to smash a hole through The Citadel wall with his bare hands and he couldn't coax so much as a flicker of movement out of it.

At last, the master stood in front of Damien, a final wooden sword clenched in his massive right fist. All down the line, every eye focused on him. The master raised an eyebrow a fraction. Damien gave an equally minute shake of his head. The master closed his eyes and heaved a sigh. Damien's collarbone was about to get broken. Again.

He held no ill will toward the master; he was only doing his job. The failure lay with Damien and no other.

The wooden sword went up over the master's head. Damien tensed, determined not to pass out this time. The sword came down. At the instant of impact, Damien let his knees buckle to absorb some of the force.

It didn't help.

Bone snapped and pain raced through his body. His vision swam. He clenched his jaw to hold in a scream of pain. Despite his best efforts, a groan escaped his lips. He didn't collapse this time, didn't tumble to the ground unconscious and wake up in the healer's quarters. He salvaged some pride from that.

Slowly, painfully, Damien climbed back to his feet, left arm useless at his side. The master held up the unbroken sword. "Fail."

He didn't know who laughed first, but that first chuckle was joined by another and another, soon his whole class was laughing at him. Damien didn't say a word, didn't dare, fearing if he opened his mouth a scream would erupt.

So much for the army's famous motto: "For the person beside you." Damien believed in that motto. He'd heard it his whole life. His classmates either didn't believe in it or didn't consider him a comrade. Either way, he just stood there, left arm hanging limp at his side, and waited for the master to give him permission to go to the healer.

The master shook his head. "Go on."

Damien nodded an acknowledgement, a proper bow beyond him at the moment. He walked across the yard, his boots scuffing through the dirt, toward the towering stone fortress that gave The Citadel its name. It served as a school and home for both the students and the masters and their families.

Like all the fortresses in the kingdom, sorcerers had built The Citadel out of dark gray granite, quarried in the northern mountains. The blocks were transported south, then fused together to make a single, solid piece of stone.

The main door stood open during daylight hours, thank all the angels in Heaven, so Damien didn't have to wrestle the giant oak-and-iron thing open with one hand. Beyond the door, the entrance hall was empty, no surprise given the early hour.

Straight ahead, a flight of stairs led to the second-floor living quarters. On either side lay passages deeper into The Citadel. Damien eased his way down the right-hand hall. He knew the way to the healer's quarters almost as well as he knew the way to the family suite upstairs.

The first door on the right led to the servants' barracks. He passed it and went to the first door on the left. It was open and inside, holding a healing elixir and wearing a familiar, sad smile, stood Miss Ella, The Citadel's healer.

Damien and Miss Ella had spent a great deal of time together since he began his training. She wore her usual white healer's robe, a red cross embroidered over her heart, her gray hair up in a bun. Behind her sat six empty cots separated by curtains. A locked chest against the far wall held all her healing supplies, not that she needed many. Warlords could heal themselves from almost any injury with soul force, so besides looking after the new students and Damien, Miss Ella had little to do. Maybe she was so nice to him because he provided her with job security.

"I figured you'd be along." The wrinkles around her blue eyes crinkled in concern. "How bad was it?"

Damien caught himself before he shrugged. "I didn't pass out this time."

She handed Damien the vial filled with red, bubbling liquid. "Drink up, then I'll adjust the bone."

He tossed back the potion. The strong peppermint flavor burned his throat a little. Damien didn't care. The instant the healing elixir touched his mouth, the raging pain in his shoulder cooled to a dull ache. Whichever sorcerer had enchanted the potion, Damien owed him a thank you.

Miss Ella gave him no chance to savor the loss of pain. She put one hand on his neck and the other on his shoulder and guided his collarbone into the proper position. When the broken ends of bone touched, they vibrated as they knit back together. No matter how many times it happened, Damien never got used to feeling his body heal.

Damien sighed, the pain nearly gone. "Thanks, Miss Ella."

She waved a hand, her face stern. "You know the drill. No strenuous activity for a day while the bones finish healing. Anything doesn't feel right, come see me."

"Yes, ma'am. Dad's not going to be very happy with me failing again."

Miss Ella's lips turned down. "That man expects too much from you. You try your best, no one can ask more than that. He gives you any grief, you send him to me. Master of The Citadel or not, I'll set him straight."

She sounded so fierce, Damien thought she might daunt the great Fredric St. Cloud, King's Champion and Master of The Citadel. But more than likely, his father would ignore her, the same way he did everyone who said something he didn't want to hear. "Guess I'll head home and get a nap."

"Make sure you drink a couple glasses of milk at lunch, you need the minerals to help the bones heal."

"Yes, ma'am." He bowed to her and left the infirmary.

Damien retraced his steps back to the staircase and went up to the second floor. Well away from the public and student areas of the school sat the quarters assigned to the masters and their families. Damien, his sister and his father lived together in the largest suite: one of the few perks of being the son of the Master of The Citadel. On the downside, it was all the way at the end of the hall. That made it quiet, but when every step jarred his healing shoulder, quiet wasn't as important as proximity.

He pushed the unlocked door open—no one would be stupid enough to mess with Dad's room—and went in. He'd barely shut the door behind him when the mental voice of Lizzenwar, his father's demon-possessed sword, appeared in his head.

You're hurt again.

Damien smiled at Lizzy's concern. She hung over their little fireplace in her lacquered black scabbard. If Dad hadn't taken her today, he must be training with the fifth years. Damien walked between the couch and Dad's favorite ragged, overstuffed chair to the fireplace and ran his index finger along the cool, smooth scabbard. Lizzy's mental shiver tickled his brain. He didn't know if she actually felt it when he touched her, but she liked to pretend.

"It's just a broken collarbone. Miss Ella patched me up."

That's the third time this year. How many times are they going to hurt you?

Damien sprawled on the couch, kicked his shoes off, and closed his eyes. An instant later, he floated in a star-filled night sky. Lizzy flew beside him, black-feathered wings spread, tail lashing behind her, and naked as a newborn. Damien smiled. She liked to try to shock him by appearing nude, but she'd done it so many times, he hardly twitched. Not that Lizzy wasn't worthy of a great reaction. She had a perfect, voluptuous figure, smooth pale skin, bright red lips and smoldering red eyes. She was easily the most beautiful woman he'd ever seen. The fact that she was a mental projection didn't bother him in the least. When she brought his consciousness into her psychic world, they were both real.

"I get one more chance to pass the test of endurance. If I fail it again, I can't advance to fourth-year studies and will have to repeat the third year. I can't see much point. If I haven't accessed my power by now, what are the chances another year will make any difference?"

"None, I'm afraid." She had a husky, sultry voice that oozed sex. Centuries ago, before her first lover bound her soul to the sword rather than let it return to Hell, Lizzy had been a lust demon, her purpose to seduce and corrupt mortal sorcerers. He suspected she was really good at it. "What will you do?" she asked.

Damien shrugged. In this world, his shoulder caused him no pain. "What can I do? I'll train hard and hope something jars my power loose. If I fail, I'll be back in three months with another broken collarbone."

The air around Lizzy shimmered and she cloaked herself in sheer black silks. She stuck out her bottom lip. "Don't say that. It kills me a little every time you come home hurt. Maybe if you spoke to Fredric, you could convince him this isn't the right path for you."

Damien laughed. “Dad decided this was the right path for me ten seconds after I was born and Mom died. I have to become a great warrior to make her death mean something. If I fail or quit, then she died for nothing. If I tried to walk away, I think Dad might kill me.”

Lizzy flew over and hugged him, her wings wrapped around him. She felt so warm and soft and real. He closed his eyes and breathed in the spicy, cinnamon scent of her hair. “I wish I could stay in this world with you.”

She drifted back. “You know you can’t. Human souls can’t be bound to objects like demons. Your place is out in the real world. But you can visit me as often as you like.”

She lashed her wings and raced through the infinite night sky. With a thought, Damien flew after her. In this place, anything he imagined became possible. He chased her and they played tag through the sky. For a few minutes, he forgot about the test, his father, and everything else beyond Lizzy’s mental world. He loved her for that gift, among many others.

Lizzy stopped and hovered in the sky, her head cocked slightly as if listening to something beyond his hearing. Damien stopped beside her. “What is it?”

“Your sister’s coming. I’m afraid our play time is over.” She sounded as disappointed as he felt.

Damien kissed her, savoring the softness of her lips. “I love you.”

He blinked, and found himself back in his physical body, lying on the couch, shoulder aching, and wishing he could go back to the only place he was ever really happy.

He shook that depressing thought out of his head a moment before the door opened and a tall, stunning girl with long, flowing blond hair, a slim build and a uniform just like his, rushed through. His sister Jennifer kicked her shoes off next his and sat on the couch beside his feet.

“I heard about the test. Are you okay?”

“Yeah, nothing I haven’t dealt with before. Dad’s going to be pissed when he finds out.”

Jen grinned. “Also something you’ve dealt with before. What happened?”

"Nothing, that's the problem. No matter what I try I just can't get the power to respond." He ground his teeth. "What's wrong with me?"

She squeezed his knee. "Nothing. You'll make it work eventually."

The door slammed open. Damien didn't have to look to know his father stood there, scowling. "Another failure, boy."

Damien sat up and peaked over the back of the couch. Sure enough, Dad stood in the doorway glowering, shaved head red with anger, his uniform flawless, his commandant's gold shield gleaming. If he got any madder steam would probably shoot out his ears. "Yes, sir."

"You're a disgrace." He stepped into the room and slammed the door closed. "A disgrace to me, your sister, your mother's memory, and the name St. Cloud."

Damien winced at the barrage, but held his peace. What could he say? If Dad measured his worth by his ability as a warlord, he certainly was a disgrace.

"On your feet when I'm speaking to you!"

Damien jumped up and clasped his hands behind his back at parade rest. "Sir?"

"I've had enough of you embarrassing me. One more failure and you're done. The Citadel is a school for warlords. Weaklings have no place here."

Damien blinked. Was his father threatening to expel him? For another student that would be bad enough, but he could always go back home to a normal life. But Damien didn't just study at The Citadel, it was his home. Maybe it wasn't much of one, but he had nowhere else to go.

Chapter 2

Damien leaned on the table in the little kitchen in their quarters and nibbled on a slice of bread covered with blueberry jam. The normally sweet jam seemed bitter this morning. He hadn't slept much last night. After his father's pronouncement Damien had thought of little else. Jen and Lizzy both tried to convince him Dad didn't mean it, but after seeing the disgust in his face Damien knew he did. Barring a miracle Damien would be homeless in a few months.

He flexed his shoulder; the pain had vanished overnight, but it still felt a little stiff. His class had sword drills this afternoon and he felt good enough to join in, though he'd have to sit out morning calisthenics or face Miss Ella's wrath. From behind the door to his sister's room came the sound of hard-soled shoes on stone. Damien covered a second slice of bread with jam and poured a glass of milk. Jen appeared in a swirl of blond hair. He handed Jen her breakfast and they ate for a while in silence.

Halfway through her bread Jen said, "I heard you tossing and turning last night. Did you get any sleep?"

Damien shrugged and washed the last of his breakfast down with a swallow of milk. "Not much. Busy mind, you know?"

"I'm sure he didn't mean it, Damien. Dad would never kick you out. He was just upset."

Damien washed, dried, and put away his dishes. "He didn't come home until early this morning and stayed just long enough to grab Lizzy. He can't even stand to be in the same room with me. I think he meant every word."

"Try not to worry about it. Walk with me to strategy class?"

"Sure."

They left their quarters and went downstairs. Students from all years milled around the entry hall, talking, arguing and flirting. Every boy and many of the girls turned their heads to stare when Jen walked down the stairs, the boys in open awe and the girls with a combination of annoyance and jealousy. She ignored them all with her usual cool indifference. No one gave Damien so much as a second glance. Walking with Jen he never had to worry about getting too much attention.

They turned down the left-hand hall towards the strategy room. Damien had a class there once a week, though they only covered basic, small-scale stuff. He loved strategy class. Since it didn't require soul force he excelled at it.

Jen stopped halfway down the hall. "Damn it! I forgot my paper. I'll be right back." She turned and ran back down the hall about three times as fast as a normal person. She must have pushed soul force into her legs to enhance her speed. He shook his head as she disappeared around the corner. Just once he'd like to run that fast.

"Well, well, well."

Damien turned to find a pair of fourth-year students ambling his way, soul-force-enhanced muscles straining against their uniforms. The tall blond with close-cropped hair was Dirk and the shorter bald one his idiot cousin Donk. Now would be a good time to be able to run like his sister.

"Our favorite punching bag, out and about without his big sister to protect him," Dirk said, prompting an evil chuckle from his cousin. "Word is you failed your endurance test again."

"What's it to you?"

Dirk's lips curled into an ugly sneer. "Tsk, tsk, you should show your seniors more respect. Perhaps we can give you some practice toughening up. What do you say, Donk?"

Donk chuckled again and cracked his knuckles. Damien grimaced. This could get ugly in a hurry. "Don't you two have anything better to do than bother me?"

The two bullies shared a look then turned back to him. "Not just now. We need our morning workout and you're it."

Damien brought his fists up in a futile gesture. He had no chance of beating them one on one much less together and judging by their grins, Dirk and Donk knew it.

They lunged for him. Damien ducked and shot between Donk's legs. He scrambled away then spun to face them. The older boys weren't using any speed enhancements, which was the only reason Damien managed that move.

"Slippery, ain't he?" Donk said.

"Indeed. Shall we try again, cousin?"

Dirk blurred and before he could react Damien slammed into the wall, Dirk's fist snarled in his uniform. His captor leaned forward. "A weakling like you didn't think you could get away from us, did you?"

Damien flicked a glance down the hall and grinned. "I wasn't trying to escape. I was trying to delay you."

Dirk frowned as he tried to understand. "Why?"

Damien nodded back toward the entry hall. Dirk turned his head just in time to catch Jen's fist with his face. Dirk flew down the hall, bounced twice, and crashed to a halt when he reached the far wall. Damien straightened his uniform. "That's why."

Jen turned her furious gaze on Donk. Dim as he was, Donk had brains enough to make himself scarce. He ran to collect his cousin as fast as his soul-force-enhanced legs could carry him. When they'd gone Jen relaxed. "You okay?"

Damien nodded. "I figured you'd be back in a hurry. Funny, they didn't seem so interested in fighting two on two."

Jen snorted. "Those two aren't interested in anything resembling a fair fight. Are you good to go to training on your own?"

"Sure. I doubt those two will bother me for a while."

Jen scowled. "If they do I won't go so easy on them."

Chapter 3

Fredric watched the gold griffin circling in the bright noon sun. It was hot again today, too hot for this early in the year. If they didn't get some rain soon the crops would wither in the fields. He stood just inside the great granite wall that surrounded The Citadel grounds, next to the open space—nothing more than a patch of dirt really—they'd set aside for visiting sorcerers. Far from the fortress and training grounds, sorcerers were able to arrive with a minimum of disruption. That suited Fredric as he despised anything that interrupted the smooth operation of his school.

Master Shen's griffin got lower with each circle. As sorcerers went he was a good one. They fought together during the last northern invasion. He both liked and respected the man, one of the few sorcerers whose company he enjoyed. Master Shen had a case of healing potions for the infirmary, luckily for his incompetent excuse for a son. Why couldn't the boy be more like his sister?

Damien works harder than any two students in The Citadel. He's kind, courteous, and has more pure skill than men twice his age. You're far too hard on him.

Fredric scowled, not appreciating having his sword commenting on his thoughts. That was the price you paid for having a demon living in your weapon. "You're always making excuses for him. If he's trying so damn hard, why can't he do what he needs to?"

I don't know, but threatening to kick him out of the only home he's ever had is hardly likely to improve his focus. He didn't get more than a couple hours' sleep last night.

"I'm desperate. The masters have tried every trick in the book to coax Damien's power out and they've all failed. Perhaps the fear of losing everything will force him to break through whatever's holding him back." The griffin landed in the dry patch of dirt, kicking up a cloud of dust. "Now be silent. I have to deal with the sorcerer."

Master Shen hopped off the griffin and waved a hand. The great golden beast vanished. Fredric shook his head. He'd never get used to sorcerers. Creating something out of nothing wasn't natural. Master Shen wore loose-fitting gray trousers and a matching tunic. His long dark hair hung in a tail that reached down to the middle of his back. That'd make a handy place for an enemy to grab and yank his head off. Over his shoulder the sorcerer carried a leather satchel.

Fredric held a hand out. "Master Shen, welcome."

They shook; he had an excellent grip for a sorcerer. Some of the soft, doughy saps they sent turned Fredric's stomach. "Commander St. Cloud. What's it been, three years?"

Fredric grinned. "Almost four. It's good to see you, Lon. How long are you staying?"

The slender sorcerer shrugged. "As long as I can be of use. Training your students to deal with sorcerers is important, even if the best strategy for them is to escape as fast as possible."

Fredric's grin faded at the implied insult. "I've killed a sorcerer or two."

Lon laughed and shot a pointed glance at the sword at his waist. "You're hardly an average warlord, Fredric. What's practical for the King's Champion is a little different than what's practical for most of your students."

Fredric grunted. Lon had a point; he just didn't like the idea that there were things out there a skilled warlord with a sharp sword couldn't handle. He started toward the fortress, angling toward the training yard to let Lon have a look at the second and third years that would get their first taste of sorcery over the next week or two.

A hundred plus boys and girls stood in neat rows, practice swords in their hands, as they made the five primary slashes, one after the other, over and over again. In another year they'd be able to make all those cuts, as well as any variations, without needing to think. At the far end of the first row his son performed them flawlessly. Fredric watched the boy flow from cross cuts to diagonal to vertical and back to the beginning. Despite his failings with soul force, Fredric found nothing to criticize in Damien's technique. He allowed himself a moment of pride. His son wasn't a complete failure.

You should tell him that sometime.

Lon stopped, his gaze locked on Damien. Fredric ignored Lizzenwar's comment and moved to join his old friend. "Something wrong, Lon?"

The sorcerer nodded toward Damien. "Why is that boy training as a warlord?"

Fredric stiffened. "That's my son."

Lon tore his gaze away from Damien. "He's a sorcerer, Fredric. A very powerful one."

It wasn't possible.

If Lon had hit him over the head with a sledgehammer it wouldn't have stunned Fredric as much as that statement. Shala had been a mistress of the spear and a warlord almost as powerful as Fredric himself. That they'd had a son who was a sorcerer defied belief. "The seer. When Damien was born, the seer said he'd be a warlord."

"That much power contained in an infant's tiny body, I doubt the seer got an accurate reading of which direction Damien's power flowed. He figured you and Shala were warlords and so assumed Damien would be as well. It's rare, but seers aren't perfect. Your son is an external soul force wielder: a sorcerer, just like me."

It took all Fredric's considerable will not to fall to his knees on the spot. He'd pushed the boy so hard, threatened to kick him out of their home, all because he couldn't make his soul force work. To find out now, after all these years, that no matter what he did or how hard he pushed, Damien would never be a warlord...

His stomach churned and he feared he might be sick. All the masters had tried everything. It never occurred to any of them that Damien might have gotten misclassified.

"My friend, I'm aware this is a shock, but Damien needs to go to Sorcery. If he should accidentally tap that massive power and release it with no control he'd level The Citadel and kill everyone here, including himself. I have to take him as soon as he can get ready."

Fredric nodded, pulling himself together. An untrained sorcerer was a grave danger. Lon had the right idea. Damien needed the proper training as soon as possible. He put his fingers in his mouth and blew a shrill whistle. The masters looked his way and Fredric pointed at Damien then gestured for him to come over.

Chapter 4

Out of the corner of his eye Damien watched his father and the strange man chat as they walked along the edge of the practice field. A moment later he felt the weight of the stranger's regard. Damien turned his head and locked gazes with the long-haired man. What the hell did he want?

The stranger broke the connection between them and said something to his father. He wished he could hear what they were saying.

While Damien watched, his body kept making the proper cuts without conscious direction from his mind. He'd been doing them since he could stand. They required no more concentration than breathing. His father raised his hand to his mouth and blew a whistle.

Everyone stopped. His father pointed at him and waved him over.

What had he done now?

The Master of Swords turned to Damien. "You saw the commander, move out."

Damien sighed and trotted over to join his father and the stranger. Behind him the others resumed their training. Damien clasped his hands behind his back and faced his father. "Sir?"

"Relax, Damien, you're not in trouble. This is Master Shen, an old friend of mine. He has something important to discuss with you."

Damien turned his focus on Master Shen. "Sir?"

The strange man smiled, a warm expression filled with kindness. The sort of expression his father never wore. "I understand you've been having trouble with your soul force."

Damien nodded. So this was some expert Dad had brought in to fix whatever was wrong with him. "Yes, sir, it doesn't work."

"That's because you've been using it wrong. Do you know about sorcerers, Damien?"

He hesitated at the odd question. "A little, from what I've read and rumors, of course."

"Would it surprise you if I said you were a sorcerer, like me, and not a warlord?"

A sorcerer! He snapped a look at his father, who nodded.

It's true, Damien. I'm sorry I didn't realize it.

When Lizzy confirmed it he accepted that they weren't joking. A sorcerer. How was it possible? "Is that why my soul force doesn't work?"

"It works fine, Damien, just not the way you've learned. Sorcerers like us use our powers outside our bodies, the exact opposite of a warlord."

Damien tried to process what Master Shen was saying, but failed. "What happens now?"

"You're going to train at The Tower of Sorcery, the school for sorcerers," his father said. "Go pack your things and Master Shen will take you."

"Yes, sir." Damien ran for the fortress before they changed their minds. He leapt once as he ran. A sorcerer! He wasn't a failure after all. His father and all the masters thought they knew so much and not one of them realized he couldn't do what they wanted him to. It wasn't that he wasn't trying; his power just didn't work like theirs. Everything finally made sense.

He ran through the front door, up the stairs, and down the hall to their quarters. He didn't have much in the way of clothes or possessions; Dad thought things just held you down and forced his preferences on him and Jen.

Damien's bedroom held little save a bed, table and chair for studying, and a chest of drawers for his clothes. He dug his rucksack out of the bottom drawer and set to filling it. Small clothes, two tunics, two pairs of pants, and dress boots. A horn comb that had belonged to his mother he wrapped carefully in the tunics. Of his meager belongings, he treasured that one the most.

He opened the top drawer and hesitated before taking the sword and dagger set his father gave him when he began training as an official cadet. The sword was almost identical to Lizzy, from its straight, thin blade right down to the lacquered black sheath. He sighed and hung it over his shoulder. The only people he'd miss were Lizzy and Jen. He touched the hilt of the sword. Too bad he couldn't trade with Dad and take Lizzy with him. He couldn't of course. She was far too powerful to leave in the hands of a kid.

The dagger had a short, curved blade and a sheath that matched the sword. He clipped it to his belt. Damien started for the door then hesitated again. He was still wearing his uniform. Only cadets and instructors wore the silver-and-blue tunics and after today he wouldn't be a cadet anymore.

Best to make a clean break. He took off his weapons, dug out his black tunic, and tossed his uniform aside. He'd never wear the damn thing again.

The door burst open and Jen ran in. "You're leaving?"

"Dad told you? I'm a sorcerer, apparently. I have to go to a school for sorcerers."

"When will you be back?" She sounded so worried it tore at him.

"I don't know. I don't know anything except that I have to go. Hopefully, when I finish my training, I'll be able to come home." Damien turned toward the door, his father stood in their watching. "Of course, I may not be welcome."

She put her hands on his shoulders. "You'd better come back. This is your home whatever anyone says."

Damien hugged her and whispered in her ear. "I'll miss you too."

What about me?

Just for a moment Lizzy brought him into her world so they could talk without anyone overhearing. "I'll miss you even more, Lizzy."

She hugged him with both arms and wings. "What will I do without you?"

"I was thinking the same thing. I love you, Lizzy. As soon as they let me I'll come see you, I promise."

"You'd better." The instant before she returned him to his body he could have sworn she was crying.

Master Shen entered the room. Damien kissed his sister on the cheek and stepped away. "I'm ready, Master."

He walked out past his father. They exchanged no words, didn't even make eye contact. Dad was probably as glad to be rid of him as Damien was to leave his father's disapproving glare behind.

Chapter 5

Damien walked across the training yard beside Master Shen, his rucksack slung over his shoulder. It took all his focus to maintain a stoic expression. He'd never need to stand in line waiting to get a broken bone again. No more orders and instructions he couldn't carry out. He was through with the place and all his father's expectations. If Jen and Lizzy could've come with him he would never even consider returning.

The stables sat at the rear of the grounds, the opposite direction from their path. Was Master Shen planning to walk all the way to The Tower or had he brought horses of his own? Or better yet, did he plan to summon a flying beast? Damien figured it wouldn't hurt to check, just in case he had gotten lost. The sorcerer didn't live here after all.

"Master, shouldn't we collect mounts before we leave?"

Master Shen chuckled. "No need for that, Damien. Sorcerers have faster means of travel."

They reached the dirt patch near the edge of the grounds where the sorcerers alway landed. Damien's heart raced. Master Shen was going to summon a flying beast. Damien could hardly contain his excitement.

Master Shen raised his right hand and a golden glow appeared in the air in front of him. The glow expanded and shifted, forming into a great griffin. Damien stared at the huge beast. Would he be able to create such a thing? The prospect thrilled and terrified him in equal measure.

Master Shen lowered his hand. "Have you ever flown, Damien?"

Flown? He'd never considered such a thing possible for him outside Lizzy's psychic world. "No, Master."

"I think you'll enjoy it." Master Shen waved his hand again and three golden steps appeared from the ground. "Climb aboard."

Damien went up the steps and found a pair of saddles had formed on the creature's back. He swung his leg over the back saddle and found it every bit as comfortable as sitting on a horse. The weirdest thing was the griffin didn't breathe or tremble. It felt like sitting on a statue.

Master Shen climbed up in front of him and a moment later a golden belt appeared around Damien's waist holding him tight. Right, if they were flying the last thing he wanted was to fall off the back of this thing.

"Ready?" Master Shen asked.

Damien nodded and the griffin leapt into the air. Seconds later Damien peered over his shoulder. The Citadel looked like a child's toy; the students training, bugs gathered around a sugar cube. Master Shen circled The Citadel once, perhaps imagining that Damien wanted a moment to say goodbye. If Master Shen believed that he was seriously mistaken. Damien was happy to leave the place, with its bullies and expectations, far behind.

Master Shen made one last pass then turned east, the beast picking up speed. After a minute Damien realized there wasn't any wind and the griffin's wings, while spread, never beat.

"Master, why does your beast not breathe or beat its wings?"

"It's not alive, Damien. The griffin is a soul force construct. I like to use a griffin, but I could have made it look like anything." Master Shen put his hand beside the griffin's flank and the creature flowed like soft clay. A moment later the griffin had shifted and Damien sat on a horse with no wings. The movement and feel of the thing hadn't changed a bit. "See, nothing to it. The construct is just to give us a place to sit while we fly. I could've shaped a couch for all the difference it would make, but a flying couch is beneath the dignity of a sorcerer."

Damien couldn't see his face, but he suspected from Master Shen's tone he was smiling. "Why is there no wind?"

"Since I don't care to pick bugs out of my teeth, I wrapped us in a windscreen."

Amazing. The things a warlord could do astonished Damien, but this, this seemed impossible. "Will I be able to do this sort of thing, Master?"

"Of course, conjuring soul force constructs is a basic skill for a sorcerer. You should be able to manage a flying mount by the end of your first year."

A year? Damien goggled. In a year he'd be able to fly around like a bird whenever he wanted to? It was beyond comprehension.

He looked down and watched the green treetops whiz by. That had to be the Great Green, the largest forest in the kingdom. It was over a day's ride from The Citadel and they were already well into it. How fast did the griffin fly? Ahead of them the edge of the forest raced closer, the lumber camp that sat beside the tree line resembling nothing so much as markers on the map in strategy class.

"We're almost there." Master Shen turned his head to look at Damien. "How are you?"

Damien grinned. "Eager to learn how to fly on my own."

Master Shen smiled as well. "I remember that feeling. Hang on to it when you get frustrated."

The sorcerer turned back and pointed ahead and a little to the right. A great black tower jutted into the sky. Around it several smaller buildings huddled in the shadow of the surrounding wall. North of the complex sat a circular amphitheater, a well-worn path connecting it to the northern gate. A few miles distant from the tower, a little town had sprouted up. Like the one near The Citadel, it sat close enough to provide services for the masters, but far enough away to keep from tempting the students to sneak out and play.

Their mount descended and as they flew closer to the school Damien got a sense of just how huge the tower was. It had to be a hundred and fifty feet tall and a hundred feet on each side. Though the shape differed he suspected the tower was every bit as big as The Citadel.

Master Shen brought the horse in for a gentle landing. The belt holding him in place faded away and Damien hopped down to the ground. The sorcerer joined him and a moment later the horse vanished. Damien turned a slow circle. The yard was empty. Up on the wall he saw an occasional guard carrying a crossbow and wearing a sword strapped to his back. The way they were slumped suggested to Damien they didn't expect trouble. Lucky for them his father wasn't here. Even if they weren't expecting trouble he'd have given them a thorough talking to about staying alert on duty.

"Where is everyone, Master?"

Master Shen glanced at the shadow of The Tower. "It's about three so I'd guess they're in class. Sorcerers don't train much outside. The yard is used during flight practice as a place to take off and land. Sometimes the guards drill, or the students get a game of Long Ball going, but other than that it's usually empty. Come on."

Master Shen headed toward the tower and Damien followed a step behind and to his left as was proper for a new student. Halfway to the tower the sorcerer noticed him and laughed. "No need to hang back, Damien. You'll find Sorcery a good deal less formal than The Citadel."

"Yes, sir." Damien quick-stepped until he reached the sorcerer's side. "I've gotten so used to the rules of The Citadel it'll take a while to learn new ones."

A set of double doors made of some dark wood Damien didn't recognize marked the entrance to the tower. Master Shen pushed them open and they swung inward without a sound and the two of them stepped through, the doors shut behind them.

The tower's entry hall was smaller than the one at The Citadel. Polished black stone with silver veins running through it covered the floors, walls, and ceiling. It felt like standing in the night sky. Doors made of the same wood as the outer doors waited on each wall. Master Shen turned left and pushed a door open. Behind it, a hall covered in the same black stone led deeper into the tower.

"Down this hall are the administrative offices." Master Shen led the way. "I sent a message to the headmaster so he should be expecting us."

They passed several closed doors before stopping in front of one marked with a silver pentagram. On a bench opposite sat a boy Damien's age, with sandy brown hair, a brown tunic, and tan pants. Brown eyes stared at Damien, unblinking.

He was about to ask the kid what his problem was when Master Shen pushed the door open. "Come on."

Damien put the boy out of his mind and stepped into the headmaster's office. A huge cherry desk dominated the room, covered with books, parchments, quills and ink. Behind it waited a tiny man with a pointed white beard, dressed in a black robe embroidered with stars. Two small, dark chairs waited in front of the desk and matching bookcases stuffed from top to bottom with leather-bound books lined the walls.

Damien bowed. "Sir, Damien St. Cloud reporting for instruction, sir."

The little man hopped out of his chair and rushed around the desk. He couldn't have been over four and a half feet tall. He grabbed Damien's hand and pumped it enthusiastically. "No need for such formality, my boy. Have a seat." His voice matched his stature: small and squeaky. "Excellent work finding him, Lon, thank you."

"My pleasure, Thomas," Master Shen said. "I'm heading back to The Citadel to resume their training."

"Of course, of course." The headmaster waved his hand towards the door.

Master Shen turned away from the desk. Damien said, "I don't know how to thank you, sir, for telling me what I am."

"As I said, it was my pleasure." Master Shen favored him with his warm smile. "If you put in half the effort training in sorcery that you did at The Citadel, you have a bright future ahead of you. Good luck."

Master Shen left the office and closed the door behind him. Damien swallowed, suddenly nervous. This place was different from home in every way and the only person he knew at all had just left.

"You seem a bit anxious. Sit down, please," the headmaster said. He stepped back around his desk and Damien eased into one of the chairs. It seemed wrong, sitting in the master's presence. He'd have taken five lashes back home if he'd dared sit in one of the masters' offices.

"I suppose I am, sir. This is all so new, so different. I'll do my best to settle in quickly."

The headmaster waved an indifferent hand. "Don't worry about it. Everyone has a first day and everyone's nervous. Some settle in fast, others less so, but sooner or later everyone settles in. When Lon said he found you I was pleased to have a fourth member for the first-year class."

Damien blinked. Perhaps he'd misheard. "Excuse me, sir, did you say my class is only four people?"

The headmaster nodded. "That's about average. Last year we had five, the year before only two. We currently have twenty-three students in various stages of training."

Damien had over thirty in his class alone at The Citadel. "Why so few, sir?"

The tiny sorcerer chuckled. "No need to add 'sir' every time you address me, son, Thomas is fine."

Thomas? He'd never considered calling a master by his given name. Damien doubted he could force himself to do it. "Yes, sir."

The headmaster shook his head. "We'll work on it. As to your question, the reason we have so few students is that a sorcerer is born only rarely. In any given year only a handful of children with externally flowing soul force are born, and often fewer than half of them are powerful enough to serve as an effective sorcerer. The biggest first-year class we've ever had was six and that was over a hundred years ago."

Damien had no idea so few sorcerers were born every year. He'd thought warlords were rare, but compared to sorcerers they were common. "How do you have classes with so few students?"

"We don't have formal classes, not the sort you're used to. Some students learn best with a study partner, others in small groups, and still others benefit from individual instruction. That's what you'll be receiving, at least for the foreseeable future."

"I'll be receiving individual instruction, sir?" Were they afraid he'd slow down the other students? He'd never been popular back home, but he liked having comrades to train with, even if, later on, he couldn't fight at their level.

"That's right. I fear you don't realize just how tremendously powerful you are. Until you can control your power it's very possible you might accidentally hurt or kill an unskilled partner. Working one on one with a skilled teacher will give you the best chance of bringing your power under control with the minimum amount of danger to anyone else. Okay?"

Damien couldn't fathom that these people thought he was powerful enough to be a danger to the other students. No one had ever considered him powerful, much less a threat. "Yes, sir."

"Any questions?"

"No, sir."

"Excellent." The headmaster gestured and the door swung open. The boy on the bench stood up and at the little man's beckoning entered the office. "Damien, this is Eli. He's another first year. You two will be roommates and Eli will help you settle in. Once he's shown you around he'll take you to Mistress Ann's training room. She's expecting you so don't dillydally."

Damien stood, bowed to the headmaster, and slung his rucksack over his shoulder. "Thank you, sir."

The little man nodded again. "Off you go."

Damien followed Eli out of the office and the door closed behind them on its own. That would take some getting used to. The boys walked back to the entry hall.

"Sorry for staring earlier. I've never seen soul force as dense as yours, not even the masters'," Eli said.

"That's fine." Damien didn't know what dense soul force meant, but Eli seemed impressed. He pointed to the right-hand door. "What's back there?"

"Meeting rooms. When the masters meet with nobles or merchants or whoever, that's where they do it. The first floor is the public portion of the tower. Everything above is for sorcerers and students only."

Eli opened the center door and behind it waited a curved staircase leading to the next floor. Damien took the steps two at a time and halfway up had to stop to let Eli catch up. The boy didn't look like he was in bad shape, but he wasn't warrior trained either. They continued up to the second-floor landing where they found yet another dark wood door. Inside was a black stone hall branching left and right. Eli went left.

When they reached an arch he turned right down a door-lined hall. "This is the students' dormitory." Eli went to the third door on the right and pushed it open. "Here's our room."

Damien followed his guide inside a rather plain room. Brown carpet covered the stone floor and two narrow beds sat ten feet apart. There was a footlocker for his gear and two tables and chairs. Spartan, even by Damien's standards.

"I thought my room back home was empty." Damien stowed his gear, putting his sword and dagger at the bottom of the trunk and covering them with his clothes.

"We just sleep and study here, so we have all we need."

"I guess. How long have you been here?"

"Two months. I was the third to arrive this year and everyone figured I'd be the last."

"What are the others like?"

"Amanda's the only girl and she's fierce, she wants to be an artillerist. Blowing things up with sorcery is her fondest wish. Jaden's quiet, short and round. He's decent enough as long as you're not into conversation. He likes books. In fact, he has a flawless memory for anything he reads. You'll meet everyone at dinner. Come on, I'll show you the dining hall then we can go up to Mistress Ann's room."

They left their shared room and retraced their steps back to the stairway, and down the hall the opposite way. The scent of garlic and cooking meat reached them long before they arrived at a pair of swinging double doors. They pushed through into a large open room with tables and benches in neat rows. At the far end was a counter with plates and utensils. Damien grinned. This at least was the same as back home. Even sorcerers needed a place to eat.

They went back to the staircase and climbed up another floor. The third floor looked much like the second: halls and doors and no people. Straight across from them was a door labeled Master Stine in silver letters. Eli led the way to a door labeled Mistress Ann.

Chapter 6

"Can you find your way back to our room on your own?" Eli asked.

Damien spared his roommate a glance. It was one floor down and two turns. He'd manage. "Yeah, no problem. Thanks for the tour."

Eli patted him on the shoulder. "Good luck."

His guide walked back down the hall and soon disappeared around a corner. Damien adjusted his tunic and knocked. The door swung open and standing behind it was a beautiful, dark-haired woman about thirty. She had a slim, graceful figure and wore a long black dress slit on both sides up to mid-thigh. A plunging neckline revealed her considerable cleavage.

Damien bowed. "Damien St. Cloud reporting for instruction, ma'am."

She laughed—more of a witchy cackle really—and said, "So formal. I'm Ann and since we'll be spending a lot of time together you should probably relax. Come on in."

She moved aside and let him enter the small, nearly empty room. The teachers were certainly strange. They had no interest in any sort of discipline that he could see. Ann led him over to the two chairs set three feet apart that were the room's sole furnishings. She sat in one and gestured to the other.

When Damien took his seat she said, "I assume Thomas explained the school rules to you."

Damien shook his head. "No, ma'am, no one's explained much of anything to me beyond the fact that I'm to live and train here for some time. Everything's so odd. There are no uniforms, no classes, no real structure. The headmaster wants me to call him by his first name. If any student called the Master of The Citadel by his first name he'd soon be picking himself up off the floor."

Her smile held the same warmth as Master Shen's. "I see. You're the first student we've ever had that spent time at The Citadel. We're not as rigid with our training because we can't be. Every sorcerer learns their art at a different pace and in their own way. All sorcerers must find his or her own path. Our job as masters is to teach the basics, offer advice, and keep everyone from getting hurt. The last one is the most difficult. The only hard and unbreakable rule is that you're not allowed to use your powers on another student or master. Break that rule once and you get twenty lashes. Break it a second time and the punishment is banishment in the Northlands. Clear?"

"Yes, ma'am. If we're not to use our powers on other students how do we practice?"

"Practice is different. Training in combat techniques with a master overseeing happens all the time, though not until you finish your first year of training. What I'm talking about is unsupervised mischief or violence. Also your movements are restricted to The Tower grounds until you complete your training."

As rules went those two seemed fair, after all the last thing they'd want is two boys fighting over a girl to blow up the dining hall. But it didn't sound like he'd be visiting Jen and Lizzy anytime soon. "Is there anything else?"

"Not really. Want to try a basic technique?"

Damien's heart fluttered. To finally tap his soul force was something he'd dreamed about for years. Now that it was going to happen his mouth felt dry and his hands trembled. "What do I do?"

"Imagine a bit of your power, about the size of a grain of rice, above the palm of your hand."

Damien imagined the speck of energy flowing through his arm and out his palm. Nothing. His soul force remained as inert as ever. He slumped in his chair. It wouldn't be any different here.

"Not like that."

Damien looked up at his teacher. "Ma'am?"

"Don't try to push the energy through your body. That's the way warlords use soul force. Our power can't travel through our bodies. Picture the grain of energy appearing just above your hand like it came out of nowhere."

Damien frowned, held out his hand, and imagined the power just appearing. A blinding light like a second sun burst to life above his hand. He looked away and squeezed his eyes shut.

"Douse it, douse it!"

How the hell was he supposed to do that? Damien clenched his fist around the speck of energy and willed it to return to where it came from. He opened his eyes and spots danced before them. At least the light had vanished.

Ann gaped at him.

"Sorry, ma'am. What did I do wrong?"

She threw back her head and laughed. "Not a thing, Damien. In fact you did something amazing. You recovered your unused energy and returned it to your core. That's a rare skill. The excessive light was my fault. You used the exact right amount of energy; I failed to allow for how dense your soul force is. I need to adjust my instructions down by at least four times when I work with you."

She held out a hand and a ball of warm, golden light appeared above it. "This is what I expected. I used the same amount of soul force as you, but mine is so much less dense it only makes this little light."

"I see," Damien said, though in truth he had no idea what she was talking about.

"Don't worry about it now. Let's try something else. This is a mental trick unique to sorcerers that lets you see another's soul force." She held her hands together in a circle just above her belly button. "Focus here and try to look through my dress, skin, and muscle to the core of my body."

Damien stared, trying to imagine the thin black cloth parting, then the skin and muscle under it. He squinted and soon a ball of golden energy became clear. He flinched and it vanished. It seemed so different from what he sensed inside himself. His power felt roiled and agitated while hers seemed smooth and calm.

When he pointed this out she said, "Everyone's power is different. Yours will calm in time. Part of your problem is you've been prodding it to do things it can't. Now that you're using it properly it should smooth out. With time and practice you'll be able to do more than see soul force, you'll also be able to sense it as well. Now try again."

He focused and her soul force appeared at once, smooth and serene as the surface of a pond on a calm day. Then it vanished. Damien squinted, trying to get the image to reappear.

"You can stop now. I raised my shield to block your vision. That's another trick sorcerers developed to hide their power from each other. Of course, if you see someone with no visible soul force you'll know they're a sorcerer, just not how strong. Building your shield is the final thing I'll teach you tonight. You'll want to get your power hidden before you meet the other students."

Damien nodded, remembering how Eli had stared at him when they first met. "What do I do?"

"Take a small ball of soul force, about the size of a marble, and imagine it turning into a liquid. Once you have that, imagine the liquid covering your whole body, always a little above your skin."

Damien did what she said and soon a golden second skin covered him. "Like this?" He couldn't be doing it right. Her shield was invisible.

"Exactly. I can't see your core anymore. Now we just need to make your personal shield a little less obvious. Focus on the shield and imagine it turning clear, like water."

Damien did as she said. The light vanished, but he could still sense his shield. It was wavering like it wanted to shatter. "The power's running out." He tried and failed to conceal his concern.

"That's okay. You have to do one more thing to make it sustaining. Do you sense the power flowing into your core to replace what you used?"

He turned his focus inward and sensed a rushing power, like a river with no origin, flooding into the small empty space in his core. "Yes."

"Good. Now imagine most of that flow going to your shield instead of your core."

Damien frowned as he tried to redirect the river. He divided it into small streams and sent them out just above his skin and below the shield. He sent a stream to each of his extremities, then some to his back and chest and finally his head. With the streams in place he sent little tendrils of power into the shield and it stopped wavering. He let out a breath he didn't realize he'd been holding. Sweat covered his back and neck. He'd run ten miles without getting this worn out.

Ann was staring at him again. Now what had he done? "Ma'am?"

She gave herself a little shake. "Sorry, but whatever you've created here is far more than a simple shield to hide your core. Your body generates more soul force every minute than some sorcerers can contain in their core. With that much power running through your shield I could probably drop a boulder on you and not break your skin. It's absolutely amazing."

"Thank you?"

Ann smiled. "I know a little about warlord training. While our powers work differently, the focus and mental discipline you've gained through your earlier training has clearly made this transition easier for you. I've worked with many students and no one has used their power as naturally as you. I think you'll find your training serves you well as we continue your studies."

She yawned and stretched. Damien tried to ignore her breasts straining to escape out the top of her dress. "I'm beat and you look all in. Let's call it a night. Come back in the morning after breakfast and we'll pick up where we left off."

Damien leapt to his feet and bowed. "Yes, ma'am. Any time in particular?"

She got up and waved a hand. "Whenever you get done eating is fine."

They walked together to the staircase. When they reached the landing she turned to continue up. "Good night."

Damien nodded. "Ma'am." He started down the stairs to his room.

He'd only gone a couple of steps when he heard her mutter, "So formal."

As he walked down stairs he reflected on what Mistress Ann had said. Maybe all the time he spent meditating and failing to move his power would turn out to be time well spent after all.

When he reached the second-floor landing his stomach rumbled. He'd completely lost track of time. Was dinner over? Damien turned toward the dining hall, hoping he hadn't missed his chance. He smelled garlic and onions, but heard nothing that suggested anyone was in the hall. He pushed the doors open and sighed. The room was empty of students. A pair of women in black-and-white servants' uniforms scrubbed the tables and a third person, a bald man as wide as he was tall and wearing a grease-stained apron, stood behind the serving counter.

Damien put on his best smile and ambled up to the counter. "Excuse me, I was late finishing my day's training and missed dinner. Is there any chance you have some leftovers?"

The man scowled at him. "I don't know you."

"No sir, this is my first day."

"Ah, you're the one everyone was talking about. They seemed disappointed you weren't here."

Damien blinked, surprised anyone besides Eli was even aware he was here. "Well, I'm sure I'll see them at breakfast. So, do you have anything? Please?" His stomach growled its own request.

"Just a minute." He ducked back into the kitchen, grumbling all the way. Damien smiled, relieved to find at least one normal person in this place. He'd feared the kingdom had gathered up all the oddballs and sent them here. The cook returned a minute later carrying a plate with a roll heaped with meat and onions. "This'll have to do. There's water in the barrel down at the end of the counter."

Damien accepted the plate and bowed. "Thank you, sir."

He ate quickly and returned his plate and cup to the cook. He yawned and headed for his room. It had been a long, strange day and he was ready for a good night's sleep. He met no one on his walk back. Inside his room he found Eli sitting at his desk reading. His roommate glanced at him and smiled. "Got your shield up I see."

Damien nodded, sat on the edge of his bed, and kicked his shoes off. "Did you break into a sweat the first time you made a shield?"

Eli laughed and closed his book. "Are you kidding? It took me three days to get mine to work. How'd you manage it in an afternoon?"

Damien shrugged. "I just did what she said and it worked. It was one hell of a relief, let me tell you. I've been beating my head against the wall for a year and a half trying to get my power to move. It helps if your teacher tells you the right way to use it."

Eli snorted. "I imagine it does. Everyone will be jealous of you. Not only did you get your shield to work on your first day, but you got assigned to Mistress Ann. Talk about lucky."

"Lucky?" Damien thought he understood what the other boy meant, but wanted to be certain.

Eli held his hands out in front of his chest. "Don't tell me you didn't get a good look at her. It's a wonder you could concentrate on your lesson."

Damien thought about Lizzy constantly appearing naked whenever they met. A woman with her clothes on, even one as well proportioned as Mistress Ann, wasn't enough to break his focus. "She certainly wasn't what I was expecting."

Chapter 7

Damien woke at five. There was no window in the room he shared with Eli, but he'd woken at five every day for as long as he could remember and, sunlight or not, his body knew when to get up. In the pitch-black room the only sound was Eli's deep, steady breathing. Damien slid out of bed, dressed by feel, and slipped out as quietly as he could. Outside, glow balls hanging from the ceiling in glass jars lit his path. Damien walked down to the dining room hoping to get his breakfast and get to training.

He pushed through the swinging doors and found the hall silent and empty. He'd have thought the cook would be up and started at least. Maybe he could get in a workout before breakfast. Eli hadn't shown him a gym yesterday, but they had to have something.

Damien went down to the ground floor and out into the yard. The morning was cool and clear, the sun just turning the sky above the wall gray. It was a beautiful late spring day.

A few guardsmen stood on the wall and Damien ran up the steps to talk to them. If anyone knew where he could find the gym it seemed like it would be the guards. He trotted up to the nearest man, a middle-aged fellow with a pot belly and salt-and-pepper beard. On closer inspection maybe he wasn't the best one to ask.

Not wanting to be rude now that he'd approached Damien said, "Excuse me. Do you know if there's a gym or somewhere for the students to exercise?"

The guardsman laughed. "Not so far as I know, young sir. Sorcerers aren't much for exercise."

Coming from a fat guardsman that was a laughable statement. "Would you guys mind if I ran the wall?"

The guardsman waved his hand. "Be my guest."

Damien shook his head and jogged away. He did ten circuits, about five miles give or take. The guards all stared at him in disbelief as he kept running. It was like they'd never seen someone exercising before. Given their lack of conditioning Damien guessed most of them certainly hadn't run in a while.

He stopped beside the same guardsman. "What time is breakfast?"

The man grumbled and glanced at the sun just peeking over the wall. "Another hour at least."

Damn, they didn't get started very early here. He grabbed the lip of the wall and swung over, hanging by his fingers. He did forty pull ups, then reversed his grip so his back was to the wall and did forty more. Damien pulled himself back up on the walkway and rolled his shoulders. What was he supposed to do for another hour?

He jogged back inside and up to the dining hall. Pots were clanging in the kitchen, so that was progress. He dropped to the floor and did some crunches. The doors squeaked and a familiar voice said, "I figured I'd find you here."

Damien grinned and kipped up to his feet. Standing by the door, a matching grin on his face was a boy a year older than him with long brown hair, a lean, fit build, and a chiseled, handsome face. John Kord, his oldest and best friend.

Chapter 8

"John! What's it been, three years?" The boys bumped fists. Damien hadn't seen his childhood friend since he started training at The Citadel and had forgotten John was supposed to be studying at The Tower. "How's it going?"

"Good, turns out I've got a gift for healing. The old man didn't like it much, he wanted an artillerist. What about you? I thought you were going to be a warlord."

"You and everyone else. Apparently the seer screwed up when I was born." Damien shook his head and sat on one of the benches. "A year and a half trying to use internal soul force and all the time I was a sorcerer. To say Dad wasn't thrilled would be an understatement."

"I can imagine. How many generations of your family have been warlords?"

"Since the first colonists came over from the old empire."

John laughed at his impression of his father. "Well, we can't help how we're born, can we?"

"Nope. Anyway, Jen can carry on the family tradition. She's a better warrior anyway."

John's expression turned wistful when Damien mentioned his sister. His friend had always had a crush on Jen. That she was completely indifferent to him made it even worse. "She can't inherit the demon sword though, can she?"

"No, Lizzy won't work with a female partner. What's the general up to these days?"

John sat across from Damien. "Dad's up north, keeping an eye on the ice trolls and ogres. Some days I'd swear he wants them to attack just so he'll have something to do."

"Really?"

"Nah, he's too fond of his men to want any of them to die in some stupid war. He's just bored."

Damien got up and did a handstand followed by pushups. Between reps he said, "This is a weird place, John. There's no gym, no real schedule. Mistress Ann said to just show up for training whenever I finished breakfast."

"You got paired up with Ann? Lucky dog. She's the best-looking teacher in the tower."

It looked like Eli wasn't the only one with a crush on his teacher. Of course, John had a crush on most every woman he laid eyes on. Pots clanked in the kitchen and Damien rolled to his feet. "So I've heard. Who's your master?"

"I'm in a group of three studying healing with Master Jones: tall, skinny and bald." John sighed. "Still, he's regarded as one of the finest healers in the kingdom."

"Is he by any chance in charge of making healing potions?"

John nodded. "Yeah, why?"

"I wanted to thank him. I've drunk enough of the damn things over the last year and a half."

John laughed again though Damien found nothing funny in his broken bones. The kitchen door swung open and the cook came through carrying a steaming pot. Behind him the two women he'd seen the night before followed with trays covered with bread, fruit, and jars of golden honey. Damien turned and jogged to the pile of bowls at the start of the line. His morning exercise had left him starving. The cook filled his bowl with oatmeal which Damien then topped with blueberries and honey. He added a slice of bread, collected a cup of water, and headed back to their bench. John joined him a moment later and they set to eating.

Damien hadn't managed more than a mouthful when the doors swung open and half a dozen students poured through. John waved to one of the girls, a cute brunette, before turning back to his meal. Damien raised an eyebrow.

"Marie's in my healing group. She's a third year. Nice girl, but kind of shy."

Damien had eaten half his food before the door squeaked again. He looked up to see Eli leading two others into the hall. There was a girl with flaming red hair and a tiny build and a stout boy with sandy hair and a dusting of freckles across the bridge of his nose. Those two had to be the other first years. Eli waved and Damien returned the gesture.

"Friends of yours?" John asked.

"My roommate and the other first years. Eli said he'd introduce me today. Have you met them?"

"John!" The redhead leapt at his friend and wrapped her arms around his neck. "How's my sweetie pie this morning?"

John grimaced and disentangled himself from the girl. "I'm not your sweetie pie."

Eli set a bowl down in front of the girl. "Amanda, behave yourself. You know John doesn't like it when you do that."

She stuck her tongue out at Eli. "I'm going to marry him, just wait and see."

The blond boy with the freckles sat beside Damien across from Amanda. He held out a hand and Damien shook it. "Jaden Orn, my dad's the cook."

Damien nodded. The family resemblance was obvious. "Damien St. Cloud. It must be nice to have your family so close."

He nodded. "We're both real busy, but at least I can sleep in my own bed."

"Hey!" Amanda leaned across the table so her face was only inches from Damien's. "I want to see your soul force. Eli said it was really strong. Show me."

Eli grabbed the back of Amanda's tunic and yanked her into her seat. "That's so rude. You're not supposed to ask people to show you their soul force. I'm sorry, Damien."

Damien shrugged. He didn't realize it was rude to ask, so it never occurred to him to be offended. He turned his focus inward and found his shield and the flows sustaining it working just like he left them the night before. Truth was he didn't know how to lower his shield without removing it completely and he didn't want to do that since putting it up was such a chore. He said as much to Amanda.

"It's not fair." Amanda glared at Eli. "You got to see it. How come I don't get to?"

Eli looked pained as he tried to think of an explanation.

"I'll show you as soon as Mistress Ann teaches me how to open a hole in the shield. Okay?"

She whipped around to focus on him. "Promise?"

Damien nodded.

Amanda grinned. "I like you. We're going to be friends."

Without giving him a chance to respond she darted across the table and kissed him square on the lips. Too stunned to speak, Damien stared at the odd girl. Who kisses someone they just met on the lips?

"There." She nodded, seeming satisfied. "Now it's official, we're friends."

Eli put a hand over his face and sighed. Damien finished his breakfast before anything else strange happened. Which, considering what he'd seen so far in this place, was a small miracle.

He was about to get up and take his dishes to the counter when the door opened again and a blond giant walked in flanked by two smaller, but still huge boys. The blond boy had to be over six feet tall with broad shoulders and thick legs. Damien had seen a picture of an ogre once in one of his father's books, and this boy wasn't much smaller.

"That's Sigurd Iceborn," Eli said. "His father's the duke of the northern territory. He's very proud, so watch what you say to him."

Damien shot a look at John who shook his head. "Sig's an ass, just like his father. Dad says it's a wonder they have any snow up north considering the amount of hot air the duke blows."

Eli winced at John's lack of tact and Amanda laughed. The shrill noise caught Sig's attention and he angled away from the counter and toward their table, his companions flanking him. A slender dark-haired boy started to get up, but Sig shoved him back into his seat. Damien tensed. He knew this type.

Sig stopped a few feet from their table, hands on his hips, looming over them. The dining hall fell silent. The giant Northman turned his ice-blue eyes on Amanda. "Something funny, first year?"

"John told us a joke."

Sig turned his gaze on John and his lips twisted. He couldn't count on his rank helping him with John, whose father, the general, was equal in rank to the duke. Technically Damien's father, as King's Champion, outranked both the duke and the general, but it didn't filter down to Damien.

"John." Sig inclined his head a fraction, acknowledging John as his equal, but clearly resenting it.

John returned the gesture. "Sig."

No love lost between those two. Sig shifted his gaze again and Damien found himself under the nobleman's intense glare. "You must be the new guy. You don't look like much. Rumor is you've got strong soul force, but I doubt you're anything special."

Damien shrugged. "That's your opinion."

The minion on the left stepped closer to Damien. "Mind your manners when you speak to Master Sigurd."

Damien stood up. These weren't warlords he had to run from. They were just boys. Arrogant boys who thought they could push around anyone they wanted. Well, Damien had gotten pushed around enough. He'd be damned if he let a new batch of bullies pick up where the last bunch left off.

He took a step closer, so he was nose to chin with the older boy. "Or what?"

The minion glanced at his master and Sig nodded. The boy grabbed Damien's tunic with his left hand and reared back with his right. Damien crouched, tucked his chin, and leapt up, driving the top of his head into the bully's nose. Cartilage crunched and blood gushed. The boy's grip on Damien broke and he clasped both hands to his face, trying to stop the flow of blood.

Minion number two rushed toward Damien, intent on avenging his bleeding comrade. He stopped, planted his front foot and threw a punch at Damien's face. Damien slipped past the clumsy blow and kicked the boy in the side of his locked knee. Another crunch echoed through the silent hall and the second henchman fell to the floor howling and clutching his busted knee.

Damien looked at Sig and raised an eyebrow. "Well?"

The muscles in Sig's jaw worked as he glared at Damien. Finally he said, "Pity you're only a first year. If you had a little more experience we could have a proper duel and I'd show you your place."

Damien shrugged. "There are other sorts of duels. Hand fighting, swords, bows. Name your weapon and I'll accept the challenge."

Sig threw back his head and laughed. "You'd dare take me on with a blade? I was trained by the finest sword master in the north. A runt like you wouldn't last ten seconds against me."

Damien smiled. "You choose swords then?"

Sig stared at him. "Did you not hear what I said?"

"All I hear is a lot of noise. If you don't have the guts to back up your big talk, get lost. I've got to get to class."

"Fine, swords. Where and when?"

John got up and stepped between them. "If you two are serious about this I know a master that specializes in creating soul force weapons. The blades only interact with each other, they won't cut flesh. I doubt either of your fathers would be happy if you killed each other. I'll speak to him and if he agrees, tomorrow at noon in the arena. Sound good?"

Damien nodded, not in the least concerned about Sig's skill. "Works for me."

"Fine. Tomorrow at noon I'll crush you in front of the whole school." Sig spun and snarled at his bleeding companions. "Get yourselves to the healers."

Damien watched the three of them walk, and in one case limp, out of the dining hall without bothering to get something to eat. "Charming fellow."

"I see you've inherited your father's tolerance for fools," John said. "Did you really have to pick a fight your second day here?"

All around them conversation picked up. Damien suspected he was the main subject. "Technically I got here yesterday afternoon, so this is still my first day."

"You know what I mean."

"Sure. Let me know what the master says?"

"You bet." They bumped fists and John left to handle the details.

Whatever he said, Damien felt certain John would persuade whoever he needed to in order to make the fight happen. Damien grinned. He hadn't fought a normal person in a couple of years. Tomorrow promised to be fun.

"Are you crazy?" Eli stared at him, his face pale.

"No, why?"

"Why? You just picked a fight with the biggest kid in the school and the son of a duke at that. He'll kill you."

"You think? John said the soul force weapons wouldn't cut flesh."

"That's not what I–"

"Don't pay any attention to him." Amanda talked over Eli. She swung her tiny fists around, barely missing giving Eli a black eye. "That was amazing the way you took those two down. I bet you can beat Sig with one hand tied behind your back."

Damien smiled. "Thanks for the vote of confidence. I need to get to class."

He left the dining hall and made his way to Mistress Ann's training room. He knocked on the door and it opened on its own. His teacher sat in the same chair as the day before, wearing a similar dress only in red instead of black.

Damien bowed. "Ma'am."

She smiled and waved him over to the empty chair. "You're an early riser. I saw you running the wall this morning. That sort of thing isn't required here."

"Yes, ma'am, but at some point I assume I'll return home and if I show up at The Citadel out of shape I'll never hear the end of it." He sat and faced her.

"You're the first boy I've taught who focused above my neck and not below. Do you not think I'm pretty?"

Damien coughed, trying to cover his discomfort. What kind of question was that for a teacher to ask a student? He wasn't sure how to answer her. "You're very pretty, ma'am, but my girlfriend wouldn't appreciate me ogling another girl."

"You have a girlfriend, how sweet. Back at The Citadel?"

"Yes, ma'am."

"What's she like?" She leaned forward, her cleavage once more threatening to spill out of her dress.

How did one describe a demon soul bound to a sword that you could only interact with on a mental level? Damien had never really thought about it. He'd loved Lizzy for as long as he could remember. "She's beautiful, sharp, with a wicked sense of humor. She doesn't always get along with Dad though."

"That's nice. Okay, I see your shield is holding. Let's try the trick with the light again. Remember, a quarter of a grain of rice."

Damien did as she said and this time the light didn't blind them. He grinned. He could do this.

"That's excellent, Damien. Now let's try a simple soul force construct. You understand what I mean by that, right?"

"Like Master Shen's griffin?"

"Exactly, though we'll try for something a little simpler. Watch me."

Damien focused like she'd taught him and watched her form a blob of golden energy into the crude likeness of a cat. It landed on the floor and ran around the training room, jumping and batting the air with its paws.

"Now you try."

"Do you want a cat?"

She waved her hand. "Whatever you want, just not too big."

Damien took his own blob of energy and formed it into a four-legged shape with a muzzle and tail. When he finished, the golden dog towered over the little cat, its head barely missing the ceiling. He winced. "Too big?"

"A little. Try compressing it. Don't take any energy away, just squish it down smaller."

Damien concentrated and the dog shrank, but glowed brighter. "Like that?"

She smiled and nodded. "Amazing. Well done."

They spent the rest of the day trying different shapes, sometimes having them battle and chase each other around the room. A few times he lost control and his construct ran into the wall and bounced off. He understood now why the room held minimal furnishings; anything other than stone would probably end up smashed to bits. When Mistress Ann called a halt to the training Damien felt like he'd spent a day in the field digging trenches. "That's harder than it looks."

"You did well and the more you practice the easier it gets. Your homework is to make the little light until you can conjure it without having to think through each step. Any questions?"

"Do you know a sorcerer who specializes in making soul force weapons?"

She frowned. That was apparently not the question she expected. "Yes, his name's Sagan. Why?"

Damien told her about the duel and John making the arrangements. "I just wondered if he'd be a fair judge of the contest."

"Sagan's an honorable man, you need not fear on that score. What were you thinking, challenging that brute to a duel?"

"I was thinking I was sick of people pushing me around. I hope this will nip it in the bud."

She nodded, her face troubled. "If Sagan agrees you'll need a master to serve as your second. I'd be happy to stand beside you."

"I'd like that, Ann."

Chapter 9

Someone jostled John from behind as he tried to make his way down the stone steps. Eli had gone early to grab their little group seats above the south entrance where Damien planned to enter. Everyone else should be there already, but he'd stopped to buy a bag of glazed walnuts on his way and was running behind. The sun shone bright in a clear sky. All in all it was a lovely day to make some easy money.

The excited chatter of students and sorcerers entering the stands filled the air. The main topic of conversation seemed to be how fast Sig would crush Damien. John grinned. Man, were they in for a surprise. None more so than the kids who'd been taking bets for the last day. When he'd bet his and Damien's money he'd gotten five-to-one odds and the sixteen-year-old oddsmaker had almost hugged him when he proved willing to take the other side of the wager. He'd be considerably less thrilled in a few minutes.

John dodged a chubby third year and finally reached Eli and the others. They'd gotten seats directly above the doors, perfect. Amanda smiled as he approached and patted the leather seat between her and Eli. John sighed. Maybe not perfect. The moment he sat, a tiny hand shot in and snatched some walnuts.

"If you weren't so cheap you could get your own."

She popped the sweet treat into her mouth and ignored him. He shook his head and ate a few before she stole them all.

"Did you make a bet?" Eli asked.

He swallowed his snack. "Yeah, a hundred royals on Damien, got five to one against. I'm going to clean up."

Eli stared at him. "You bet on Damien?"

John smiled at his incredulous tone. He clearly had no idea what Damien could do with a sword. "You didn't?"

"I put five on Sig."

John turned to Amanda. "What about you?"

"Ten on Sig." She snitched another walnut.

"What about all your cheering for Damien and telling him how great it was that he beat up those two thugs?"

She shrugged. "Cheering's one thing, money's another. I'll cheer my lungs out for Damien, but Sig's huge."

John looked across Eli at Jaden. "How about you?"

Jaden shook his head. "I don't have any spare money for gambling."

John grinned. That was a nice way of saying he didn't want to bet against Damien. Jaden would be feeling better about that decision soon.

"Damien St. Cloud!" The announcer's voice, amplified with soul force, echoed through the arena. Time for the fun to begin.

When Damien and Ann entered John and the first years cheered. Damien looked bored and Ann looked stunning. Where did she get those outfits? It was going to be hard to concentrate on the match and not stare at her. Damien spoke with Master Sagan for a moment.

"Sigurd Iceborn!" the announcer said.

Sig entered from the far doors, his chest bare, and a pretty, pale master a step behind. No surprise Sig would choose Mistress Ingrid as his second, she was the only master from the northern duchy at the tower. She was cute, but nowhere near as beautiful as Ann. Judging by the little frown on her otherwise expressionless face she'd rather be just about anywhere else. But when the son of your duke asks you to be his second you couldn't exactly refuse.

Beside him Amanda shook her head. "Look at the size of him. I'm afraid you threw your money away."

"Want to make a side bet?" John asked.

She narrowed her eyes at him. "What kind of bet?"

"If Damien wins you don't hug me anymore and if Sig wins I'll give you a kiss."

She blushed then frowned. "You really think he's going to win?"

"I know he will."

"Then no bet. I like hugging you too much to risk it."

Chapter 10

The sun was high overhead as students and sorcerers made their way to the arena. The founder of Sorcery had shaped the arena out of a single huge chunk of granite. It was amazing. He'd cut it out of a mountain then ten sorcerers combined their power to bring it back here where he carved it out over four days. Damien couldn't imagine someone having that much control.

Word had quickly spread about Damien's duel with Sig. John told him over breakfast that he was a huge underdog. Damien had given his life savings, twenty-three gold royals, to his friend to bet on him. If the odds against him were as bad as John said he stood to make a nice bit of coin.

Damien stretched and bounced in place, trying to get his blood pumping and his muscles loose. He wore a simple black tunic and pants, the same set he'd worn the day before in fact. According to John, Master Sagan's weapons were harmless unless he wished it otherwise so protective gear was unnecessary.

"Are you sure you want to go through with this?" Ann stood beside him just outside the south entrance to the arena. Instead of her usual dress she wore tight black pants and a red silk top. She'd informed him that red and black were the proper colors for this sort of occasion.

"Yup. Watch this." He made the little light appear in front of him without even raising his hand then drew the power back in. "Not bad, huh?"

"How can you be so calm? He's three times your size."

Damien shrugged. "Size doesn't mean much in a sword fight. It just makes him a bigger target."

A roar went up from the crowd and a much amplified voice said, "Damien St. Cloud!"

Damien grinned. "Shall we?"

Damien went first and Ann followed a step behind and to his right. The tall double doors opened at their approach and the roar of the crowd washed over Damien. One hundred and seventy-five sorcerers and students filled the seats. In the sand at the center of the arena floor a grizzled old man with a scruffy beard and missing left hand waited, Master Sagan, Damien assumed.

He bowed to the master. "Thank you for doing this, sir."

Master Sagan shook his head. "Boy, I'm not sure if you're brave or stupid. I know the man that trained Sig and he's one of the best in the kingdom."

"Really? The man who trained me claims to be one of the best as well. This should be a good match."

"And who might that be?"

Before Damien could answer the announcer said, "Sigurd Iceborn!"

The doors on the opposite end of the arena opened and Sig entered, his chest bare to show off his muscles. He had plenty of them, Damien wouldn't deny that. Lucky for him they weren't having a wrestling match. The crowd cheered even louder, telling Damien everything he needed to know about how they'd bet. Behind Sig a master Damien didn't know, a woman with pale skin and hair so blond it almost looked white, regarded the whole scene with bored, half-closed eyes.

He turned to Ann. "Did you bet on me?"

She looked away. "I don't like to gamble."

"I'll take that as a no."

Sig reached the center of the arena and stopped a couple of paces from Damien, a grin plastered across his pale face. “Well you had the guts to show, I’ll give you that.”

“I was about to say the same thing.”

Sig’s grin turned to a snarl. “I’m going to crush you, you little speck.”

Damien nodded, not at all impressed.

Master Sagan raised his hands and the arena fell silent. “Here are the rules. I’ll provide the weapons. Any hit I deem fatal will count as a point. Three points wins. Clear?”

They both nodded and Master Sagan turned to Damien. “What’s your weapon?”

“Dai Chi long sword.”

Master Sagan blinked, seemingly surprised by the choice of such an exotic weapon. He recovered quickly and a long, thin, straight blade appeared in front of Damien. It looked exactly like Lizzy, right down to the sharkskin wrapping on the hilt. He grasped the hilt and swished it around a couple times like a kid with a stick playing knight. The weight and balance were perfect. When did Master Sagan get a chance to see Lizzy? He’d have to ask after the match.

Seeing him swing the sword Master Sagan whispered, “Do you know how to use that weapon?”

Damien held up the sword and gave it a close look. “I believe so.”

Sig laughed and Master Sagan shook his head. He turned to Sig. “Weapon?”

“Claymore.”

A four-foot blade a hand wide with a two-handed grip appeared in front of Sig. He grasped it, whirled it around over his head and roared to the crowd. They cheered and he waved like he’d already won the match. Damien smiled at the display. Sig was so overconfident he could probably win using his off hand.

“Take your positions.”

Damien stood four feet from Sig, his sword in front of him, wrist cocked. Sig took a wide stance, sword raised at middle guard.

“Begin!”

Sig flinched back to begin his swing. The instant he moved Damien lunged, burying a foot of illusory steel in Sig's throat. The arena fell silent. Damien recovered and returned to his position. He glanced at Master Sagan and raised an eyebrow. The old man shook himself and said, "First point to Damien."

Damien smiled. "See, nothing to it. I didn't get a chance to answer you earlier. My father trained me. His name is Fredric St. Cloud. You probably know him better as Fredric the Lightning, King's Champion and Master of The Citadel. You guys must have met at some point. The sword you created for me is an exact replica of the demon sword he carries."

Master Sagan stared at him, Sig stared at him, and it seemed everyone in the crowd was staring at him. Guess they really hadn't thought he had a chance. He faced Sig and resumed his stance. "Ready when you are."

Chapter 11

John rubbed his hands together, eager for the match to start. Down on the sand Master Sagan conjured a long thin sword for Damien. It looked just like his father's demon sword. Did Master Sagan know or was it just a coincidence? Damien swished it back and forth, playing around. Beside him Eli groaned.

Sig got his weapon and roared for the crowd. They took their positions. "Begin!" Master Sagan said.

John blinked and Damien's sword was in Sig's neck. Stunned silence surrounded him. Students and sorcerers gaped at Damien's speed. From the intense look on several of their faces he suspected they were trying to figure out how Damien used his soul force without them noticing. Amanda grabbed his sleeve and tugged. "What happened?"

"Damien won the first point."

"I barely saw him move then it was over."

John nodded. He'd dueled Damien once when they were little. He was nine and Damien eight, and he hadn't fared any better than Sig. If the match lasted another full minute he'd be shocked.

Chapter 12

"Luck won't save you this time." Sig raised his blade so the hilt was near his right ear and the point aimed at Damien's chest. Why didn't he just put a sign around his neck saying he was going to thrust the instant Master Sagan gave the signal?

"Begin!"

Sig thrust, just as Damien expected. He spun and parried, pushing the huge blade to the left. Sig staggered past and Damien slashed him across the back of the neck.

"Second point to Damien."

Sig regained his balance, spun and snarled at Damien. Such a scary face. Damien smiled. "I don't imagine this is how you expected our match to go."

"My master said I was his finest student, the best in the Northlands. I can't lose to a skinny runt like you."

"Did your father pay him to train you?"

Sig's snarl turned to a look of confusion. "Of course."

"You don't think his continued employment might have depended on him telling you and the duke what you wanted to hear?"

"He lied to me?"

"Either that or the Northlands are in serious trouble the next time the Ice Queen sends her army south."

"No! I will beat you." Sig took his stance, sword held in a two-handed grip on his right side. This one was a little harder to read at least.

Damien raised his sword and nodded once.

"Begin!"

Sig roared and swung his blade in a horizontal slash that would have cut Damien in two if the blade was real. Damien leapt straight into the air, pulling his legs up tight. The sword passed under him with inches to spare. He landed and thrust his weapon through the side of Sig's head.

"Match to Damien."

And that was that. He tossed his fake sword to Master Sagan who let it fade away. "Thanks for overseeing the match, Master."

Master Sagan inclined his head. "An impressive performance, young man. Your father would be proud."

Damien smiled. His father would be disgusted that he'd wasted his time fighting someone as unskilled as Sig in the first place. He could hear Dad now. Find someone worth your effort. Getting praise for defeating that boy is worthless.

The crowd stood, getting ready to leave the arena and cry over their lost money. How much would he and John collect for his trouble? Damien started for the doors.

"Stop!" Sig faced him, his face red and furious. "This isn't over. I'll pound you with my bare hands. Your tricks won't help you then."

A murmur ran through the crowd and they turned back to the arena.

"You fought a fair duel and lost," Master Sagan said. "Don't dishonor yourself with this tantrum."

"Stay out of this, old man. I'm going to teach this snot you can't insult the heir to the North and get away with it."

Sig ran toward him, arms out wide. It appeared he planned to crush Damien like a great bear. Damien waited, perfectly at ease, until the last second when he dodged left, grabbed Sig's outstretched arm and dropped his full bodyweight to the sand. He dragged Sig down with him, twisted his arm and wrenched it up, stretching the shoulder joint just short of dislocation. He planted his knee in his opponent's back. Under him Sig groaned.

"It's not fair," the giant boy whimpered. "I'm the strongest."

"Strongest?" Damien stood up and pulled his tunic off. A gasp from behind him said Ann saw the scars crisscrossing his back from his failure to master iron skin. His chest sported a matching set. "You dare claim to be strong yet you haven't got a single scar. Your master didn't train you, he let you play with a sword and told you you were a soldier. We're done here. Leave me and my friends alone or so help me I'll send you to the healer for a month."

Sig buried his face in the sand and his body shook. Damien slipped his tunic back on and walked away. The last thing he wanted was to sit and listen to the boy cry.

Ann came over to him and put her hand on his shoulder. "Are you okay? Your back..."

"I'm fine and the scars are old." He looked at his feet, embarrassed that he'd lost control. "Thanks for standing with me."

"You didn't need much help. I feared I might have to carry you out of the arena."

Damien smiled and held out his arm. "Your confidence in my skills warms my heart."

She linked arms with him and they walked out of the arena together.

Chapter 13

Damien sat on the edge of his bed holding his sister's letter and read it again. He'd been studying at The Tower for a little over three years and would be taking his final exam in an hour. Ann said she had no doubt he'd pass with flying colors and have all his restrictions removed. That would be nice since Jen wanted him to come home for the summer solstice the day after tomorrow and celebrate with her and Dad. Unless the masters removed his restrictions he wouldn't be allowed to leave the tower.

He grimaced and tossed the parchment on his desk. It would be great to see Jen and Lizzy again, but he didn't know what sort of reception to expect from Dad. Maybe it wouldn't be too bad. Now that there was no chance of him becoming a warlord there'd be no pressure on either of them. They could just be father and son rather than master and student.

A quick pace around his little room did nothing to relieve his anxiety. He stopped in front of his footlocker, dug out a pair of thin leather gloves, tossed his tunic on the bed so it wouldn't get sweaty, and pulled on the gloves. A pair of curved sabers appeared in the air in front of him. Damien grasped the hilts and ran through some basic forms. He'd discovered after his duel with Sig that if he wore gloves he could grip weapons he conjured himself, as long as they didn't actually touch his skin.

He leapt, spun, and twisted, swirling the blades around his body. Lost in the movements, his worries fled to the back of his mind and vanished, at least for a few minutes. A thin sheen of sweat soon covered his chest. Though he'd never be fast enough to stand toe to toe with a warlord, Damien felt pleased that he'd maintained his form for three years without a sparring partner.

After a couple of minutes he stopped and blew out a breath. "Enjoying the show?"

"I didn't think you'd noticed me." Ann pushed the door the rest of the way open and sauntered in. She wore one of her typically snug, low-cut dresses. "With everything a sorcerer can do, why do you insist on using those swords?"

Damien reabsorbed the energy in the blades, stripped off his gloves, and dug a towel out of his trunk. Why did he keep using swords? With what he'd learned the last few years he could destroy a small army with a thought, but somehow the sword still called to him. "I guess it's the discipline. To be a good swordsman you need perfect focus and balance. When I do forms it drives out all other thoughts."

He finished drying off and reached for his tunic. It jumped out of his hand. He looked up at Ann, who smiled. "No need to put that back on so soon."

Damien shook his head. He'd have to introduce Ann to Lizzy, they were a lot alike. With a thought he formed a bubble around his tunic and severed whatever thread of energy she'd attached to it. He pulled it back to his side of the bed and threw it on.

She stuck out her bottom lip. "You never let me have any fun."

"Staring at your students without their shirts on might get you into trouble."

She looked around. "There's no one here but us. Are you going to turn me in?"

Damien grinned. He thought of Ann as an older sister; a somewhat perverted, often inappropriate older sister. He'd never do anything to get her in trouble and would happily cut the throat of anyone that did. "Of course not. Should we head up? Eli's probably just getting started."

She heaved a dramatic sigh. "I suppose, if you're not going to leave your shirt off so I can enjoy the view, we might as well."

They left Damien's room and headed for the stairwell. It was fifteen floors up to the testing chamber. Damien could have jogged up easily enough, but Ann wouldn't appreciate it, especially since she wore her ridiculous four-inch heels. "Want me to handle transportation?"

"Save your strength for the test."

Damien raised an eyebrow at that. He could replenish any power he used carrying them up in seconds and she had to know that by now. "Is it that bad?"

She turned serious for the first time. "No, it's not bad, exactly, just challenging. I know you can handle it. You're the most gifted student I've ever trained and your power still terrifies me a little."

She conjured a little basket around them and it lifted them up one floor after another, until they reached the fifteenth-floor landing. The basket vanished and Damien opened the door for her. Beyond the door waited a short, black-stone hall. No silver broke the dark surface of the tiles. A little shiver ran through him. The atmosphere gave him chills.

At the end of the hall a black door marked with a rune of forbiddance blocked their path. Except on test days no one but the high sorcerers entered the chamber. A few feet from the door, as though to lift some of the foreboding a student must feel on his approach to the testing chamber, rested a pair of perfectly ordinary leather chairs.

Ann sat in one, but Damien was too anxious to sit down. He paced the short hall, eager to get on with it. After his tenth trip back and forth Ann said, "Will you please sit down? You're making me nervous."

He sat beside her and patted her knee. "Sorry. I don't do well with waiting."

"I see that. Have you heard from your friend?"

"Not since he left this spring." John had passed his tests and gone north to apprentice to the master healer in the northern army. He'd also be stationed close to his father, which might be good or bad depending on the general's mood. "I'm sure he's fine. John has a knack for getting along with people. So, how does one go about becoming a high sorcerer?"

"It's simple enough. Every ten years all the sorcerers in the kingdom come to The Tower for the gathering. Any full sorcerer interested in the job can stand for high sorcerer. We then hold a vote and the five with the most votes become high sorcerers for ten years."

"I thought there were only four high sorcerers?"

"We select five then they chose amongst themselves who to promote to archmage. The archmage heads to the capital to advise the king on supernatural matters and oversee the Crimson Legion, the sorcerers in charge of protecting the king. There's a lot of politics involved and most sorcerers aren't interested in the job. That's why Lidia has held the post of archmage for the past sixteen years."

The black door creaked and swung open. Damien leapt to his feet a moment before a slumped-over Eli walked through. He looked up at Damien and shook his head. He'd failed. Damien clapped him on the back as he headed for the stairs. Eli was a solid sorcerer, and even if he failed this time he could try again in six months and pass it for sure.

"Damien St. Cloud." A disembodied voice spoke from inside the testing chamber. "It's time."

He glanced at Ann, who shook her head. "You're on your own. I'll be here when you finish."

Damien entered the dark chamber and walked to a circle of light in the center of the room. Looming over him, one at each of the four cardinal directions sat the four high sorcerers. Three women and one man, all older than Ann, but not by as much as he'd expected. He put them all in their late forties or early fifties.

He bowed to each in turn then clasped his hands behind his back and waited. He didn't have to wait long.

"Mistress Ann has recommended you for the final examination," the Master of the South said. "Do you feel you are ready?"

Damien faced the master. "Yes, sir."

"Very well," the Mistress of the East said, her voice almost as deep as the master's. "You must demonstrate competence in four of the six primary skills. Where do you wish to begin?"

"Shielding." Protection and attack were Damien's strongest skills so he planned to start there and make a good first impression.

"Form your shield and we will attack. Resist as long as you can," the Master of the South said.

Damien conjured a golden globe around himself, wasting neither time nor energy to make it invisible. He spent a quarter of his power on it and felt certain it would hold against anything but a full-power assault. Energy blasts from each master struck his shield in succession. Their attacks didn't even cause it to flex. So far so good.

Next they attacked it together. Dents formed, but the shield held. Damien let out a breath. A moment later a golden giant appeared, a club in its hand. It swung down at him and an instant before it struck he reinforced the top of the sphere. The club skipped off without breaking through.

"Well done," the Mistress of the North said. "You pass the first test."

Damien reabsorbed the shield energy remaining and diverted some of the power from his personal shield to restoring his core. It wouldn't take long for his power to replenish.

Damien passed attack easily, hitting multiple moving targets and shattering every shield they conjured. Detection was harder, but he found the poison in every sample they brought and neutralized it. He was almost through. Sweat stained his tunic and stuck it to his back.

"Next?" the Mistress of the North asked.

"Shaping." Damien took a few deep breaths to steady himself and a chunk of stone floated down from somewhere in the darkened recesses above him. "What do you wish me to make?"

"Whatever you like," the Mistress of the East said. "Impress us."

Damien studied the stone, both with his eyes and his soul force. It was taller than it was wide and a couple of fissures ran through it. If he hit those wrong the rock would crumble and he'd fail the test. Luckily for him both flaws ran along the edge of the stone so he could use most of it. When he had the image of what he wanted firmly in mind he sent out streams of soul force and carved.

He had no sense of time as he worked, his focus on the task absolute. When he finally finished, a statue of a nude, winged female sat on the floor. The face was a little crude and the feathers on the wings could have used more texture, but overall it was a pretty good likeness of Lizzy.

Around him the masters applauded. "The finest example of shaping we've seen from a candidate in many years. That's four passed out of six," the Master of the South said. "Congratulations, you've passed your final test."

The master looked at the three women and each nodded. He continued. "We remove all restrictions from you. You are now free to use your powers at your discretion. Finally, you'll need to find an experienced sorcerer to mentor you for two years of field work before you'll get missions of your own. Well done."

The door behind him opened, he bowed to each of the masters, and left. Ann stood beside her chair, a worried frown on her face. Damien grinned and she smiled. "You passed?"

"Sure did. All credit to my teacher. How long was I in there?"

"Three hours. I was afraid they'd killed you for a little while." They went back downstairs in her basket. As they descended Ann asked, "What will you do now?"

"I'm going home for a visit. Jen invited me for the Solstice festival and I'm eager to see her and Lizzy."

She leered at him. "You're not afraid your lover has moved on in three years?"

Damien had never told Ann Lizzy was a spirit bound in his father's sword and he didn't feel the need to now. "I don't think so."

"Well if she has, let me know. After today you're not my student anymore so anything goes."

Damien shook his head and the basket hit the second-floor landing. She never quit. "Thanks. Though I'd be too afraid of the other guys to try anything with the object of their affections."

She laughed, hugged him again, and rose up to the sixth floor and her apartment. Damien sighed. When he got back from The Citadel he'd have to find an apartment in the upper levels. He was a sorcerer now, which meant he couldn't stay in the students' rooms anymore.

He made the familiar walk back to the room he shared with Eli and pushed the door open. His roommate lay on his bed, an arm over his eyes. When Damien entered he rolled on his side. "How'd you do?"

"Passed. Took damn near three hours. What happened to you?"

"My shield broke, I missed half the moving targets, and my construct lost its mock battle."

Damien winced. He'd failed attack, shield, and conjuring, the three primary skills for a sorcerer, not good. "What about the rest?"

"I passed detection and shaping no problem and I could have passed healing, but I failed the other three first."

"Sorry. Want some advice?"

Eli shrugged, sighed, and said, "Sure, what could it hurt?"

"Chose one of the three you failed and focus on it for the next six months. When the time comes you'll have your skills ready to go."

Eli got up and they shook hands. "Thanks, Damien, you've been a good roommate and friend. I suppose I'll get a new bunkmate now."

"Only for six months, then you can get an apartment on my floor, whichever one I end up on. I'm heading out for a few days. See you later."

"I saw your sister's letter on your desk. You must be excited to finally go home again."

"Yeah, excited and terrified, the same as when I arrived here."

Chapter 14

Damien circled The Citadel once to have a look around. It was late afternoon on a dull, gray summer day. He'd gathered his gear and taken off a couple minutes after his talk with Eli. His rucksack and weapons hung off his shoulder, just like when he'd left, but he didn't bother with a mount. Instead he flew on his own like a bird, his shield keeping the bugs out of his mouth and nose. He went full blast, pushing as hard as he dared. He ended up making the return trip in under an hour.

Below him, tiny figures practiced their forms in the training yard. A wave of nostalgia hit him, just for a second, before he remembered all the bad things he had to put up with. He descended and landed on the dirt patch beside the wall. No one greeted him, of course. He'd come early hoping to surprise Jen and Lizzy.

He skirted the practice field, pausing a moment to look the students over and make sure no one was a sorcerer. Nope, all happy little warlords. That was good. He wouldn't have wished the frustration he went through on anyone.

He angled toward the fortress. Classes would end soon and Damien wanted to avoid the press of students in the entry hall.

He walked through the doors and sighed in relief. The hall was empty; he'd beaten the rush. He jogged up the stairs and down the hall to his family's quarters. He raised his hand to knock then hesitated. Three years, what would it be like to walk through that door again after three years?

Stop being such a wimp.

He pushed the door open.

Jen stood in the kitchen setting the table, her familiar golden hair swirling around her as she worked. She'd grown since he last saw her. She stood close to six feet tall now and her figure had filled in. He suspected the guys still drooled when she walked by. Especially if she walked by wearing an outfit like the one she had on now. Sheer blue fabric billowed around her and slits in the arms and legs revealed smooth skin. A lot of female warlords dressed in revealing outfits to distract their opponents, their iron skin defense better protection than any armor.

"Hey, sis."

The plate in her hand fell to the kitchen floor and shattered. She spun, eyes filled with tears. "Damien."

She covered the distance between them in an instant, lifted him off the ground, and spun him around. She cried openly as she hugged him. He had a tickle in his throat, but managed not to cry. "It's good to see you too."

She set him down. "I didn't know if you were coming. Why didn't you write?"

"I didn't know if I was coming either until I passed the final test this morning. I'm a full sorcerer now. I still have to do fieldwork with a more experienced sorcerer for two years before they'll give me my own missions, but I have no restrictions on my power beyond good sense."

"Congratulations." She stepped back and looked at him. "You've grown so much."

"So have you," he said, eyeing her ample chest.

"Ugh! Why is it every boy, even my brother, notices those first? I swear they're nothing but a nuisance. Still, they make an excellent distraction when I fight men."

"I bet. What's for dinner?"

"Roast venison and vegetables. I need to clean up that plate."

"I'll get it." Damien focused on the plate and the pieces glowed and lifted off the floor. He heated the edges and fused the chunks together. The small bits he melted and used to fill the cracks. Finally he polished the surface and it looked good as new. "There, all fixed."

She looked at him then at the plate floating in the air in one piece. "Neat trick."

"Thanks." He lowered the plate into the sink and released his power. "How's it feel to be a proper warlord?"

"Great." Jen finished setting the table, adding a place for him. "They gave me my own squad. There's only five of us, but I'm in command."

Damien sat in his usual place at the table. "Congratulations. From your letters I got the impression you didn't care much for working with the watch in Port Valcane."

She grimaced. "No, the commander was grabby and it took all my self-control not to knock him through the wall of his office. That was a long year."

"I'm impressed you managed it. What's your squad like?"

She grinned and sat across from him. "They're great. Tough, smart, and determined. One of them graduated this year, two are my yearmates, and the fourth is a veteran of twenty years."

Damien offered a knowing smile. "Is he there to keep an eye on you?"

"Probably, but he's never undercut me with the others and he follows orders like any other soldier so I can't complain."

A creak from the door stopped Damien before he could ask another question. He glanced over his shoulder to see his father walk into the room, Lizzy held easily in his left hand. He spotted Damien and stopped. Here it comes.

"Hi, Dad, I'm home."

"Damien. You've completed your studies?"

Not the warmest greeting, but at least he hadn't yelled or threatened to throw him out. "Yeah, I'm a full sorcerer now." Damien conjured a little light and made it vanish.

His father hung Lizzy over the fireplace and took his seat at the head of the table. "Sending you there was the right decision. Good. When's dinner?"

Chapter 15

Damien lay on his old, lumpy bed, legs crossed, staring at the ceiling. Dinner had been an interesting sort of awkward. He and Dad had no idea how to react to each other. Jen had tried to fill the silence, but only sounded pained. They ended up eating without conversation and after he helped Jen clean up Damien retreated to his room. It would be a long visit if he and Dad couldn't figure out some way to get comfortable with each other.

He closed his eyes and found himself floating beside a beautiful, naked Lizzy. He sighed at the sight of her. They stared at each other for a moment then came together. The feathers of her wings tickled the back of his neck and her tears soaked his shirt. He held her, her body soft and familiar in his arms. Damien had dreamed of this reunion for three years.

When they parted she wiped her eyes. "I wasn't sure you'd ever come back."

"You didn't think I'd forget about you, did you?"

She sniffed. "Not really, but we were so far apart. You might have found another girl."

Damien grinned. "As though a girl exists that could compare with you."

She smiled. That appeared to have been the right thing to say.

"In fact I used you as the model for my shaping final. The masters seemed impressed with the little statue I made of you." He concentrated and a replica of his final project appeared in the air between them.

She flew around the statue, looking it over. "Not too bad."

She lashed her wings and flew away. Damien let the statue vanish and chased after her. They played the old game, racing through the endless sky. When he caught her this time, she made his clothes vanish and wrapped them both in her wings.

Later they drifted together, her wings around them like a blanket. Damien had always known this day would arrive, but now that it had, it felt more perfect than he'd dared hope. Lizzy rested her head on his chest and he put an arm around her. Not for the first time Damien wished he could stay with her like this forever. It would certainly be preferable to having to try to talk to his father again.

"He regrets having been so hard on you." Lizzy's glowing red eyes looked up at him. She must have read his thoughts. "He just doesn't know how to fix it. Emotional matters have never been Fredric's strong suit."

Damien laughed, short, bitter and humorless. "No kidding. After the Solstice I'll head back to The Tower and he'll be free of me again."

"Do you have to leave so soon?"

He stroked her hair. "I've got to start my fieldwork. I wish I could take you with me."

She sighed and nuzzled his neck. "I can't project myself more than fifty feet, and I know of no sorcery that would allow us to connect over such a distance."

"I can try to visit more often. Maybe me and Dad can figure out some way to talk to each other that doesn't resemble pulling teeth."

"I think he would like that. I certainly would."

Lizzy's head lifted off his chest and listened to something beyond his perception.

"What is it?"

"Someone came to the door and now your sister's getting dressed."

"Trouble?"

"It's after midnight, so I assume so."

Reading his mind again Lizzy returned him to his body. Damien rolled out of bed and went to the door in time to see Jen walk out of her room, her sword strapped to her back. Just inside the door stood a tall, broad-shouldered boy with a maul over his shoulder. "What's up?"

She turned back. "Goblins. They burned a farm eight miles north. I'm taking my squad to investigate. Go back to bed."

"Be careful."

She threw a wave over his shoulder and walked out with the stranger. Damien went back to bed and sighed. Goblins, so close to The Citadel. That was certainly strange. Usually they kept to the wild lands. The green-skinned monsters were stupid enough, but he thought they had more sense than to hunt near a cluster of warlords. He fell asleep still musing on what had prompted the little brutes to do something so foolish.

Chapter 16

Jen cinched the buckles on her back sheath tight as she walked down the hall beside Edward Mark, one of her squad members. They strode through the hall outside the living quarters, the only sound this late at night their boots on the stone floor. Glow globes set every twenty feet lit their path. Edward had drawn the short straw and received the task of fetching her when word of another goblin raid arrived at The Citadel. A little after midnight a night patrol had seen flames and when they went to investigate, discovered the attack. The little bastards had burned a farm an hour's ride away. They did it to mock her, she knew it.

The raids had started two weeks ago. Local patrols had failed to deal with them; three soldiers were killed in the first attempt to handle the green-skinned monsters. After that the patrol leader put in a request to have warlords handle the matter. Hunting down a few goblin raiders should have been a simple matter, so Dad assigned Jen and her squad to the mission, her first as a commander. Three burned farms later Jen had begun to doubt their ability to even find the miserable wretches.

She clenched her jaw and sent soul force through her brain to burn the last of the sleep from her mind. She needed her full focus tonight. No way would her prey escape this time. Outside the fortress's main doors the rest of her squad waited with saddled horses. Dim light from a near-full moon lit the yard. Jen sent soul force to her eyes to enhance her vision and the scene before her became clear. Three warlords sat astride their horses, weapons and other gear secured, eager and ready for a fight. Jen leapt onto the back of her black gelding. None of them were more eager than her.

"Let's go!"

They thundered through the main gate and turned up the dirt road, following the directions the patrolman provided. Between the moonlight and smooth road they made good time for the first part of the trip. Sparks leaping into the air showed the location of the burning farmhouse. Jen reined in her mount and turned off the main road and onto a rutted wagon path that led down to the farm.

As they got closer the smoldering remains of the house came into view along with three patrolmen who were placing a shroud over an uncovered body. Jen frowned. More bodies on her watch. Each one pained her, as much because of the failure they represented as the loss of life. Jen hated failing, probably because she'd done so little of it. That's what Damien would say if he could hear her thoughts.

She didn't yet know what to make of her little brother. He'd changed in the three years he spent at Sorcery. His trick with the plate showed he'd learned to use his soul force. She smiled at that. He'd struggled so long to get his power to work. That he'd finally found a way forward pleased her.

The group stopped short of the patrolmen and dismounted. Jen caught Talon's eye and nodded toward the farmhouse. The lanky warlord nodded and rushed over, soul-force-enhanced eyes scanning for tracks. Talon had a knack for hunting, having grown up the son of a woodsman at the edge of the Great Green. If anyone could figure out where the goblins went it was him. The patrolmen left their grisly task and walked over to the warlords.

"Report," Jen said.

Two of the patrolmen looked at the third man, an older fellow with a salt-and-pepper beard and tired eyes. He cleared his throat. "We were riding our usual patrol an hour or so before midnight when we saw the glow from the fire. When we arrived the house was fully engulfed and we saw no goblins. This is the second farm attack I've seen so I figured it had to be the same bunch as before. I sent Mica to The Citadel and the rest of us searched for survivors." He nodded toward the bodies. "Didn't find any."

Jen patted him on the shoulder. "Thank you. We'll take it from here."

"Get them bastards, ma'am. Don't know how many more farmers I can tell to lock their doors at night and they'll be fine before I throw up."

Jen knew just how he felt. Every time they arrived too late to save a family then failed to track down the creatures responsible she felt sick and angry, mostly angry. "We'll get them. They can't hide forever. Head back to town and get some rest."

"If it's all the same, I think we'll finish our patrol. Doubt I'll get any sleep tonight anyway."

Jen nodded. "Whatever you think best. Thanks again."

Talon stood by the corner of the burning farmhouse. When she finished with the patrolmen he waved her over. When she arrived he pointed at the dirt. Short, wide prints covered the ground. She'd visited enough goblin victims to recognize their tracks. "Talk to me."

He pointed northeast. "They came from that way, across the farmer's fields, and smashed down the back door. They dragged two people out here and the third ran toward the outhouse. Looks like the goblins ran that one down about halfway across the yard. They didn't haul away any loot. They came, killed, burned, and left. I can't see much point to it."

"Since when do goblins need to make sense?" The others had gathered around and they chuckled at her comment. Talon had a point though. These goblins acted even stranger than usual for their insane kind. Not that it mattered to her why they did it, all she cared about was finding them and putting an end to it. "Which way?"

"Same way they arrived, back across the fields. They didn't make any effort to hide their tracks. It's like they don't care if we follow them. It's kind of insulting."

They left their horses tied to an old elm a safe distance from the burning ruin. In the dark, moving across rough ground, they'd be better off on foot. Talon led the way, the others a few steps behind. They left the yard and entered a field with what Jen guessed was wheat; most of the farms around here grew wheat. She shook her head. What a stupid thing to think about.

Focusing on the situation at hand, she used her soul force to sharpen her hearing and smell, either one of which would be more likely than her sight to warn her of an approaching enemy in the dark. Talon led them on, never hesitating, along the goblin trail. From her position behind him she saw the path the goblins had left as clear as the wagon ruts that led to the farmhouse. Talon was right, they didn't seem to care if anyone followed them. If she was following an enemy that wasn't obviously insane she'd fear an ambush. In this case she'd welcome it, at least they could come to blows with the goblins instead of chasing them all over the countryside.

They arrived at the edge of a forest. It was of fair size and consisted mainly of evergreens. No one had bothered to name it since, despite its size, it was tiny compared to the Great Green. Talon paused a moment at the edge of the forest and crouched down for a closer look at the tracks. A couple minutes later they were on their way again, angling more east than north. For an hour they marched through thick, young evergreens. Finally they stopped at a thicket of brambles and blackberry bushes. Some of the vines had inch-long thorns.

"What's the problem?" Jen asked.

"The tracks lead in there." He pointed to some broken vines where the goblins had pushed them aside. "Gonna be a bitch forcing our way through. You want to stay on their trail or circle around and try to cut it on the opposite side?"

"Keep on them." There was no way she'd let the little bastards have a chance of sneaking past them now. "Our iron skin will protect us from the thorns."

Talon nodded and pushed his way through the brush. Jen followed a step behind. She felt the sharpness of the thorns, but when she yanked them aside they broke off on her impenetrable skin. Her very penetrable clothes, unfortunately, grew ever more shredded with each step. Jen grimaced and kept going. She had plenty of clothes back home. Fifteen minutes of hard slogging later Talon stopped and stared at the ground.

"What's wrong?" Jen stood beside him and looked where he was looking.

"The trail ends here."

She studied the area, but saw nothing except brambles and thorns. Where the hell could the goblins have gone that their trail just vanished? It didn't seem possible. "Explain."

He shook his head. "The trail ends. One minute it was there, now it's not. I can't explain it."

Rhys yawned. They'd been at it for hours. Jen hated to quit, but with no trail to follow she couldn't think what to do next. She snarled at the heavens. How did they do it? Every time she thought she was close the trail vanished.

"Let's go back, get some food and new clothes, and head out again," she said. Maybe her brother the sorcerer would know something. Heaven knew she needed the help.

Chapter 17

When Damien walked out of his room he found Dad and Lizzy already gone and Jen not back yet. He sighed. So much for a family breakfast. He found bread and jam along with milk from the icebox and fixed himself a snack. He'd finished half of it when Jen pushed the door open and trudged through, her clothes torn and her sword dragging behind her.

"Hard fight?"

She shook her head and tossed the sword on the couch. "We tracked them through the forest, brambles, and thickets for hours then lost them. I don't know how they do it! It's like magic."

Damien fixed her a slice of bread and jam then poured a second glass of milk. He didn't have enough hands to carry everything over to the couch so he conjured an extra pair. Glowing, golden hands zipped Jen's breakfast over to her. She flinched when the disembodied hands appeared before her, then took the food. Damien joined her and they ate together on the couch.

"Dad would have a fit if he saw us eating on the couch," Jen said around a mouthful of bread.

Damien finished his breakfast. He was in too good a mood after last night to care what his father thought about him eating on the couch. "What are you going to do?"

"I don't know." She sipped her milk. "We've tried everything, but we always lose them after a few miles. Can you take a look? You don't have to fight, just help us find them."

"If they're using sorcery there might be residual energy I can track. I'm not sure what the masters would say, but since this isn't a proper mission there shouldn't be any problem with me helping you out. When do you want to go?"

"Right now." She kissed his cheek, leaving a spot of sticky jam. "Let me wash up and get some new clothes. My team's getting breakfast and we were planning on heading back out anyway."

"Okay. I'll meet you in the hall."

Damien left Jen to get cleaned up. He locked the door behind him so no one would walk in on her and headed down the hall toward the entry. He didn't bother with his sword. In a real fight a steel sword was about his weakest option. In the entry hall a couple dozen students stood around chatting. He saw no one he knew. His class would have graduated last year and received their first assignments so it was no surprise everyone was a stranger.

"Well, well, what are the odds?"

Damien groaned at the familiar voice. He turned and saw Dirk and Donk coming from the general direction of the mess hall. He hadn't expected those two idiots to be here. They were a year ahead of him and should be out on whatever assignment the military had chosen for them. "Dirk. What's the matter, no one want you two in their command?"

Donk clenched his fist, but Dirk laid a restraining hand on his shoulder. "On the contrary, we completed our third successful mission and are waiting for our next assignment. Good of you to come home and provide us a little entertainment while we wait."

Damien grinned. He wasn't some scared kid looking to run this time. He was a sorcerer, with full access to all his powers. If these clowns thought they could push him around now, they were in for a surprise. "All right, let's play that game you two liked so well. You remember, the one where I hit you as hard as I can then you hit me as hard as you can. I'll even let you go first."

"Brave of you, punching bag." Dirk balled his fist.

"What're you two doing?" Jen stood at the top of the stairs. She had changed into an identical outfit, this one free from rips, and carried her sword over her shoulder.

Dirk and Donk stepped back from him. Damien looked up at Jen. "It's okay, sis, we're playing a game. No need to worry."

Damien poured power into his shield. "Don't worry, boys, she won't interfere. Right, Jen?"

Jen looked at him. She wasn't a sorcerer and couldn't see the power surrounding him, but she must have gotten a sense of his confidence. "You sure?"

"Absolutely." Damien tapped his chin. "Go ahead, give it your best shot."

Dirk shrugged. "Your funeral."

He swung with all his might. Soul force coursed through his body as he put everything he had into it. Dirk's fist hit Damien's shield and stopped. He could have punched a mountain and done more damage. The dumbfounded Dirk pulled his fist back and stared at it like it had betrayed him.

Damien turned to Donk. "Your turn."

Donk tried an uppercut to Damien's stomach with the same results as his cousin. They looked at each other then back at Damien. It would have been comical if it wasn't so pathetic.

"My turn."

Damien shaped a golden gauntlet around his right fist, then covered his arm and shoulder in more golden armor. He pumped a third of his power into the construct. Little sparks and jagged mini-lightning bolts sparked off the armor. Excess power caused the floor and walls to vibrate and dust to fall from the ceiling. It seemed like the whole fortress was shaking. He drew his fist back.

Dirk and Donk ran back the way they'd come as fast as their soul-force-enhanced legs could carry them. The assembled students and Jen all stared at him with wide eyes. Damien reabsorbed the power and the vibrations stopped. He glanced up at his sister. "Ready?"

Chapter 18

Damien and Jen walked out the doors together and turned toward the stables. He couldn't stop grinning about the way Dirk and Donk had run off. That made his visit home even sweeter.

"What would have happened if you'd hit one of those idiots with that thing you made?"

Damien had been pretty confident the cousins would run at the sight of his construct, so he hadn't given it much thought. "It probably would have blasted them into a fine red mist. Don't worry, if they hadn't run I would have pulled the power back enough to only break a few bones."

"You scared me half to death when you let them hit you. I guess you don't need me to protect you anymore."

Damien reached out and squeezed her hand. "I'll always need you to protect me. That's what big sisters are for."

She squeezed back. "Thanks."

Damien winced when the familiar stink of the stables reached them. The Citadel kept fifty horses on site for the masters and students to use in their training and on missions. The stable itself was a long narrow building with an exit on either end. Four men stood beside five horses near the door. They had the horses saddled and ready to go. When they spotted Jen they snapped to attention. Good discipline, Dad would approve.

"Guys, this is my brother, Damien. Damien, this is my squad." She named them one after another. The tall one with the maul on his shoulder was Edward Mark. He had come to fetch Jen the night before. Next came Talon Wrath. He wore a pair of swords belted at his waist and had a fit, but not bulky build. Talon regarded Damien with cool, appraising eyes. Standing beside Talon was a grizzled, scarred veteran who looked older than Dad, named Rhys. He carried a mace in a loop on his belt and wore a shield on his back. Last was a whip-thin kid Damien's age with a staff, named Alec Wright. The way he looked at Jen told Damien everything he needed to know about Mr. Wright. He'd fallen head over heels for his lovely sister.

"Why'd you bring the kid?" Talon asked.

"Damien just finished his training at Sorcery. He's going to help us find the goblins."

"More likely he'll slow us down," Edward said.

Damien hadn't expected a warm welcome, but he figured at least they'd give him a chance. "If you guys think you can find the goblins on your own that's fine, but so far all you've done is make my sister look bad."

Edward's hand tightened on his maul and soul force coursed through his body. Damien sighed. None of them had enough power to concern him. He could lay them all out without breaking a sweat, but that wouldn't help Jen deal with the goblins.

"Kid's got a point," Rhys said. "I don't fancy spending another day thrashing through the woods with my thumb up my ass. If he can find them I'm glad to have him along."

Jen grabbed Edward's leather shirt and yanked his head down so his eyes were level with hers. "Damien's coming. We're not having a debate or a vote, clear?"

"Yes, ma'am."

Damien forced himself not to smile. She had a way of getting her point across.

"I'll saddle another horse," Alec said.

"No need." Damien concentrated and a golden horse appeared beside him. He spent another moment turning it black to match his sister's then leapt up into the saddle. "Ready when you are."

The others mounted up and Jen led the way through The Citadel's main gate. She guided them north along a well-worn dirt road. The horses went at an easy canter and Damien matched their pace. His construct's hooves never touched the ground, instead he glided along just above the road. It made for a smooth ride, certainly better than bouncing along on a living horse.

He eased up beside his sister. "Where are we going?"

"The thicket where we lost the trail."

"It'll be better if we go to the site of the attack so I can track them from the beginning. If they are using sorcery they might have led you down a false trail."

She looked over at him. "Can you do that?"

He nodded. "Easily. Make some fake goblins the way I did my horse, send them off through the nastiest patch of forest around, and laugh while you guys got shredded by thorns."

"You think that's what happened?"

"Maybe. Best not to take chances."

They reached the still-smoldering farmhouse an hour later. Blackened timbers stuck out of the basement and three shrouded bodies lay on the ground a few feet away awaiting burial. It was a mess. Damien studied the ground. Small tracks covered the soft dirt. A strange black energy swirled around the bodies; not much, more like the remnants of a casting.

Damien had never seen the soul force of a goblin and had no idea if that's what the energy was. He circled the ruins and soon found wisps of the same power leading toward the distant woods. He guided his mount in that direction, following the wisps. When he reached the edge of the trees, thicker blobs of dark energy went left while fainter flecks went straight ahead.

He turned to his sister. "Which way did you guys go?"

She pointed left and Damien nodded. "They laid a false trail for you. The real path goes straight ahead, deeper into the woods."

"There're no tracks that way," Edward said. It looked like he was going to play the part of second guesser.

"Look under my horse's hooves. Do you see any tracks? If the goblins have a sorcerer, which it's clear they do, then hiding their path is simple. I'm tracking the remnants of the sorcerer's casting and it goes straight ahead."

"The forest is too thick for horses." Jen swung down off her mount. "We'll leave them and continue on foot."

Damien dismounted and reabsorbed the construct. While the others hobbled their horses Damien concentrated on the trail. The sorcerer must have surrounded the goblins with a shield that brushed the branches aside and let them snap back into place without breaking. That was tricky work, making a path through the thick evergreens and breaking no branches. The enemy sorcerer had skill, no doubt.

When they'd finished tending the horses Jen said, "Lead on."

Damien expanded his shield so it was outside his clothes and started forward. The prickly spruce limbs made no more impression on his shield than Dirk's punch. The little group tromped through the forest until well past noon, following the twisting trail of dark energy.

"Look here." Talon bent down to examine the ground. "Tracks."

Sure enough, as though out of nowhere, the tracks of a group of goblins appeared in the soft dirt of the forest floor. "They must have figured they were far enough away that we wouldn't stumble over their trail." Jen patted Talon's shoulder.

Talon assumed the lead, his eyes focused on the now-obvious trail. Damien made no complaint about the warlord taking over the tracking duties. He focused on the dark energy, making sure it continued to follow the tracks and they didn't veer off on another false path.

They continued on for another hour, the residual energy getting thicker with each step deeper into the forest. Around them the scrubby evergreens had given way to towering, mature pines. If they got the goblins cleaned out, some loggers would drool over the tall, straight trees.

"Damien." Jen walked by herself a little ways from the rest of her squad.

He went over to join her. "What's up?"

"I wanted to thank you. We'd have never found their trail this deep into the forest."

Damien grinned. "No problem. This is the sort of thing we're trained for. Maybe you can write me a little recommendation for whichever sorcerer I end up serving with."

"Of course, I—"

He held up a hand to stop her. Up ahead a pillar of dark energy rose out of the forest. No goblin sorcerer put out that much energy. Whatever they were approaching it was powerful, and evil. "We're getting close, sis. Whatever's out there, it isn't just goblins."

"What do you see?"

Damien described it to her. "We need to be real careful."

She nodded. "Talon! Don't get too far ahead. Weapons out and eyes focused. Alec, you're on rear guard. Damien, stay with me in the center."

The squad drew their weapons, formed up, and made their cautious way onward. The closer they got the thicker the miasma appeared. Damien's stomach clenched. He'd never seen anything so wrong. Around them the trees reflected the corruption; bark peeled and drooped from drying trunks, the limbs twisted like arthritic hands. The grass and shrubs had withered and curled up. He tapped a dry bush with his toe and it disintegrated.

They climbed up a little rise and stopped. Ahead of them, in a clearing, sat a jumbled up pile of trees, branches, and mud. Easily forty yards in diameter and twenty feet tall, the goblin lair resembled a giant beaver lodge. Like a lodge, the inside would be hollow with chambers and passages. A large opening about eight feet in diameter faced them and to Damien's enhanced sight it looked like a chimney belching corruption.

"Let's go get 'em." Talon started down the far side of the bank.

"Wait." All Damien's senses screamed that danger waited in the lair. "At least let me scout it so we have some idea what we're walking into."

Edward looked at him, a dubious frown twisting his lips. "You think you can sneak in there?"

"Not me." Damien held out his hand and a golden wasp appeared above it. He concentrated and the color shifted so it looked like a black wasp. "A scout bug. They'll never notice it and we can see what's in there."

"Good idea." Jen motioned them back down the bank. "Send it in."

"It's nothing but a bunch of stinking goblins. Just because they set up in this nasty stretch of woods doesn't mean anything. We go in and carve them up, like we were trained." Talon stood a little below the top of the bank, his swords clenched in his fists. He looked tempted to ignore Jen. Heaven help him if he did.

Jen glared at him. "Get down here and keep quiet. They've got at least one sorcerer and who knows what else. A little scouting seems like just the thing to me. It's not like the ugly monsters are going anywhere. Go on, Damien."

He nodded and conjured a flat rectangle of soul force and connected it to the wasp with a hair-thick strand of energy. An image of the surrounding forest appeared on the viewer. Satisfied with the connection, Damien made the thread invisible and sent the wasp toward the mouth of the lair. The image shifted as the wasp flew, showing whatever the little construct looked at.

Jen stood beside him and studied the image on. "That's amazing. I didn't know sorcerers could do something like this."

"It's a handy trick."

The wasp entered and the image went dark. Damien frowned and adjusted the wasp's eyes through the link, making them bigger and reflective to increase the light they collected. The image brightened. The inside of the mound looked just like you'd expect a hollowed-out pile of wood to look like. Branches jutted into the tunnel and a rough, worn path led deeper into the lair. Damien had expected the tunnel to narrow soon after the entrance. Given the goblins' small stature a narrow tunnel would give them an advantage in a fight, instead it maintained its size the whole way.

Ten feet in, the bug reached the first branch in the tunnel. Damien guided it down the side tunnel. A couple feet further on it widened into a round room filled with trash, animal skins, and half-eaten gobbets of meat. Damien shuddered, glad he couldn't connect a thread to transmit smell.

No other paths led out of the chamber so he guided the bug back to the main tunnel. Over the next five minutes they passed two more branches leading to living chambers like the first, but still no goblins. The main tunnel led to another round chamber three times the size of the smaller ones. Ten goblins gathered around a giant creature seated on a crude wooden throne. It had curved tusks and long six-fingered hands ending in black talons. Rolls of fat under coarse black fur covered its body. Through the link Damien saw the corruption rolling off the monster. The goblins' eyes resembled black pits as they stared, enraptured, by the horror on the throne. They'd absorbed the monster's corruption.

"What the hell is that?" Jen asked. She stared at the monstrosity on the projection, her mouth partway open as though she wanted to say more but couldn't find the words.

"It's a demon. That's the source of the corruption." Damien shuddered. Demons were an abomination that had no place in the mortal world. Over time, just by being here, they twisted everything and everyone around them, turning their surroundings into a little slice of hell on earth. Only rarely could a demon overcome its innate corruption and transform into something purer, a risen demon, like Lizzy. "Looks like it's taken control of the tribe. See the especially wrinkled one closest to it?"

"Yeah. Man, that's one ugly goblin."

The withered goblin beside the demon's throne had bones driven through its earlobes, lips and nose. Sharp fangs protruded from its upper lip. Withered, sagging breasts argued it was female, but Damien had no intention of getting close enough to make sure.

"That's their sorcerer. There's a connection between her and the demon. She's not a full warlock, but her power's been enhanced by the demon's corruption. The regular goblins have absorbed it as well. They'll be much more dangerous than anything you're used to."

"They're nothing but shit-stinkin' little goblins." Talon's knuckles were white, he was gripping his swords so tight. "Let's go get them."

Jen ignored Talon and pointed at a pair of dark arches at the rear of the throne room, for lack of a better word. "What are those?"

Damien guided the wasp along the ceiling, hoping neither the sorcerer nor the demon would notice it. It reached the closest arch and flew through. A long, narrow, twisting tunnel led to a small opening to the surface. Looked like a back door. He searched beyond the second arch and found another exit. It was too small for the demon, but the goblins could escape through them easily enough.

"That's it." Damien let the wasp dissolve. "A demon, a sorcerer, and nine corrupted goblins. We should get out of here and collect some reinforcements. I can fly to The Tower, get some more sorcerers, and be back in a day."

"What if they attack another farm tonight?" Edward said. "While you're collecting reinforcements people might die. We're here now. Let's deal with them before they do any more harm."

"I agree," Talon said.

"I don't know." Alec chewed his lip. "If there's a demon..."

Rhys remained silent, his gaze on Jen. Whatever the others thought, it was her call. Damien watched the muscles of her jaw work as she thought. "Edward's right," she said at last. "We need to deal with them before anyone else gets hurt. We can't fight them in their lair. Damien, can you flush them out so we can fight in the open?"

"Sure, I can blast them out easy enough. What are you going to do about those other exits?"

She turned to Edward. "Take Alec and cover the left side. Talon, you and Rhys take the right. We'll cover the main entrance. Kill anything that comes out then fall back here to reinforce us."

"How are we supposed to find them?" Talon asked.

Damien conjured two glowing spheres. "Follow the lights. When you're in position crush them and I'll sense it. My blast will follow a minute later. Be careful. Their aura of corruption will make your iron skin vulnerable. Don't count on it to protect you."

"How about you let us worry about the fighting?" Talon said.

Damien sent the orbs out toward the small tunnels. It would take a couple minutes for them to get in place. He wished Jen had let him get help. During his studies he'd read a lot about demons. Even a weak one would be a huge challenge. If he had to fight the sorcerer at the same time he didn't know what might happen.

"We can do this, right?" Jen sounded like she needed some encouragement. In truth he didn't know if they could do it and he didn't want to lie to his sister.

"It's not too late. You can call them back, we can retreat, and return with more help. There's no guarantee they'll attack again tonight."

"But there's no guarantee they won't. Edward was right about that much. We've been hunting these monsters for a week. The people rely on us to protect them and we've done a poor job of it. We'll take them down together. I can count on you, right?"

"Do you even need to ask?"

They shared a smile. A few seconds later the first then the second orb shattered. The others were in place. Damien conjured a ball of energy and hurled it at the entrance.

Chapter 19

A golden ball of energy raced toward the entrance to the goblins' lair. It flew out of sight down the tunnel and Damien detonated it. The explosion shook the clearing and sent bits of wood flying out. Dust and debris marked the openings of the secondary exits. Jen drew her sword and he increased the power to his shield.

Damien focused on the entrance. When the demon came he'd have no trouble detecting it. Beside him Jen held her long sword in a two-handed grip, soul force surging through her body, strengthening her muscles and bones to many times the power of a normal person.

He grabbed Jen's arm and yanked her behind him.

A golden shield appeared before them an instant ahead of a blast of dark fire. Raging black flames swept by on either side of them. They didn't feel hot so much as wrong, an abomination that didn't belong in this world.

When the flames subsided he absorbed the minimal energy remaining in his shield. From within the lair three small energy sources raced ahead of two bigger ones.

Sounds of battle from deeper in the forest indicated the others had engaged their opponents.

"Here they come."

Three goblins, their eyes filled with corruption, the tips of their crude spears burning with the same black flames that had shot out of the tunnel, came screaming out of the exit.

Quick as thought, golden swords fell from the sky and pierced them through the head and chest. Damien reclaimed his power the instant the goblins died.

"Aren't you going to leave any for me?"

"You'll get your chance. You have to keep the demon busy while I deal with the sorcerer."

As if summoned by his call the goblin sorcerer flew out of the mouth of the tunnel. A beam of darkness streaked toward Damien. He raised a shield to deflect it and leapt into the air after the goblin.

Streaks of golden energy shot from his fingers, detonating around the monster, but never making a solid hit. They chased each other through the late afternoon sky, golden energy hammering dark barriers.

The little bitch was fast, Damien had to give her credit.

Damien conjured a wall in her path. If he could slow her down and get in a clean hit he'd be able to end this fight.

The goblin surrounded herself with an aura of dark power and smashed right through his wall.

So much for that.

At the edge of his awareness the seething power of the demon raged. He hoped Jen could keep it busy. A dark beam streaked past his head, missing by inches.

He didn't dare worry about his sister now. If he did his opponent might get lucky and hurt him and then they would all be in serious trouble.

The goblin dodged another of his blasts. The thing was too fast to hit that way.

He conjured a pair of golden angels and sent them after the goblin. He didn't worry about them getting hit, instead focusing on getting them close to the enemy sorcerer.

Lances of dark energy punched holes through his constructs, but they didn't falter. Damien poured more power into them, closing the holes and increasing their speed.

One of them got a hand on the goblin's ankle. She turned to blast it. The moment the goblin stopped, the second angel grabbed her arms.

Damien released the power in both constructs. The double explosions tore the little goblin to bits.

Chapter 20

Jen stood, trembling, watching her brother exchange blasts with the wrinkled goblin. When the blast of dark fire shot out of the tunnel and she took cover behind Damien's shield, she had feared they'd be incinerated. That his power blocked it amazed her.

Jen knew her brother was powerful, his demonstration in the hall that morning made it clear enough, but the ease with which he blocked those flames then killed the goblins without batting an eye amazed her. It had always been her job to protect Damien, but now it seemed she was the one who needed protection.

A roar sounded from the tunnel, drawing her back to the matter at hand. The demon lumbered into view. Its head brushed the top of the tunnel as it stepped out into the clearing, yellowish-green saliva dripping from its tusks. The sight of an enemy she could fight jolted Jen out of her stupor.

She was a warlord and she had a job to do.

She pushed soul force into her legs and sprinted toward the monster. Her sword sliced across its chest then she was past, its claws missing her by inches. The demon spun to face her, the wound on its chest closing as she watched.

Jen shook her head. Her father didn't even heal that fast.

She lunged toward it and sliced its knee. A taloned hand swooped down to tear her apart.

Too slow.

She leapt back and before it recovered darted in again, cutting its arm.

It went like that for half a minute, her darting in to cut it and the demon healing the shallow wounds an instant later. She put some distance between them and took a deep breath. She could keep this up for hours, but it didn't seem like she was accomplishing anything.

Jen blinked and the demon was before her, its clawed hand rushing toward her stomach.

So fast!

She got her sword between her and the monster's talons an instant before it sent her flying halfway across the clearing. The rough ground tore her clothes, ripping the left sleeve of her tunic off as she skidded through the dirt.

She sprang to her feet in time to meet the brute's next charge.

Claws met steel.

Jen poured more soul force into her muscles to hold the demon back.

How could it be so strong? She'd hoped to save some power in case she needed it later, but if she held back the demon would kill her.

Power flooded her body as she let all her soul force go. She shoved the demon back and hacked a chunk out of its side.

Her sword blurred and thick black ichor flew as she hacked at her opponent.

The demon took a step back and roared.

Got you now, you ugly monster.

Dark power rushed from the demon, its wounds closed in an instant, flames burst from around its hands and the ground under its feet blackened.

Her body trembled as corruption poured from the beast. It had just been playing with her.

Standing face to face with the demon, its full power revealed, Jen saw her death.

Why hadn't she listened to Damien?

This creature was so far beyond anything she'd ever imagined. She felt like a little girl. A terrified little girl, facing a hungry bear.

She would be devoured and there wasn't a thing she could do about it.

Chapter 21

A surge of dark power drew Damien's attention back to the ground. Jen stood a few feet away from the demon, staring at it and not moving.

Its power had overwhelmed her.

Damien had read about that in his studies, but never imagined it happening to his sister, strong as she was.

The demon raised a claw.

Damien drew out half his remaining power and conjured a golden serpent. His construct wrapped around the demon, binding it in place.

He let out a breath. He'd made it in time.

The demon's corruption was rotting his construct by the second. He needed to finish it, but didn't want his sister to feel like he'd saved her. She needed to be part of its defeat to regain some of her confidence.

"Jen!"

She shook herself and looked up at him. Damien dragged his finger across his throat and pointed at the demon. Jen looked at the bound monster and nodded.

She leapt.

All her power flowed into her arms and back as she swung her sword at the demon's neck. Its head shot up into the air and Jen rolled clear.

The serpent snapped the head out of the air and Damien detonated it, sending the power into the sky instead of outwards into the clearing. A great pillar of golden light consumed the demon so nothing of it remained.

Damien sighed. He sensed no other sources of corruption outside the lair.

It looked like they'd won.

Thank heaven for that. He only had a third of his power left.

Jen knelt a little ways away from the shallow crater that marked the demon's grave. He landed beside her, taking a moment to shift the flow of his soul force so half went to replenishing his core rather than the usual trickle. "You okay?"

She stood, sheathed her sword, and nodded. "It didn't hit me. Damn, that thing was strong. I know Dad's killed a demon or two, but I can't see how he managed it. I couldn't do much more than scratch the thing."

"For one thing, Dad's got more soul force than you. Not a lot." He raised his hands when she glared at him. "He's also got Lizzy, which doubles his strength. She can also send her power through the blade so it cuts better than normal steel. Those are huge advantages."

She didn't seem convinced, but screams, growing closer by the second, ended the conversation. Rhys burst into the clearing, Talon slung over his shoulder. The younger man was clutching his leg and screaming with each breath.

"What happened?" Jen rushed over to check on her subordinate.

Rhys lowered Talon to the ground. "One of the goblins got through his guard and jabbed him in the leg. Didn't look like much of a blow, but the spear pierced him deep. He fell screaming on the spot. I killed the little bugger, but I couldn't do anything for Talon."

Jen tore the cloth away from the wound. The goblin had stabbed Talon in the lower thigh, six inches above his left knee. Black lines ran out from a raw, red wound. Talon gritted his teeth, trying to hold in the screams.

He managed it for a couple of seconds.

Jen put a hand on his forehead. "Talon, you have to focus on healing."

He thrashed and gasped. "Can't. Hurts, so much pain."

Edward and Alec emerged from the woods and rushed over. While Rhys filled them in Jen led Damien off to the side. "Can you heal him?"

Damien shook his head. Despite his considerable skills, healing was the one thing he couldn't do. His soul force was too dense for such fine work. "I'd be more likely to blow his leg off than cure him. There's one thing I can try, but I make no promises. The corruption's deep in his flesh."

"He's dying. Do whatever you can."

Damien nodded and knelt beside the thrashing Talon. He put his hand above Talon's wound and sent his soul force into the injured man's body, blocking the flow of pain from his injury to his brain. Talon went still and lay back. He sighed. "The pain's gone."

"It's not gone," Damien said. "I blocked it so you can concentrate. Now focus on healing. The corruption is still spreading. Purge the darkness first, don't worry about the wound."

Talon closed his eyes. Soul force flowed from his core down to his leg. His muscles shrank as he pulled every drop of power and sent it to battle the corruption in his leg. The dark lines drew back ever so slowly.

Over the course of three minutes Talon purged the corruption and partly closed his wound. He fell back, covered in sweat, every speck of excess soul force used up.

"You've cleansed the wound. I'm going to restore the link between your leg and brain. Brace yourself."

Damien removed his barrier and Talon winced, but didn't thrash or scream. A little blood oozed out of the remaining gash, clean and red, with no sign of infection. Rhys dug a healer's kit out of his satchel and set to work binding the injury.

Damien started to get up, but Talon grabbed his sleeve. "Thanks. You saved my life. You were right. That goblin's spear went through my iron skin like it was nothing. I've never felt such pain."

"Save your strength." He patted Talon's hand. "You've still got healing to do."

Jen turned to Edward and Alec. "Get a stretcher built. He won't be walking anywhere for a while."

Damien left them to their work and walked through the late afternoon shadows toward the goblin's lair. That demon hadn't appeared from nowhere. He needed to search the lair for a clue as to its origin.

He hadn't taken three steps when Jen grabbed his wrist. "Where are you going?"

"To have a look around." He nodded toward the lair entrance.

"I'll come with you. The guys have things under control out here."

They continued on together. At the mouth of the tunnel Damien conjured a globe of light without breaking stride. He winced at the stench of rot and corruption. He hadn't expected a goblin lair to smell of perfume, but this was nasty.

They turned down the short branch to the sleeping chamber. It looked the same as they'd seen through his bug's eyes.

"Thanks for helping Talon. He might be a jerk, but he's a good soldier."

Damien turned back toward the main corridor. "I'm glad I could do something. If John were here he'd have purged that wound and had Talon sealed up in ten minutes."

"Could he have handled the demon too?"

Damien headed toward the central chamber. "Probably not. The best healers rarely have dense soul force. It lets them refine their power enough to affect a body on the cellular level, but that sort of control doesn't help much in a fight."

"If we stumbled on this place alone, could my squad have beaten that demon?"

"Maybe."

She grabbed his shoulder and spun him around. "Tell me the truth."

Damien looked into his sister's eyes and saw something he never thought he'd see, doubt and fear. The battle with the demon had shaken her more than he realized. “No, I don’t think so. The sorcerer would have cut you to pieces while you tried not to get killed by the demon. The goblins, even corrupted as they were, you could have managed. But the demon and sorcerer, with their ability to use external soul force, no.”

Her lips trembled and he thought she might cry. “My decision to attack might have gotten them all killed, might have gotten me killed.”

Damien covered her hand with his. “We’re all okay. The goblins are dead and no longer a threat to the people. You held your own against a demon. Things could have been much worse.”

“Thanks, little brother.”

The central chamber, like every other chamber in the place, was a mess. Damien’s explosion hadn’t helped any. Bits of broken wood mixed with rotted flesh and strips of skin. Damien ignored most of that and went right up to the throne.

It was a crude thing, roughly built from scraps of wood and bound with leather thongs. It was a wonder it supported the demon’s weight. At its base was a stone slab.

Damien leaned in for a closer look. On the edge of the slab it looked like someone had engraved runes. He conjured a blast of energy to smash the throne off the slab. On the top of the altar was a carving of a horned skull.

“What is that?” Jen asked.

“A sacrificial altar. A cult of the Horned One must have operated here at one time. The goblins built their lair around the altar. The question is, did the cult summon the demon or did it enter the area on its own?”

“How would you know?”

“I wouldn’t, but there are sorcerers who specialize in this sort of thing. I’ll report what we found and they’ll send someone out to investigate. But first I have to ward this place so no one wanders in.”

Damien conjured a ball of energy and left it floating in the central chamber. As they walked back out, he put a similar ball in each chamber they passed, linking them together with strands of energy. When they reached the exit he put up a barrier so no one could enter.

"There. Can you guys make it back to The Citadel on your own?"

Rhys had Talon bandaged up and Edward and Alec were putting the finishing touches on a stretcher. Jen nodded. "We'll make camp and head back in the morning. Will you return for the festival tomorrow?"

"Depends what the masters have to say, but I'll try." Damien leapt into the sky and flew back towards the tower to report.

The sun had set when Damien landed in the empty yard outside the tower. He hoped the headmaster would still be in his office as he had no way to get in touch with the high sorcerers on the top floor. The doors opened at his approach; he'd gotten in the habit of opening them unconsciously using his power.

He turned down the left-hand corridor and found the headmaster's door closed. He knocked and when there was no response tried the handle and found it locked.

Damn it! Where could he be?

He left the administrative area and headed upstairs to the dining room. Perhaps the old man was getting something to eat. He pushed through the double doors and looked around the room. Nothing but students.

He ground his teeth in frustration. Where else? Ann would know, if he could find her.

Damien made his way up to the third floor but when he reached her training room found it empty. Cursing the universe in general and teachers in particular, Damien went up to the sixth floor to try her apartment. He knocked on the closed door and after a few seconds, to his immense relief, it opened.

"Damien?" Ann stood in the doorway, dark hair dripping, wearing a short robe that left her legs bare. "I thought you went to see your family."

"I did. I helped Jen and her squad track down some goblins. Turns out they were led by a demon. We killed it, but inside their lair I found an altar to the Horned One. I couldn't tell if the demon was summoned there or not, so I came back to report after I warded the lair against intruders."

"Slow down. You killed a demon? By yourself?"

"Jen helped."

"Really?"

"A little."

Ann stepped away from the door. "Come in. I need to get dressed then we have to go talk to Thomas."

Half an hour later found Damien and Ann seated at the headmaster's coffee table, warm cups of tea in their hands, and Damien repeating his story for the second time. When he finished the headmaster said, "This is troubling news. We've seen nothing from the Horned One's cult in years. I'll send a team to investigate first thing in the morning."

Chapter 22

Damien walked down the familiar black-and-silver hallway towards the dining room. A pair of first-year girls saw him and crossed to the other side of the hall, their eyes wide. He sighed.

Two months had passed since the demon incident and word had spread that he'd killed it on his own. The reactions to the news varied from fear to awe, with fear being by far the most common.

Having the people you saw every day regard you as a monster made life awkward to say the least. Even worse, none of the more experienced sorcerers would take him on as an apprentice. He asked everyone he saw and to a person they found some excuse to deny his request.

Well, he couldn't do anything about it, so he trained on his own and hoped for the best. The truth was Damien didn't really know what he wanted to do with his new skills. He had power enough to serve almost anywhere, but he hated the idea of being stuck in a fort somewhere, waiting for trouble to find him. Joining the inquisitors appealed to him. Wandering the kingdom, rooting out corruption, generally helping the people who didn't have connections among the rich and powerful. Damien couldn't imagine a more satisfying use for his power.

He pushed through the dining hall doors and the room fell silent as every gaze focused on him. Damien wanted to shout boo, just to see if they'd flinch. Eli was sitting at the end of one of the benches and waved to him. Damien collected his meal, mystery meat and potatoes covered in gravy, the same as usual, and went to join his friend. The three students seated at Eli's bench made themselves scarce when Damien arrived.

"Maybe I should just eat in my room."

"Don't pay any attention to them. Have you heard anything more about the cult?"

Damien sat down. "No one has said anything to me. You'd think since I was the one who discovered them they'd keep me in the loop."

"I'm sure if there's any fighting to be done you'll be the first to hear. What've you been doing to keep busy?"

"Practicing on my own. Ann recommended a book on shaping. I'm going to check it out after lunch."

"What's it about?"

"Shaping materials other than wood and stone. She says working with more complicated materials will help me learn to better control my power."

Eli shook his head and smiled. "I can barely manage stone and you're already looking for more complex materials to work with. I'm jealous."

"Don't be. At least no one's terrified of you." Damien hated the bitterness in his voice. He'd thought Sorcery would be different than The Citadel, and it had been. For three wonderful years he was just another student, stronger than average, sure, but nothing extraordinary.

Now, thanks to the demon incident, he found himself alone most of the time, the other students too uncomfortable to want to be near him. Even Amanda and Jaden treated him like a snake that might bite them if they did something wrong. Only Eli still acted the same as before. They finished their meal in silence, Damien's bitter comment having spoiled the mood.

Damien got up to return his plate and Eli grabbed his arm. "You're joining us tonight for Jaden's after-testing party, right? We'll either congratulate or commiserate depending on whether he passes or not."

"You sure you want me to come? I know I make the others nervous."

"Don't worry about it. They need to get used to the new reality. It's one thing to know you're strong and another to learn you can kill a demon by yourself."

"It doesn't seem to bother you."

Eli offered a rueful grin. "Remember, I saw your unshielded soul force the day you arrived. I've had over three years to accept the fact that you terrify me. Give the others some time. They'll come around."

Damien laughed. "All right, everyone's meeting in our room, right?"

"Yeah, and Jaden's dad is fixing the food. See you tonight."

Damien nodded, returned his plate to the counter, and went to the library to fetch the book Ann recommended. His quarters were on the eighth floor. As he walked down the silent hall he shook his head. The reason they assigned him this room was because all the other sorcerers living there were out in the field. He essentially had the whole floor to himself. Well, to hell with them, he'd enjoy the peace and quiet.

The apartments they provided for full sorcerers weren't much of an improvement on what they gave the students. Same bed, same minimal furniture; the only difference was no roommate and if he wanted to pay for it he could decorate however he wanted. His twenty gold royals a month stipend would buy some nice furniture, but Damien preferred to save his coin. You never knew when the government might decide sorcerers needed a pay cut.

He kicked his shoes off and plunked down on the narrow, lumpy bed. Perhaps he'd splurge on a nice featherbed at least. The book he'd retrieved from the library had a black leather cover and measured at least two inches thick; not exactly light reading.

He opened to the table of contents and scanned down the list of chapters. Shaping organics, crystals, living animals and plants. He stopped when he reached the last entry: forging weapons without heat. Damien had read about swords created by a sorcerer using only soul force. Lizzy was soul-forged and her blade was the purest steel in existence.

Troubles forgotten, Damien flipped to the back of the book and started reading. Jen's name day was coming in a few months. What would be a better gift than a soul-forged long sword?

Chapter 23

Eli sipped cider and wondered when Damien would arrive. Amanda had walked in fifteen minutes ago wearing a typically gaudy orange-and-red dress. She pounced on the plate of little sandwiches Jaden's dad had prepared for them the moment she spotted it. He didn't bother scolding her. Amanda did what she wanted regardless of what anyone said. He'd begged a couple of extra chairs from one of the masters so no one would have to sit on a bed.

They'd decided to have the little party in his room because the masters hadn't assigned him a new roommate yet. In fact he didn't expect to get a new roommate this year as they only had three first years and they were all girls. That suited Eli fine as he was an only child and enjoyed being alone. Not that Damien had been a bad roommate, even though he got up every morning at five.

"Is he coming?" Amanda had a half-eaten almond butter sandwich in her left hand and an untouched ham sandwich in her right.

Eli didn't need to ask who she meant. "Damien said he'd be here. I didn't tell him a specific time so we'll just have to wait and see when he shows up. Try not to act so nervous when he gets here."

"I can't help it! No one should be that powerful. It's not natural. The fact that he's also good with a sword makes it worse. Damien could kill you so many different ways it's terrifying."

"Don't say things like that. He's our friend...he's my friend anyway. John's not afraid of him, that should tell you something."

"I guess."

The door swung open and a stiff, sweat-soaked Jaden stood in the doorway, his round face glistening. Eli was starting to ask if the test was that bad when Damien appeared behind him. If Amanda was nervous around Damien then Jaden was flat-out terrified. Eli couldn't figure out why since Damien had done nothing remotely aggressive toward either of them. If anything, he stood up for them when Sig picked on them. Maybe to them it was like living next to a volcano; you never knew when it might erupt and when it did you couldn't do a thing about it.

Eli set his cup down and shook both boys' hands. "I wasn't sure if you'd make it, Damien."

Damien smiled. "I got to reading. I wish the tower had windows so I could tell what time it is. I met Jaden on my way downstairs. Tell them the good news."

Jaden opened his mouth to speak, but no sound came out. He cleared his throat. "I passed."

Eli grinned and clapped him on the back. "That's great. Apparently everyone's going to pass on their first try except me."

"Don't jinx me." Amanda came over with the tray of sandwiches and offered one to Damien. "They're pretty good."

"Thank you." Damien took a ham sandwich. Eli handed him a mug of cider and he nodded, his mouth too full to speak. When he swallowed he said, "Which disciplines did you choose?"

Jaden sat in an empty chair and sipped cider. "Detection, shaping, healing, and attack."

Damien raised an eyebrow and Eli knew how he felt. He figured the last skill the shy young sorcerer would choose would be attack. Eli would have guessed shielding.

Seeing their surprise Jaden offered a weak smile. "Master Zora recommended I do attack over shielding or conjuring since it requires less sustained power." He glanced at Damien. "What book were you reading?"

Damien finished his sandwich and sat across from Jaden. "Advanced shaping. There's a chapter on soul-forging weapons. Since I have nothing better to do I thought I'd make a sword for my sister's name day gift."

Jaden smiled and the tension seemed to melt out of him. "That's nice. I should shape something for my mom. Her name day is next month."

The next hour passed with no tension and lots of laughs. Damien yawned and asked, "Do you have a master lined up?"

Jaden nodded. "I volunteered to do a one-year posting on Lookout Island. The master there knows how to shape a viewer powerful enough to let you see a hundred miles away. I want to learn that conjuring. Besides, nothing ever happens out there. That's the sort of job for me."

Damien grinned and everyone stood. They all shook hands and somehow Amanda made off with the leftovers. How did she eat so much and still remain so tiny? When the others had gone he and Damien stood by the door.

"Thanks for this," Damien said. "I think they're a little more comfortable with me now. When I met Jaden on the stairs I was afraid he might have a heart attack before we got here."

Eli smiled, glad he could ease a little of his friend's worry. "It was fun. I think when you mentioned your sister it reminded everyone that you're just a regular guy who has a huge soul force. Good luck with her sword."

Damien started down the hall, his step lighter than Eli had seen it since before the demon. He threw a wave over his shoulder and Eli thought Damien would be okay after all.

Chapter 24

Damien flew towards the Crimson Caldera. After the get-together he felt better than he had in a while and he'd slept like the dead. He woke up rested and eager to get started on his project. He'd left the tower at first light hoping to make the long journey in one day. Noon had come and gone an hour ago along with any chance of getting home before nightfall. Below him the mountains of the Crescent Range sped by.

Situated in the northeast corner of the kingdom, the Crimson Caldera took its name from the red-scaled drakes that nested on the lip of the pit. In the bottom magma bubbled, providing the heat necessary to hatch the great winged lizards' eggs. What drew Damien to the inhospitable place was a report in the library that said a meteorite had struck the caldera a decade ago and no one had gone to collect it for fear of the drakes.

Meteoric iron was the purest in the kingdom and he wanted to get enough to make Jen's sword. A shimmer of heat rose from the pit and Damien angled toward it. Though it was still August, this far north it was already getting chilly. It felt like they'd have a bad winter this year. He was eager to slice off a chunk of iron and head back.

Along the rim of the pit sat half a dozen stone nests formed from boulders as big as Damien was tall. Three of the nests held mature female fire drakes, their dull red scales, small head crests, and forty-foot length separating them from their brighter, smaller mates. Damien wrapped himself in invisibility. If the females were sitting on their nests they must have eggs and he certainly didn't want to anger a nesting drake.

He flew over the pit. Down in the bubbling magma, bobbing like a cork on a pond, floated the meteorite. It was twice as big as his head and glowed cherry red. Damien conjured a thin disk of energy, set it to spinning, and launched it toward the chunk of iron.

It hit with a wicked shriek and started cutting into the metal. On their nests the drakes screamed and arched their necks toward the sky. Guess they don't like the noise. He didn't blame them, the blade squeaked worse than nails on slate.

A bright red shape hurtled down out of the sky, missing Damien by a couple feet. The male drake rushed toward the cutting blade, intent on killing whatever was bothering his mate. Its wings snapped open a five feet from the magma and it lashed out with a talon.

The black claw hit Damien's disk and got sliced off. The drake shrieked and swooped around for another pass.

Stupid beast, it couldn't hurt his blade. It could only cut up its talons. Damien poured more power into the blade, hoping to get the metal he needed before the drake finished wheeling around for another pass.

The increased speed of the blade's rotation made the screeching even louder, prompting the drakes to scream at greater volume. Damien conjured ear covers before he went deaf. The male finished its turn and once again dove at the blade, this time with its fanged mouth leading.

Not good.

The beast was about to lose its bottom jaw. He didn't want to hurt the drake; he just wanted to get the iron.

Damien wrapped the drake in soul force and sent it plunging into the magma. It flopped around, annoyed but unharmed by the intense heat.

His blade finished cutting and the small chunk of iron slipped into the magma. Silence fell in the caldera, much to his relief. He formed a bubble of soul force around the small chunk and lifted it out of the magma. On a whim he grabbed the sliced-off talon as well. It might make a nice pommel for the sword.

Damien flew off with his prize and when he was a safe distance away released the male drake. The creature roared, trumpeting its victory over the now-vanished blade.

Chapter 25

Damien focused on the lump of iron sitting on the heavy table he'd dragged up to his room. He'd already removed all the impurities, leaving behind nothing but clean metal. Now he had to shape it.

He inserted his power into the ore and felt the molecules of iron. They seemed jumbled up, going every which way. Before he aligned them he needed to mold the lump into a blade. Pushing, pulling and stretching, Damien slowly coaxed the metal into a rough bar.

He gasped and let his focus lapse. He'd used three quarters of his power and all he had to show for it was a bar of metal. Better than a lump, but he still had a long way to go. Damien leaned back in his chair and wiped the sweat from his brow. He hadn't even moved and look at him: sweat drenched his body and his limbs were trembling. It might have been less work to beat the metal into shape at a forge. Of course, that wouldn't help him improve his shaping technique.

For the next two weeks Damien labored on the blade from the time he got up in the morning until he went to bed at night. He'd gotten it shaped into a proper blade, albeit a blunt, unbalanced one. He was about to dive back into his work when he heard steps outside in the hall. Who could be visiting him up here? Ann was the only one he knew that might, and she should be training her new student.

Curious, Damien went to the door and poked his head out into the hall. A woman he didn't recognize stood two doors up from him, a glowing key in the air in front of her. She must be one of his floormates back from assignment.

Maybe she hadn't heard about his adventure with the demon. If he got her to commit to taking him as an apprentice before she found out he could finally start his fieldwork.

He darted out the door and strode toward her. "Excuse me. I'm—"

"The demon slayer, I heard." She turned to face him. Her hair was going gray and fine wrinkles lined her face. Despite her apparent age her gaze was firm and she stood straight and tall.

On the inside he winced, but he let nothing show on his face. "That's been completely blown out of proportion."

She laughed at that. "Kid, there's no way the statement 'he killed a demon all by himself' can be blown out of proportion. If you did it, you did it. There's no other way to say it. Did you do it?"

He hung his head. "Yes, ma'am. I didn't set out to, it just sort of happened. I don't suppose you're looking for an apprentice?"

"No, and even if I was, there'd be no point in me choosing you. On my best day I wouldn't last ten seconds against a demon, even a weak one. If you killed one at your age, with such limited experience, you're at a different level than me. I wouldn't know where to begin teaching you. I'm sorry."

He sighed. "Thanks anyway. At least it'll be nice to have some company up here."

"I doubt I'll be good company. After three months in the field without a break, I plan to sleep then sleep some more. I'm Maria von Kade." She held out a hand.

"Damien St. Cloud." They shook and he left Maria to her rest.

After yet another rejection he didn't feel like working on the sword anymore. In fact he didn't feel like staying in the tower. He needed to get out. Damien went to the stairwell and flew down to the sixth floor to see if Ann had finished her training for the day.

He knocked on her closed door and it opened a few seconds later. Ann smiled and leaned against the door frame. "Everything all right, Damien?"

"I need a change of scenery. Have you had dinner yet?"

"No, I just finished my lessons a little while ago. What did you have in mind?"

"Dinner at the Dancing Pony, my treat."

She beamed. "A date with my favorite student, how lovely. Let me get my cloak."

Damien started to say it wasn't a date, but she had disappeared back into her apartment. She returned a moment later wrapped in a midnight-blue cloak. They left the tower and Damien flew them to the little town just down the road.

The founders, creative souls that they were, named the place Tower Town. Most of the commerce revolved around supplying the tower with everything it needed to function, mainly food and other mundane supplies. Several inns and taverns catered to the visitors that had business with the masters, along with sorcerers that got sick of the food in the dining hall.

When they landed in the packed dirt street just outside the Dancing Pony, the finest inn the village had to offer, no one spared them so much as a second glance. It spoke to how often sorcerers visited Tower Town that two people landing in the middle of the street didn't rate so much as a pause in stride.

The Dancing Pony was a two-story inn with a dining room on the first floor and rooms for rent on the second. You could find a similar building in every town in the kingdom just about. Damien held the door for Ann then closed it behind them. Half a dozen people sat in the common room. They had beaten the dinner rush which suited Damien fine. He wasn't much in the mood for noise or crowds.

A fire blazed in the fireplace taking the chill off the cool night. They found a table near the hearth and Damien helped Ann take her cloak off. The waitress came over to take their order then left them alone.

"So what's the matter? You never want to go out."

Damien slumped in his chair. "I'm sick of being turned down. Every sorcerer I talk to is unwilling to take a chance on me. What are they afraid of?"

"Some are afraid you'll show them up, and others honestly don't know how best to help you. You just have to be patient. Eventually you'll find the right mentor."

"I guess. Has anyone ever quit before? Just given up on the whole damn thing?"

Ann's normally cheerful face went dark as she frowned. "A few quit every decade, moving on to work for merchants traveling through rough country, or going off to explore some distant corner of the kingdom, but most sorcerers consider it an honor to serve on the front lines, protecting the people. The ones that choose to leave the crown's service still keep in touch with The Tower to remain in good standing with the government."

"Yeah, I know about the ones that go into private service. I mean has anyone left it all behind, just vanished and made a new life having nothing to do with sorcery?"

"It's not something we advertise, but it happens. Since the school's founding less than ten sorcerers have vanished. Most left the kingdom, but there are a handful we've lost track of entirely. Those are the ones we fear the most. If they're hiding it's probably because they're up to no good. The most recent was sixteen years ago, a young man named Connor Blackman fled ahead of a group of sorcerers coming to arrest him on charges of trafficking with demons. No one knows where he went after that. It's like he just disappeared."

They finished their meal in silence. Damien couldn't stop wondering what would happen if he decided to run away. Would they send a group of sorcerers to kill him rather than let him go? It wasn't the sort of thing he liked to think about. He understood the masters' point of view. It would be horrible for all sorcerers to have a rogue running around doing whatever he liked.

After dinner they flew back to the tower and Damien walked Ann to her apartment. They stopped outside her door. "I'm sorry, I wasn't very good company tonight."

She smiled and patted his cheek. "That's okay. Are you feeling better?"

"I'm not planning on running away if that's what you're asking. I'll finish Jen's sword and if I still haven't found someone willing to take a chance on me, I'll try to convince the high sorcerers to assign someone."

Chapter 26

Damien focused on the edge of his sister's sword. It was already sharp enough to shave with, but he wanted to get the edge a little finer, make it a little harder so it lasted longer. He'd been working on it almost nonstop for the last two months. The balance was flawless, the blade strong and flexible. It wasn't as polished as Lizzy, but Damien didn't think you'd find a better weapon anywhere in the kingdom. Even the fire drake talon he'd set in the pommel looked like it was meant to be there.

Fine grains of iron fell to the tabletop as he ran his soul force along the edge. He made ten more passes before he felt certain he couldn't get it any sharper. He lifted the sword and wiped a cloth along the blade to remove any remaining iron filings. The hilt felt warm in his hand. According to the book that was because he'd put so much of his soul force in the iron a little had remained behind. That was one of the unique properties of a soul-forged blade. He would also be able to sense it anywhere in the world.

He made a couple of swings, careful not to damage any of his room's minimal furnishings. Satisfied with his creation Damien placed it in the cherry wood box he'd had the carpenter in town build. The sword nestled down into the crushed velvet lining, the deep-gray metal stark against the red cloth. Like Ann said, black and red were the colors for battle. He hoped Jen liked it. The hasp clicked shut and he tucked her gift under his arm. He was eager to see her reaction and, since he had nothing else to do, he decided he'd take it to her right now. He could fly to The Citadel in time to have lunch with her.

Damien left his apartment, flew down to the first floor, and went out onto the steps. It was only mid October, but a foot of snow covered the grass and the guards huddled under thick cloaks. Sunlight reflected off the snow forcing him to narrow his eyes. This was the time of year when the guards earned their money. At each corner of the wall a brazier burned so they could warm themselves as they walked the perimeter. Most of them spent more time standing around the fire talking than they did patrolling.

Damien shook his head. No one had yet explained to him why they even bothered with guards on the wall. He still leaned toward it being some sort of punishment.

He expanded his shield so it was six inches away from his skin then vibrated the air trapped between his skin and the shield, creating a pocket of warm air around his body. He couldn't raise his body temperature like a warlord, but this was a good alternative. He leapt into the air and turned toward home. A few hundred yards from the tower he increased his speed, pushing with everything he had. The ground became a blur of white and green. He wished he had some way to measure his speed.

Half an hour later The Citadel came into view; a new personal record. If he kept practicing he might make the trip in fifteen minutes. Below him in the training yard tiny figures ran around, carrying parcels. Saddled horses pawed the ground outside the stables and no one was training.

What the hell was going on? He remembered training in snow twice this deep

He landed beside the door, not bothering with the official landing zone. A pair of first years brushed past without seeming to notice him. Inside, students and full warlords jammed the entry hall. They stood talking in clusters, the unsteady flow of their soul force revealing their anxiety.

Some wore travel gear and had their weapons belted on. Many of the younger ones looked nervous. Damien saw no sign of Jen. He ran up the steps and down the hall to their quarters, hoping to find her.

He knocked once and pushed the door open. "Sis? Dad? Anybody here?"

Jen emerged from her room. She wore her standard slashed blue tunic and pants, her sword jutted up behind her head and a rucksack was slung over her shoulder. "Damien? What are you doing here?"

"I brought you your name day present early and I thought we might have lunch together. It looks like I came at a bad time."

"I'll say. Haven't you heard? The Ice Queen's army is on the move. General Kord expects to make contact within the next couple of weeks. Eight squads are being deployed to help and another ten are going to handle any stragglers that slip through the line."

"I'm glad I got here before you left. If you're going into battle my gift will come in handy." He held the five-foot box out to her.

"I don't have time."

"Please. You won't regret it, I promise."

Jen set her bag down, took the box, and opened it. She gasped when she saw what was inside. "It's beautiful. Damien, how did you afford this?"

"I didn't buy it, I made it. It's soul-forged from meteoric iron. Took me two months to craft it."

Jen removed the long sword from the box. "It's amazing. The handle's warm."

Damien explained about how a bit of his soul force remained in the blade after he finished with it. "Even when we're apart a little bit of me will always be with you."

She set the sword and box on the kitchen counter and hugged him. "Best present ever. Thanks, little brother. But now I've really got to go."

She replaced her old sword with his soul-forged blade, put the box and her old sword on the couch, and started toward the door.

"Got room in your squad for one more?"

Jen looked over her shoulder. "You volunteering?"

"The masters have me sitting around the tower sucking my thumb. Maybe I can do some good up north."

"You don't have any gear or weapons."

Damien let a little power blaze around his body. "I am a weapon, and anything else I need I can scrounge up in camp."

"I'm convinced. After that business with the demon I'm sure the guys won't complain. Come on."

They left The Citadel and walked around to the stables. Jen's squad was readying their horses. The scene reminded Damien of when they'd gone hunting the goblins, only this time forty other warlords readied their mounts all around them.

"Guys," Jen said when they were close enough. "We've got an extra recruit. I trust no one will complain if my little brother rides with us again."

Unlike last time, smiles and handshakes greeted Damien, none warmer than from Talon who walked without even a limp after his close encounter with the goblin spear. A horse appeared beside Damien and he climbed aboard. "Where's Dad?"

Jen swung up onto her own horse and nudged it over beside him. "The king called him back to the capital to take command of the reinforcements in case our line breaks."

"How many did the Ice Queen send south?"

"Word from the scouts is twenty thousand mixed ogres and ice trolls along with a hundred strong frost giant artillery. It looks like she's serious this time."

Damien frowned. "Damn. That's more than last time, isn't it?"

"A lot more. That's why we're heading north. Eight squads of warlords can make a big difference. Rumor is they're ordering fifteen sorcerers to help as well."

Damien nodded. Fifteen sorcerers would make an even bigger difference. He hadn't heard about it, but that didn't surprise him. Nobody told him anything. Still, twenty thousand was a lot of monsters.

Chapter 27

John bustled around the healers' tent, a chest filled with healing potions clutched in his arms. Cots filled the bulk of the tent. Empty for the moment, and everyone hoped they'd stay that way, but even John knew better. Four nurses sat in a circle bundling bandages and chatting about husbands or lovers, offering prayers that everyone would make it through the battle safely. John sighed. You'd have thought there'd be at least one single nurse.

He'd arrived the day before with his father, the other healers, and the general's support staff. The bulk of the army had arrived and set up camp ten days earlier, but Duke Iceborn wanted to discuss every fine point of strategy with the general and, despite his disdain for the duke Dad was enough of a politician to keep his opinion to himself on the cusp of a war.

And they were on the cusp. John had read the scouts' reports and it sounded like the Ice Queen planned to send the largest army in several generations against them. If Dad had suffered from boredom in years past he certainly wasn't now.

"John!" Master Kane, the army's chief healer and John's mentor for the past year and a half, shouted at him from the tent flap.

John set his burden down on a cot and jogged over to the gray-bearded sorcerer. "Master?"

"We've got wounded just over the border, let's go."

"Yes, Master." John conjured a shield and stepped out into the cold.

Despite the protection he shivered. Wind and snow blew out of the north, a bitter chill that wore on the men and sapped their strength. John spent an hour every day tending frostbitten soldiers. The couple hundred warlords handled the cold easily enough, but the ordinary men suffered.

John narrowed his gaze and spotted the familiar wisps of blue soul force threaded through the wind and snow, remnants of the Ice Queen's power driving the storm on. Maybe when the main force of sorcerers arrived they could shield the camp from the worst of the weather.

Master Kane conjured a chariot and John stepped up beside him. The master's shield blocked the storm and they shot into the air. "What happened, Master?"

"Scouts on their way back ran into an ambush. One man made it through uninjured and ran for help: that's us. The others were alive when he left, but in no condition to move. The cold will work for us today. Remember, just get them stabilized enough to move. We'll handle the rest in camp."

"Yes, Master." John shivered, but not from the cold. He seldom left the relative safety of camp. His soul force wasn't dense like Damien's. If something went wrong and he had to fight, his power wouldn't hold out very long.

Below them white spread out as far as he could see, broken by the occasional spot of green where a spruce hadn't been covered up. He scanned ahead, looking for some sign of the wounded soldiers. First, he looked for red, as the blood from a large battle would show up well in the snow, but he soon gave that up for a fool's errand. The way it was storming any sign of battle would vanish in minutes.

The chariot veered right and descended. John saw nothing remarkable, but Master Kane must. Halfway to the ground a huge ice boulder came flying out of nowhere. Master Kane veered and John blasted, and between the two of them they avoided the missile. Below them a twenty-foot-tall, blue-skinned frost giant shimmered into view. It wore armor made of ice and between its raised hands another boulder of ice took shape.

"Did you know they could turn invisible?" John readied another blast, but held it in reserve. He doubted he had enough power to kill the giant and he wanted to be able to help turn aside any missiles that came their way.

Master Kane sent a blast at the giant that blew his half-formed boulder to bits. "Yes, but I figured I could still spot its soul force. Join your power with mine and we'll attack together."

John sent half his soul force to a point just in front of the chariot, and the master's power appeared an instant later and entwined with his. Master Kane formed the attack while John provided power. A golden lightning bolt lanced down at the giant.

The bolt struck its icy armor and shattered it. The armor served its purpose, slowing their blast enough that the giant had time to dive to the side and avoid the worst of the attack. The only damage they inflicted was a deep crease along its ribs.

The giant staggered to its feet and raised both hands. Shards of ice shot up at them, shattering against the chariot's underside.

Master Kane grimaced and sent more power to reinforce his construct. John hated to leave the wounded, but he was about to suggest retreating before they ended up needing rescuing as well.

Man, he wished Damien was here.

"We need to hit it again," Master Kane said.

"I'm only good for one more, Master."

"It'll have to be enough."

John joined most of his remaining power to Master Kane's. This time the master conjured a golden dragon and sent it swooping down at the giant. When the giant tried to dodge, Master Kane adjusted his construct's path and drove its claws into the giant's wounded side.

The construct got a secure grip and the master sent a pulse of energy through the dragon and detonated it. When the snow settled all that remained were a pair of blue-skinned legs.

Panting, John bent over and urged his soul force to recover faster. That had been too close. The chariot descended and he straightened up. Below them, leaning on a spruce, a soldier with a bandaged leg waved. Master Kane landed the chariot and allowed it to vanish after they climbed down.

"Lucky you came when you did," the injured soldier said. "I thought that giant was going to squish us."

John bent down to examine the man's leg, but was waved off. "Check the others first. They're all hurt worse than me."

He left the wounded man where he stood and went deeper into the small stand of evergreens. The coppery tang of blood and moans from the wounded reached him at about the same time. Soldiers lay on cloaks thrown over the snow. Five men and two women clutched wounds and in one unfortunate fellow's case, the stump of his right arm.

John had studied and thought himself prepared for the aftermath of a battle, but this was worse than he imagined. None of the wounded were warlords so they wouldn't heal quickly on their own.

Forcing himself to work through the nausea, John went to the man with the stump first, leaving a nasty stomach wound for his mentor. "So what happened?" John asked the grimacing man. He insinuated his soul force into the man's body and blocked the flow of pain. A sigh of relief passed the man's lips.

"Ice trolls happened. They dug themselves in under the snow. We didn't have a clue until ten of them burst out of the ground all around us. Just damn lucky we had numbers on our side or they would have killed us all. As it was we lost over half the patrol and the rest of us are hardly in any shape to fight."

While he talked John sealed veins and accelerated regeneration of muscle and skin over the stump to prevent infection. He frowned and burned away a nasty spot of bacteria, probably left over from the troll's spit. A quick scan of the rest of the man's body showed no other injuries or infections. He squeezed the soldier's remaining hand. "You're going to make it."

John and Master Kane spent an hour tending the wounded before loading everyone on a soul force wagon and flying back to camp. If this was what they had to look forward to it would be an especially ugly war.

Chapter 28

Two weeks of hard riding found Damien and the others at the edge of the northern army's war camp. Hundreds of tents sprawled along the length of a river valley. A cloud of wood smoke rising from the camp made a dark gray day even darker, so many fires burned to keep the regular warriors warm. The scent of burning pine reached them even from a mile away. He felt bad for them, huddled around their fires, trying to keep warm while they waited for an eight-foot-tall monster to try to take their heads off. The only good thing about a winter camp was it kept the stink to a minimum.

Damien and his companions only bothered with a fire when they set up camp to enjoy a hot meal. Both warlords and sorcerers could keep themselves warm through the use of soul force. The warlords sped up their metabolism to generate heat, and Damien simply heated the surrounding air to a temperature he found comfortable. It took such a tiny portion of his power he didn't think twice about the effort.

The other squads had fallen a day behind as they didn't have Damien to create a road above the snow for them to ride on. They had to resort to forcing their horses to plow through ever-deeper drifts of snow the farther north they went. If the other members of Jen's squad hadn't already gotten to like him, the fact that he could keep them out of the snow would have made him their best friend.

The squad reined in at a checkpoint half a mile out from the camp. "Halt and name yourself." What Damien had initially thought was a snowman spoke and raised a snow-covered spear.

Jen urged her mount a little closer, forcing Damien to extend his platform so her horse wouldn't sink in up to its knees like the unfortunate soldier. "I'm Jennifer St. Cloud and this is my squad, reporting as ordered."

The guard lowered his spear. "Where are the rest of the squads and how is your horse standing on top of the snow?"

"The others are about a day behind us and my brother's a sorcerer."

Damien waved at the guard. The poor snow-covered guy just stared at him. Perhaps he'd never seen a sorcerer before.

"Can we go?" Jen asked. "I imagine General Kord is anxious for us to report in."

The guard scrambled out of their way and waved them through. They rode past the still-staring guard. Damien smiled at him as he rode his conjured horse past, but got no reaction. On closer inspection Damien guessed the guard was about his age and someone had probably assigned him to guard their rear line to keep him away from the fighting. He always knew John's father was a good guy and this was more proof of it.

They reached the first of the tents and Damien let his portable road vanish. Some unfortunate had shoveled the area down to the dirt allowing them to move around without trudging through snow. Jen led them toward the center of camp where a tent twice the size of Damien's quarters back at the tower waited, a flag with a snow-covered mountain crossed with a claymore flapping in the breeze above it. Was the duke in camp or was he leaving it to General Kord?

When they arrived, two young men standing outside the command tent rushed over to collect their horses. Damien waved them off and reabsorbed the energy from his mount. The pages were younger than Damien, but they didn't give the squad a second look. Stationed outside the command tent they probably saw all sorts of unusual people come and go. The boys led the horses off to the temporary stable.

Jen brushed the tent flap to one side and led the way in. A huge table covered with a map of the Northlands dominated the central chamber of the tent. General Kord stood beside it, talking with a soldier who dripped on the floor as the snow melted off his uniform, and adjusting the positions of models representing the Ice Queen's troops. Jen, Damien, and the rest of the squad stood with their hands clasped behind their backs, waiting for the general to finish with what Damien assumed was a scout.

Finally the scout bowed to the general and brushed past them back out into the cold. General Kord noticed them standing by the tent flap and smiled. "Jennifer, and Damien too, this is a pleasant surprise. Come in, come in, no need to be so formal."

They approached the map and bowed. John's father was a big, broad-shouldered man, with a thick beard, dark hair and hard green eyes. He looked nothing like his son, who very much favored his mother. The general came around to their side and hugged Jen when she straightened. He shook hands with Damien and nodded to the rest of the squad.

"Reporting for duty, sir," Jen said.

"I wasn't sure your father would send you. Well, I guess everyone's got to fight their first war sometime." The general turned to Damien. "Where's your mentor? You were a year behind John so you can't be acting alone yet."

"I was visiting Jen and tagged along. I can't seem to find a mentor and we did good work together this summer, so I thought I could lend a hand."

"I heard. Killed a demon, impressive. Still, you'd best report to the sorcerers' commander after we finish here. I wouldn't want to step on her toes."

Damien nodded. He'd check in, but whatever the woman said, he had no intention of letting his sister face whatever was waiting out there without him.

"What's the situation, sir?" Jen asked.

General Kord returned to the map and the rest of them gathered around. He pointed out two model ogres a few miles north of the kingdom's border. "They've divided their army. Half will attack through Frozen Hell pass and the other half are climbing up and over an ice ridge here. We have to defend the pass, but we need to keep enough men in reserve to handle the force climbing the ridge."

Jen pointed at another gap in the mountains. "What about this one?"

"We've seen no activity in the middle gap. My guess is they're trying to spread us out. That's a new trick. Maybe the dragon isn't as stupid as we hoped. This is the first time she's divided her army, usually they try to overwhelm us with numbers at one of the passes."

"What's our assignment going to be?" Jen asked.

General Kord pointed at six white circles ten miles behind the enemy's line. "Our sorcerers spotted these supply depots while long range scouting. Food and weapons are gathered there before going on to the monsters on the front line. I want your squad to destroy them. I don't know if it'll slow them down much, the ice trolls fight with their claws anyway, but if we can eliminate their food supply it might make them desperate enough to make a mistake."

"Understood. When do we leave?"

"It's too late in the day to go now," the general said. "Why don't you find a tent, get a hot meal and a good night's sleep, and head out first thing in the morning."

"Yes, sir," Jen said. "Where might we find an empty tent?"

"I have no idea. Ask the pages out front, one of them can help you."

"Where are the sorcerers camped?" Damien asked. He wanted to get the meeting over with so he could focus on the task at hand.

"When you go out take a right and go until you see the big blue tents. That's them."

Chapter 29

Damien parted ways with his sister and her squad and headed toward the sorcerers' tents. As he walked he considered how best to approach whoever was in charge. He'd be polite but firm. Damien wanted to help and he had the power to make a difference.

The six blue-dyed tents looked pretty near identical to those used by the rest of the army. Unfortunately that made it hard to figure out which one was the command tent. A dark-haired girl in her mid twenties with no visible soul force dressed in a dark-blue tunic and pants left one of the tents.

Damien sighed and jogged after her. "Excuse me."

The sorcerer turned back to face him. "Yes?"

"I'm looking for the commander. Can you help me out?"

"Who are you?" Her gray eyes narrowed. "I haven't seen you around camp."

"Sorry, I'm Damien St. Cloud. I arrived with my sister an hour ago. General Kord sent me to check in."

Her narrow eyes went wide. "You killed the demon. I didn't realize you'd been assigned here. The commander's tent is there." She pointed at a tent a little ways down the row. It had a plaque with a black tower carved on it above the flap. How had he missed that?

"Thanks." He left the gaping sorcerer where she stood and jogged over to the command tent.

Some tents had a board outside for visitors to knock on, but not this one. He shrugged, brushed the flap open, and ducked inside. A pale woman with white-blond hair sat at a table with two male sorcerers. The woman looked like the master that had served as Sig's second in their duel. They fell silent and looked up at Damien.

"Hi. I'm Damien St. Cloud. General Kord sent me to check in."

The men muttered amongst themselves and he picked out the words demon slayer. Was that the first thing everyone he met would say? The woman hissed and the men fell silent. "Why are you here?" she asked.

"I thought I could help. I've fought with my sister's squad before and we did good work. This seemed like an opportunity to do that again."

The woman's pale lips turned down in a frown. "My sister spoke of you. You embarrassed my lord's son in a duel. For that insult alone I should send you back to the tower."

"I saved Sig's life," Damien said. Annoyed by the woman's attitude he went on. "He thought he knew how to fight. With his meager skills he was liable to get killed in a real fight. I showed him the truth. Where's the insult in that?"

She stood up; the woman was easily as tall as Jen, with a slender, boyish figure. "You have no mentor and no place here."

Damien walked deeper into the tent. If she thought he'd just walk away on her say-so she'd miscalculated. "I don't have a mentor because none of the more experienced sorcerers have the guts to take on an apprentice more powerful than them. I've been sitting on my hands for four months waiting to find someone with the stones to work with me. Now there's a war on and you want me to go home and sit around some more?"

She stepped around the table and soul force gathered around her. "What do you think you can do that we can't?"

Damien gathered his own power, enough to make the tent shake. "Nothing, but since when is having an extra set of hands a bad thing in war? I'm not planning to sit around camp getting in your way. I'm going out with my sister in the morning. Just pretend you never saw me. Every ogre I kill is one less for you to deal with."

She spun away from him and released her power. "Do what you will. I don't care." She dismissed him with the back of her hand.

Damien reclaimed his power, bowed to her back, and left.

Chapter 30

When they crossed the border it felt like the temperature dropped twenty degrees. The wind blew waves of loose snow, obscuring their vision beyond forty feet. The Ice Queen's magic controlled the weather, hindering her enemies and aiding her own forces. Only a dragon had that much power. The kingdom was fortunate she'd never come against them herself. If that ever changed he feared for their survival.

They'd been running at a brisk pace all morning, Damien's power allowing them to travel on the surface of the snow. They'd seen no signs of ogres or ice trolls; the general's information looked good. If he was right about the locations of the supply depots it would make their jobs a lot easier. Hunting around in a blizzard would be a miserable process.

"Can anyone tell where the hell we are?" Talon asked.

"I'm not sure." Jen squinted into the wind. "But we've got to be within a mile of the first depot."

"Want me to see if I can find it?" Damien asked.

Jen nodded and Damien conjured a remote viewing construct. Instead of a bug this time he conjured an invisible sphere and sent it flying in the direction they believed the depot lay. The rest of the squad gathered around to watch. For several minutes the only images the sphere sent back were white and empty. As Damien guided it through the empty terrain he passed something dark.

With a thought he moved it back. The dark object turned out to be the head of an ogre. Beyond the ogre several large tents sat in a clearing free of wind and snow. The orb circled the clearing revealing seven more ogres guarding the tents. They had found the depot. Jen clapped him on the shoulder.

Following the link to his orb, Damien led the squad to their target. They crouched forty yards away from the clearing. It looked like someone had set up an invisible wall blocking the storm.

It wasn't fair.

Still, the blowing snow made for good cover, allowing them to approach without the ogres noticing. Jen used hand gestures to direct her squad to surround the depot.

"What should I do?" Damien asked.

"Wait here and keep your eyes open. We can handle eight ogres. I just don't want anything sneaking up on us."

She waited a full minute, let out a shrill whistle, and charged, drawing her sword as she went. Damien stepped out of the storm to better watch. Before he got clear of the wind the first ogre lay in two pieces in the snow, staining it red. Their speed and strength enhanced by soul force, the warlords finished the guards in less than a minute. It was an impressive bit of work. The power of a warlord never ceased to amaze Damien.

He ambled into the clearing in time to see Jen flick the blood off her sword and slip it into the sheath on her back.

"How did it work?" Damien asked.

"Like a dream. It cut through them with hardly any resistance."

Talon slashed open one of the tents, revealing rows of heavy spears standing upright in wooden racks. The next tent held slabs of meat—no one wanted to inquire too closely about type—hanging from what looked like a clothesline. They tore open the other tents and found either weapons or food in each of them.

"What now?" Edward asked. "We can't exactly make a fire out in the snow."

"I'll handle it." Damien conjured bubbles around the tents and yanked them together in the center of the clearing, merging the bubbles into one. He drew a heavy portion of soul force and squeezed. The bubble shrank to the size of a large boulder, crushing everything inside and fusing it together in a solid mass. The bubble shifted, turning into a catapult with the crushed supplies as the stone. Damien launched the mass out into the storm where it vanished.

He dusted off his hands, reabsorbed the leftover energy, and grinned. "All done. Where's the next depot?"

They set out for the next target but it was too far away to reach before dark. They made camp in the storm. Talon found a stand of spruces that cut the wind a little and Damien augmented it with an invisible barrier that blocked both the wind and the light of the little fire they made from dry branches broken off the nearby trees.

Damien reclined on a bed of soul force while Rhys fixed them a warm meal, the savory scent of simmering meat mixing with the smoke from the fire. It was nice, feeling like part of a group. His solitary studies at the tower and later spending months alone forging Jen's sword had denied him that camaraderie. He hadn't realized how much he missed being part of a team.

Jen came over and he conjured a replica of the couch in their quarters for her to sit on. She sprawled on it, one leg hanging over the arm. "You have a thoughtful look, little brother."

"Just enjoying the moment. I never realized how much sorcerers did alone. I think I prefer being part of a team."

She nodded. "That's left over from your time at The Citadel. Warlords are trained to fight for the person beside them. When you're alone you have no one to fight for."

"I suppose. I—" He sat up. Something powerful was nearby.

Damien scrambled to his feet, trying to locate the source. He moved around the camp, ignoring the confused looks from the others.

Where was it?

The power felt defused rather than focused like a sorcerer's conjuring. He stopped.

There!

East and a little north. It wasn't too close, but it wasn't that far either.

"What is it, Damien?" Jen stood beside him, squinting into the storm outside their shelter, trying to see what he saw. She could strain as hard as she wanted. What Damien sensed wasn't visible to anyone besides a sorcerer.

"Power, lots of it. Headed toward our lines. It's still a ways out, but in a day, maybe two, it'll reach our people, assuming it doesn't change course. I can't get a fix on it. We need to check it out."

"It's dark and there's a blizzard. We're more likely to get lost than find something in this storm. Let's wait until morning and if you still sense it we'll investigate."

Damien wanted to argue, but Jen made a good point. They'd be able to tell more in the morning, though she was wrong about them getting lost. He could follow something that powerful blindfolded.

Chapter 31

They were up and moving at first light. The storm had let up during the night, the blizzard dying down to flurries. Apparently even an immortal dragon couldn't maintain a storm of that power forever. Damien hoped the Ice Queen would need a nice long rest; being able to see where you were walking made a nice change.

They'd planned their route to the supply depots carefully so as not to waste any time, but the power Damien felt last night lay well off their chosen path. Whatever was generating the power had stopped some time during the night, before resuming its slow, steady progress at dawn. The others grumbled about abandoning their mission, but Jen pointed out their mission included scouting enemy movements. Whatever Damien sensed almost had to be something to do with the enemy forces.

"How much further?" Edward asked.

Damien shook his head. "It's moving again. Not as fast as us, but steadily south. If whatever it is doesn't speed up we should catch it in an hour, two at the most."

"It better be worthwhile," Talon said. "We could have reached the second depot by now."

They continued on in silence. Whatever they thought about going off course, the squad members were too professional to give their position away to a potential enemy.

An hour and twenty minutes later they reached a snow and ice covered ridge. The power he'd felt earlier screamed in his head and all around them flecks of bright-blue soul force streaked the air. It wasn't far now.

Damien motioned the others to stop. They gathered around and he whispered, "It's right over the ridge."

They eased up and poked their heads over the crest of the ridge. In a valley below them a column of thousands of ogres and ice trolls marched shoulder to shoulder. None of them gave off much power individually. Damien saw nothing that looked like a sorcerer or warlord, though ogres and trolls all had stronger soul forces than normal humans. It was what accounted for the ogres' great strength and the trolls' rapid healing. Even so, it wasn't enough to account for the power that emanated from the army below. The question was, what did?

They ducked back down and Jen pulled a rough map of the territory out of her tunic and unfolded it. She touched the map and said in a low voice, "We're about here. There's nothing on the map to indicate a valley exists here. Nevertheless that's a third army and judging from its direction of travel it's headed for the unguarded pass. We need to warn General Kord he's going to have company."

"I can get the message to him if you have pencil and paper to write on," Damien said.

Rhys rummaged in his ever-present satchel and pulled out a stubby pencil and a two-inch square of parchment. Jen nodded her thanks, scribbled a note, and rolled the paper up. Damien conjured a bird and when Jen held out the note, had it grasp the rolled-up parchment in its beak. The bird raced into the air, far faster than a flesh-and-blood animal.

Damien conjured a rectangle so he could see through the bird's eyes and guide it. Ten minutes later the camp came into view. He guided the bird to the general's tent. The two pages standing outside the tent gaped at the bird hovering in the air in front of them.

The pages looked at each other, then back. One of them must have noticed the note gripped in the bird's beak as they pulled the flap open for it. The bird flew in. The general sat in a camp chair eating a bowl of something that steamed in the cool air. Damien guided the bird to land on the edge of his bowl.

That might not have been the best idea as the general sucked in a surprised breath and choked on his breakfast. When the coughing subsided he took the scrap of paper and unrolled it. A few seconds later his eyes widened.

Damien had only linked his sight to the construct, but he was good enough at reading lips to know the general asked if the information on the paper was accurate. The bird nodded its head. General Kord ran out of the tent, his food forgotten.

Damien let the construct dissolve. He'd done everything he could for now.

Chapter 32

The little group crouched in the snow above the monster army, their message successfully delivered. Whatever else happened at least the army wouldn't get caught by surprise. Whether they could defeat a third army was another question altogether.

"We should follow them," Jen said. "If they change course or join up with another force we haven't yet seen we have to be able to warn the general."

"I agree," Damien said. "If we're in position I might be able to break their charge and give the soldiers a better chance to hold the line when they attack."

"Do you really think there might be more of them?" Alec asked. Damien had never met a nervous warlord, but the youngest member of Jen's team came close.

Jen shook her head. "I don't know, but we need to be ready for the possibility. No one has any idea how many monsters live in the Ice Queen's territory. Some people speculate the reason she attacks every decade or two is to keep the numbers of her army at a reasonable level rather than to try to conquer the Northlands. I think that's bullshit, but we're all just guessing."

Quiet from over the ridge brought their conversation to a halt. They peeked over the edge and saw the end of the column marching out of view. The squad jogged along, never letting the back of the column out of sight. Trailing the enemy force was slow, tedious work, but they kept at it until the sun hung low in the sky and the army stopped for the night. The enemy force set up tents made from fur-covered hides. They made no fires, but passed around what looked like gobbets of raw meat and ate them cold.

Damien shuddered. How did anyone live like that? The monsters were little better than animals, slaves to be pointed south to kill and die on the whim of an indifferent mistress. He would have pitied them if they weren't on their way to murder people he'd sworn to protect.

One ogre, a big, blue-skinned monster wearing nothing but a loincloth and standing a head taller than anything Damien had seen up to now, moved a short distance from the camp, a club of carved ice slung over his shoulder.

That had to be the commander. Commander might be too generous. He was probably the one that pointed and roared when he wanted them to attack.

"We should make camp and get some rest," Talon whispered.

Before anyone could reply a dragon's head made of ice rose up out of the frozen ground. The soul force Damien sensed gathered around it. This was the source he'd been tracking. It wasn't the Ice Queen. As overwhelmingly powerful as this beast was, it wasn't strong enough to be her. This must be one of her sons. The books Damien had read suggested she had at least two, though she hadn't sent one against the kingdom in over one hundred years. The dragon's eyes glowed bright blue, the same color as the soul force swirling around everywhere. It stared at the big ogre who looked back at it, mouth agape.

They ducked down out of sight. "Where the hell did that thing come from?" Edward asked.

"It's been there all along," Damien said. "The dragon's power is what I sensed, I just didn't realize it."

"Are there tunnels under the snow where it travels out of sight?" Jen asked.

Damien shook his head. He'd read everything in the library about dragons. "Dragons are nothing but energy bound into matter, ice in this case. It can send its energy through the ice then rise up, forming a new body as it goes. That's why they only attack the kingdom in the winter. There's no ice in the summer and it reduces their strength to have to maintain the integrity of their bodies outside their element."

Jen's eyes went wide. "They mean to surprise our forces. No one will know the dragon's there until it's too late. We have to send another note."

Rhys already had parchment and pencil out. Jen jotted down a quick note and when she finished Damien had a bird ready to go. It clamped on to the paper and flew off. His construct hadn't gone more than a couple hundred yards when it shattered, shards of energy scattered everywhere, the note disintegrated.

"What happened?" Jen must have seen the bird explode.

Damien was about to explain when Talon said, "Guys?"

Damien had never heard a tremor in the arrogant warlord's voice. He and Jen inched up the slope to join him. When they peeked over the dragon's glowing blue eyes were staring right at them.

"Shit!"

They slid down to rejoin the others. The beast must have sensed Damien's conjuring and raised a barrier to stop the message from going through. The scrabbling of claws on ice reached them a moment before a bluish-white face, its lips peeled back from a fang-filled mouth, scraggly black hair trailing down its back, appeared over the slope. A reflexive burst of soul force from Damien blew the ice troll's head to bits. A second later half a dozen more popped up like gofers on the plains.

Damien blasted two more, but the rest made it over the ridge and charged, claws raised to slaughter anyone that got close. Behind the first wave, more trolls appeared, and behind them yet more.

It looked like a troll avalanche and the six of them were about to get buried.

Jen cut the arm off one and gutted a second. "Can you fly us out of here?"

"No." Damien conjured curved blades of dense soul force and sent them flying into the mass of trolls. The spinning blades decapitated half a dozen in the first pass. "If we break cover the dragon will turn us into frozen treats. I'm not strong enough to shield us all from something that powerful. Plus I don't know if I can get through its barrier."

Jen chopped the head off a troll attempting to reattach its arm to the oozing stump on its shoulder. "Damn it! I guess we'll have to run."

"I can hold the trolls off, go." Damien guided his spinning swords into another clump of trolls and sliced them into bloody chunks.

"I can't leave you here alone." A troll clawed Jen's arm, but failed to penetrate her iron skin. She punched it in the face, crushing its skull and driving shards of bone into its brain, killing it instantly.

"I'll be fine, trust me." Damien raised a golden wall between the squad and the trolls. "Go!"

Jen gave him one last look, concern plain on her frowning face, and then she and her squad sprinted away in a cloud of snow.

Good, now that they were clear he didn't have to hold back. Damien dropped the wall and shaped the energy into a bubble around him. Trolls raced toward him, foot-long purple tongues hanging out of their mouths, spit flying and freezing on the side of their faces. Ugly things, no doubt about that.

The first pair of trolls reached his bubble and scraped their black claws against the impenetrable barrier. More trolls gathered around until nothing but rough, pebbly skin, claws, and fangs filled his vision.

He waited another minute for good measure then conjured a pair of twenty-foot-long blades, one on either side of the bubble, and set them spinning as fast as he could. In an instant he ground over a hundred trolls into so much fertilizer, spattering the snow red for fifty feet in every direction.

It looked like a butcher shop had exploded.

A quick look around revealed no more trolls and the dragon's power moving away. It must have decided to push on through the night. That wasn't good. If the army reached their line before Damien and the others warned General Kord about the dragon it would be a slaughter.

He couldn't allow that to happen.

Chapter 33

Jen ran, soul force blazing in her legs, the world a blue-and-green blur. She glanced back over her shoulder in time to see Damien surrounded by a horde of ice trolls. She clenched her jaw and kept going. If her brother could handle a demon, a bunch of trolls wouldn't bother him. Jen trusted him to survive and catch up. If he didn't make it she'd kill him.

"Captain!" Talon pointed at a patch of evergreens a little ways ahead.

Jen nodded, that would be a good place to rest and wait for Damien to catch up. They raced through the first few rows of spruce and skidded to a stop in a clearing in the center of the stand. It looked like someone had cut some trees and not that long ago if the fresh stumps were any indication. She'd never heard of ogres or trolls cutting timber; they lived in ice caves, at least according to everything she'd read.

"How long do we wait?" Edward asked.

Jen wanted to snarl, *until my brother catches up*, but that wouldn't be practical with the dragon and its army on the march. "We'll give him fifteen minutes. If Damien hasn't caught up by then he isn't going to."

No one argued, which was just as well given her mood. She'd left her brother surrounded by trolls! What kind of sister did that?

It didn't matter if he told her to go, or that he was the strongest sorcerer she'd ever seen, he was her brother and she'd left him on his own.

A branch snapped, jolting her out of her recriminations. That hadn't taken long. Jen figured even Damien would have needed more time than that to deal with so many trolls. A nine-foot-tall, blue-skinned figure wearing a mask of ice carved to look like a dragon stepped into the clearing, an icy club held loose in one hand. A moment later eight more stepped out of the trees. The silent figures pointed their clubs at Jen and her squad.

Jen drew on her soul force, enhancing her perception and preparing her body for battle. She raised her blade, eager to take her frustration out on ogre flesh.

She recognized the ogres standing before them. Numerous reports mentioned the masked berserkers that served as the Ice Queen's elite troops. They were essentially the monstrous equivalent to warlords.

The first ogre blurred and attacked her in a rush. Ice club met soul-forged steel with a resounding crash. If she hadn't sped up her awareness she wouldn't have gotten the blade up in time.

All around her the crack of ice on steel filled the clearing. Jen pushed the ogre back half a step and counterattacked. It matched her blow for blow as they raced around the clearing fighting for an advantage.

She leapt at a spruce, twisted in midair so her boots hit the trunk, and pushed off with enough force that the tree cracked down the middle. At a blinding speed that even her father, the great Fredric the Lightning, would be hard pressed to match, Jen raced toward her opponent.

The masked ogre raised its club a fraction too late and her sword found its heart. She kicked the brute off her blade in the nick of time as a second berserker barreled toward her with murderous intent. Jen met it head on and the battle began again.

If any normal person entered the clearing all they would have seen were blurry images racing around in clouds of snow. To Jen's soul-force-enhanced perception the battle unfolded in real time. This ogre didn't have the same skill as the first and she soon had it on the defensive. She gashed its leg then cut a shallow groove in its chest.

Out of the corner of her eye she spotted an ogre coming up at high speed behind Rhys. A second ogre had a death grip on his shield.

The elder warlord beat on the brute's arm, trying to force it to let him go, but he'd never turn in time to block the incoming berserker.

Jen abandoned her wounded opponent and raced to cover Rhys's back. Her sword came up and the ogre's club came down. Steel met flesh at its wrist and the ogre's club went flying, hand and all. Her back cut took its head half off.

A wet crunch made her spin around in time to see Rhys yank his mace out of the second ogre's skull. At that moment Damien flew into the clearing.

Jen tried to shout a warning as her wounded opponent, his injuries all closed up, raced toward her brother, club cocked and ready.

Chapter 34

Damien focused on Jen's sword and quickly sensed the fragment of his soul force several miles distant. He frowned. Why weren't they still moving? Damien gathered his power and blasted toward them, flying along only a few feet above the ground. He skimmed the fluffy snow, blowing waves of white to the left and right. He reached the edge of a spruce grove and had to slow to weave his way through the trees. Unlike a warlord he couldn't use his soul force to speed up his reactions.

A minute later he burst into a clearing and found the squad battling a bunch of masked ogres. Damien sensed at once that this lot had warlord-level soul force. Even if he couldn't sense it the fact that nine ogres were giving Jen and her team a real fight would have told him everything he needed to know. The dragon must have sent a squad of berserkers to deal with them.

Damien barely had time enough to register the situation when a club appeared out of nowhere and came swinging at his head.

It bounced off his shield without hurting him, but the force of the blow sent him flying across the clearing toward a second berserker who had his club raised like a forester getting ready to chop down a tree. Quick as thought Damien sent a scythe of pure soul force spinning toward the berserker.

With the speed of a warlord the ogre dodged the worst of the attack, taking only a shallow gash along its ribs. At least the attack forced it to move aside and gave Damien a chance to get his uncontrolled flight righted.

He managed it not a moment too soon. The first ogre was sprinting across the clearing, its club cocked and ready.

Not this time.

Damien expanded and softened his shield. The club struck and sank into the energy web instead of bouncing off. Unlike last time Damien didn't go flying, instead he stuck to the berserker's club.

In the brute's instant of confusion he blew a head-sized hole through its chest. His opponent crumpled to the snow.

Four other ogres lay dead or dying while another five battled Jen and her squad at speeds so fast Damien could just follow the battle. The only reason he knew how many fought was by counting the different soul forces. In a fight where he couldn't even see where the combatants stood from one instant to the next he didn't dare launch an attack, he'd be as likely to hit one of his comrades as an ogre.

A second later an ogre appeared out of the scrum, unmoving, its leg half severed below the knee. Before Damien could blast it, its head went flying off into the trees. He didn't know which blur killed it. He guessed his sister given the smoothness of the cut.

Warlords and berserkers raced around the clearing at speeds he could hardly process. Damien stood, surrounded by his shield, and let the battle play out without him. An ogre went down, and another a second later. It looked like his side was winning.

The final berserker appeared directly in front of Damien, perhaps thinking him an easier target than the warlords, and brought its club down on his head. The blow drove him, shield and all, a foot into the snow. Damien narrowed his eyes and a dozen spears of soul force pierced the ogre's body.

The rest of the squad stood, panting, surrounded by dead ogres. Edward's arm hung at a funny angle, attesting to the fact that at least one ogre got a solid blow in. He walked over to a good-sized spruce and slammed his shoulder into it. The joint popped back into place and healing soul force rushed to repair the remaining damage.

Jen straightened and hurried over to Damien. "You okay?" Ogre blood dripped from her sword and spattered her face.

She made a gruesome sight, like a warrior goddess of legend, worshiped by primitive people with blood sacrifices.

"I'm fine, you?"

She bent down and cleaned her sword off with a handful of snow. "I'm good. Never fought berserkers before. They had some skill."

Edward grunted, but made no other comment. It appeared he was the only one injured. "What about the trolls?" Talon asked.

"I shredded them. The dragon's marching through the night. If we don't hurry they'll reach the pass ahead of us."

Chapter 35

After an exhausting night of running the team finally left the Ice Queen's territory behind just as dawn lightened the ever-present clouds. The only sign they'd crossed over into the kingdom was the sun finally breaking through the gloom. They saw no soldiers, not even the pickets assigned to the perimeter. The general must have called everyone to the central pass.

After the fight with the berserkers a reluctant Damien had tried to fly back ahead of the others to warn the general. He hated leaving the others behind, but as his sister pointed out he could make the trip faster than any of them. He didn't get over fifty feet off the ground before he slammed into a barrier. The dragon must've conjured it to keep them from rushing back to warn their army. With no other options they'd run along as fast as possible and hoped for the best.

They took a moment to catch their breath then the squad turned north. Damien didn't know how the dragon managed it, but it had raised a sheer wall of ice, blocking them from making a direct run to the central pass. The wall forced them to travel miles out of their way, delaying and exhausting them.

Damien didn't know what difference a handful of warlords and a single sorcerer would make, but they were determined to make the effort. The squad hadn't gone more than a hundred paces when a wide-eyed soldier came running towards them as fast as the deep snow would allow. Every few seconds he glanced back over his shoulder, as though he expected to find an ogre on his tail.

Jen raised her hand. "Hey, what's going on?"

The soldier turned his terrified gaze their way. "A dragon! A bloody big dragon appeared out of nowhere."

They surrounded the trembling soldier. "Slow down. Just tell us what happened." Jen rested a reassuring hand on his shoulder.

He took a deep breath and let it out slow. "A third army arrived just before dawn. Thousands of monsters came howling down the pass. We was ready for them though. The sorcerers hammered the first wave, broke their line, and left the stragglers for us to clean up. We was winning, 'til that dragon rose out of the ground. It sent a blast of ice across our line, froze better than a hundred of our boys solid. The commanders shouted orders, but we'd had it. Last I saw that damn dragon was stomping on the stragglers. Looked like it was having fun too."

Jen let the soldier go. They couldn't blame him for running. "We're too late."

"Maybe not." Damien gathered his power. Since they were clear of the Ice Queen's territory the barrier should be clear. It was probably a suicide mission, but if he couldn't kill the dragon a lot of soldiers would die. "At the very least I've got to try."

"Damien!" She shouted after him, but he'd already leapt into the air and turned toward the battle.

Damien raced through the sky. The central pass lay a couple of miles from the army camp. Below him tiny figures of fleeing soldiers raced away from the battlefield. The army had routed, pure and simple. No discipline or direction influenced the men, just a need to escape the horror of the dragon. Damien understood, he'd felt the beast's power in its unfocused state and it dwarfed the demon he killed last summer. The plain truth was Damien doubted he could kill the dragon. He'd probably hit it with everything he had and get a laugh for his trouble. But what choice did he have? If all those people died and he did nothing he'd never be able to face himself again.

It took less than a minute to reach the pass. The dragon's forces had blocked the retreat of the majority of the kingdom's soldiers. Towering over everything was a horror of icy spikes, horns, and fangs. The dragon had to measure over fifty yards, not counting its sinuous tail. Beside and behind it thousands of ogres and trolls watched it slaughter the trapped humans.

Damien gathered his soul force. Golden energy rushed out of his center and collected in a seething ball in front of him. Any moment he expected the dragon to sense his power and look up, but it was having too much fun to spare Damien a glance. As his power grew the dragon raised a taloned foot and brought it crashing down on half a dozen men, crushing and slashing them to ribbons.

Bastard!

He drew deeper, pulling the power out in a river.

When he'd drawn every drop of energy he had, Damien loosed the blast at the dragon in a single focused lightning bolt.

He fell.

The world went black and the ground rushed to meet him.

Damien hoped he'd pass out before he struck. Hitting the ground from this height would hurt, for a moment at least.

Chapter 36

"Damien!" Jen shouted after her brother again. He ignored her, racing off to do something very brave and stupid.

She drew on her depleted soul force and sprinted after him. Despite her speed Damien pulled away from her.

She dodged spruce trees that seemed to appear from nowhere, her accelerated senses allowing her to make decisions ten times faster than a normal person. What was he thinking, trying to take on a dragon on his own? They should gather reinforcements, especially more sorcerers, and make a proper counterattack.

Jen leapt an eight-foot boulder. But if they did that they'd lose the forces fighting in the central pass along with General Kord, who almost certainly had led the soldiers himself. Damien must have realized that as well.

Idiot!

A tear froze on her cheek. If anything happened to him... No, she wouldn't allow anything to happen to him. She was his big sister and it was her job to keep him safe, even if he didn't think he needed to be kept safe anymore.

A line of retreating soldiers streamed past her. She was moving so fast most of them didn't even notice her. In the sky above, Damien had come to a stop. He floated, facing toward the pass, still a mile away. In front of him golden energy gathered. He wasted no effort disguising his conjuring.

She clenched her teeth and ran faster. She had to get to him before he released his power. If Damien gave it everything he had there'd be nothing left to hold him up

She was still a hundred yards short of her brother when a thunderous explosion shook the ground. The energy he'd summoned crackled like a lightning bolt toward the pass. Damien fell. He had no power left to stay in the sky.

She gathered herself and leapt. As she flew toward her brother she glanced into the pass in time to see his attack slam into a massive dragon made of ice. It roared louder than the explosion, bits of its body flying in all directions.

Damien thudded into her arms.

He groaned. "Hey, sis. I think I overdid it." Then he passed out.

She landed in the snow, turned, and sprinted toward camp. There'd be healers there. Someone could do something for him. Jen ran so fast a wake of snow rose and fell on either side of her, washing over the occasional group of soldiers she passed, their shouts and curses drowned out by the wind in her ears. She dodged the sparse trees and weary soldiers with equal indifference. Her only thought was to get Damien to the healers as fast as possible.

A couple minutes later the first tent came into view. "Hang on, little brother, we're almost there."

Damien gave no sign he heard her. He lay in her arms, limp and still. If not for the rise and fall of his chest she would have thought he'd died. She clenched her jaw and headed toward a sprawling white tent with a red cross on the side. Wounded soldiers in torn armor surrounded the tent. Jen shouldered her way through them.

"Hey!" A big bald man with an arm hanging limp at his side grabbed her and spun her around. "What do you think you're doing, cutting to the front of the line?"

Jen narrowed her eyes and snarled. "Take your hand off me or you won't need a healer."

Whether the look in her eye or the cold tone she used, something made the wounded man take a step back and raise his good hand. The others must have noticed the altercation because when she turned around a path had opened for her to the front of the tent. Jen hurried inside.

Dozens of cots filled the inside. Healers of all sorts, both mundane and sorcerers, tended moaning, groaning, and bleeding soldiers.

The stink of blood and death almost overwhelmed her.

Six cots to her right, John Kord knelt beside a wounded woman, his hands glowing as he sealed a gash on her side.

"John!"

He turned his handsome face in her direction and his eyes went wide. John and Damien had been close when they were little and her brother mentioned they'd gotten reacquainted at the tower. He finished with the woman then ran over to them. "What happened?"

She told him as they walked over to an empty cot. Jen laid her brother down and John made a pass with one hand over his chest. He nodded to himself.

"Well?" she asked, a quiver in her voice.

John smiled. "Don't worry, he'll be fine. Channeling that much soul force all at once exhausted his body. It looks like he used a little of the energy he needed to maintain his life functions, which explains why he passed out. He'll be sore as hell for a few days, but other than that I don't expect any lasting impact."

"How long until he wakes up?"

John shrugged. He didn't seem at all worried, which set her mind at ease. "Your guess is as good as mine."

"Can I stay with him?"

"Sure, grab a stool. I've got to get back to work. Hey, when this is over we should get something to eat."

Jen shook her head. He never failed to ask her out when they met, and no matter how many times she turned him down he kept trying, even in the middle of a war. She had to respect his persistence. "I'll pass."

He sighed, apparently having expected her reply. John left her alone with Damien. Jen glanced around and found a forgotten three-legged stool half hidden under a torn cot. Not ideal, but it was better than standing. She settled down beside her brother, took his hand, and closed her eyes to try to nap until he woke up.

Chapter 37

Damien hurt everywhere. From the tips of his toes to the top of his head he was one giant ache. Even his hair hurt. He and pain were old and bitter acquaintances, but for all the injuries he'd taken at The Citadel he'd never before hurt everywhere all at once. This was a new experience and he didn't like it at all.

Around him groans of pain filled the air. It sounded like he wasn't the only one that got hurt, though he was probably the only to sustain self-inflicted injuries. He opened his eyes and a white roof filled his vision.

The healers' tent, of course. Somehow he always seemed to end up with the healers. He turned his attention inward and found his soul force regenerated, but his shield hadn't recovered. He drew a little soul force and winced. How long would it hurt to use his power? He supposed it didn't really matter. He focused through the pain and recreated his shield. When he finished drawing on his power the pain faded a little.

"Damien?"

He turned toward his sister's voice and found her sitting beside his cot. "Did I get it?"

"You hit the dragon, but I didn't see what happened to it. Don't ever scare me like that again."

Her eyes were red like she'd been crying. It was a rare thing, seeing his powerful, fierce sister with tears in her eyes. He hoped to never see it again, much less be the cause of it. "Sorry, sis. I couldn't think what else to do."

A cough sounded and Damien turned to see General Kord and the pale sorcerer that led the army's sorcerers standing near the entry of the tent. Damien tried to sit up, but Jen put a hand on his chest, forcing him back into bed. "Sir?"

The pages entered a moment later carrying a pair of folding camp chairs. They set them up and the general and sorcerer sat beside his bed. "I was on the field when you blasted that dragon," General Kord said. "You blew a hole big enough to drive a wagon through in its side and somehow our sorcerers say it escaped."

"I tried to shape the blast so it wouldn't hit our soldiers. Is everyone okay?"

"You didn't catch a single one of my men in the blast, but you killed thousands of ogres and trolls. When the dragon fled the monsters lost their enthusiasm for the fight. We swept the field clear and according to my scouts they're still running. I suspect the war's over for this year, thanks to you. I dispatched a letter to His Majesty and the king insists on having a feast and award ceremony in your honor. You, Jen, and her squad are to head south as soon as you're able to travel." He shot a look at the sorcerer.

Her face twisted in a grimace. "Well done, young man. You blew away over half the dragon's soul force with your attack. It'll take centuries for it to recover. The Northlands owe you a great debt. You have my thanks and the thanks of my lord duke."

Damien smiled. What sort of threats had General Kord made to get her to say that? Whatever he said, Damien appreciated it. "I'm just glad I made a difference." He brought his fist to his heart. "For the person beside you."

The general grinned and returned the salute. "For the person beside you. You're welcome in my army any time, Damien. Your father would be proud."

"Thank you, sir."

The general nodded and he and the sorcerer left. When they'd gone Damien turned to his sister. "How long was I out?"

"Most of a day. John said you'd be fine, but I was starting to wonder."

"I didn't mean to worry you." Damien grinned. "Did he ask you out?"

Jen sighed. "Of course. That boy won't take no for an answer."

Damien laughed even though it made his whole body hurt. "What do you expect, he's in love."

Chapter 38

Damien managed another day resting before he couldn't stand it anymore. He still ached, but it was bearable and getting less painful all the time. In another week, hopefully, he'd be recovered. It still hurt to draw his soul force. John said it was because he'd used too much all at once, but he hadn't done any permanent damage. Better yet, if Damien had to do it again it would hurt less since he'd done it once already.

Damien, Jen, and the rest of her squad rode for the better part of three weeks before the walls of the capital rose in the distance. Damien would have preferred a conjured mount, but John assured him riding a real horse would be better under the circumstances. So here he was, on a rolling, breathing, stinking mount ten miles from the capital. Snow blanketed everything; trees, fields, and fences were reduced to white blobs.

He hated winter. Anything might be hiding out under that white expanse. A clever, patient enemy could sneak within a few feet of his target before he struck. Of course, anyone stupid enough to sneak up on Damien and his companions would end up dead in very short order. At least the traffic to the city had tromped down the snow covering the road so the horses didn't have to slog through knee-deep piles of the stuff.

"What are you thinking about?" Jen asked.

"Assassins."

She frowned. "What about them?"

"I'd rather fight half a dozen than go to some stupid feast."

She laughed. "It'll be fine. Just smile and nod, shake some hands, and plead exhaustion. You could probably escape inside an hour."

He grimaced. An hour? How would he manage an hour of smiling and listening to those idiots talk about the battles they watched like they had some part in the fighting? At least the food should be good. After a month plus on the road and eating in camp Damien wanted a hot, well-cooked meal in the worst way.

Not tiny sandwiches covered in cold cucumbers either, but meat and hot bread. And a mug of mulled cider, he'd sell his soul for a mug of hot cider.

"Looks like they sent out a welcoming committee."

Jen's words shook him out of his thoughts. A dozen horsemen cantered out from the main gate toward them. Damien squinted, but couldn't tell who it was.

"It's Dad." Jen must have used her soul force to sharpen her sight.

Damien warped the air in front of his eyes to mimic the lenses of a spy glass. A little twinge of pain coursed through him, but nothing to bother about. Sure enough, through the magnification field, he saw his father riding at the head of ten horsemen dressed in blue-and-silver tabards, a gold crown embroidered on their chests. They carried lances with matching pennants flapping in the wind.

An escort of royal guardsmen, how nice. It looked like the king, or as he preferred Jen and Damien to call him in private, Uncle Andy, was going all out.

They reined in when the two groups were ten yards apart. Jen and her squad saluted his father, their fists touching their chests. Damien waved. He wasn't a warlord and he didn't answer to his father.

Dad returned the salute. "Congratulations on your successful mission." He turned his intense gaze on Damien. "I understand you made a good showing for yourself, son. His Majesty wishes to extend his most sincere thanks for your efforts on his behalf. Well done."

The pride in the old man's voice surprised Damien. He'd never had much use for sorcerers and even less for Damien himself. He considered them cowards for the most part since they didn't fight the enemy face to face. "Thank you, sir. It'll be nice to see Uncle Andy, I mean the king, again."

Dad winced at his slip. Damien had to remember not to act too familiar with Uncle Andy when other people were around. Sometimes he forgot the kind man that used to run around with Damien on his shoulders as a child was also his king. Of course Uncle Andy would have a fit if he acted too formal in private so he had to balance it, so complicated. Stupid court, with all their rules and propriety. It would be so much easier if everyone could just be friends instead of lords and vassals. The fact that a lot of them hated each other might have something to do with it.

The guardsmen formed up on either side of the group and they rode toward the gate. Dad eased his mare over beside Damien.

Taking on that dragon was very dangerous.

Damien smiled, but didn't reply. It was good to hear Lizzy's voice. He hoped they'd have time to catch up later. Dad hated it when he talked out loud to her when others were around, so he contented himself with sending her warm thoughts.

"General Kord said you saved the northern army all by yourself." Dad sounded a little dubious and Damien didn't blame him. All he'd ever seen was Damien the screw up.

"I did the best I could and things worked out. I was lucky Jen was there to catch me since I didn't have a drop of power left after I blasted that dragon. I was hoping to kill it, but the spotters said it got away."

"An impressive feat just the same." Dad patted him on the back.

Damien smiled at the awkward attempt at affection. Of all Dad's myriad of talents, showing affection to his son was not among them. It was nice that he'd made the effort though. Maybe they'd manage to be civil for however long they were in the capital. "Thanks, Dad. Did any of the monsters get through?"

"Reports say a few groups snuck past our line. I've got squads out hunting them down. You've done your part. Let others handle this."

"Yes, sir." That was one order he'd be happy to follow.

Chapter 39

The city gates consisted of foot-thick oak timbers held together with iron bands. The walls loomed fifty feet above them. Twenty feet thick and constructed of granite blocks fused together with soul force, the wall was almost a solid piece of rock. Beyond the gate the citizens had shoveled the cobblestone streets clear of snow, making traveling easy.

Hundreds of people walked in both directions up and down King's Way, the central road from the gate to the castle, on their way to one of the many shops and taverns lining the street. Noon fast approached, so this was probably the lunch rush. Many people waved at the stoic guardsmen, hoping for a reaction.

Damien remembered doing the same thing when he was little and visiting the capital with Dad and Jen the first time. They never flinched despite his youthful efforts.

He sighed. It had been too long since they visited the castle together. Did the cook still make the honey butter biscuits he and Jen used to steal as kids? He hoped so and if she did he planned to steal some more.

"You look nostalgic."

He glanced at his sister who wore a smile that no doubt matched his. "How long has it been, six years?"

"About that. Do you think Princess Karrie will be happy to see you?"

Damien's smile soured. Princess Karrie was Uncle Andy's daughter, heir to the throne, and a year younger than Damien. On his last visit she'd developed a crush on him and followed him and John everywhere. She even proclaimed to anyone that would listen that she intended to marry him. He'd had no use for girls at the time and now he only had eyes for Lizzy. He really hoped she'd grown out of it. "Not too happy I hope."

Jen laughed. She'd always gotten a kick out of the little princess chasing him around. Funny, she didn't seem to find John chasing her around nearly so amusing. Not wanting to ruin the warm fuzzy feeling he was enjoying Damien kept that observation to himself.

Fifteen minutes brought them to the inner gates. A second, thirty-foot wall surrounded the residential district and served as a second line of defense if the outer wall should fall. As far as Damien knew that had never happened.

King's Way continued on through the neat rows of cedar-shingled multifamily houses. The further they went the nicer the buildings. In the distance the imposing gray stone castle loomed. A third wall, this one twenty feet tall, surrounded the castle just inside the dry moat. A single drawbridge allowed access to the castle.

With their escort of royal guards no one challenged them as they rode across the heavy planks of the drawbridge. Damien glanced up at the spiked bottom of the raised portcullis. How big a force would it take to penetrate this far into the city?

A bigger danger would be sorcerers flying in over the walls. Of course anyone attempting to fly into the castle would have to deal with the archmage and her Crimson Legion.

Inside the wall was an empty courtyard. Long, low barracks sat along the walls and housed the royal guards. Now that they were inside their escorts peeled off and rode towards the barracks. Perhaps they'd get the rest of the day off.

Four boys rushed out of the keep to collect their horses. When they'd dismounted and the stable boys had led the animals away Damien asked, "What now?"

In answer to his question an old man with a knobby staff wearing long blue robes hobbled out of the keep. A wispy white beard grew from his chin and he wore a golden key around his neck.

Damien grinned. Dale Alan, the castle seneschal, looked exactly as he remembered from all those years ago.

"Dale!" Damien waved.

The old man smiled. "Master Damien, it's been far too long. And Jennifer as well. Wonderful to see you both. The king is expecting you."

Dale led them into the keep, his staff tapping along on the stone floor. Inside, a long hall lined with suits of armor led to a set of double doors that opened into the throne room. Halfway down, a door on either side led to the rest of the castle. A pair of royal guards, their halberds resting on the floor, stood beside the doors.

They looked more like doormen than guards. As if reading Damien's mind the two men pulled the doors open as they approached.

The throne room wasn't as big as you might have expected, reflecting the fact that when they'd built the castle defense came before pomp. A red carpet ran down the center of the room between rows of empty, hard wooden benches that sat facing the raised throne where Uncle Andy sat beside another pair of guards.

Those two carried well-worn long swords and judging from their soul force were powerful warlords. Not that Uncle Andy was any slouch. His soul force almost matched his guards and he was still strong and fit, his dark hair streaked with gray. He wore a simple gold circlet, blue-and-silver tunic, black pants, and a purple robe trimmed with fox fur. When they reached the end of the carpet everyone took a knee.

"No need to stand on protocol in private, please rise."

Damien got up and found Uncle Andy on his feet and walking down the two steps from the throne. He shook hands with Jen and her team. "I understand you did good work finding the dragon and its army and warning General Kord of its approach. Well done."

They all bowed their heads and murmured words of thanks. Besides Jen none of them had met the king before and they seemed uncertain what to say. Uncle Andy realized it as well. "I'm sure you're tired from your journey. Perhaps you'd like to rest in the barracks."

"I'll join you later," Jen said.

The guys bowed and fled like men who'd just received a reprieve from the gallows. When they'd gone and the doors closed behind them Uncle Andy laughed. "Am I so intimidating?"

Damien grinned and shook his hand. "They just don't know you like we do. Can we skip the award ceremony and just have the feast?"

"Same Damien, always thinking with his stomach. Unfortunately, we have to have the ceremony. General Kord put you up for the Medal of Valor and after reading his report I believe you deserve it. Don't worry, it won't take that long. Karrie's around here somewhere. I believe she mentioned wanting a dance at the feast."

Damien managed not to grimace.

Chapter 40

Two days after his meeting with Uncle Andy, Damien stood in a short hall that led to a balcony where the king would place a gold trinket around his neck. The voices of the gathering crowd reached Damien despite the distance.

He tugged at the collar of his formal robes. A shrill, wrinkled woman had spent an hour yesterday evening measuring him and attempting to poke him with needles. If not for his personal shield he'd look like a pin cushion. He'd never met the woman before, but he felt certain she hated him on sight. When she left an hour later he returned the feeling.

Why couldn't they just get it over with already? He couldn't see the sun from where he stood, but he figured he had at least another half hour of waiting. Damien never imagined wishing for a demon attack, but it might be a welcome change right about now. He conjured a chair and slumped down in it.

"Damien St. Cloud?" A slender, older woman with blond hair, a mess of fine wrinkles around her sharp green eyes, and a crimson robe appeared as if out of nowhere. He saw no soul force so she must be a sorcerer, probably a member of the Crimson Legion.

Damien blinked in surprise. “Yes, ma’am, can I help you?”

“I’m Lidia Thorn, archmage of the kingdom.”

Damien scrambled to his feet, reabsorbed the speck of power he used to form the chair, and licked his lips. The archmage! What was he supposed to do, bow, salute, no one ever told him. “Nice to meet you.” That was almost certainly not the proper reply.

She smiled at his unease. “Please relax or you’ll make me nervous. I’ve been reading about you. You completed your training in the minimum required time, killed a demon a few days later, and now you almost killed a dragon. An impressive start to your career.”

“Thank you, ma’am. I haven’t had much luck finding a mentor despite my efforts. If I can’t find one soon I don’t know what sort of career I might have.”

She waved her hand as though that was of no concern. “Show me your power.”

“Ma’am?”

“Channel half your power into your shield and make it visible. Reading reports isn’t the same as seeing for myself.”

Damien saw no reason to refuse, and even if he did he wouldn’t dare object to her order. He made his shield visible and suddenly the world took on a golden tint. Half his power went flowing down the channels he’d made. All around him stones vibrated, and cracks ran along the floor as the power he didn’t fully contain spilled over. The archmage’s hair and robe blew back from the breeze his power whipped up.

“That’s enough.” She waved her arms like he couldn’t hear her.

He drew his power back in and returned his shield to its original state. “Was that okay, ma’am?”

She smiled and straightened her hair. “Better than okay. You’re stronger than me. I suspect you could take any three of my Crimson Legion in a duel. How about you come work for me?”

“Ma’am?” He had to have heard wrong. There was no way the archmage would want a kid six months out of the tower to serve in her legion.

"I want you to come work for me. The others are too gutless to take you as an apprentice. Well, that's their loss. You're far too valuable to waste sitting in The Tower waiting for a mentor. I'll be your mentor and you'll answer directly to me. You've certainly proven yourself a capable field agent. What do you say?"

Damien didn't have to think long. "I'd be honored, Master."

She nodded once. "Excellent. I've arranged a room for you in the castle. When I have something I'll summon you. In the meantime keep practicing and make yourself useful around the grounds. I'm sure you can find something to do."

Damien blinked and she vanished. He squinted, trying and failing to penetrate her invisibility screen. What an odd woman. He'd assumed the archmage would be more intimidating, but she reminded Damien of a kindly aunt.

Oh well, at least he didn't have to go around begging for a master anymore. He was working with the archmage. He restrained himself from jumping for joy. After this even the award ceremony would be bearable.

Book Two

Border Betrayal

Chapter 1

Damien St. Cloud leaned against the wall in the back corner of the throne room, the stone rough through his black tunic, and watched the line of peacocks waiting their turn to suck up to Uncle Andy. Silk and lace draped the soft, flabby bodies of thirty of the richest and most powerful people in the kingdom while gold and gems glittered in the light of the glow globes hanging from the ceiling. They'd arrived to present themselves to the king. Probably so, despite his best efforts, he wouldn't forget they existed.

A slight breeze from the invisible fan he'd conjured blew the overwhelming stink of perfume mingled with sweat away. When he first entered, the stench had about knocked him over. You'd think people that rich could afford a bath. He didn't know how the regular guards stood it. The warlords used soul force to block their sense of smell. Damien could see the flow of energy that separated their brains from their noses. That had to be how Uncle Andy kept from throwing up.

For his part the king sat on his simple wooden throne, a big, fake smile plastered on his face as he shook the hand of a fat, bald nobleman in acid green silks. Damien couldn't hear what the fawning fop was saying nor did he care enough to conjure an eavesdropping sphere to listen in. He assumed the man wanted something, the same as the rest of the leeches in line. Rich as they were, you could always count on a noble to want more.

Damien narrowed his focus, curious about the nobles' soul force. The fat man in green seemed ordinary enough, likewise the woman behind him. The man behind her, one of the few without a giant stomach, had a weak internal soul force. Not strong enough to train as a warlord, but enough to give him an edge over an ordinary person.

He kept scanning. A surprising number of the nobility lacked any significant soul force. Maybe nature made a point of balancing their wealth with a lack of real power. Damien frowned when he reached the second-to-last man in line, a potbellied fellow with oily black hair and watery blue eyes. He had no soul force at all. Which meant he had to be a sorcerer. Curiosity piqued, Damien studied the man even closer. A faint soul force aura surrounded his body. Some kind of illusion maybe.

Why would a noble need an illusion to present himself to the king? Something was wrong. Along the far-side wall stood the captain of the royal guard in his immaculate blue-and-silver tabard over practical mail armor. Damien didn't know the man well. He'd stood beside Damien's father when Uncle Andy presented him with the Medal of Valor last week. The captain had a strong internal soul force, nothing compared to Dad, but better than average. Most important, his loyalty to the king was beyond question. He'd know if the nobleman was hiding something.

Damien worked his way around the back of the throne room. The guards all knew him and moved out of his way. A minute later he leaned against the wall beside the guard captain, arms crossed, trying to look casual. "Captain."

"Damien. Something I can do for you?" The captain pitched his voice low so no one would overhear them.

"The second-to-last man in line, do you know him?"

"Dominic Santen. He's a merchant prince, bought a title, but doesn't hold any land. What about him?"

"Is he a sorcerer?"

"No, he's a weasel, liar, thief, and cheat, but not a sorcerer."

"Then we have a problem, because that man's a sorcerer and I suspect he's using an illusion to look like Mr. Santen."

The captain eased his hand closer to the well-worn hilt of his sword. "Are you certain?"

"Yeah." Damien wanted to tap his soul force, but didn't dare for fear of warning the imposter. "How do you want to handle it?"

"Can you break the illusion so we can see what we're dealing with?"

The imposter had moved so he stood only ten people from the throne. They needed to act fast, before he got any closer to Uncle Andy. "Sure, but if he's strong this could get ugly fast. Do you want me to shield the nobles or take down the sorcerer?"

"Take down the sorcerer. I know enough about sorcerers to know my men won't have much of a chance against him. We'll deal with the nobles. Blasted Crimson Legion! They were supposed to screen all the guests before they entered the throne room."

Damien nodded. The captain's plan made sense. Part of him wanted to defend his new comrades, but he couldn't think of a good argument. How had the sorcerer snuck into the castle? Damien hoped whoever the imposter was, he was just filling in for the real Dominic Santen and didn't mean any harm. "Understood. When do you want me to go?"

The captain made several subtle gestures with his off hand and all around the room guards tensed. "Now."

Damien drew power and sent a stream of it at the imposter. He formed the blast so it would only shatter the illusion, not harm the person under it. The image of an out-of-shape merchant vanished. In his place stood a female figure. Tight gray pants and shirt hugged a curvy figure. A half mask covered her face from the nose down. She wore thin black gloves and heavy leather boots.

Her cold gaze locked with Damien's. This woman was a killer, he knew it. She leapt toward the throne, a golden blade appearing in her right hand. Damien conjured a wall in her path, but the blade made short work of it. He'd never seen a soul force construct that dense. It looked like she put all her power into it.

Uncle Andy had leapt to his feet and pulled his sword. It appeared he wanted to fight, but his guards were standing in front of him, shielding him from the assassin. Whimpering nobles fled for the exit, royal guards attempting to keep them under control. Damien had no time to worry about them. With his barrier demolished the sorcerer rushed the guards.

They attacked and an instant later found their swords in pieces, only their enhanced speed keeping them from getting gutted. Damien drew half his power and conjured golden chains that wrapped tight around her legs and body. He matched the density of her blade and when she tried to cut the bindings away she only nicked them.

Uncle Andy's guards hustled him out the back exit. Half a dozen guardsmen approached the woman as she furiously hacked at the chains. Damien poured more energy into them to repair the damage she was causing.

"Somebody hit her! I can't keep her bound forever."

The captain of the guard raced in at warlord speed and brought his pommel down on the back of her head. Her sword vanished and she slumped in Damien's chains. He studied the flow of her soul force to make certain she wasn't faking before he let the chains vanish. Two guards caught her before she hit the ground.

Chapter 2

Every castle had a dungeon. Damien felt sure it was a rule. He'd never visited one before so he had no idea how Uncle Andy's compared to someone else's. In some of the stories he'd read, the authors described dungeons as dank, smelly places filled with torture chambers and hooded guards that entertained themselves by beating the prisoners. By that standard this dungeon was a pleasant spot.

Cool and dry, without a bit of standing water, the dungeon under the royal castle had a dozen cells outfitted with simple cots and mess buckets. A faint odor of sweat and human waste filtered through the halls, but nothing unbearable. In fact, to Damien, the smell offended less than the nobles' perfume. Steel doors with small view slits kept the prisoners from wandering off. Ten guards in blue-and-sliver uniforms patrolled the halls, heavy truncheons hanging at their belts.

On their way to the interrogation chamber Damien and the archmage passed three guards on patrol. Was "interrogation chamber" a euphemism for "torture chamber"?

When she heard about the attempt on the king's life his master had about hit the roof. Damien wouldn't have wanted to be whichever Crimson Legionnaire had let the assassin sneak into the castle.

"You did well to spot and subdue her, Damien," the archmage said. "Since you took her alive, hopefully we can find out who hired her."

"Thank you, Master." Damien allowed himself a moment to bask in his mentor's praise. "I've never seen anyone who used their soul force like she did."

"I'm not surprised." They rounded a corner and found three red-robed sorcerers facing into an open room. Soul force streamed from the sorcerers. Every time the assassin tried to draw power from her core they severed the link and her conjuring collapsed. He wasn't familiar with that technique. Inside the room a fourth sorcerer in identical robes sat at a simple wooden table facing the assassin.

"She's a member of a group called the Soul Knives," the archmage said. "Assassins for hire that specialize in creating soul force weapons of great destructive power. They're based down south in the badlands. Whoever hired her must have a lot of coin as they don't work cheap."

They stopped just beyond the interrogation chamber. Someone had removed the assassin's mask and outer clothes, leaving her wearing nothing but small clothes. Her thin lips were turned down in a sullen frown. Pale, freckled skin covered a lean, wiry body. Several thin scars marred her flat, well-muscled stomach. She might have been attractive but for the flat, emotionless brown eyes; killer's eyes. Damien's father had eyes like that when he fought.

The sorcerer in the room slammed his fist on the table. "Who are you working for?"

The assassin's cool, indifferent gaze raked him over and dismissed him. Damien doubted just asking would be enough to get her to talk. Maybe they'd need a torture chamber after all.

"I don't think she's going to tell us anything," Damien said.

His master smiled, a tiny, evil curl of her lips. "We haven't begun the interrogation yet. Alden's just giving her a chance to talk and save herself some pain. I wanted you to see how he proceeds. This isn't the sort of thing they teach at Sorcery. Pay close attention."

She whistled two sharp notes. Alden drew a thin stream of power and drove it straight into the assassin's brain. She tried to conjure a shield to block the probe, but one of the other sorcerers countered her.

The assassin's back arched and she screamed. Damien recognized the place Alden stabbed: the pain center of the brain. In healing class they'd learned how to block the flow of pain from a wound to that area, like he'd done for Talon last summer. This looked like the exact opposite of that technique. It never occurred to him to do that.

The questioner shifted his probe to another section of her brain and the screaming stopped. "Who hired you?"

She opened her mouth to speak, but no sound came out. Damien glanced at his master.

"She's trying to lie, but Alden's blocked her access to that area of her brain. If she wishes to speak she can only tell the truth. This part of the technique is more important than the pain. If you can't keep them from lying torture does no good."

Damien winced when Alden switched his probe back to the pain center, drawing another scream. For her sake, killer or not, he hoped she told them what they wanted to know. "Do you think she'll break?"

"They all break eventually." Her cold, emotionless tone sent a chill up Damien's spine.

Chapter 3

Damien sat at the intricately carved mahogany table in the dining room of the royal quarters. Roast pheasant and a variety of sides covered the table. Uncle Andy sat to his left, Princess Karrie across from him, and Queen Audra to his right. After the attack that morning Uncle Andy had insisted he join the family for supper, as a reward or for protection Damien couldn't say. For his part Damien was glad to have an excuse to escape the marathon torture session in the dungeon.

He'd never considered himself squeamish, but after two hours of listening to that woman scream he had been happy to beg off and get ready for supper. The assassin was tough, he had to give her credit. Alden had to quit after an hour and a half. While he recovered, a stunning young woman—blond hair, blue eyes, and a perfect figure—took his place.

The sight of perhaps the most beautiful woman he'd ever seen after Lizzy, torturing someone without blinking, amazed him. The strangest thing about the whole process was the lack of blood. Aside from a hoarse voice you'd never know anything had happened to the assassin.

"What's wrong, Damien?" Queen Audra asked. She wore a blue gown, her long dark hair hanging loose down her back. Damien had never been as close to the queen as he was to Uncle Andy. Whenever his family visited the capital she spent most of her time gossiping with her ladies. Uncle Andy liked to play with him and Jen. "Isn't the pheasant to your liking?"

Damien looked down at his almost untouched plate. Everything tasted like ashes after the torture session. As far as he knew the assassin was still screaming under their feet. Thinking about it soured his stomach.

"Everything's delicious. I guess after the attack I don't have much appetite."

He looked up and found Karrie staring at him with her bright, green eyes. She batted her eyelashes, trying to play the flirt. Since he'd last seen her Karrie had grown into a pretty girl. Straight black hair framed a heart-shaped face and a slim body was just starting to show signs of the woman she'd be. In a couple more years, when she finished filling out, the noble boys would be fighting over her and not just because she stood to inherit the throne.

"It's a good thing you were there today." Uncle Andy took a sip of wine. "A lot of people might have gotten hurt otherwise."

"My master said to make myself useful. Capturing assassins seemed useful."

Uncle Andy laughed and dug back into his meal, an attempt on his life insufficient to blunt his appetite. Damien nibbled a few more bites. The pheasant really did taste wonderful. To his surprise, five minutes later, he'd cleaned his plate. He fought a yawn and lost. It had been a long day.

"You look all in," Uncle Andy said. "What do you say we call it a night?"

Before Damien could respond a tremor ran through the room, setting the silverware to rattling. The little quake lasted for maybe five seconds.

"Bloody tremblers," Uncle Andy said. "I swear, if it's not one thing it's another."

Damien stood and stretched. The tremors were a nuisance, but basically harmless. "I think I'll head to my room. I'm afraid I wasn't good company tonight."

Audra patted his knee. "Don't give it another thought. Go get some sleep."

Damien bowed to the queen and shook Uncle Andy's hand.

"I'll walk you to your room." Karrie popped out of her chair.

Damien's jaw clenched and released. He tried to think of a polite way to refuse, but nothing came to him. The walk only took a couple of minutes. He could tolerate her unwanted attention for that long. It wasn't that he disliked Karrie, she was a sweet girl, he just didn't like her the way she wanted him to.

"That's a good idea, sweetheart," Uncle Andy said. "You need to spend more time with people your own age."

Damien glanced at Uncle Andy. Was the king trying to set him up with his daughter? By heaven, he hoped not. Karrie had unreasonable ideas enough without her father encouraging her.

Karrie grabbed his arm and tugged him toward the door. He swallowed a sigh and let her lead him out of the royal apartment. Outside the sumptuous quarters waited the same plain gray halls as everywhere else in the castle. Damien loved visiting Uncle Andy, but it felt good to get back into surroundings he found comfortable. Now if he could just get Karrie to loosen her death grip on his arm so he could walk without tripping on her.

Damien turned right. His quarters sat on the same floor as the royals', but in the opposite wing. "Could you give me a little space before we fall?"

"Are you sure?" She rubbed her small, firm breasts against his arm.

Damien hesitated a moment before he pulled gently away. He needed this complication right now like he needed to wrestle a demon barehanded. "I'm sure."

She released his arm and pouted. "Why? There are half a dozen boys that would cut their best friend's throat to walk with me."

Damien didn't doubt it, especially if she acted with them the way she did with him. "I believe it. You're a beautiful girl, and a princess too."

"Then what's the problem?" She reached for his arm again and Damien sped up.

He needed to get back to his room before he said something wrong. He doubted Karrie heard no very often and he didn't know what sort of reaction he'd get if he told her straight out he didn't like her that way.

She hurried to walk beside him then laughed. "If you keep speeding up we'll be running through the halls." Karrie took his hand. "There, that's not so bad, is it?"

"No." A right turn and three more doors and he'd be at his room. He'd hold her hand for a couple of minutes and call it a night.

They finished the walk in silence. Damien tried to let go and reach for the door, but Karrie didn't let him. "Aren't you going to invite me in?"

Damien had no intention of inviting her in. He barely had to force a yawn. "No, I'm beat."

Karrie stood up on her tiptoes and kissed him, her tongue darting in his mouth for a moment before she stepped back. Damien stared at her, no idea what to say, no coherent thought in his head beyond wondering where she learned to kiss like that.

"I told you when we were little I would marry you one day and I meant it. I hate those arrogant, soft boys, with their fake compliments and eyes on Daddy's throne. Daddy already thinks of you like a son, Mom likes you too, and I like you a lot. The only one that seems to have a problem with this is you. I have to marry in three years, and get betrothed in two. I have no interest in fending off smelly, grabby noble boys for two years. You're a hero and you saved Daddy's life today. No one would complain if he announced our engagement after all you've done."

Damien did his best to process her speech, but it overwhelmed him. After the battle and what was happening under their feet right now, he didn't have the wherewithal to deal with this right now. "Good night, Princess. Sleep well."

He freed his hand and fled into his room, closing the door firmly behind him. He took slow, deep breaths, trying to get his heart rate down. He didn't know what to feel, what to think. He didn't love Karrie, but that kiss... The pounding in his ears didn't fade until the click of her heels moved beyond his hearing. He sighed and stepped away from the door. What was he going to do?

Something sparkled on his desk, distracting him from the princess. He locked the door and crossed the dark room to his plain wooden table. Glowing words sat on the top. They read: She broke. My office. Dawn. So the archmage convinced the assassin to talk. He wondered for a moment what shape the woman was in then dismissed the thought as irrelevant. She had tried to kill Uncle Andy. She deserved what she got.

Chapter 4

Damien strode down the hall toward the archmage's office. She'd chosen a place well away from noise and people. In fact, judging by the smell, he figured at some point in the past the small room had served as a storeroom for chamber pots. Damien hadn't been brave enough to point that out.

He absently took a bite of the egg and cheese sandwich he'd begged from the kitchen, his mind elsewhere. Damien had come to an arrangement with the cook. In exchange for not stealing her rolls he could get a snack whenever he wanted. This suited Damien as he usually woke up early and hated waiting to eat. His master rose early as well and he hoped she'd enjoy the second sandwich that floated along beside him in a soul force bubble.

Damien fought off a yawn. He hadn't gotten much sleep last night. The attack and torture had pumped him full of adrenaline. Add the princess's proclamation that they were getting married, his preferences be damned, and it was a wonder he slept as much as he did. Surely the king could have found a better match for Karrie than him.

On the other hand, having seen some of the elder members of the nobility, maybe he couldn't. Nevertheless Damien had no intention of marrying Karrie, he just had to find some way to make that clear to her and the king. Right. Damien wished he had time to make a quick trip to The Citadel to visit Lizzy and see what she thought about all this. The demon spirit understood relationships better than he did. Getting to be with her, even for a little while, would soothe his nerves as well. Heaven's mercy, he wished they could spend more than an hour here or there together every few months.

Nothing marked the door as belonging to the archmage. It just looked like a plain oak door with an iron pull. It didn't even have a lock. Not that it needed one. If she didn't want anyone inside, a soul force barrier would keep people out better than any normal lock.

He popped the last of his sandwich in his mouth and stepped up to the door. Muffled voices, neither of them sounding happy, filtered out into the hall. Damien frowned. She must have had a meeting before him. He moved a few steps away and leaned against the wall. He didn't want his master thinking he had been eavesdropping.

A minute later the door slammed open and a tall, fit young woman in her early twenties, with short brown hair stalked out, her face twisted in an angry scowl. She wore leather pants, knee-high boots, and a blue shirt that showed her figure to good effect. She stormed past Damien, glaring at him as she went. What had he done?

She turned a corner that led to the main gate. Damien shrugged. Whatever her problem, it had nothing to do with him. He pushed off the wall, walked over to the open door and poked his head in. The archmage sat in her chair behind a battered desk, head in her hands.

"Is this a bad time, Master?"

She looked up and offered a wan smile. "No. Is that for me?"

Her gaze locked on the sandwich floating beside him. Damien guided it over, transforming the bubble into a plate and landing it on her desk. "I thought you might be hungry."

She took a giant bite out of the sandwich. "You were right."

Less than a minute later the food was gone. She sighed. "Thank you. I always intend to get breakfast, but something often comes up. Sit down."

Damien dropped into the padded mahogany chair in front of her desk. To his right a cherry bookcase held hundreds of leather-bound books. "Was the unhappy young woman I saw what came up today?"

"My daughter, Lane. She's one of the kingdom's leading diplomats. I just gave her a new assignment."

"The moment I saw her I thought diplomat, either that or berserker. I take it she didn't care for her new task?"

His master smiled. "No, the assignment didn't bother her. She's mad because I assigned you to be her bodyguard. Lane doesn't like sorcerers."

Damien raised an eyebrow at that. "The daughter of the archmage doesn't like sorcerers? That sounds awkward."

"We've made peace. I don't know if you noticed, but she doesn't have any extraordinary power. Being born the daughter of a leading sorcerer and having no power of her own was hard for Lane. Spending time around sorcerers reminds her of what she doesn't have."

Damien could relate to that. "What about the assassin?"

"Right, that's the reason you're accompanying Lane. Baron Trasker hired the assassin to kill the king. He's a border baron, one of ten. They've been complaining about taxes and threatening to secede from the kingdom, leaving us open to raids from the bandits living in the badlands. Lane's going to their annual meeting to try and negotiate a settlement."

Damien nodded. "And I'm going to keep her safe from Trasker."

"Partly, but mainly you're going in case she fails. If the barons can't be persuaded to see reason you're to remove them from their positions."

"As in"—Damien drew a finger across his throat—"permanently?"

"Exactly. Keeping the border secure is too important to jeopardize because of petty, noble greed. It will also make a good example for their eventual successors. I've spoken to the king and you have full authority to resolve this with whatever force necessary."

Damien nodded again. She wasn't starting him off with an easy mission, to say the least. "Does Lane know my real job?"

"No, and I prefer you not tell her until the last possible moment. I don't want her to think I don't have faith in her abilities."

"Okay. Anything else?"

"Don't forget to check in at each stop. If I have new information I'll pass it along. Keep my daughter safe and come home in one piece. Good luck."

Chapter 5

Damien left his master to brood in her office and followed Lane to the main gate. He couldn't stop smiling. Even if she hated him, any assignment that got him out of the capital for weeks or maybe months was right up Damien's alley. When in doubt, delay. Sound, if not especially brave, tactics.

He didn't meet another soul until he reached the gate guards who waved him through. Since the ceremony last week everyone knew Damien and he could go wherever he wanted with no trouble. He shivered in the chill breeze as he passed under the raised portcullis, and through the open gates. A thin blanket of snow covered the ground, but the riot of footprints made it impossible to tell where Lane had gone.

Damien frowned and turned back to the guards. "Did you fellows see an attractive, pissed-off looking woman with short brown hair come this way?"

"I believe she was headed for the stables," the right-hand guard said.

Damien touched his forehead in salute and headed left, expanding his shield and heating the air around him as he went. The stink of the stables, though reduced by the cold, still made them easy to find. Why would she bother with horses when he could fly them to the border in a day?

He found Lane in a fur-lined cloak right outside the stables, adjusting the straps of the saddle on a bay gelding. Her breath puffed in the air with each tug of the strap. Damien strode up and stopped a few feet away. "Morning. I'm Damien St. Cloud, I'll be your bodyguard for this mission."

Lane gave the strap one last yank and straightened up to face him. Jade eyes flashed in the bright morning sun. "So my mother said. I'll tell you what I told her, I don't need a bodyguard and I certainly don't need a sorcerer tagging along on a diplomatic mission. All you people are good for is blowing things up."

Damien certainly had a knack for blowing things up, but he liked to think that wasn't the extent of his talents. "We don't need horses, you know. I can fly us to the border by nightfall."

"Ha! If we fly in there they'll know you're a sorcerer and they'll think you're along to intimidate them into doing what the king wants. If the barons feel threatened the negotiations will be over before they start. Besides, the meeting isn't until March first. If we ride and take it easy, we should make it just in time."

Ten weeks on the road and away from Karrie, that sounded fine to Damien. "Do you have supplies?"

"The grooms are loading a mule. There are army supply posts every ten days where we can get more food and swap horses. Are you ready?"

"I need to pack my gear and grab a sword so I'll pass for a regular bodyguard. Other than that I'm good to go."

"Well hurry up, I want to be out of here inside the hour."

Damien nodded and jogged back toward the keep. When he'd moved past the guards he wrapped himself in an invisibility screen and flew a few inches off the ground so his steps wouldn't draw attention. A lot of sorcerers forgot that part when they turned invisible. Clomping steps from thin air drew people's attention. Not that he'd get in trouble if someone caught him, he just didn't want to deal with the princess.

He flew through the halls at the speed of a brisk run, dodging servants and messengers as he went. The halls quieted as he approached the living areas. A single chambermaid carried a pile of towels toward the laundry. Damien floated silently as she hurried past him, then he turned toward his room.

He landed outside the door and let his screen fade. Getting ready shouldn't take long. He could pack everything he owned in five minutes. Two minutes later he had a change of clothes, a spare set of boots and his curved dagger tucked away in his rucksack. His sword he strapped to his back then covered it with a heavy fur cloak. He wore both for appearances rather than need. Damien glanced in the mirror and nodded. He looked like a proper bodyguard.

"Where are you going?"

Damien spun to face the door and found Karrie standing there, arms crossed and frowning. He'd been visible for two minutes. How had she found him? "I've got a mission, guard duty for the archmage's daughter. Your father knows about it."

Her frown deepened. "He didn't say anything to me. I know Lane Thorn. She's very pretty. I suppose you prefer spending time with older girls."

Damien would have preferred spending time with Lizzy, who had existed since the dawn of time, so he supposed that made her an older girl. Lane, on the other hand, appeared to hate him on principle. He doubted it would be an especially pleasant trip. "Guarding Lane is a job, and I assure you she hasn't the slightest interest in me, nor do I have any in her, beyond keeping her safe. We have a task to complete. When it's finished we'll come back, so relax."

Her frown softened. "I don't like you hanging around with another girl, but I suppose it is your job. See that you keep it professional. We'll continue our conversation when you return."

Karrie turned in a swirl of silk skirts and sauntered down the hall back toward the royal residence. Damien wanted badly to shout at her back that she wasn't his girlfriend and it was none of her business who he spent time with, but she might come back if he did, so he held his peace.

Damien retraced his steps back to the stable and found Lane sitting in her saddle, reins held in one hand, the lead of an overloaded mule in the other. "Ready?"

Damien nodded and started to conjure a mount.

"What are you doing?" Lane's disagreeable voice stopped him halfway through the process. "You're posing as a regular bodyguard, remember? No sorcery; you ride the same as me."

He grimaced, both at her patronizing tone and the idea of having to ride a bouncing, jostling, uncomfortable horse for ten weeks. A stable boy led a saddled roan mare out of the long building. Damien accepted the reins, nodded his thanks, and checked the saddle straps. Everything looked good and tight.

He hung his rucksack from the pommel and swung up into the saddle. "Satisfied?"

"Hardly." She clucked her tongue and led the way toward the outer gate.

Damien tapped his mount's ribs and followed her. This was going to be a long trip.

Chapter 6

Damien figured they managed fifteen miles before the sun dropped so low in the sky that they had to stop and make camp. The roads this close to the capital had little snow to bother them, the tread of hundreds of horses and wagons having stomped it down to nothing. Damien appreciated that almost as much as he appreciated the invisible soul force pad he'd conjured between him and his mare. Lane couldn't see it and what she didn't know about she couldn't yell at him for.

She led them off the road into a caravan cutout, a little open patch where travelers could make camp. The clearing could accommodate ten wagons and fifty people, so the two of them and their three animals made little impression.

Six inches of fresh snow covered the ground. No one had used this cutout for a week or two at least. The ring of stone surrounding the fire pit looked like a circle of miniature snowmen.

"Do you want to tend the horses or clear off a spot for us to sleep and start a fire?" Lane asked.

"I'm good with either." It surprised him that she'd bothered to ask what he wanted instead of just giving him his marching orders.

"I'll take the horses."

Lane dismounted and he joined her, passing his reins over. She led the animals to a small clump of pasture pine at the edge of the cutout. Damien kicked around through the snow like he was using his feet to clear it off. Beside him an invisible broom ten times the size of a normal one brushed the ground clear in a couple of minutes.

Damien left the now-clear campsite and went to join Lane by the trees. Maybe he could find some dry branches to get a fire going. When he arrived she had the horses unsaddled and was busy rubbing his mare down. She looked up as he approached; she must have heard him tromping through the snow.

"What?" She sounded mad. The woman sure carried a lot of anger.

Damien held his hands up in surrender. "I'm just looking for firewood. Unless you'd rather eat a cold dinner and freeze tonight."

She mumbled something and went back to rubbing his mare.

"What?"

Lane looked back up. "I said, I'm sorry. I'm not really mad at you, I'm mad at Mom for assigning a sorcerer as my bodyguard. She knows I don't like being around people like you."

Damien chuckled and kicked through the snow, looking for fallen branches. He picked up a few and when he straightened Lane stood three feet away, hands on hips. "What's so damn funny?"

"You. You and everyone else. They all want to define me by my soul force. Dad's disappointed because I'm a sorcerer and not a warlord. Most of the other sorcerers don't want anything to do with me because of how dense my soul force is. And it's the only reason your mother took me on as an apprentice, despite knowing nothing else about me. There's more to me than my power, you know."

Now it was Lane's turn to laugh. "I have the exact opposite problem. People judge me by my lack of power. My whole life I've been held up to the example of my mother and been found wanting. Now you come along. Yeah, I know all about the demon and the dragon and every other thing you've done in your short career. You're everything I was meant to be."

Damien collected some more sticks. "Don't be jealous of my power. All it does is separate me from everyone. Aside from my sister and a few friends, no one will look at me as anything but a threat or tool. If that's the life you're pining for you're welcome to it."

Chapter 7

Jen strode down the hall toward her father's office in The Citadel, the hard soles of her boots tapping on the stone floor. He'd summoned her earlier and she hoped he had a new mission planned for her and her squad. The war had ended after Damien blasted that dragon and while the feast and all the compliments had been nice, she wanted to get back out in the field. Maybe he'd send them out to hunt down some stray ogres, that would be a good workout.

She reached back and brushed the hilt of her new sword where it jutted up over her shoulder. It still felt warm from the remnants of her brother's soul force. She shook her head. Some of the things Damien had done boggled her mind, and crafting the sword was the least of them. Her little brother had grown strong. Jen went back and forth between pride in all that he'd accomplished and sadness that he no longer seemed to need her.

The cadets were all in class or outside training and the empty halls agreed with Jen. It seemed like she couldn't take a step out of her room without attracting stares. The boys had always stared, of course, she'd made peace with that years ago. But since the war, the stares had a different quality. The desire was still there, but now there was a little awe and fear mixed in. She didn't really understand it since her brother had done most of the extraordinary stuff, but she'd been there and survived, so maybe that was enough. Damien told her how people at The Tower avoided him after the demon incident and she wondered if she was going through something similar. Whatever it was she'd be glad to get out of The Citadel for a while.

Her father's office door had a golden shield nailed to it, a replica of the badge of office he wore pinned to his uniform. She knocked and pushed the door open. The spartan room matched Dad's personality. He sat at a simple oak desk in a hard, straight-backed chair. A stand for the demon sword—she'd never gotten comfortable with Damien calling it by its nickname—rested at his right hand. She knew Dad could have the blade out and at a person's throat faster than she could blink. A three-shelf bookcase filled with military manuals along with a pair of chairs for guests completed the furnishings.

Jen ignored the two empty chairs in front of the desk and stood with her hands clasped behind her back. "Reporting as ordered, sir."

Dad looked up for the first time. "Jennifer, sit down. I have your next mission."

Eager now, Jen slid into the left-hand chair. "Yes, sir."

He steepled his fingers and looked at her through the gaps. "What I'm about to tell you doesn't leave this room. Unfortunately a number of people know already, but I'd just as soon not spread the information any faster than necessary. An attempt was made on the king's life two days ago."

Jen's breath caught in her throat.

"Andy's fine," her father hastened to add. "Your brother was there and he captured the assassin. The report I received says he saved a lot of lives. If they didn't want to keep it quiet I suspect he'd be up for another medal."

Jen caught the barest hint of pride in her father's voice. Maybe he and Damien would finally become a little closer. "That's a relief. Do you want my squad to track down whoever hired him?"

"Her, not him, and no, I don't. The interrogators persuaded the assassin to talk. They know who hired her. Your brother's looking into that end."

Jen frowned. If Dad didn't want them to track down whoever hired the killer, what was their mission?

"Are you familiar with a merchant prince named Dominic Santen?"

"Of course, anyone that's spent any time in Port Valcane knows the Santen family. They own a third of all the businesses in the city and rumor is they control another third indirectly. Why?"

Dad drummed his fingers together. "The assassin used an illusion of Dominic Santen to sneak into the throne room and now, according to the Valcane watch, Dominic is missing. Your job is to find him and determine if he's collaborating with the assassin or if he's a victim."

"Why us? The Valcane watch is competent, never mind that their captain is a pig. Surely they can track down a missing merchant."

Dad nodded. "I'm sure they could. The problem is we have no idea how many of them have divided loyalties. Since the Santen family controls so much of the city we can assume they have more than a few watchmen in their pockets."

"And if they're working with whoever hired the assassin we can't count on the watch's loyalty." Jen saw it clearly now. "I understand. It'll take us a month to ride to the coast."

"No, it won't. You remember Master Shen?"

Jen nodded. The good-natured sorcerer had taught her class the basics of surviving an encounter with a sorcerer. Run the other way as fast as you can.

"Master Shen will fly your team to the city then remain there in case you need sorcerous backup. The assassin they hired was a sorcerer after all. Questions?"

"No, sir." Jen stood. "Dead or alive, we'll find him."

Dad nodded. "Be careful. I have no idea what sort of mess you're walking into."

Chapter 8

The wind streamed through Jen's hair when she leaned over the side of the golden chariot. Her heart raced and she couldn't stop smiling. She'd never flown before and the sensation exhilarated her.

Below them the sprawling expanse of Port Valcane squatted in the dying sunlight. The oldest city in the kingdom, Port Valcane was the first village the settlers carved out of the wilderness when they arrived from the Old Empire. It had grown a thousand times since then, and now covered a mile north to south and three-quarters of a mile east to west.

She'd gotten to know the city well in her year there, from the stink of the fish market to the perfume of the merchant villas. Jen preferred the fish. At least they weren't apt to bite you. Most of the merchants she'd met would put a dirk in your kidney for an extra copper.

Jen's good mood dimmed a little when she considered what awaited her down there. Her former commander, Watch Captain Tosh, expected them to report in the moment they landed. A competent administrator, Captain Tosh had a bad habit of touching his female subordinates. If he laid a hand on her this time she'd knock his teeth down the back of his throat. She was visiting the city as an independent investigator for the crown and he had no authority over her. Of course, he could make her job a lot harder if he ordered his watchmen not to cooperate.

A groan pulled her mind back to the present. Edward slumped against the side of the chariot, his skin a sickly green. They hadn't flown out of sight of The Citadel before he'd thrown up over the side. To say flying didn't agree with him would be putting it mildly. She knew people got sick on boats, but she'd never heard of anyone getting sick while flying. In Edward's defense, the only other person she knew that had flown before was Damien, and nothing much bothered him.

She patted her subordinate on the shoulder. "Just a few more minutes."

"Yeah, after we check in we should get something to eat." Alec grinned. Like Jen he seemed to have enjoyed the flight. "I hear good things about the fish stew."

Edward scrambled to get his head over the side of the chariot before he gagged. Rhys and Talon laughed.

Jen shook her head and frowned at Alec. He winked back. She turned away so he wouldn't notice her smile. The youngest member of her team had a crush on her and she didn't want to do anything to encourage him. Romance between teammates never ended well and once in a while it ended with someone dead. If she could help it, no one in her command would die.

The chariot descended toward the city. From the front Master Shen said, "You enjoyed the flight. You and your brother have the same smile."

She left Edward to his gagging and moved up beside the dark-haired sorcerer. "It's wonderful."

Edward let out an especially loud gag.

"I enjoyed it anyway. I can't speak for everyone."

Master Shen laughed. "I know a couple sorcerers who don't like to fly, though neither of them so loudly as your man. It's not for everyone."

He reached into an inside pocket of his gray cloak and pulled out a six-inch stick of pale, polished wood. She took it and found it warm in her hand. "What's this?"

"It's a call stick. I infused enough of my soul force into it to last a week. Just break it if you need me and I'll come as fast as I can. If the investigation takes more than a week we'll need to meet up so I can reenergize it."

Jen slipped the stick into the pouch on her belt. "I assumed you'd be working with us."

Master Shen shook his head. "Sorcerers make people nervous. You'll have better luck on your own. I have a task of my own, straight from the archmage no less."

He offered no details so Jen assumed he had orders to keep them to himself. That didn't bother her. She had things of her own she couldn't talk about. "Do you want to plan a spot to meet in six days to compare notes and recharge the call stick?"

"Good idea. Are you familiar with The Mermaid?"

"Sure, everybody knows The Mermaid. They have the cheapest drinks and best food in the city. Not exactly a private place for a meeting."

"On the contrary, it's a perfect place for a meeting. The crown owns the tavern. We have a sorcerer on duty at all times, listening in to the gossip. You'd be amazed what you can learn if you just listen. When you arrive, ask the barman for the capital suite. He'll give you a key and walk away. Go to the third floor and turn right, it's the last door on the left. If I'm not there when you arrive, I will be shortly."

Jen tried not to stare and failed. She'd worked in the city for a full year and had no idea the government owned The Mermaid. "Does Captain Tosh know about this?"

"No one in the city government knows." Master Shen turned to face her, his usually smiling face serious. "The city government doesn't always have the capital's best interest at heart. Don't mention the tavern to anyone. You never know who might be listening."

Jen stepped back to let Master Shen concentrate on landing the chariot. What had seemed a simple mission now looked a good deal more complicated.

Chapter 9

Captain Tosh's office looked just the same as Jen remembered it. A huge mahogany desk covered with curlicue inlays filled with gold dominated the center of the room, a single chair for guests in front of it which she ignored, preferring to stand with her men. A bookcase filled each corner, curios rather than books covering the shelves. The captain had never been one for study. He always claimed he read enough reports over the course of the day that the last thing he wanted to do was read books in his spare time. Behind the desk a window looked out over the glittering city.

The sun had set just as Master Shen landed the chariot, and now glow lamps twinkled on every street corner. Captain Tosh's office sat on the top floor in the northeast corner of watch headquarters. It took up a quarter of the floor all by itself, though she couldn't pin that one on him. The office hadn't changed in two hundred years.

Behind the garish desk Captain Tosh reclined in a soft leather chair and looked at them through half-closed eyes. A short, barrel-chested man, with an oiled goatee and polished fingernails, the captain considered himself the angels' gift to women. Whether the women agreed or not concerned him little.

He leaned forward and smiled. "I can't tell you what a pleasant surprise it was to hear my favorite former subordinate was leading the investigation into Dominic's disappearance. Jennifer, you're looking as beautiful as ever."

Tosh's oily grin turned Jen's stomach in a way the flight hadn't. The less time she had to spend in the pig's presence the better for both of them. "Have you made the arrangements for us to speak with the family?"

He heaved a dramatic sigh. "Always right to business with you. Same old Jennifer. The family has agreed to see you at ten tomorrow morning. Dominic's widow...ahem...wife, have to stay optimistic, is too distraught to talk, but the eldest son, Mikhail, has agreed to meet with you."

Good of him considering they had a royal charter to investigate this matter that gave them the authority to go anywhere and talk to anyone they wanted, whenever they wanted. "I appreciate that. I won't take up any more of their time than necessary."

"Go easy, Jennifer. The boy's lost a father after all. I trust you'll keep me informed of anything you discover."

Jen nodded, intending to tell him as little as possible. "As time permits. I assume you'll inform your men to provide whatever help we need."

"As long as it doesn't interfere with their duties. I still have a city to keep safe."

So, they understood each other. Jen would offer him as little information as she could and he would offer her as little help as he could. She and her squad were basically on their own, which she'd expected.

"Best of luck with your investigation, Jennifer."

"Thank you, Captain."

Jen led her team out of Tosh's office, into the hall, and past his assistant, a pretty blond girl about half Tosh's age. How many bruises did she have from the captain's pinches? They left the bored girl behind and headed toward the stairwell.

"Talk about sleazy," Talon said.

Jen held a finger to her lips. They needed to stay quiet until they left headquarters. They arrived on the first floor and, luckily for them, avoided the main processing area where the watch brought in criminals, handled interrogations, and basically took care of business. A back door by the staircase led to the street. Jen took a deep breath of cool night air.

"Can we talk now?" Alec asked.

"No." Jen turned north toward their inn. She wouldn't feel comfortable until they had locked the doors behind them and checked for spies.

Chapter 10

Princess Karrie marched away from Damien's room, a frown creasing her forehead. What had Daddy been thinking, sending Damien off on a mission so soon? She'd only just begun working on him and it would take weeks to wear him down enough that he'd accept the inevitable. She would marry him, and that was that.

A servant scurried out of her way, but Karrie paid her no more attention than she did the paintings that decorated the walls every few feet. It would have been ideal if Damien wanted to marry her as much as she did him, but it didn't look like that would happen. If she knew who she was up against it would make it much easier to turn him to her way of thinking.

Maybe he preferred older girls, like Lane. Karrie chewed her lip. That didn't seem likely. He hadn't shown any great interest in her when Karrie had said something. Damien clearly regarded Lane as a job and nothing more. Maybe someone from The Tower? It made sense that he might have another sorcerer for a girlfriend. How could she find out?

She barged through the door to the royal quarters, eager to take her father to task over sending Damien away. The kitchen and dining room sat empty and spotless, no doubt thanks to the efforts of the servant she'd seen earlier. She took a couple of steps and peeked into the sitting room. Empty, though a small fire burned in the hearth. Daddy must have had a meeting.

"Mom!"

"In the sewing room, dear." Her mother's faint voice came from the back of their quarters.

Karrie rushed down the carpeted hall, past their bedrooms, to her mother's sewing room. The small room had a pair of windows that let in the morning sun. Her mother sat at her square embroidery hoop, her delicate stitches creating a scene of dragons flying through a clear sky.

Mom set her needle down and looked up at her. "What's wrong, dear?"

Karrie plopped down on the floor facing her mother. "Dad sent Damien on a mission. I just started working on him. How can I convince Damien to do what I want if he's not here?"

"My dear girl, badgering the boy won't convince him to do what you want. You need to tease him and seduce him. It takes time. When he comes back try playing hard to get. Maybe invite one of those boys that's always chasing after you to visit the castle. Make him jealous. Ideally you want him to come to you."

"It's bad enough I have to deal with those idiot boys at the stupid balls the nobles and merchants are constantly throwing. The last thing I want is to have them hanging around the castle as well." Karrie chewed her lip some more. "And what if it doesn't work? I'm not sure Damien likes me that way. If he doesn't he's likely to feel relieved instead of jealous."

"Hmm." Mom tapped her chin. "That's a good point. I'd assumed every boy would want to marry you. You are the heir to the throne. But that probably doesn't mean much to Damien. He's too much like his father. Fredric always hated politics. Well, if the usual tactics don't work we'll try something more drastic. One thing is certain. If you wish to secure your reign and not become some man's arm candy, you need Damien. His power, combined with a disdain for politics, make him perfect. With him at your side no one would dare challenge your rule."

Chapter 11

The Santen family villa covered more ground than the king's castle back at the capital. Painted white and trimmed with gold, the main house stood two stories tall. White marble statues beside elaborate topiary animals decorated the sprawling, manicured grounds. From the main house, two single-story wings spread left and right. The whole thing together had enough space to house an army.

The squad stood across the street from the estate's iron gate. Jen crossed her arms and studied the place. How much had it cost to build? A gilded red carriage rolled down the cobblestone street. A pair of stunning white geldings pulled it, guided by a coachman in black-and-red livery. Aside from the carriage the streets in the Lord's District were quiet. No street vendors shouted, no kids ran around playing, she hadn't even seen a servant out running an errand. They were far enough inland that the creak of the docks and rush of the waves didn't reach them. Only the faint tang of salt in the air mixed with the yeast and cinnamon from the bakery behind them gave any sign that the ocean was close.

The district felt dead.

She shuddered. Dead as Dominic Santen most likely.

"What's the plan?" Talon asked.

They'd arrived a little early for their meeting with Mikhail Santen so they could scout the place. "You and Rhys will come with me to interview the son. Talon, you focus on his heart rate. Rhys, watch his pupils. You two will be my lie detectors. Edward, stay here and keep an eye out for trouble. I don't expect any, but better safe than sorry. Alec, I want you to snoop around the grounds. Check out security, get a feel for how hard it would be for someone to sneak in, grab Dominic, and escape."

Everyone murmured their agreement, though Edward grumbled about getting stuck as lookout. He'd also left his maul at the inn. It made him stick out too much to be practical in the city. He'd settled for hiding a handful of daggers about his person.

"Let's go." Jen strode across the street with Talon and Rhys beside her. Alec seemed to vanish as he accelerated away from them. Edward leapt up to the roof of the bakery behind them and crouched down behind the chimney.

The gate was unlocked and swung open at Jen's touch. Either it served no purpose beyond decoration or the family had unlocked it in expectation of their arrival. Jen thought the former more likely than the latter. A white gravel path wound through the grounds toward the curved steps up to the front door. A pair of guards, the first Jen had seen, armed with spears and short swords, stood on either side of a set of massive, intricately carved double doors.

The men crossed their spears. "Name and business?" one asked.

"Jennifer St. Cloud here to see Mikhail Santen. He's expecting me."

They moved their weapons aside and the guard who'd spoken nodded. "Yes, ma'am. We just needed to be sure who you were."

They pulled the doors open and Jen walked into a foyer twice the size of her family's quarters at The Citadel. A garish marble fountain shaped like a dolphin sprinkled water out its blowhole into a pool at its base. On either side of the room, curved staircases led up to a second-floor balcony. Jen half expected to see Mikhail standing there, looking over them. Closed doors to the left and right opened into the mansion's wings. Straight ahead a short hall led deeper into the main house. A slim, pretty brunette with short, curly hair, wearing a servant's black-and-white uniform with a too-short skirt appeared from deeper in the house.

The servant curtsied. "Master Mikhail said to bring you to the sunroom. Follow me, please."

Jen nodded and motioned for her to lead the way. They went through an arch, turned left, and continued down a white, marble hall lined with carved busts of men Jen didn't recognize, probably past heads of the family. At the end of the hall an open door led to a round room, the walls consisting of solid glass. A young man dressed in a fine black tunic and trousers, a long, drooping mustache decorating his face, sat in a blue-upholstered armchair. A matching chair three feet away faced him.

"Mikhail Santen?" Jen asked.

The young man nodded and waved an indifferent hand at the empty chair. The servant bobbed another curtsy and scampered out. Jen frowned at the lack of courtesy shown to an agent of the crown, but kept quiet. She sat facing the arrogant merchant, Talon and Rhys taking up positions behind her.

"I'm here investigating your father's disappearance. Is there anything you can tell us about it?"

He leaned forward, his bloodshot brown eyes half covered by long brown hair. "You say disappearance, but you mean murder. My father has never been out of contact for this long. Only death would cause him to worry Mother so."

"I say what I mean. Since no body has been found I assume he's alive somewhere, perhaps being held against his will." Jen tried to force sympathy she lacked into her voice. "Does your family have many enemies?"

Mikhail threw back his head and laughed. "No one gets as rich as us without making enemies. And the richer you are the more enemies you make. We have many."

"I don't suppose you could narrow it down a little for us?"

"The Blackman clan despises us for forcing them out of the shipping business, as though it's our fault their ships are outdated and often arrive late. The Corno clan nurses an old grudge over timber rights in the Great Green. There are many others, but those two are the most vocal."

"Did your father travel with bodyguards?"

"Always. Six men led by a female warlord, Citadel trained, like you lot. We've heard nothing from them either. Probably eaten by sharks."

"What were—"

Talon laid a hand on her shoulder bringing Jen up short. "What?" Jen asked.

"Someone drew steel outside."

Chapter 12

Jen sharpened her hearing and the distant ring of steel on steel reached her. She leapt to her feet and pulled her soul-forged blade from its sheath.

Footsteps pounded outside, getting closer.

"What's the meaning of this?" Mikhail asked.

Jen grabbed the merchant and yanked him behind her. Soul force flowed, strengthening her muscles and hardening her skin. Not a moment too soon.

The windows shattered as an armored figure leapt through them. Glass shards bounced off Jen's iron skin.

The stranger wore a full helm, gauntlets, and a mail coat that covered him from neck to knees. He carried a four-foot-long great sword. He whirled the blade around his head and sliced one of the chairs in half.

Jen rushed forward at full speed. Her sword streaked toward the invader's neck.

His speed a match for hers, the great sword rose to block her attack. Unfazed, Jen continued the assault, her weapon a blur as it slashed and stabbed.

High, low, left, right, the armored man blocked her every effort.

Damn, he was fast.

Talon streaked in from the side, his double blades driving for the man's unprotected legs. The invader leapt straight up, six feet into the air, carrying seventy pounds of armor.

Impossible.

Talon caught a boot to the back as he went under his target. The powerful kick sent him flying out the shattered window and into the yard.

Jen darted back into the fray. At the rear of the room Mikhail cowered behind Rhys. "Get him out of here!"

Rhys grabbed Mikhail and slung him over his shoulder. They raced away at warlord speed.

Good, now she could focus on her enemy without worrying about the merchant. She drew deeper from her soul force. A tingle from the hilt ran up her arm, her brother's soul force reacting to her power.

She swung with all her might. The invader caught the blow on his blade and staggered. He hadn't had time to set his feet after he landed.

Jen swung again. All power and no finesse.

Every blow drove the armored figure back. It took everything she had just to manage that. This guy was strong, stronger than any warlord she'd ever faced. Almost as strong as the demon.

At the edge of the shattered window he bound her sword. Their guards locked and they jockeyed for position.

Jen pressed against him with every ounce of strength she could muster to no avail. Dark sparks shot from his gauntlets. He grunted and forced her back a step.

Jen leaned in, trying to hold her position.

The gauntlets burst into black flames, just like the demon's claws.

He forced her to retreat another step. Jen put everything she had into holding him, but he kept on coming. She couldn't beat him and Damien wasn't here to save her this time.

The tips of two blades burst out of his chest. The black flames flickered.

This was her chance.

Jen disengaged and spun. Her blade sheared the stranger's head off. A fountain of black blood geysered out of his neck before his body collapsed to the floor.

Talon stepped on his back and ripped his blades out. Jen gasped for breath. She'd used everything she had.

"You okay?" Talon asked.

She straightened and nodded. "Stay here. Don't let anyone touch the body."

Jen left Talon standing guard over the corpse. Rhys wouldn't have gone far. She needed to make sure Mikhail was okay. Jen pulled the call stick out of her pocket and snapped it. Master Shen needed to have a look at those gauntlets.

She found Rhys and his terrified charge in the foyer along with Edward and three more dead bodies. She kicked one over so she could see his face. He didn't look like much. Dark brown skin, beard, leather armor, scimitar, and a crushed skull.

"What happened?"

"I saw these three run through the front gate and followed," Edward said. "I got two, Rhys got one."

"It's not a competition," Rhys muttered.

"Hey!"

They all looked up. Alec stood on the second-floor balcony, blood spattered on his white shirt.

"You okay?" Jen asked.

"Sure, it's not mine. There's three more dead guys up here. Looks like they were trying to reach the wife."

"Okay. Stay with her just in case. Edward, sweep the grounds, make sure we're done."

He nodded and vanished.

Jen turned her attention to Mikhail. "Who are they?"

He held his hands out. "I have no idea."

"What about the big guy in the sunroom?"

The merchant gave her a blank look. Jen flicked a glance at Rhys who shook his head. Either the merchant was telling her the truth or he was so terrified Rhys couldn't read his heart rate. Either way he was useless.

Edward appeared as though out of nowhere. "We're good. I found six dead guards, but no more like this bunch."

"Good. Watch the front. Alec!"

The young warlord dashed to her side. "Yeah?"

"Go to watch headquarters and fetch a patrol. Maybe they'll know who these people are."

He nodded. "You want 'em here double quick or should I take my time?"

"Take your time. Hopefully Master Shen will turn up soon and he can take a look around before the locals show up."

"Got it." He ambled out the front doors, hands in his pockets, looking for all the world like a teenager out for a morning stroll. Only the blood on his shirt spoiled the image.

Chapter 13

Jen paced in the Santen's elaborate foyer. Mikhail flinched every time she drew close, like he expected her to kick him. Two hours had passed since she sent Alec to fetch the watch and still no Master Shen. Where in the world was he? He'd given her the call stick in case she needed him and now that she did he was a no-show.

Edward appeared beside her. "There's about twenty watchmen headed this way, your friend Tosh in the lead."

"Damn it!" Jen walked back to the sunroom. Talon sprang up from the undamaged chair when she entered. "Grab his gauntlets and go. We'll meet you a block north."

"Will do." Talon yanked the dead man's gauntlets off and sped away.

Grumbling about unreliable sorcerers, Jen returned to the foyer. A minute later Captain Tosh strode through the door at the head of a war party of watchmen plus Alec. He looked down at the three dead men, a frown of distaste curling his lips.

He glanced at the cowering merchant. "Who's this asshole?"

Jen glared at the merchant cowering behind Rhys like her subordinate would protect him. "Mikhail Santen."

Tosh barked a laugh. “Mikhail’s about six inches taller and twenty pounds lighter than this guy.”

“Well?” Jen said.

The imposter scrambled back a few feet before Rhys grabbed him by the scruff of the neck and lifted him off the ground. He shook the imposter like a dog with a rat. “Speak up!”

“I didn’t do anything.” The prisoner flailed at Rhys’s impassive form. “She paid me fifty royals to pretend to be the merchant for a day.”

“Who paid you?” Jen moved closer so she stood only inches from the squirming man.

“The girl. You know, in the servant’s outfit. It seemed like easy coin.”

Jen glanced at Alec and Edward and the two warlords accelerated away. It wouldn’t take them long to search the grounds.

“Who is she?” Tosh asked, butting his way into her interrogation.

“How do I know, man? I was getting a drink at The Drowned Rat when this girl sidles up to me and whispers in my ear about a job, coin up front. I got here this morning real early like she said and found her in that servant getup. Thought maybe it was some kind of sex thing, you know. I wouldn’t have complained either. She was gorgeous.”

“What about the job?” Jen asked, failing to hide her annoyance.

“Take it easy. She said some people wanted to talk to the merchant, but he wasn’t in town. She gave me these fancy duds, a sack of gold, told me what to say, and then put me in the sunroom to wait for you. Like I said, easy money, at least till that armored guy smashed the windows in.”

Tosh looked at her. “Armored guy?”

Jen nodded toward the arch. “He’s not going anywhere. Any of these slobs look familiar to you?”

Tosh bent down and yanked one of the dead men’s sleeves up to the elbow. He had a tattoo of a raven on the inside of his forearm. “The Unkindness. They’re a group of thugs and skull crackers that hire out to anyone interested. They usually work the docks.”

Jen grunted. A moment later Edward and Alec arrived, causing Tosh to flinch.

"No sign of her," Edward said.

"She probably took off as soon as she left us with him." Jen jerked a thumb at the imposter. "I think it's time we had a word with the grieving wife."

"Maybe I should handle it," Tosh said. "She's bound to be terrified."

Jen waved him toward the stairs. If Tosh wanted to lead the way he was welcome. She followed the captain up the curved staircase to the balcony. At the top they had a choice of left or right.

Tosh looked at her and raised an eyebrow. Jen enhanced her sense of smell and caught the coppery tang of blood to the right. She nodded that way and Tosh took the lead again.

A short hall ended with a closed white door. The three dead men on the floor in front of it had gotten blood all over its pristine surface. Jen was glad she didn't have to clean the place.

Tosh knocked on the door. "Mrs. Santen? This is Watch Captain Tosh. Open the door please, it's safe now. Ma'am?"

Tosh glanced at her and she shrugged. What could she tell him? It wasn't like she could see through the door. He tried the handle, but it was locked.

"Move." Jen brushed him aside, reared back, and kicked the door off its hinges. It flew ten feet into the room and skidded to a halt at the foot of a canopy bed the size of Jen's whole bedroom.

"Are you trying to give the poor woman a heart attack?"

They stepped through the doorway into a cavernous white room empty of all furnishing save the giant bed. Surrounded by white pillows, with her body buried under a white comforter, Mrs. Santen's face looked tiny. Her eyes never opened despite the crash and clatter of the door. Jen didn't like the feel of this.

She looked over at Tosh and from his slack-jawed expression suspected he had the same feeling. "You wanted to go first, so go on."

"Thanks." Tosh favored her with a sour grimace. "Mrs. Santen?"

They eased closer, each taking a side of the bed. They drew closer still. The woman's gray, sallow complexion combined with the blue lips told Jen all she needed to know. She grabbed the giant blanket and yanked it back.

She flinched. There was nothing but the woman's head in the bed. A dried pool of blood stained the white sheets under the blanket. "So much for a heart attack."

Tosh frowned. "Show some respect." He flung the blanket up over the remains.

"Is that at least the correct person's head?"

Tosh nodded and they retreated from the bedroom back toward the foyer. "I met her a couple of times at government functions. What's going on in my city?"

That's what Jen wanted to know. It looked like something bigger than a missing merchant. "Someone has it in for the Santen clan. I doubt we'll find Dominic alive."

"You mean to continue the search?"

"That's the mission. Until I find a body or someone tells me to stop, I'll keep looking."

"What if I tell you to stop looking?"

Jen laughed.

"That's what I figured. Try to keep the breakage to a minimum. We'll clean up here and notify the surviving family."

She stopped halfway down the stairs. "There are more of them?"

"A daughter. She married into another merchant house. I can't recall which."

"Sounds like a good suspect. I assume she stands to inherit all this."

"Probably. You want to come along when I talk to her?"

Jen frowned. She needed to track down Master Shen and have him look at those gauntlets. Much as she wanted to hear what the daughter had to say, the sorcerer came first. "I'll leave her to you. What do you say we meet up tomorrow morning and compare notes?"

"My office?"

"Fine. Do you still not get started until midday?"

"Funny. See you tomorrow."

They left the watch to deal with the villa and headed north to catch up with Talon. They found him leaning against the wall of a general store, the gauntlets tucked under his arm. "What took you so long?" Talon asked.

"We went to talk to Mrs. Santen and found her head, but no body. Tosh is going to talk to the daughter. We need to get to The Mermaid and find out what in the world is going on with Master Shen."

"What about Mikhail?" Talon asked.

Jen grimaced. They'd left the imposter with Tosh. She doubted they'd drag anything more out of him. "He was a dupe. A disposable tool the girl probably meant to have die in the attack along with the rest of them. The real one's still in the wind along with his father."

"What?" Talon stared at each of them in turn.

"I'll explain on the way."

They walked out of the alley and headed toward The Mermaid. When they left the Lord's District behind the streets grew crowded. People hurried along the sidewalks, running errands. All of them made way for Jen and her squad, many throwing sidelong glances at their weapons.

The shouts of vendors filled the air. It seemed like the city came alive around them. It gave Jen a moment's pause, being surrounded by so much life only minutes after leaving a house full of bodies. Life went on and a house full of dead merchants and thugs wouldn't slow it down.

The Mermaid lay in the Shipping District abutting the docks. The tang of salt grew stronger the closer they got to the water. The acrid hint of smoke mixed with the normal ocean smells. Jen looked up. Black smoke billowed in the distance. "You've got to be kidding."

"What?" Edward asked.

"I think The Mermaid's on fire."

Chapter 14

It took less than a minute to reach The Mermaid at warlord speed. Black smoke billowed out of the roof and flames shot from broken windows on the third floor. All around the burning building locals were gathering. People came running up the street with buckets. They'd have a bucket brigade going soon. The fire hadn't spread too far yet. They might save some of the building. More likely they'd just try to keep it from spreading to the neighboring businesses.

Jen took a moment to orient herself. Unless she was badly mistaken the flames came from the capital suite. What were the odds of someone attacking the secret crown listening post and Jen's squad on the same morning?

"Talon, Rhys, fan out and look for the servant girl. Alec and Edward, with me." She accelerated to the burning inn, her subordinates right behind her.

They rushed past the gaping crowds so fast she doubted they even registered their presence. A quick glance showed the common room was empty, all patrons having sense enough to flee. Jen heightened her hearing, but the only sounds were shouting outside and the crackle of flame above them.

She pointed toward the kitchen and Alec raced to check it out. She and Edward sprinted up the steps. At the second-floor landing she pointed again, leaving Edward to clear the floor. Jen continued up to the third floor and down the hall to the crown suite.

Smoke filled the hall and the heat resembled an over-fired oven. She strengthened her lungs and ran on.

The door to the suite was smashed. Judging by the damage someone had broken it in. Flames filled the doorway.

Jen crouched down, trying to see into the suite. Even with enhanced vision the smoke and flames obscured too much. She needed to make sure.

She drew power and slammed her palms together. The blast of wind blew the flames back from the doorway for an instant and she ducked through the gap.

Flames seared her skin, forcing her to put more power into her defenses or get roasted. Even strengthened by soul force she needed to hurry. The common room held nothing valuable, just burning furniture. The first bedroom was empty and she began to fear she'd wasted her time.

Jen kicked down the door to the last bedroom. A woman lay on the floor, her skin blistered and her clothes reduced to charred scraps.

She scooped the woman up and fled the burning room as fast as her soul-force-enhanced legs would carry her. She reached the second floor a moment later. Away from the flames, Jen sent healing energy to soothe her seared skin. Edward joined her a moment later. He took one look and left again.

He returned a second later with a pink fur-lined robe which he slung around her shoulders. Apparently her clothes hadn't stood up to the flames as well as her skin. "Thanks. Take her."

Jen passed the unconscious woman to Edward and adjusted the robe so it covered her better. Pity he couldn't have found anything a little less garish.

"She's alive," Edward said.

"Let's collect the others and get out of here."

Ten minutes later found them in Jen's room at their inn. They'd collected a fair share of stares when they rushed through the common room. Despite the guys' best efforts you could only do so much to hide one burned woman and another in a pink robe. Rhys examined the woman while Jen changed into her spare outfit.

"How is she?" Jen asked.

"Alive. Don't ask me how given all these burns. She needs a healer. The sooner the better."

Jen nodded. The only healer she knew was at watch headquarters, but if she brought the woman there it might lead to some uncomfortable questions. She needed more information and she needed it now.

"Can you wake her?"

"Maybe, but it won't be a kindness."

"We don't have the luxury of kindness. Do it."

Rhys nodded and dug a bottle out of his satchel. He passed it under the woman's ruined nose. She choked, gasped, and tried to sit up.

"Easy, you're safe now." Jen sat beside her on the bed. "Is there somewhere we can take you? The only place I can think of is the healer at watch headquarters."

The woman gave a vehement shake of her head. "Secret," she gasped.

"I understand. Master Shen told us about your work. Can we take you to him?"

Another shake of her head. "Missing."

"Shit! Can we take you somewhere else?"

"Underbridge. Secret place. Emergency..." She passed out again.

Jen stood up and paced. What should she do?

"Any of that make sense to you?" Talon asked.

She stopped. "Not much. There's no Underbridge district. There is a bridge across Cold River. Maybe they've got a bolt hole there. That's all I can think of."

"Whatever we're going to do, we need to do it quick. She won't last long with those burns," Rhys said.

"Let's go for it. Rhys, you carry her. Edward, you're with me. Talon, take Alec and watch our back trail. I don't want to be followed."

Edward went to his room to retrieve his maul and this time Jen didn't object.

Chapter 15

They wrapped the unconscious woman in blankets to keep her from freezing before they reached...wherever they were going. Jen's window opened into an alley so they went out that way, leaping down from the second floor with no trouble. The Cold River bridge was north of the city, maybe half a mile past the gate. Jen had only ridden over it once during her previous posting to Valcane.

They raced through the quiet streets at half speed; Jen didn't dare try full speed with the injured woman over that distance. The timing worked out well. Most people were inside eating their noon meal. Those unfortunates who had to work outside in the cold went in to warm up, leaving the city a ghost town for half an hour, plenty of time for Jen's team to pass through.

The north gate stood open and they ran out, the two guards standing beside a burning brazier not giving them a second look. The dirt road beyond the city was clear of snow thanks to the nearly nonstop traffic coming and going from the port. Talon and Alec accelerated to full speed and zipped back to make sure no one was following them. Jen and the others ran on, the bridge waiting only a minute away.

The Cold River bridge was a tall, arched thing of fused stone and steel wide enough to accommodate two wagons side by side. The ravine it crossed wasn't especially wide or deep, but the chill of the river made fording a dim prospect. Even in summer the mountain streams kept the river frigid; at this time of year it was frozen solid.

"Stay here, I'll call if I find anything." Jen skidded down the side of the ravine to the river bank. Fine gravel crunched under her feet when she hit bottom.

She jogged over to the base of the bridge. The engineers had fused the legs to the cliff face. Even with her enhanced vision Jen couldn't tell where the cliff ended and the bridge began. She also couldn't find where this secret whatever was. Why couldn't the woman have stayed conscious long enough to tell her something useful?

Jen studied the striated stone, mostly gray with a few streaks of pink. Nothing stood out. When she ran her finger over it looking for a seam she came up empty. After five minutes she'd covered the whole area under the bridge and found exactly nothing. Had she misunderstood the woman's message? Was there a place named Underbridge she didn't know about?

"Shit!" She looked across the frozen river at the far side of the ravine. There was nothing for it, she had to check. At least the river was frozen so she didn't have to swim.

The river ice felt as hard as stone under her feet as she made her way to the far bank. She slid sideways, caught her balance, and continued on. Jen reached the other side with no further trouble. Her breath steamed into the air as she searched. Every second reduced the woman's chances of surviving.

The stone on this side matched the bank. Jen ran her fingers over the rough cliff face. There had to be something. If she couldn't find anything she didn't know what she would do.

There!

Something gave under her fingers. She pressed harder and a hand-sized section of stone pressed inward. A catch popped loose and a stone door swung in on concealed hinges.

Jen threw a fist into the air in silent celebration. On the opposite side Rhys and Edward had seen her success and begun their descent into the ravine. She had no idea what they'd find, but the cave had to be warmer than out here. Rhys crossed the river first, the woman cradled in his arms like a child. You wouldn't think it to look at the grizzled old veteran, but he could be surprisingly gentle.

Movement caught her eye. At the top of the ravine six figures in long, dark coats stood staring down at them. They looked like cousins of the goons they'd killed at the villa. Jen put her fingers in her mouth and blew a piercing whistle. Both her men looked her way. She pointed up at the bank.

Edward readied his maul. Jen gathered her legs and poured soul force into them. She leapt, covering the width of the river in a single bound, to land beside Edward.

She glanced back at Rhys. "Keep going! We'll handle this lot."

He nodded once and continued toward the cave.

Jen drew her sword. Edward grinned beside her. "Think this crew will be any tougher than the bunch from this morning?"

"I hope not. I want to finish this and have a real talk with that woman. And where the hell are Talon and Alec?"

Edward shrugged, his already huge shoulders even larger as he poured soul force into them. "Beats me. Maybe they got lost."

"It's only a mile and a half to the bridge and there's a road. How could they get lost?"

Another shrug. The six thugs slid down to the bank and halted about fifteen feet away. They rolled up their sleeves, revealing the black ravens. As one they dragged their thumbnails across the tattoos. Blood welled and the black ink came alive.

Midnight flames danced along their arms. Several threw back their heads and howled, in pain or ecstasy Jen couldn't say. The black flames reminded her of the dark power that flowed from the gauntlets of the armored attacker.

"Be careful."

Edward grunted. "Reminds me of those goblins we fought."

"Yeah, only my brother isn't here to help us this time."

"Ha! We can manage without the kid."

Jen wished she shared his confidence. The battle with the armored man had shown her how strong her opponents could be. If they weren't careful they might end up dead.

The gang members had gotten themselves under control. Black flames surrounded their hands, ran up their arms, and burned in their eyes.

They pulled short swords from hidden sheaths in their coats. The flames flowed from their hands down the blades.

Jen clenched her sword and drew deep from her core. Soul force flowed, accelerating her perceptions, and strengthening her body. She raced forward at ten times her normal speed.

She swung at the center thug. He leapt back and the two beside him thrust at her sides. Jen spun and slashed, gashing one across the thigh.

The ground shook when Edward's maul missed its mark and struck the bank. She didn't dare spare a glance to check on her subordinate. Her original target darted back in, his swords thrusting high and low, fast as rattlesnakes.

But not as fast as lightning. Jen drew more power and vanished. She appeared an instant later behind her opponent and hacked his head off.

The others gave her no chance to celebrate. Three of them attacked her at once. Jen used every trick she knew and all her speed to keep clear of the darting blades.

Damn, they were quick.

Two came in from her left, their blades lunging toward her chest. Jen spun away from them and hammered the right-hand attacker with the side of her blade.

He staggered left, his weapons tangled with one of his partners.

Jen thrust her blade through the first thug's back and continued on into the second's chest. Before they died her opponents twisted, yanking the sword from her hands.

Unarmed, Jen retreated before the third man's furious assault. She wove through rapid-fire thrusts, some missing her by inches.

She needed her sword.

Her opponent knew it too. He kept between her and his dead companions. It was a standoff.

He lunged, swords leading. A length of wood flew down between his legs.

Her opponent stumbled, his swords lowered for an instant. Jen hardened her knuckles and punched him in the side of the head, caving in his skull.

She spun and found Edward standing over the crushed remains of his opponents. He threw her a little wave as if to say see, we didn't need Damien. She smiled, appreciating the gesture.

Alec landed beside the dead man and collected his staff. "You okay?"

"Yeah." Jen retrieved her sword and cleaned the blade on one of the dead thug's coats. Talon skidded down to stand beside Edward, the gauntlets still tucked into his belt.

"Where have you two been?" Jen asked.

Talon jerked a thumb toward the bodies. "These guys had friends. We just killed another four of them. Tough bastards. They put up way more of a fight than the bunch from the villa."

"I noticed." Jen led the way across the ice at a brisk walk. She wasn't certain she had enough soul force left to jump it. If the others hadn't gotten back when they did, the fight might have been a lot closer. "Let's see if Rhys has her patched up yet."

Chapter 16

The inside of the bolt hole reminded Jen of a small flat; they'd even brought in a cheap carpet to cover the stone floor. There were two cots against the back wall. The unconscious woman lay on one, a blanket tucked around her. Her burns had healed enough that only white patches of skin remained and those would flake off in short order. Even her nose had grown back. Whatever healing supplies they cached here must have been potent.

A fire burned in a little iron stove in the far corner, a full coal scuttle beside it. The stovepipe went through the side of the cave wall to vent who knew where. Rhys sat on a three-legged stool beside his patient, a half-full coffer of healing potions at his feet.

Jen sat cross-legged beside her cot. "How is she?"

"I rubbed three vials on her burns and she woke up long enough to drink three more. I think she'll be fine, but I'm no expert. I heard fighting."

Talon and Edward leaned on either side of the tunnel back to the secret entrance. Alec had drawn guard duty and stood just inside the entrance to make sure no one snuck up on them. Jen had no idea how many members the Unkindness had, but she didn't plan to take any chances.

"Yeah, the thugs found us. This bunch had a new trick." She described the black fire. "It made them a damn sight tougher than the last group."

"Sounds like the goblins," Rhys said, echoing her earlier thoughts. "How do you suppose they gained access to power like that?"

She shook her head. "You got me. We need to find Master Shen. I'm so far out of my depth I'm drowning."

The woman groaned and tried to sit up. She failed and flopped back on the cot. "Thirsty," she said in a rough voice.

Rhys shrugged off his water skin and handed it to her. She tried to sit up again and he put a gentle hand on her back, easing her into a sitting position. She drank deep and sighed. "Thank you." Her voice sounded better already.

"You're welcome. I'm Jennifer St. Cloud. My squad and I were sent to find Dominic Santen. Master Shen said we could find help at The Mermaid."

She laughed, dry and bitter. "That didn't work out very well. I'm Mariela. I was sent to consult with the observation team a week ago. I'm not sure how much I can do to help you, but anything within my power is yours for the asking."

"Are you a sorcerer?" Jen's heart leapt at the thought of getting some extra power on their side. Maybe she wasn't as strong as Damien, but even a weak sorcerer would be a huge asset.

Mariela laughed again. "Hardly. I'm a scholar. I specialize in supernatural threats, demons and angels, along with their cults. The team had seen an increase in cult activity in the city and wanted my opinion. I wish I'd told them to take a flying leap."

Rhys chuckled and Mariela smiled up at him. Now that her face wasn't a mass of burns Jen realized she was an attractive woman with bright blue eyes, full lips, and prominent cheekbones. When her eyebrows and hair grew back she might even be beautiful. They looked close in age, maybe Rhys had found a girlfriend. Jen cleared her throat. "Can you tell us what happened?"

"Sure. I was reading in the back bedroom when something exploded. I stuck my head out and saw a girl standing in the flames.

Marco, our lead sorcerer, lay dead at her feet. The other two members of the team were slumped against a wall bleeding out. She spotted me. I slammed the door, but she punched through it and stabbed me with a blade of power that surrounded her hand. The next thing I remember is seeing you standing over me."

Jen frowned. "What did the girl look like?"

"Pretty, petite, short curly hair. She wore a short black dress and went barefoot of all things."

Jen nodded, sounded like the servant girl was a sorcerer. "What happened to Master Shen?"

Mariela shook her head. "No idea. He gave us a report about the attempted assassination and your search for Dominic. He said you should receive any help you needed and left. He mentioned something about spying on ravens. It made no sense to me."

It made sense to Jen. Master Shen had gone to spy on the Unkindness and ended up captured or killed. That wasn't good, but at least now they had a place to start looking for him. "Can you tell me anything about Dominic Santen?"

"Not much. He was the head of the local cult of The Binder in Chains. Many of the richest merchants are members. It's as much social club as cult."

"I'm not familiar with that demon lord. Can you tell me anything about him?"

Mariela smiled. "The Binder isn't a demon lord, he's an archangel. His cult preaches absolute obedience and always following through on a contract. That's what makes him so popular with merchants."

"Tyrants and slavers too, I imagine," Talon said.

"Yes. The Binder's teachings are unleavened by any mercy or kindness. He's considered the harshest of the archangels. Some of the paladins I correspond with think if he doesn't find some way to soften his message he may fall."

Jen shuddered. A fallen archangel would be a horrible threat, easily as great as any of the five dragons. "Do you think Dominic was a willing participant in the assassination attempt?"

"No. Absolute obedience, remember? Turning against the king would be a breach of his beliefs."

Jen didn't laugh, but it took some effort. She'd seen more than once that belief often gave way to ambition.

Chapter 17

The docks at night were a dangerous part of the city, especially with Jen and her squad sneaking through the shadows. Mariela had fallen asleep shortly after their conversation and she hadn't woken when they slipped out of the cave at dusk. Jen hated leaving the woman alone, but didn't dare spare one of her team to stand guard. They took four healing potions with them and left the other two for Mariela. Jen had no idea how many members the Unkindness had or how many could use the black flames, but she suspected they had enough that even together her team would have a tough fight.

This close to the water the stink of fish guts mingled with salt and rum to assault her nose. Scores of ships creaked in their slips, everything from tiny sloops to three-masted caravels. The streets were practically empty. Anyone they met after dark in this part of town would mean them ill.

The glow-ball lanterns had been smashed years ago and no one bothered to replace them. The only light came from the windows of the raucous taverns lining the streets. Dark as it was, to Jen's soul-force-enhanced eyes it might as well have been daylight. Despite her night vision she saw no sign of the Unkindness and she had no idea where they hung out. If they had to search every vomit-scented tavern in the docks it would be a long night.

Jen leapt from her perch on the roof of a sail maker's shop to a tavern roof across the street where Talon crouched.

"See anything?" she asked.

He pointed at a tavern three doors down. "There's a pretty barmaid down there. If we live through the night I might introduce myself."

She slapped his shoulder. "See anything useful?"

"Nah." He patted the gauntlets on his belt. "How long am I going to have to drag these around?"

"Until we find someone to check them out. What's the matter, they too heavy for you?" She leapt away to check on the others before he could respond.

Alec stood behind a meat smoker's chimney, the mouthwatering scent of rendering pork filling the air. Jen landed softly beside him. "Anything?"

He shook his head. "I really want some bacon."

"We can have some for breakfast after we rescue Master Shen."

Jen leapt away. Three blocks further on she reached Rhys. The oldest member of the team stood in the shadows of a snow-clogged alley. "Anything?"

"Edward slunk by a minute ago. He was tailing a likely looking fellow, but I have no idea if it panned out."

"Which way?"

He nodded to the right.

"I'll see what he found. If we need help I'll whistle, so keep an ear out."

He nodded again and settled deeper into the alley. Jen leapt to the roofs and ran along above the street, eyes straining for any sign of Edward. She gritted her teeth. He should know better than to tail someone on his own, especially after seeing what the thugs could do.

At last she spotted him standing in the shadows of an empty alley, his maul leaning against the wall behind him. His gaze was focused on a two-story brick building across the street. A glow lamp hung above a closed door at the top of a short flight of steps. Nothing about the place seemed remarkable to her.

She leapt down and landed beside him. Edward never flinched. "Report."

“I followed a guy in a coat like the ones the thugs were wearing to that building across the way. He knocked and when the door opened he rolled up his sleeve and showed the raven tattoo. The door guard let him in then slammed and locked the door. That was about a minute ago.”

Jen grinned in the dark. This was the best sign they’d found so far. “Do you think this is their base?”

He shook his head. “No idea. I couldn’t see past the guard. You want to go kick the door down?”

Kicking the door down was the last thing she wanted to do. If the Unkindness heard them coming they might kill Master Shen, assuming he was still alive. “Do you remember the knock he used?”

“It didn’t sound like a code if that’s what you mean. He just knocked, the door opened, and he showed off his tattoo.”

“Perfect. All we need is to get the door open. I’ll fetch the others. If anyone comes out before I return take them into custody. And for heaven’s sake keep it quiet.”

Chapter 18

It took ten minutes for Jen to collect the rest of her people and rejoin Edward. When they arrived, a dead man lay on the ground beside him. Jen grimaced. "This is not what I meant when I said take him into custody."

"You said keep him quiet. He shouted when I grabbed him so I punched him. I may have hit him a little too hard."

"No kidding," Talon said.

"Did he have anything on him when he stepped out?" Jen asked.

Edward shook his head. "My guess is he's a messenger."

Jen eyed the dead man then turned to Alec. "You look about the right size. See if his jacket will fit."

Alec leaned his staff against the wall and shrugged into the dead man's long coat. It was a little short, but not bad. "What now?" He reached for his staff.

"Leave it." Jen pointed to the hilt of a dagger sticking out of the top of his boot. "Use that. Knock on the door and when the guard opens it, take him out. We'll be right behind you."

Alec walked across the street, the boot dagger in his right hand behind his back. He climbed the steps and knocked.

Jen held her breath. If the guard raised the alarm they'd had it, and most likely so had Master Shen.

The door opened and the guard said something. An instant later Alec drove the dagger up under his chin and into his brain. They rushed across the street. Edward shouldered the body and dumped it with the first one. Jen tossed Alec his staff and they slipped inside, locking the door behind them.

Beyond the door was a small room with a hard wooden chair and rickety table with a broadsheet on it. Apparently the guard enjoyed reading gossip while he waited. Jen glanced at the front page. Two months out of date; maybe he covered his eyes with it while he napped. A second door led deeper into the building.

"What if someone knocks?" Alec tossed the nasty jacket into the guard's chair. "Won't they wonder where the guard is?"

"We can't worry about that, unless you're volunteering to fill in." Jen raised an eyebrow.

Alec waved his free hand. "Just asking. What now?"

"Now we have a look around and see if we can't figure out what's happening in this city. Talon, take point. Edward, rear guard. Let's move."

The second door opened on well-oiled hinges. Behind it a long, narrow corridor led deeper into the building. Talon went through first, silent as a hunting cat. Jen let him get a short lead before she followed, the others right behind her. As she slipped down the hallway she trailed her fingers along the wall. Whoever built it had faced the walls with rough-cut lumber. Whatever business fronted this place it wasn't high end.

Talon stopped at the end of the hall. It ended in a T. "Which way?"

Jen couldn't see that it mattered. They'd have to search both directions anyway. "Right."

They continued right maybe five paces before coming to a door. Talon gave it a tug and it creaked open. Jen winced at the noise, which certainly sounded louder to her soul-force-enhanced ears than it really was. Inside they found crates, coils of rope, and block-and-tackle sets hanging from pegs on the wall. Apparently this building served as an outfitter for sailors. That made sense. There were probably another two or three just like it further down the street.

"Keep going, unless you hear a heartbeat," Jen said.

Talon nodded and continued down the hall. He paused at two more doors before continuing on. The hall ended at the rear of the sales floor. Everything you could imagine a ship needing filled the open space. Sails, rope, crates of nails, even barrels of withered apples.

Whatever the Unkindness were up to, it had to be either upstairs or in the basement. Jen enhanced her hearing as much as she could and lay down on the floor. She pressed her ear to the boards and held her breath. A faint grinding reached her along with some muffled grunts. Someone was doing something down there. Whether the gang or some unlucky worker sharpening harpoons they'd learn soon enough.

"Someone's in the basement. Fan out and find the stairs."

With their enhanced senses it didn't take her team long to locate a door built into the wall. Rhys opened it and Talon had slipped through before she could say anything. Jen stood by the door, waiting for Talon to finish his scouting. The grinding she heard earlier sounded louder by the open door.

A minute later Talon returned, his face pale. "You won't believe it."

"What?" Jen asked.

He shook his head. "I don't have the words. Come on."

Jen followed her shaken subordinate down the short flight of stairs, the rest of the squad on her tail. What could he have seen that shook him so bad? At the bottom, a short hall led to a doorway through which came a dark, crimson glow. Something about that light chilled Jen to the bone.

Talon motioned "down" with his hand and they crouched as low as they could. Jen eased down the hall and peeked through the doorway. Her breath caught in her throat and her stomach twisted.

The doorway opened out onto a catwalk that ran around the perimeter of a deeper room. Down in that pit people, both men and women, lay strapped to vertical tables.

Their clothes hung in tatters. Hundreds of shallow cuts covered their bodies. Gags kept them quiet as people in long coats circulated amongst the prisoners. When a wound stopped bleeding one the torturers would slice a fresh grove in their flesh. Most horribly, the blood running out of the wounds flowed up toward a black circle in the ceiling a few feet from Jen's head.

Every so often a drop of some black liquid dripped out of the circle and into a stone bowl placed under it.

Jen stepped back from the doorway and clenched her fists. It took every ounce of self-control she had not to run down there and kill every one of those monsters.

They needed more information. She didn't see any sign of Master Shen or the servant girl or for that matter Dominic Santen. It didn't look like they planned to kill those unfortunate people, just bleed them. Judging by the number of scabbed over wounds some of them had, they'd been prisoners for a while.

"What now?" Talon gripped his swords and looked as eager as she felt to go down there and do some cutting of their own.

"I noticed a door on the far side of the catwalk. There must be some cells around here where they keep their prisoners. We have to try and find Master Shen. Whatever's going on down there it's beyond my comprehension. If we go stumbling into something blind some of us are going to get killed. Rhys, Edward, and Alec, stay here and keep watch. Talon, you and me are going scouting."

They left the others by the doorway and slipped out onto the catwalk. Whoever built it had bolted it securely to the wall; it didn't creak or wobble when they put their weight on it. Jen inched along, careful to make no noise. She glanced down into the lower level. A gang member was sharpening knives on a grindstone. That explained the noise.

A woman with long, limp brown hair looked their way. Jen froze and motioned Talon to as well. They stood in the shadows and the woman was close to one of the braziers that provided heat and light for the torture chamber. She doubted the woman could see a thing in the deep shadows close to the ceiling.

Jen let out a silent breath when the woman turned her attention back to the horrors close at hand. The door was only fifteen feet away, but it took Jen and Talon five minutes to reach it at the crawling pace they set. Jen pressed the dark wood and the door swung open without a peep. She looked up and sent a silent word of thanks to whatever angel watched over crazy warlords. Talon closed the door behind them.

Beyond the door waited a pitch-black hall. Even with her enhanced sight Jen couldn't make out much. Her nose, unfortunately, wasn't hindered in the least. The stink of sweat, waste and blood filled the hall. She hated to risk it, but they needed more light.

"Open that door back up."

"You sure?" The doubt in his voice came through loud and clear.

Jen wasn't sure of a damn thing except that she was blind in the dark. They couldn't help anyone if they couldn't see them. "Open it."

He eased the door open and dim light filtered through, just enough to let her see the row of cells lining the hall. Her lip curled in a snarl. If she'd wanted to kill the Unkindness before, now she really wanted them dead, and not necessarily quickly.

Ragged figures filled the left-hand cages, their bodies covered with freshly scabbed-over cuts. Grime covered them and from the smell she guessed their chamber pots had been emptied...never. She squinted, trying to make out the details of their faces. Master Shen had to be here somewhere. He'd only been gone a day so he should be in better shape than the others.

Jen worked her way down the hall. None of the pathetic figures reacted to her. Whether they couldn't see her, or they didn't have strength enough she didn't know. She reached the end of the prison and someone groaned from her right. She turned and, alone in a cell, lay Master Shen.

They'd stripped him to the waist and cut a bunch of gashes in him. He wore no restraints and didn't stir when she moved closer to him. She grabbed the door and pulled. Even with her enhanced strength the steel door didn't budge.

"Master Shen." She spoke just above a whisper and even that seemed far too loud.

He groaned and turned his head toward her. His face was a mass of bruises and one eye had swollen shut. She winced and tried again. "Master Shen, I can't open the door."

He crawled toward her, but only managed to get a few feet closer. He muttered something.

"I can't understand, Master."

"Drugged."

Of course they'd drugged him. He couldn't use his powers if he couldn't concentrate. Jen fished a healing potion out of her pocket and reached as far into the cell as she could. He stretched out a trembling hand, fumbled, and finally got a grip on the vial.

He ripped the cork out of the top with his teeth, spat it out and drank the potion in one gulp. His bruises faded and the gashes on his chest shrank. A minute later he sat up and rotated his arm, and nodded.

"Thank you, Jennifer. I feared I'd die in this awful place."

Relief flooded through Jen. "Can you open the door?"

He conjured a golden key and fit it into the lock. A second later it clicked and she pulled it open. He stood up and joined her in the hall. "What do you say we escort these people out of here?"

Chapter 19

Master Shen pointed at the wall. A lance of golden energy shot out and he cut a circle in the wood. The disk fell into the snow outside with a dull thump. Jen glanced back at Talon who stood just inside the doorway. He shook his head. No reaction from the torturers.

Jen hurried over and crouched beside him. "Fetch the others. We're getting these people out of here."

"With pleasure."

Talon eased out onto the catwalk and Jen went back to join Master Shen. "You've regained your power."

"I never lost it." He spoke in the same low tone. "I just couldn't focus enough to use it. I'm eager to hear how you found me, but this isn't the time."

Jen seconded that. He conjured keys for the other cells and unlocked them. The rest of her squad arrived a moment later. "Get 'em out of here," she said.

Rhys went in the first cell and helped people to their feet. Alec helped them to the door and Talon and Edward guided them out the hole in the wall. The prisoners staggered and shuffled down the hall. This was taking too long. Jen gritted her teeth and kept quiet. They could only move as fast as they could move.

They emptied the first cell. It held ten of the sickest, scrawniest looking people she'd ever seen. While Talon half-carried the last prisoner out into the alley Rhys moved on to the second cell.

"Where do you think you're going?" The servant from the Santen's villa floated at the entrance to the cell block. Power sent her short hair flying every which way. She'd traded her servant's outfit for an equally short black dress. Like Mariela said, her feet were bare.

"You!" Master Shen sent a blast of raw soul force down the hall, barely missing Jen, and sending the enemy sorcerer hurtling back into the far wall. He raced after her and explosions followed a moment later.

Jen grimaced. This was getting out of hand fast. She grabbed Edward as he passed. "I don't care if you have to carry them, but we need to speed this up. If we don't hurry, those two will bring this dump down on our heads. Spread the word."

A crash sounded from upstairs and shattered boards rained down into the pit. Come on, Master, fight her in the air, away from the building. A bald, broad-shouldered gang member with black fire burning in his eyes leapt up onto the catwalk. He carried a four-foot-long double-bitted ax and was running toward Jen.

She drew her sword and forgot all about the dueling sorcerers.

Jen met her opponent at the doorway. She had to keep him out of the cell block. He swung the broad-bladed ax with all his might. Jen hopped back. The ax tore a two-foot chunk out of the doorway.

She lunged, hoping to finish him before he recovered. Somehow the man batted her attack aside with the haft of his ax.

Jen recovered and blocked his back cut. This guy moved every bit as fast as the other bunch they'd fought. She slashed high, low, high. He blocked every attack. Jen repeated the series with the same result, a lot of noise and no blood.

Her sword went high then low again. The thug raised his ax, anticipating her high slash. Just as she'd hoped.

Jen spun and cut low again. Soul-forged steel sliced through the flesh of his thigh, taking the unfortunate man's leg off above the knee. Jen kicked him in the chest. He flew over the edge down into the pit.

She walked to the railing and leaned over. Like rats fleeing a sinking ship the thugs rushed down a hole in the floor. Jen leapt over the rail. Maybe she could capture a couple of them.

Two rushed her, short swords drawn. They lacked the black flames and she cut them down in seconds. Those seconds proved expensive. The door to the secret passage swung shut and a lock engaged. She stomped on it, but the thick metal lid didn't budge.

"Damn it!"

She could do nothing about the escaping thugs so Jen turned her attention to the bound and bleeding prisoners. She sheathed her sword and grabbed a fallen knife. An emaciated man flinched at her approach.

Jen cut his hand free. "Easy, I'm here to help."

She freed the second hand and he slumped against her. "Heaven bless you, girl." He gasped the words out like it took the last of his strength.

Edward landed beside her and took the unconscious man out of her arms. Another blast shook the building. It sounded farther away. Maybe Master Shen realized he was about to collapse the place on them.

Jen moved on to the next victim. It took her team two minutes to free all twelve prisoners and carry them up and out of the pit. Jen paused as Rhys carried the last woman up the iron steps. The black disk on the ceiling shimmered like water and a drop of darkness fell into the bowl.

Jen grimaced and kicked it over. The nasty stuff oozed across the floor, sizzling and burning stone. She shuddered. What could they use that crud for?

Maybe she didn't want to know. Jen leapt up to the catwalk and followed Rhys out the hole in the wall. Above them streaks of energy lit the sky. She couldn't tell who was winning.

"Did we get everybody?" Talon asked.

"All the prisoners, but some of the gang escaped." Not a perfect victory, but when she looked at the huddled figures shivering in the snow Jen figured maybe it was close enough. "Let's take these people somewhere warm."

An explosion shook the night and Master Shen fell from the sky. Jen leapt and caught him eight feet from the ground. They landed close to the hole he'd cut in the wall. "You hurt?"

He grunted and looked up. Jen followed his gaze. Hovering above them, an armored figure sat astride a black horse with glowing red eyes and flames around its feet and tail. The knight wore a great sword strapped to his back and a full helm shaped like a leering demon that hid his face. Inscribed on his breastplate was a huge, horned skull.

Beside him the sorcerer floated, a little pout on her pixie face. "You spoiled my fun, Mikhail."

Mikhail!

This was the missing Santen heir?

"Don't call me that!" Mikhail said. "Mikhail Santen is dead. I am Sir Darkness, a demon knight."

The sorcerer grimaced. "I am not calling you Sir Darkness, Mikhail, or anything equally pretentious."

Black flames gathered around his bare hands. "You dare question my commands?"

Jen hoped they'd kill each other and save her a lot of work, but the sorcerer raised her hands. "Of course not, my lord. Hey, how about that? 'My lord' would be a good thing to call you."

He nodded once and the flames vanished. "It will do."

"Hey!" Jen shouted. "Where's your father?"

Mikhail turned his attention to her and a chill ran through Jen. His eyes were pits of fire. "Dead. I cut his heart out and his blood fueled my ascension to greatness. I'll never again have to listen to his prattle about obedience and following the rules. I make the rules now."

His gaze shifted. "I wondered what became of those." He held out his bare hands and the gauntlets on Talon's belt flew up and slid over them. He flexed his fingers. "Now die, worms."

A black ball of crackling energy formed in the air in front of him.

Jen grabbed Master Shen and ran back to the others.

The sphere shot toward the alley. Master Shen raised a golden barrier.

White snow and black energy washed over them. Jen braced the slender sorcerer.

The assault lasted only moments. When the snow settled, all that remained of the Unkindness's base was a smoking crater. Master Shen slumped in her arms and his barrier vanished.

Jen eased him to the ground. "Everybody okay?"

Her squad all indicated that they were, even the prisoners survived the attack. Jen studied the sky. No sign of the sorcerer or Mikhail, thank heaven.

Master Shen groaned and sat up. Jen helped him to his feet. He wobbled, but stayed upright. "Are you all right, Master?"

He nodded. "Some of the corruption penetrated my shield. It would have been unpleasant if I was in peak condition. As I am now it stunned me. Is everyone safe?"

"Yes, you did it."

"Good." He turned toward the smoking crater. "It's a good thing we were only on the edge of the blast. If his aim had been better..."

"I have a lot of questions, Master Shen."

He smiled and patted her shoulder. "I'm sure. I have my share as well, but they'll all keep until we reach somewhere warm."

Chapter 20

"I thought I told you to keep the breakage to a minimum." Captain Tosh sat behind his desk. A vein in his forehead throbbed in time with his heart. "Do you call blowing up a building in the docks minimal breakage?"

Jen and Master Shen sat across from him. They'd retreated to Jen's inn long enough to change clothes before leading the victims to watch headquarters. Some kid fresh out of training had been dispatched to fetch the captain. He'd arrived ten minutes later, shirt half tucked in and hair uncombed. Jen managed not to laugh.

The former prisoners were downstairs getting looked at by the healers. The rest of the squad had stayed with them to offer what reassurance they could. That left Jen and Master Shen to handle the inevitable explanations. She would have preferred to fight a dozen thugs.

"I didn't destroy the building. I rescued the prisoners and their jailor didn't appreciate it."

Tosh ran a hand through his rumpled hair. "Just walk me through it. Start with what happened after we parted ways."

Jen paused to gather her thoughts and try to figure out how to tell the story without revealing the secret spying operation, but couldn't see any way around it.

"I told Jennifer to look up an old friend of mine if anything happened," Master Shen said, saving her the trouble of making up a story. "Mariela told her about my efforts to investigate the Unkindness so she tracked them down and freed me along with the other prisoners. Mikhail Santen murdered his father to gain demonic powers which he used to destroy the building in an attempt to murder us. He fled with a female accomplice. Where they are now we have no idea."

"A handful of the gang escaped under the building, I assume into the sewers," Jen said.

"That's it? That's your whole explanation?" Tosh stared at them.

Jen shrugged. "That's what happened. It hasn't even been a full day since we left the villa. What more do you want?"

Tosh waved a hand. He looked exhausted. "Nothing. I don't want a thing. I trust you're finished with your investigation and will be leaving my city soon."

"Tomorrow morning," Master Shen said. "I need sleep and food before I'll have strength enough to transport us to the capital."

"Fine, just don't blow up anything before you leave."

Jen opened her mouth to protest, but Master Shen laid a restraining hand on her wrist. They took their leave of the weary captain, collected her men along with many thanks from the former prisoners, and headed to Jen's inn. She had a ton of questions, but when she started to ask, Master Shen shook his head.

They stopped outside the inn. The sun was just coloring the horizon. "Order some breakfast and wait for me in your room," Master Shen said. "I'm going to collect Mariela. I'll be back soon."

He leapt into the air and faded from view. Jen shook her head and led the way in. The smell of fresh bread washed over her and her stomach rumbled, reminding her that she hadn't eaten in a full day. A serving girl bustled around the common room, wiping tables and straightening chairs. It wouldn't be long before the other guests came down to eat.

Jen waved her over and ordered a large breakfast to be sent up to her room. She flipped the girl a gold royal and went upstairs. Fifteen minutes later a tapping sounded on her window. She saw nothing, but opened it anyway. Something brushed against her and a moment later Master Shen shimmered into view, Mariela held in his arms.

He laid the scholar on Jen's bed and sat on the edge. The woman looked better. The last of the dead skin had flaked off and her hair had grown back, only an inch long, but still. Six healing potions could work wonders.

A knock sounded on the door. Outside two serving girls held trays laden with food. Edward and Alec collected the trays and closed the door. Master Shen waved his hand and nodded. "We can speak now. I've blocked all sound from leaving the room."

Jen fixed an egg-and-bacon sandwich and leaned against the wall. "So what was that black disk in the ceiling above the torture room?"

"A hell gate. A small one, thank heaven. Someone opened it for them and they fed it blood to get demon essence."

"You mean that black stuff?" Jen finished her sandwich and moved on to the pastries. "It looked like a lot more blood went in than black stuff came out."

Mariela sat up. "It runs about a gallon of blood to a quarter ounce of essence."

"What do they do with it?" Alec asked around a mouthful of ham.

"You saw the ones with the black flames?" Master Shen asked.

They all nodded. "What are they anyway, the flames?" Talon asked.

"For the gang members the flames were simply a visible manifestation of the demonic power running through their bodies. They represent the flames of hell. For a warlock or a demon the flames are the shape their corrupt soul force takes unless they chose to transform it into something else. The gang used the essence to ink their tattoos a second time. When they shed their blood it triggered the power which took the shape of the black flames. What you missed was the aftermath. Normal humans aren't equipped to handle that much soul force, much less corrupt, demonic soul force. Most of them would have dropped dead the instant the power dried up."

"Mikhail didn't seem to have much trouble," Jen said.

Master Shen frowned. “He’s a different matter altogether. Mikhail bonded his soul to a demon, most likely that ugly flying horse he was riding. It allows him to draw on the demon’s power, but when he dies the demon consumes his soul and grows stronger.”

“Seems a little short sighted,” Rhys said.

“Usually, but demon binding grants immortality as well, so as long as no one kills him the demon doesn’t get his soul. If the binding was done correctly it can’t betray him either.”

“So what happens now?” Jen asked.

“Eat, sleep, and tomorrow we fly back to the capital where I report to the archmage then I’ll fly you back to The Citadel to report to your father.”

Jen sighed. This was one mission she didn’t regret finishing.

Chapter 21

A little after noon the first supply station came into view. It jutted up out of the snow several hundred yards ahead of them. Damien had never felt so glad to see a building, even a slumping, three-room shack like the station, in his life. Eight days of riding and sleeping in a tiny, two-person tent with a woman that barely tolerated him left him eager for a bed and someone, anyone, else to talk to. A bath wouldn't hurt either of them as well.

Behind the station a fenced-in paddock and modest stable housed about ten horses. Army patrols stopped at the station to swap injured mounts and tend to tack and shoes. No soldiers manned the place, only a farrier, stable master, and their apprentices. It struck Damien as a peaceful if tedious post.

They rode around to the paddock. From the stable a middle-aged man with a beard wearing a heavy fur-lined jacket ambled out to meet them. "Can I help you?"

"We need fresh mounts and supplies," Lane said.

"Yeah, and you are?"

She frowned and fished around in her furs. After a moment of hunting she pulled out a badge and pointed it at him like it was a crossbow. "Lane Thorn, diplomatic corps. This is my bodyguard."

No introduction for him. Damien tapped his forehead in a two-fingered salute. "Damien St. Cloud, pleasure."

The stable master studied the badge a moment then nodded. "Looks official. You two staying the night?"

"Yes." Damien didn't give Lane a chance to speak. "Please tell me you have a tub in this place."

He glowered at Damien. "Of course. Just because we're in the middle of nowhere doesn't mean we live like savages. Leave the horses and mule to me and the boys and head on in. Nigel can show you where everything is."

Damien swung down and grabbed his rucksack. Lane joined him, pausing to collect the smallest of her bags from the back of the mule. They trudged through a foot of snow to the back door of the station. An iron ring served as door knob and Damien pulled it open. He went through first like a proper bodyguard.

The main room had a big, potbellied iron stove in the center that threw off a pleasant heat, its chimney running up through the roof. Four chairs sat around a rough-hewn dinner table. Two closed doors, one straight ahead and a second to his right, led to other rooms. Not exactly luxury, but it would do.

Lane came in behind him. "What a dump."

The door straight ahead opened and a bald man wearing a leather apron stepped into the room, a crossbow at his shoulder ready to fire. "Who the hell are you?"

Damien was halfway across the room before he finished the question. Damien leapt onto the table, gathered himself, and leapt again.

His heel crashed into the man's crossbow. It clattered to the floor.

Damien grabbed the man by the throat and slammed him into the wall. "Nigel?"

Nigel croaked something then settled for nodding.

"I'm Damien, that's Lane. We'll be spending the night tonight. The stable master said you could show us where everything is. If I let you go you're not going to go for that crossbow, right?"

A red-faced Nigel shook his head.

"Good." Damien released him and stepped back. "Crossbows make me nervous."

Nigel coughed and rubbed his throat. "You didn't look nervous. Who are you again?"

Lane flashed the badge a second time. "Diplomatic corps. You must forgive my bodyguard. He can be over protective."

Nigel coughed again. "You don't say."

Damien bent down, removed the bolt from the crossbow, and uncocked it. "Here. Be careful, you could hurt someone with that thing."

Nigel managed a hoarse laugh. "Yeah, like myself. Dinner's a few hours away. Want me to set up the tub?"

"Yes!" he and Lane said at the same time.

The second door led to a supply room with an open space for the heavy iron tub. They melted snow on the stove to fill it. The whole process took half an hour. It would have taken double that, but Damien sped up the project with a little subtle sorcery.

Of course, Lane went first. She went in and slammed the door. A moment later it opened again. "I'd better not catch you peeking."

"Can I peek as long as you don't catch me?"

Lane slammed the door again. He took that as a no. Damien had only been half joking about peeking. Lane was a beautiful woman if you looked past her personality. He wouldn't have minded a closer view of those long legs. He sighed. The look wasn't worth the argument. Anyway he had more pressing matters to attend to.

Damien dug a scrap of paper and pencil out of his kit and wrote a quick, two-sentence note to the archmage. She'd taught Damien how to send his constructs to a location he knew so he didn't have to guide the message the whole way. He conjured a bird and sent it to his master's office. That little task finished he pulled a chair over beside the stove, grabbed a second one to use as a footstool and settled in to wait.

A hot bath followed by a hot meal left Damien in a much-improved mood. His good mood soured slightly when Nigel explained that they had to sleep on the floor. At least they were inside and warm.

Damien woke early as usual and found a scroll on his chest sealed with crimson wax. A reply from the archmage. How had she gotten that scroll inside the station?

He slipped out of his bedroll and headed for the outhouse. Damien shivered when the cold air hit him. With a thought he increased the temperature of the air inside his shield. It was pitch black out this early in the morning, but the short path was well marked.

Damien closed and latched the door of the rickety little building. He conjured a tiny light and settled down to read. One good thing about the cold: it kept the stink to a minimum.

Fifteen minutes later he finished reading about Jen's adventure. It sounded like she'd had a rough time. She was okay, and that was what mattered. At least they knew Dominic Santen hadn't been involved in the assassination attempt, though his son appeared mixed up in it.

Damien sighed and incinerated the message. He hated complicated things like this. He wished someone would just tell him who to blast and let him get on with it. Oh, well.

Chapter 22

Ten weeks later found Damien and Lane on the outskirts of the first good-sized town they'd seen since the capital. The roofs of two-story buildings rose above the wooden palisade that surrounded the town. This far south the worst of the cold had passed and the first buds were visible on the maples growing along the road. A single, four-story mansion towered above all the other buildings. Damien assumed it belonged to whichever noble oversaw the town.

"What's the name of this place again?"

Lane glanced over at him. "Allentown."

"Right. And we're stopping here why?"

She sighed. "Because we have another week until the meeting and I want to spend a little time getting a feel for what the people think about the barons' plan to leave the kingdom. We're only forty miles from the border. These people sit right on the edge of a potential war zone if the barons abandon their responsibilities and let the bandits cross en masse."

"Does that matter in the grand scheme of things?" Damien wanted to tell her even if she failed the barons wouldn't be allowed to leave the kingdom alive.

"Of course it matters!"

Damien raised an eyebrow.

"Okay, maybe it doesn't matter to the negotiations, but it matters to me. Looking after these peoples' wellbeing is as much my job as dealing directly with the nobles."

Damien smiled. Even if she didn't like sorcerers, she had a good heart. That made it even harder to keep his secret.

They reached a set of double doors built into the palisade that served as a gate and reined in. A pair of guards with swords and spears stood on either side of the doors. "State your business," the left-hand guard said. He couldn't have sounded more bored

"We're just passing through," Lane said. "We need an inn for the night. Could you recommend a nice place?"

The right-hand guard chuckled.

"We've only got two inns, miss." The left-hand guard ignored his companion's laughter. "And I'd never send a lady to one of them. Best head over to the Golden Stag. It's clean and they serve the best food in town. Just take the second left, you can't miss it."

"Thank you." Lane smiled in a way that made Damien jealous for a moment.

The guards pushed the doors open and they rode through. The streets were a little muddy, no surprise this time of year. All the buildings looked sturdy and well taken care of. They all had flat roofs that could also serve as archery platforms. If bandits ever attacked the town they'd find arrows raining down on them from every direction.

Damien counted the streets and turned his mount toward the second left.

"No. We don't want to go somewhere fancy," Lane said.

"We don't?"

She shook her head. "The people I want to talk to can't afford a place like the guard described. If the nice inn is to the left we want to go right."

Right, heaven forbid they stay at the nice inn. They might have soft beds and decent food. Better to find some rat hole liable to give them a disease.

Damien followed her away from where he wanted to go. The farther they went down the street the worse the buildings looked. The first couple of rows seemed okay. Then the cedar shakes covering the walls became patchy before giving way to simple rough-sawn boards covering the walls.

Shouts and music sung with more volume than skill led them to The Horny Badger Inn, a take on the name of an aggressive animal native to the badlands. The less said about what the owner had painted on his sign the better.

The sign hung at a forty-five-degree angle from a single chain. Nothing about the building looked square. The entryway cocked a few inches left and the back wall had sunk a foot into the ground. Damien seriously considered shoring the place up with soul force before letting Lane enter.

The inn had a hitching post out front, but no sign of a stable. What should they do with the horses? If they left them tied up out front he had no doubt they'd be walking the rest of the way to the gathering.

Damien dismounted and tied off his horse. "What now?"

"We'll talk to the owner." Lane dismounted and tied her mount next to his. "There must be somewhere nearby we can keep the horses."

"Right." Damien grabbed his rucksack and slung it over his shoulder. He started for the stairs, but she brushed past him. He sighed. "After you."

He feared Lane's foot might go right through the half-rotted steps, but she made it up to the landing and pushed the door open. Inside, the common room was full of people laughing, drinking, and eating. Smoke filled the air. Damien examined it with invisible strands of soul force and found only mild stimulants, nothing poisonous.

The crowd looked rough: loggers and farmers mingled with thugs and whores. Everyone carried a weapon of some sort, mostly wooden cudgels and knives. From the number of scars and bent noses it looked like they weren't afraid to use them.

Along the far wall ran a bar behind which stood a middle-aged man with one eye and not many more teeth. "Talk to the bartender and rent us two rooms. Find out what we should do with the horses. I'm going to mingle," Lane said.

Damien shook his head. Lane had too many teeth and not enough scars or holes in her clothes to mingle with this lot. She looked like a swan swimming through a pond of raw sewage.

The archmage said she knew what she was doing and Damien had to trust that. Leaving Lane to her mingling Damien ambled over to the bar. The bartender met him with a gap-toothed smile. "You sure you folks are in the right place?"

Damien set his bag down. "No, but it looks like we're staying the night, assuming you have two empty rooms."

The bartender coughed and spat something thick and black on the floor behind the bar. "We got six empty rooms. Hell, we ain't rented a room by the night in years. You best keep an eye on your lady friend. She's attracting the wrong kind of attention."

Damien glanced over his shoulder and found the men leering at Lane as she worked her way through the press. Maybe they'd be content to look and he wouldn't have to kill any of them. He returned his attention to the bartender. "Don't suppose there's a stable around here."

The bartender barked a phlegmy, congested laugh. "Only thing we do with horses in this part of town is eat 'em. You want a place to store 'em you best head back to the fancy part of town."

Damien concentrated and conjured an invisible barrier around the horses. That would keep anyone from taking them to the butchers while he figured out how to convince Lane to stay somewhere else. Maybe someone would pinch her ass and she'd realize this wasn't a good place for them.

"Still want those rooms?"

Damien sighed and nodded toward Lane. "She's the boss. I'm just a bodyguard."

The bartender whistled through his teeth. "I wouldn't mind guarding that body. Uh-oh. Looks like you've got work to do. She's caught Bonzo's eye."

Damien grimaced. Sounded like the name of a dancing bear at the summer fair. "Who or what is a Bonzo?"

"He's the biggest man in the place. Head enforcer for the Daggers. They run this town."

"What about the nobleman that lives in the mansion?"

"Ha! The Lord Mayor? The Daggers pay him off with gold and young girls. His soldiers won't lift a finger to stop them."

Damien's anger rose. When he finished with the barons he'd have to visit the Lord Mayor as well. That sort of behavior couldn't be tolerated in the kingdom.

But first Bonzo.

Damien spun around and scanned the room. It didn't take long to spot the brute leaning against the wall near the end of the bar, his gaze following Lane's every move. He stood nearly seven feet tall, broad-shouldered, with a raw-boned, weathered face. Made Sig look like a midget.

Damien looked closer. Bonzo had weak internal soul force he used to augment his strength and toughness. His technique was sloppy. Probably self taught rather than Citadel trained. Bonzo wasn't strong enough to be a threat to a real warlord, much less a sorcerer, but his ability would give him a huge advantage over a normal person.

Bonzo pushed away from the wall and sauntered across the common room toward Lane. Everyone rushed to move out of his way. Lane had her back to him as she chatted up a painted whore whose best days had come and gone before Damien was born. Maybe Bonzo would do the job of convincing her to stay somewhere else for him.

"You're pretty." Bonzo patted her ass.

Lane spun around and craned her neck to look up at him. "Watch where you touch."

Bonzo leered at her and reached for her chest.

Lane slapped his hand away and raised a fist. "Try that once more and I'll deck you."

Bonzo laughed and stuck his chin out. "Take your best shot."

Lane reared back. Quick as thought Damien wrapped her in a full-body shield and anchored her to the floor. Next he added a sphere of soul force at the end of her fist.

She swung. The sphere hit Bonzo's chin and released the stored energy.

He flew across the common room and slammed into the wall.

Lane blinked and stared at her fist. "Asshole."

Everyone held their breath, waiting for him to stand up.

They'd be waiting a while. He'd put enough energy into the blast to kill a normal person. Even someone like Bonzo wouldn't shake that off any time soon.

When it became clear the giant wouldn't be getting up again a cheer rose from the crowd. Damien reabsorbed all the energy he'd wrapped Lane in and smiled.

Damien turned back to the bartender who shook his head. "What does she need you for?"

"She keeps asking me that very same question. Truth is I work for her mother. The old lady worries and pays well. Who am I to argue?"

The bartender laughed. "Words to live by, my friend."

Chapter 23

When Lane finally finished chatting Damien waved her over. Scowling, she stalked to the bar. What was she pissed about now?

"What?" Lane asked.

"They don't have a stable in this part of town. My new best friend"—Damien nodded toward the bartender—"assures me that any horse we leave outside will find its way to the meat market in short order."

"Fine. Take the horses back up the street and find a stable. I'll wait here."

"If you think I'm leaving you alone in this place you're nuts. And if your mother found out she'd kill me. We go together and walk back together, if you insist on returning."

"It's for the best, miss." The bartender flinched when Lane turned her angry gaze on him. "Bonzo's got a lot of friends. You don't want to be here when they find out you flattened him."

Lane turned back to Damien. "What's a Bonzo?"

"The gentleman lying by the wall over yonder."

She pursed her lips. "I think I have a good feel for what the people in this part of town think. Maybe it would be useful to talk to the other side."

Thank Bonzo and all the heavens.

Lane headed for the door and Damien slipped the bartender a silver crown before he followed. He doubted it would stop the man from telling the Daggers which way they went, but he had provided some useful information.

Damien dissolved his invisible barrier before Lane reached it. He detected no sign that anyone had tried to bother their horses. Lane swung up into her saddle and Damien followed her example.

They'd gone as far back as the cedar-sided buildings before Lane said, "You used your powers back there. No way I knocked that goon out myself."

"Yeah, I sure did. Would you have preferred to break your hand on his jaw?"

"I told you not to use your powers. I know how to throw a punch."

Damien shook his head at the woman's stubbornness. "I'm sure you do, but have you ever punched a warlord? Bones as hard as steel tend to be hard on the knuckles."

Lane laughed. "If he was a warlord then I'm a princess."

"He wasn't Citadel trained, but Bonzo did have a weak internal soul force. He's what's called an instinctive user. You'll run into one now and then. The point is, trained or not, you still would have broken your hand on his jaw. After that I would have had to do something drastic to stop him from raping you on one of the tables while the whole place watched."

That shut her up. They reached the crossroads and turned in the direction the guards had suggested. The effect on the buildings was exactly the opposite of their ride toward the first inn.

Houses became nicer. Fresh coats of paint covered everything. Single-story buildings gave way to two stories. Windows got wider and more numerous.

The Golden Stag stood two stories high and sprawled over half a block. An iron fence surrounded manicured grounds. Warm light from the windows lit the yard. Three steps led up to dark wood doors, inset with colored glass.

Damien guided his mount through the open gate. Beside him Lane groaned.

"What's wrong?"

"I hate places like this."

"Oh sure. Clean, warm, good food, no thugs to attack you. Seems like a horrible place. Bet you a royal the bartender has all his teeth."

Lane offered a weary smile. "It's not the setting, it's the memories. Mom used to bring me to places like this. Everyone patted me on the head, and smiled these sad smiles, every one of them thinking how pathetic it was for someone like Mom to have such a disappointment for a daughter."

A pair of boys in blue tunics embroidered with golden stags rushed out from behind the inn. They held their reins while Damien and Lane dismounted. As soon as they had their gear the boys led the horses and mule off toward the back. Now that's what Damien called service.

"You're not a little girl anymore," Damien said. "Try to relax and enjoy the luxury. After this little break it's back to business."

"I'll try." Lane followed him up the steps. "It's only one night after all."

Chapter 24

Damien sighed and followed Lane down the steps out of The Golden Stag. She'd said only one night and meant it. Too bad. Damien hadn't slept as well as he did last night in weeks. Deep feather beds combined with the best meal he'd eaten since leaving the capital added up to nine hours' unbroken sleep. For the first time in his life Damien cursed the training that had him awake before the sun rose.

Outside dawn was just coloring the horizon. Low, dark clouds and brisk temperatures threatened a late-season flurry before the end of the day. Two new boys in identical livery waited with their horses saddled and ready. From the shine, it looked like they'd combed them out and cleaned the mud from their tails and the feathering around their hooves. The horses looked better than when Damien claimed them from the last supply depot. They'd even slicked up the mule.

He tossed the boys a crown apiece. They snatched the silver coins out of the air with practiced ease. Damien patted his mare on the neck and swung up into the saddle. He hung his rucksack from the pommel and followed Lane out the open gate.

After a moment of silence Damien said, "Best six royals I ever spent. Tell me you didn't love those beds and I've never eaten roast that tender."

Lane nodded. “Maybe I was too quick to dismiss an occasional bit of luxury. The beds were a delight.”

“Ha! Thank you very much. I guarantee we both would have ended up with food poisoning if we ate at the other place.”

They rode through the slowly awakening town, eager to finish their journey. According to Lane’s map they’d reach Baron Kannon’s castle late tomorrow, barring any unforeseen adventures. Damien hoped she could convince the barons to do their duty. Though he had no qualms about killing, he preferred to avoid it when possible.

They came to a stop a hundred yards from the south gate. Nine rough men in leathers stood blocking their way. All of them carried a weapon of some sort, with axes, swords with chipped blades, and heavy cudgels making up the bulk. In the center, a little ahead of the rest, Bonzo stood with his arms crossed across his massive chest. He looked none the worse for last night’s pounding. He’d found an ax as long as he was tall with a massive, double-bitted head that probably weighed thirty pounds. A pair of town guards stood by the closed gates leaning on their spears. It didn’t look like they planned to offer any assistance.

Damien turned to Lane. “Do you want me to handle this or do you want to try and negotiate?”

Lane frowned. “Part of being a good negotiator is knowing when negotiation is a waste of time. Could you please keep it subtle? No golden dragons or smoking craters.”

“Come on, how did you know I was going to use a golden dragon?”

A hint of a smile cracked her stony face. “This is serious.”

Damien dug his thin leather gloves out of his rucksack and pulled them on. “No it isn’t. I’ve been in a few serious situations. This is a nuisance at worst.”

He dismounted and handed her his reins. “Keep your distance just the same.”

Damien strode toward the assembled thugs. His eyes narrowed as he studied their soul force. Only Bonzo had anything more than normal.

He could kill them all in an instant, probably should, since he suspected they were all members of the Daggers. Nevertheless, he wanted to give them a chance to surrender. He just didn't know where to take them since the Lord Mayor and his men were in the gang's pocket.

He stopped halfway between the gate and Lane. Damien crooked his finger, beckoning Bonzo forward. Even from a distance the enforcer's clenched jaw was visible. If he didn't move out of the way he was about to get a lot less happy and a lot more dead.

Bonzo slung his ax over his shoulder and marched toward Damien. When he stopped Damien stared him straight in the throat. Man, he was big. Maybe he had some ogre in his bloodline.

"We ain't interested in you," Bonzo said. He had a deep, gravelly voice and breath that suggested he brushed his teeth with the contents of his chamber pot. "But the girl's got to pay for insulting me. You can have her back when me and the boys are through."

"That's a generous offer, but unfortunately I'm her bodyguard and I'm afraid handing her over to you wouldn't do her body any good. How about you guys get out of here? I don't want any trouble."

Bonzo laughed. Behind him the rest of the thugs tensed and raised their weapons. That was all the chance Damien intended to give them. He conjured a pair of swords and drove them through both Bonzo's lungs.

Blood gushed out of Bonzo's mouth and he fell to his knees, the giant ax clattering to the ground. Damien stepped back, ripped his blades free, and cross slashed.

Bonzo's head plopped to the ground.

Before the other thugs recovered from the surprise of their leader's death, Damien hurled his blades at them. He accelerated their rotation until they looked like steel disks and guided them into the assembled thugs.

Human flesh didn't stand up well to soul force blades sharper than a razor and harder than steel. In three seconds all eight thugs lay in perhaps twenty pieces. One of them moaned in pain. He'd lost both legs above the knee and would bleed out in a hurry.

Damien held out his hands and the blades flew back to him. He reabsorbed the energy, tugged his gloves off, and walked back to rejoin Lane.

She stared at him, mutely handing him his reins when he reached for them. Perhaps she'd never seen real combat and its aftermath. It wasn't pretty.

Damien swung up onto his mare. "You know how they say don't look down when you're somewhere high? You might want to follow that advice until we reach the gate. It doesn't look any prettier up close.

She clenched her teeth and stared over the top of the wall. They rode toward the gate which the two guards hastened to open. Damien stayed close to Lane in case her horse shied away when they went through the bodies. A minute later they were out the gate and on the road again.

Chapter 25

They traveled down the dirt track in silence. A mix of spruce and oak trees towered over both sides of the narrow road. Damien sighed beside her. Lane couldn't believe she'd just watched him slaughter nine men and as far as she could tell it hadn't fazed him in the least. She couldn't stop trembling. Couldn't force the image of those men being sliced apart out of her head.

Half an hour later, when Allentown was well behind them, Lane said, "I always knew the sorts of things sorcerers could do, but I'd never seen it before. You killed those men like I might step on a bug."

"Same principle I guess. You step on the bugs so they don't bite anyone else. Dealing with that bunch didn't take any particular power. My sister could have done the same thing and she's a warlord."

Lane looked at him, eyes bulging, the blood drained out of her face. "How can you talk about it so casually? You just killed nine people. Aren't you even a little upset?"

"It's unfortunate they made me do it, but no, I'm not upset. Do you know anything about training at The Citadel?"

She blinked, not certain she understood. He was a sorcerer, not a warlord. "I thought sorcerers trained at Sorcery."

"We do, but before I went to Sorcery I trained for almost three years at The Citadel. People tend to think fighting techniques and how to use internal soul force are the most important things you learn, but they're wrong."

Lane licked her lips, not certain she wanted to know. She took a breath and asked, "What is the most important thing?"

"To kill without hesitation or regret. Before we move on to the second year's training, all first year cadets are thrown into a pit with a chained goblin. The goblin is armed with a club and the cadet is given a short sword. The masters don't let you out until the goblin is dead."

She put a trembling hand to her mouth. "That's horrible."

Damien shrugged. "Second year they throw you in with an unchained goblin and this time it has a sword and you have a dagger. You have to get up close to kill it. Get the blood on your hands. It spatters on your face."

"Heaven's mercy. They do this to children?"

"Eleven- and twelve-year-olds. Third years move on to killing men, prisoners in this case. You have to cut the throat of a condemned man. I had a head start. Dad threw me in with a chained goblin when I was ten, before my official training started." Damien looked up at the sky, lost in thought, totally unaware of her growing horror. "On my tenth name day he gave me this beautiful sword and dagger set. I was so happy. It looked just like the sword he wore. That night after Jen went to sleep he woke me up and took me down to the pit. I didn't realize yet what he intended."

"You don't have to tell me," she said. A part of her wanted him to go on. She felt an almost overwhelming need to understand this young man her mother had sent to protect her, this killer in a boy's body.

Damien shook his head and continued on like she hadn't spoken. "Dad said if I wanted to keep the sword I had to earn it. He threw me in with my precious new sword. He told me to kill the goblin and become a warrior. The goblin went crazy, thrashing and beating on its chain with a useless, blunt short sword. It was making the most shrill screeches."

"What did you do?" Lane asked in a breathless voice, knowing the answer before she spoke.

"I killed it. I think as much to shut it up as anything. Dad lowered a rope, I climbed out, and he hugged me and said how proud he was. It was the last time he hugged me. I think it may have been the last time he was proud of me." Damien locked his gaze on Lane and she went cold. "That's what it means to be a warlord. I may use external soul force, but I was trained to be a warlord. To kill my enemies without hesitation or remorse. I don't go out of my way to find people to kill, but if it becomes necessary..."

Lane shook her head and offered a weak smile. The horror of his childhood stunned her. "And I thought I had a difficult time growing up. You make me feel bad about complaining that some of Mom's friends gave me condescending pats on the head. I've never had to kill anyone."

Damien grinned, seeming to shake off his dark mood. "That's why your mother sent me. If there's ugly business to be done, let me handle it. My soul is so bloodstained a few more drops won't matter."

So young and so bitter. She wanted to hold him, give him the hugs his father withheld. Lane suspected it was too late for any number of hugs to do him much good. You don't become a killer at ten without getting a permanent scar on your soul. How many scars did Damien's carry?

Chapter 26

Baron Kannon's keep loomed dark and menacing where it sat on a cliff overlooking the border five miles away. Dark clouds gathered behind it, setting a gloomy scene. Surrounded on three sides by sheer vertical drops, the only way to approach the fortress was up a steep, winding path that ended at a high, crenelated wall.

The keep itself towered three stories high. A dozen arrow slits covered the front and sides. A dark-green banner with a golden bow embroidered on it snapped in the wind from a pole on the right-hand tower. The baron's ancestors had chosen well when they built their home. Now the question was, would the current Baron Kannon make a wise decision and stick to his duty. Damien hoped so. If they could accomplish this mission without killing that was fine with him.

A soft breeze blew through the spruce, filling the air with the scent of evergreen. Damien breathed deep, enjoying the moment.

"It's so peaceful here," Lane said. She'd been a lot nicer to him since the battle with the Daggers. Was it pity or fear? He didn't know or especially care. Whatever melted her icy personality, it was a welcome change. "You'd hardly guess a day's ride south bands of murderers constantly gathered and plotted how best to kill and plunder our land."

"At least they're flesh-and-blood humans and not monsters or demons. Our soldiers can handle them. The problem is sometimes they try to cross in small groups that are hard to detect. That's why the barons need to maintain their patrols."

"Don't worry," Lane said. "I'll convince them. I can't imagine they'll want to make an enemy of the kingdom."

Lane didn't know how right she was. "Any thoughts on your strategy?"

"Not yet. I need to hear all their complaints before I can figure out how best to address them."

"I assume your mother warned you the barons might be dangerous."

Lane nodded. "I think she's overly concerned."

"Either that, or we're walking into a trap."

"Does that worry you?"

Damien shrugged. "Not especially." He'd welcome a trap. It would eliminate all the stupid politics. If they attacked he'd counterattack and they'd all die. Problem solved.

They started up the steep trail, letting their horses pick their own path. If any conventional army tried to attack this place they'd be cut to pieces by the baron's archers before they ever closed on the keep. They reached the top without incident.

Two gatehouses bracketed a double set of portcullises. A guard stood behind the first portcullis. He wore mail and carried a sword at his waist. A dark beard streaked with silver marked him as a veteran. They reined in about four feet from the gate.

Lane pulled out her badge. "I'm from the diplomatic corps. The barons are expecting me."

"Yes, ma'am. You're the last to arrive. Open the gate!" The inner and outer portcullises clanked up until they could ride underneath. "Go on in. Master Miles, the baron's majordomo, is expecting you."

"Thank you." Lane went through first and Damien followed a moment later.

Damien nodded as his horse walked past, one soldier to another. The gate guard seemed competent. Hopefully the rest of the guards were cut from the same mold.

Halfway across the yard a pair of boys came running. Damien swung down, collected his gear, and handed his reins to a blond youngster about ten. Why was it always stable boys? You'd think there'd be a stable girl somewhere.

The boys led the horses and mule away as the double doors to the keep swung open. A man in his fifties with an oiled goatee and a long, forest-green robe strode out, his staff of office tapping on the stone. He came down three steps, paused, and bowed to Lane.

"Officer Thorn, welcome to Kannon Keep. I received word from your august mother, informing me of your assignment. I do so hope you can straighten out this business with the taxes and soldiers. My lord has been so terribly upset he hasn't slept the night through in months."

Lane plastered on a fake smile. "I'll certainly do my best. After all everyone wants this matter cleared up as quickly as possible."

Miles beamed. "My thoughts exactly. Follow me, please. Your bags will be brought up presently. We've arranged for you and your bodyguard to have adjoining rooms. I trust that's convenient?"

The last was addressed to Damien and he nodded. "Perfect, sir. It seems you've thought of everything."

Miles laughed. "That's my job, young man."

The majordomo led them inside. The doors opened directly into a great hall. A huge fireplace blazed with a tree's worth of wood. A golden chandelier, its fifty candles unlit, hung from the ceiling. A second-floor balcony overlooked the hall. Miles guided them to a set of steps leading upstairs. A couple of twists and turns later they came to a pair of doors fifteen feet apart.

"Your rooms," Miles said. "Should you need anything just use the pull rope and a servant will be along in short order. I'll leave you to prepare for the feast."

"Feast?" Damien asked.

"Of course. The annual gathering always opens with a great feast. It is my lord's honor to set the finest table. Never fear, there's always plenty of leftovers for the guards and servants."

Miles trotted off, his staff tapping away, no doubt to alert his master that they'd arrived.

“I need to clean up and change,” Lane said. “Did you bring something appropriate?”

“I think I have a clean tunic. I’m a guard, remember? I don’t need to dress up to enjoy the barons’ leftovers.”

Chapter 27

Damien stripped off his travel-stained clothes and tossed them on the bench at the foot of his oversized bed. The room they'd provided was every bit as luxurious as The Golden Stag. White silk sheets covered the bed, and a glow-stone lamp of blown glass rested beside it on the far nightstand. A jug of water and a basin sat on the nightstand beside him. If this was how the barons lived he couldn't see they had any room to complain about taxes. He'd pictured hard men living in rough forts surrounded by enemies. This place was every bit as nice as Uncle Andy's castle back at the capital.

Damien filled the basin and cleaned up. The cool, clear water felt wonderful on his dust-caked skin. A soft towel hung from the drawer pull and he used it to dry off before tossing it in the pile with his dirty clothes.

Now the question was, had his change of clothes stayed clean in his rucksack? He dumped it out on the bed and sighed his relief at finding the black cloth free of dirt. Behind him the door creaked. He spun to find Lane standing in the doorway that connected their rooms, her face bright red. She was staring at him, mouth partway open.

He slung the tunic over his head. "Didn't anyone teach you to knock? Some diplomat."

"Sorry. I just wanted to make sure you had something clean to wear. I see you do." She closed the door.

Damien shook his head, pulled on his pants, and buckled his sword on his back. Lane's reaction was typical of people seeing his scars for the first time. He should be used to it by now, but it gnawed at him all the same. At least they didn't bother Lizzy. Her being a demon, he suspected she'd seen a lot worse over the centuries.

Now all he had to do was wait for Lane to finish. He didn't know how long that would take, but he suspected from the stories he'd heard from some of the masters about their wives that he should get comfortable.

Chapter 28

Lane shut the door, her face burning. Why hadn't she knocked? If Damien had opened the door on her while she was getting ready she would still be screaming at him.

She sat on the edge of the bed and tried to slow her racing heart. When she closed her eyes she could still see the scars on his back. If that was the result of his warlord training someone needed to do something about it. It wasn't human to do that to a boy.

He wasn't a boy anymore though. She tried not to smile when she thought of the hard muscle under his scars. Her face burned hotter.

Stop thinking about him!

Damien was a sorcerer and she hated sorcerers. He was her bodyguard, a killer assigned to keep her safe. Nothing more. She'd treated him badly and he probably disliked her anyway. He'd certainly been annoyed when she walked in on him.

Following his example she stripped and poured a basin of water. The water cooled her down and she sighed. What was wrong with her, anyway? They'd traveled together for two and a half months and she'd felt nothing but annoyance at having him tag along. Though he had come in handy at that grubby inn and later with the thugs, Lane could admit that.

And that story about his father! Lane shuddered to think anyone could treat their child so callously. If nothing else her mother had always loved her and showed her nothing but kindness. Maybe she felt some disappointment that Lane wouldn't follow in her footsteps, but that never got in the way.

Lane had always been bitter about what she considered a miserable childhood. Now that she'd met someone that had an actual, horrific upbringing, Lane felt like a spoiled brat. She glanced at the door, half afraid she'd find him standing there watching her bathe and half hoping he would be.

Lane sighed and dried off. Another day or two more and this business would be settled and they'd part ways. Of course, Damien worked for her mother so she'd probably see more of him.

She dug a specially wrapped parcel out of her pack and found the seal intact. Good, no dust had slipped inside. Lane unwrapped the blue-and-silver gown and smiled. What would he think of her in this?

Chapter 29

Damien paced, waiting for Lane to finish getting ready. The masters hadn't lied, women really did take a long time. For a moment he was tempted to sneak a peek, it would only be fair, after all she'd seen him in just his small clothes.

He abandoned the idea at once. She'd kill him, sorcerer or not.

Lane knocked on the connecting door. Finally. "Come in."

The door swung open and his breath caught in his throat. Lane wore a blue-and-silver gown of fine silk that shimmered in the light of the lamp. The skirt fell to just above her knees, showing the curve of her calf. The neckline plunged just low enough to show off the tops of her smooth, freckle-dusted breasts.

"Wow."

"You like it?"

"Very much. You look stunning. Where did you hide that outfit?"

She beamed. "Mom sealed it in a package with soul force to keep dust out and prevent wrinkles."

Damien shook his head, stunned for the second time in as many minutes. How much skill would it take to weave a barrier that delicate and give it enough power to last ten weeks? He couldn't even fathom how to begin such a casting.

Lane held out her hand. "Shall we head down?"

Damien took her hand and for reasons he didn't fully understand, brushed a soft kiss across it. He let go and took up a position two steps behind her. "I'm your bodyguard not your companion, remember? Much as I'd enjoy it being otherwise, we both have to play our parts."

She looked sad for a moment, but shook it off. "Right, let's go."

They left their fine suite behind. Damien placed an invisible strand of soul force across both thresholds. If anyone entered the rooms while they were gone he'd know. Lane glided along through the cool stone halls. She had to be chilly in that dress.

Ten men in fancy outfits, many of them with medals pinned to their chests, stood around chatting in the great hall. Servants in black-and-white uniforms mixed with the barons. They carried trays loaded with little sandwiches or full glasses of wine. Along the walls ten armed men stood, seeming at ease, though their eyes never stopped moving, constantly scanning for danger. To a man they had cold, dead eyes. Killers' eyes.

Damien took a moment to study the gathered men and found several guards and two barons all had modest internal soul force. No surprise to find a few warlords in such a powerful gathering. Lucky for him all the guards were in their mid to late twenties and the barons older yet. No one would recognize him from The Citadel.

Conversation fell silent when Lane entered. Damien knew just how they felt. She smiled her fake smile, grabbed a drink from a passing servant, and headed toward the closest group of barons. Damien checked her drink with an invisible thread of soul force and found it free of poison. He sent out more threads, checking the rest of the drinks as well as the food.

He didn't expect to find anything. It would be too risky to poison the food in this setting. A baron might grab something he shouldn't. Satisfied that Lane wasn't in any danger at the moment, Damien went to stand in an empty space along the wall.

The older guards eyed him, sizing up the youngest member of their cohort. They didn't look impressed. That was fine with Damien. He didn't care what they thought of him and if they believed he was weak they might underestimate him. He crossed his arms and settled in for what he hoped would be a boring evening.

His gaze wandered from Lane to the barons, to the guards, but always returned to Lane. In that outfit she drew the eye of every man in the room. Damien frowned. At least some of the barons had to be married. Where were the wives?

"Hey." A big, broad-chested warlord sidled up beside Damien. He wore leather armor despite his soul force, whether to disguise the fact that he was a warlord or just because he liked the look Damien couldn't guess. A claymore hilt jutted up beside his ear and he looked like he knew how to use it. A thick black beard covered his face and his left eye was missing. He had an imposing look which no doubt served him well in his chosen career.

"Evening. Which one are you with?"

"Baron Trasker."

That focused Damien's attention. If their information was correct and Trasker had hired the assassin his bodyguard could be a source of information, or a threat. "Which one is he?"

"The bald one with all the medals. You're guarding the woman. She's the king's representative, right?"

Damien nodded, scanning the room for Trasker. There, chatting with Lane. Man, he did have a chest full of gold. How many wars had he fought in? He was a modestly strong warlord as well.

They seemed to be having a pleasant-enough chat. The baron didn't look like the sort of person that would hire an assassin, not that you could really tell.

"Why'd they send someone so young to guard such an important diplomat?" the guard asked.

"Got me. I don't pick and choose my missions. The higher-ups tell me where to go and I go. This job's been a breeze. ten weeks of riding through the wilderness, camping under the stars with a beautiful woman, and no one trying to kill me. If it was summer instead of winter it would have been perfect. They can send me on as many missions like this as they want."

"You don't sound too attached to your charge."

Damien shrugged. “I’m attached to getting paid. Anything happens to her and I’m liable to be out of a job.”

The bearded guard grinned. “You got the right attitude, kid. Name’s Sloan.”

“Damien.” They shook hands.

Miles emerged from a door at the rear of the hall. “My lords and lady, dinner is served.”

Chapter 30

Morana adjusted her tight, black dress and fluffed her curly copper hair as she walked down the dim tunnel. After she left that idiot Mikhail to return south, she'd flown to her master's base in the northern mountains, as bleak and desolate a place as she'd ever visited.

It suited Connor Blackman perfectly.

She approached the library Connor had carved out of the mountain and paused outside the entrance to pull the neck of her dress a little lower. Morana didn't know why she bothered. Connor never noticed her no matter how short her skirt or how low her top. Was it her or did he have no interest in women in general?

Morana squared her shoulders and stepped across the threshold. As always the darkness of the place struck her like a cold fist, sending a thrill through her whole body. How she wished to join Connor in this wonderful, consuming darkness. Soon, he'd promised her. For now he needed her soul force uncorrupted so she could move about as his agent in the wider world.

Connor had carved the library out of solid stone; the tables and bookcases were simply stone he'd left behind and shaped to his needs. Ancient tomes and scrolls covered the gray shelves alongside stranger artifacts like a horned demon skull that still retained eyes which followed her every move. If it had lips she suspected it would have licked them. The entire collection radiated demonic corruption.

She reached out to touch a black gem that pulsed with power, but caught herself before her fingers could brush the cold facets. Last time she touched something in his collection Connor had been very upset with her. She had the scars to prove it.

Morana strutted down through the rows toward the back of the room, swinging her hips in her best imitation of a cheap whore. She'd tried this trick before and, of course, he'd ignored her like always. Maybe this time she'd have better luck.

Connor sat in a stone chair turned inky black after years of absorbing his corruption. Long, black hair covered his face as he looked down at the blackened metal amulet in his hands. That artifact never left his possession. Morana had asked him about it once and he just smiled and said it was the key to eternity. Whatever that meant.

She stopped a safe distance from him and after a moment he looked up, veins black in his pale face, lips blue as a corpse, and eyes as crimson as blood. She shivered, wishing she had the courage to discover for herself if those lips felt as cold as they looked. "Master."

"Morana." The emotionless, precise voice showed her neither warmth nor affection. "How fare things in the city?"

She grimaced. He wasn't going to like this. "The Unkindness is finished and the death of the Santen family has been discovered."

Blue lips peeled back from clenched teeth. "The others?"

"Still in place and undiscovered."

"That's something, at least."

"Mikhail, that idiot, destroyed the gate."

She'd expected Connor to hit the roof at that, but he just waved a hand. "Doesn't matter. It was just a proof of concept. Now that I know it works I can move on to the next phase."

"Do you have another mission for me?" Please don't send me to join Mikhail.

"Return to Port Valcane. I have agents arriving in the near future and they may require your assistance. In the meantime see about gathering up whatever remains of the gang. I'm sure we can find some use for them."

"After Mikhail destroyed their base they may not want to work with us anymore."

Connor's gaze bored into her. "I trust you to persuade them."

Chapter 31

Damien followed Lane into the dining room. A long, cherry table filled the center of the room, the surface covered with elaborate settings for each guest, including five forks, three knives of various shapes, two spoons, and an odd hooked device that looked more appropriate for a torture chamber than a formal dining room. On each plate rested a vellum card with a guest's name written on it. Lane sat at the end of the left-hand row next to Baron Trasker. It may have been meant as an insult to stick her at the end of the table, but it pleased Damien as she at least wasn't surrounded by potential enemies.

A crystal chandelier hung over the center of the table, its scores of candles casting a warm glow throughout the room. In each corner a large green potted plant spread wide leaves. Lane and most of the barons took their assigned seats. The other guards stood against the wall behind their charges and Damien mimicked them, standing behind Lane. At the head of the table, Baron Kannon remained standing. He whispered something to Miles. The majordomo nodded and hurried out through another door. Behind it Damien caught a glimpse of the kitchen. The smell of spices and roasting meat wafted through the momentarily opened door.

Baron Kannon raised his hands and the mumbled conversations fell silent. Two young, female servants emerged from the kitchen, each bearing a bottle of red wine. Damien quickly scanned the wine as well as Lane's glass, plate, and utensils. No poison. So far so good.

When everyone had a full glass Baron Kannon said, "A toast, to another year of cooperation with my fellow barons, and continued good relations with the kingdom."

He addressed that last bit to Lane, who offered a polite nod. They all raised their glasses. "Hear, hear!"

Everyone drank and Baron Kannon took his seat at the head of the table. More servants emerged from the kitchen. They carried platters covered with little disks of bread smeared with some sort of gray mush. Damien didn't know what it was, but he was glad he didn't have to eat any.

He scanned the food and found no poison. The next two courses were salads, also poison free. By the time the soup came out Damien was starting to think they weren't going to try and kill Lane tonight. One of the pretty, young servants set a bowl of deep-red soup in front of Lane.

Damien's nerves jangled when he encountered an especially nasty poison floating in the steaming liquid. Lane lifted the larger of her two spoons as Damien rushed to gather all the poison into a small ball.

He managed it with half a second to spare before she dipped in for the first bite. He wrapped the poison in a soul force bubble, turned it invisible, and dumped it in the dirt around the farthest plant. It didn't instantly turn black, so the poison must not have been quite as bad as he feared.

For her part Lane chatted away with Trasker and the baron across from her, as fat a man as Damien had ever seen. No one gave her any searching looks like they were expecting her to fall face first into her soup. The poison was probably a slow-acting one, something that would sicken her overnight. Part of Damien wanted badly to kill them all on the spot, but he had to be sure all the barons were involved and not just Trasker.

The next three courses were clean, and smelled delicious. Dessert was some sort of whipped concoction topped with flames. Another poison was mixed with whatever accelerant produced the flames. Damien purified the food again and dumped the second poison in the same pot as the first. The edges of the plant's leaves turned brown.

The second poison must have enhanced the effects of the first. That was risky. If Lane hadn't cared for either the soup or dessert their plan might have failed even without Damien's interference.

"I don't know about you," Sloan said. "But I'm starving."

Spending the evening removing toxins from Lane's food had soured Damien's appetite. "I think I might be coming down with something. My stomach is a mess."

Sloan nodded. "I hear you. Some of this rich food is poison."

Chapter 32

Lane took her seat at the end of the row. The barons had probably stuck her there as an insult, but Lane refused to let it bother her. She had a job to do and petty tricks wouldn't stop her. She felt completely at ease knowing Damien stood behind her. Though she wouldn't deny having the young sorcerer along had annoyed her at first, he'd proven himself a skilled protector and pleasant companion. He might be the first sorcerer whose company she'd allowed herself to enjoy, outside her mother.

Across from her Baron Marris couldn't take his eyes off her chest. She smiled at him. "Baron Marris, how's your lovely wife?"

He grimaced and his face went white. "Fine." His voice sounded more strained than she'd expected.

Beside her Barron Trasker chuckled. "Well struck, my dear. I'm afraid we're all missing our wives. Given the tense situation with the kingdom we thought it best to leave them at home. It's been a lonely few weeks."

He didn't sound like a traitor. Did the barons really fear the king would target their families? Even if they voted to leave the kingdom, Lane didn't believe King Andrew would do anything to innocent women and children. She'd met the king several times and found him to be kind and decent.

"Rest assured, Baron Trasker, that the king would never do anything to bring harm to an innocent."

He patted her hand in a fatherly sort of way. "It's sweet that you believe something so naive, but in war there are no innocents and no one is off limits. The king will do what he must to keep his nobles in line." Trasker's voice turned hard. "And we will do what we must to protect our families."

Lane reconsidered her initial assumption. Maybe Trasker had betrayed the kingdom. If he truly believed his family was in danger he might not consider it treason, but rather a desperate attempt at self-preservation. If that were true, what else might these desperate men be driven to? Hopefully nothing too drastic. Nevertheless she found herself doubly glad to have Damien watching her back.

Baron Kannon made a toast and the first course arrived. Lane smiled, she loved pâté. She wasn't alone and soon everyone had polished off their appetizer.

"I don't suppose you'd care to give us a preview of the king's demands," Trasker said.

"You already know what he expects: the border secure and your taxes paid on time. I'm here to listen to your concerns and work out the details of a final agreement. I'm sure tomorrow's meeting will be productive and this ugly matter will be put behind us."

Trasker's smile seemed forced. "Of course, tomorrow."

The rest of the meal passed with little more than casual chitchat. None of the nobles pressed her for information. In fact no one seemed especially interested in the meeting tomorrow. The only interesting thing beyond the delicious meal was twice she would have sworn her food moved on its own. Lane must have drunk more wine than she thought.

When the servants had cleared the remains of dessert Lane felt full to bursting. Kannon rose again and said, "Gentlemen and lady, I hope you enjoyed tonight's meal. Sleep well, for tomorrow we have much to do. If any of the bodyguards are hungry feel free to help yourselves to any leftovers in the kitchen."

The gathering broke up, and most of the barons headed toward their rooms. Several bodyguards jogged into the kitchen. Lane expected to see Damien among them, but he simply stood, hands behind his back, waiting for her.

She went over and put a hand on his shoulder. "Aren't you hungry?"

"I don't have much of an appetite this evening. Are you ready to head back?"

She'd planned to offer to wait while he went for something from the kitchen, but if he wasn't hungry there wasn't much point. "Sure. It doesn't look like they plan to do anything important tonight."

She headed for the door and Damien followed at the appropriate distance, his gaze darting around the room, trying to look everywhere at once. He looked more nervous than when they'd arrived. Had something happened she wasn't aware of?

Lane paused and looked back. "What's wrong?"

"Not a thing. Please keep going."

Lane knew a lie when she heard it, but clearly Damien didn't want the barons to hear what he had to say. Curious and a little anxious, Lane set as brisk a pace as she could and not look like she was fleeing back to her room. They arrived at their rooms and she reached for the door.

Damien grabbed her wrist and looked up and down the empty hall. He leaned in close and for a second she thought he meant to kiss her.

"Someone's been in our rooms," he whispered in her ear. "They're gone now, but they may have left a surprise. Let me go first."

Lane tried to swallow, but found her throat dry. Her over-full stomach churned. She nodded and he released her wrist.

The door to her side of the suite opened slowly. Damien still stood in front of her, shielding her from anything that might wait inside. Lane found herself glad to have a sorcerer for a bodyguard. She expected him to move, but Damien never even twitched. His body remained taut and his eyes alert as he examined the room with senses other than sight.

After five tense minutes he said, "It's safe."

Damien went through the door to her side of the room and waved her in. The moment she crossed the threshold he shut the door and threw the bolt. He concentrated for a moment then sighed. "I warded the room against eavesdropping so we can speak freely."

"How did you know someone had been in our room?" Lane sat on the edge of the bed.

"I put an invisible thread of soul force across the doorway. Someone snapped it halfway through dinner. It might have been a servant coming to see if the room needed cleaning, but I didn't want to take chances."

She smiled. "You're taking your role as bodyguard pretty seriously."

"It seemed prudent, especially considering someone tried to poison you at dinner."

Lane choked and burst into a coughing fit. She had to have misheard. Damien sat beside her and patted her back. When she could breathe again she said, "Poison?"

He nodded. "In the soup and dessert. Don't worry, I removed it and disposed of it safely."

She stared at him. "I thought my soup stirred on its own. That was you?"

"Yes. I didn't recognize the poison, but I wanted to be sure I removed it before you had a taste. Did any of the barons seem suspicious to you?"

"I only spoke to Trasker and Marris and they seemed tense, but no more than you might expect considering the circumstances. Perhaps the barons didn't know about the poison."

"Perhaps. If they're surprised when you walk into that meeting tomorrow you'll know for sure. Just make sure you don't eat or drink anything they offer."

No kidding.

Chapter 33

Damien left Lane in her room to try and sleep. Hearing you'd been targeted for murder could give a person insomnia. Still, he hoped she could get a little rest. The moment the connecting door closed behind him he sent streams of soul force around every inch of the suite. He sealed the doors and every crack so tight an ant couldn't find a way through.

In truth he didn't expect anything to happen tonight. Whoever tried to kill Lane had no way of knowing she didn't eat the poison. When she walked into the meeting in the morning, however, all hell might break loose.

He hoped it did.

The instant anyone made an overt move against Lane the negotiations would be over and he'd have a free hand to handle things however he wished. He'd gotten to like Lane and the fact that they'd tried to kill her made him want to deal harshly with the barons.

He sighed and lay down. Everything was so complicated.

Damien woke early and found his barrier intact and no sign that anyone had attempted to breach it. Good. For once things seemed to be going how he expected.

The meeting was scheduled to begin around midmorning, leaving him four or so hours to kill. His stomach rumbled. He hadn't eaten since lunch the day before. Maybe he could sneak down to the kitchen and find some untainted food for breakfast. With the suite sealed Lane was in no danger.

Damien had no interest in conversation so he wrapped himself in invisibility before leaving his room. He scanned the hall outside before he stepped out. If anyone saw the door open and close by itself they might grow curious.

The kitchens were at the rear of the castle on the first floor. Damien strolled through the empty halls, seeing no one save a servant hurrying along, carrying a mop and sloshing bucket of water, and completely unaware that he was walking a couple feet to her right. Damien smiled. It was fun walking around with no one knowing he was there.

Damien smelled the kitchen long before he reached it. The pleasant, yeasty scent of bread mingled with cooking bacon. His mouth watered. A bacon sandwich and cold mug of ale would suit him just fine. Knives thunking into cutting boards and someone shouting about burning rolls told him he was getting close.

He rounded the corner in time to see one of the bodyguards from last night grab a servant by the arm and drag her away from the kitchen door. He didn't know the man, Damien had only spoken to Sloan. What could he want with the servant?

Damien could only think of one thing and if that's what the bodyguard wanted Damien would have to step in. He followed them down a long hall toward the back of the castle. The guard pushed a door open and dragged the girl out into the yard. Damien slipped through the open door and followed them toward the stable. It looked like he had the right idea.

Damien almost canceled his invisibility, but hesitated. He didn't want to give himself away unless he absolutely had to. The girl wasn't screaming for help, but from her frightened eyes and pale face he felt certain she didn't want to be going along with him. Maybe she knew no one would help if one of the barons' bodyguards wanted to have his way with her.

They ducked into the stable and Damien hurried up behind them. If he pushed her down into a pile of hay Damien would step in, disguise be damned. He peeked through the doorway. The guard had released the servant and she rubbed a red spot on her arm where he'd gripped her.

"You didn't have to be so rough," the girl said.

"I had to make it look like I was dragging you off for a tumble. Do you have any poison left?"

Damien tensed. Were these two behind the attempt to kill Lane?

The servant dug two little pouches out of a pocket in her uniform. "There isn't much. I put two scoops in the woman's food like you said."

The man snatched the poison out of her hand and stuffed it in his pocket.

"When can we leave? If I have to put up with one more of Master Kannon's pinches I fear I may slap him."

"Soon." The bodyguard held out his arms and she went to him. The girl buried her face in his chest and he held her with one arm. The other arm reached around and pulled a dirk from a sheath at the small of his back. "Don't worry, I'm almost done."

Damien wrapped the girl in a soul force barrier an instant before the bodyguard tried to stab her in the gut. The servant's eyes went wide when his weapon bounced off her uniform. Damien wished he could have seen the look on the bodyguard's face.

He slipped into the stable, wrapped the man up in a cocoon of soul force, and stiffened the shield around the servant so she couldn't move. With his prisoners secure, Damien let his invisibility fade. The girl's eyes got even wider and the bodyguard tried to move, but only managed to fall over. Damien surrounded the stable with a sound barrier so no one would overhear them.

"I think we need to talk." He turned to the girl. "You put poison in Lane's food?"

Her lip trembled. "He promised to take me away. He said to just put a little powder in her food and she'd get sick and not be able to finish the negotiations. It's so awful here. I just wanted to escape."

Stupid girl. "You'll find the mines a good deal less comfortable, assuming they don't hang you."

She started bawling and Damien gagged her with a strip of soul force. He should feel sorry for her. The guard clearly used her and it sounded like the baron took advantage of her. Maybe if she'd poisoned Kannon he would have been more understanding.

He turned his attention to the bodyguard lying on the ground. The cocoon around his head vanished.

"Help! Sloan! James! Anyone!"

Damien crouched beside him. "No one can hear you. We're going to have a chat. If you tell me what I want to know I won't crush you into a bloody mush."

"I won't tell you anything." He spat at Damien.

Thankfully the spit slid right off Damien's personal shield. Damien clenched his fist and the cocoon shrank, squeezing the guard's body. The man gasped for breath.

"Who told you to kill Lane?"

"Go to hell!"

Damien shook his head and squeezed again. The guard moaned and fell silent when he couldn't refill his lungs. Damien let him suffocate for a minute before he allowed the guard take a breath.

"The next squeeze will break ribs. Consider your words carefully."

"All right, I'll tell you whateve—"

The guard screamed when dark fire shot out his eyes and ears. Black tar oozed out of his nose and he stopped breathing.

"Damn it!" Damien slammed a fist on the stable wall. A warlock had put a binding on him. Poor bastard probably didn't even realize it. He turned to the servant and found her unconscious on the stable floor. "Damn it!"

Now who could tell him what was going on?

Chapter 34

Lane yawned, stretched, and rolled out of the soft, warm bed. After Damien's revelation about the poison it had taken her a while to relax enough to fall asleep. Her beautiful dress hung in a wardrobe. She wouldn't be wearing it to today's meeting. This would be all business.

She debated telling the barons about the poison, but if they were behind it she'd be alone in a room with ten men who wanted her dead. If she kept her mouth shut it would probably be safer. Safe was good.

Her stomach groaned and she reached for the pull rope. Her arm was halfway to the silk cord when she caught herself. What if they brought more poisoned food? Better wait until Damien was up and could check it. She pulled a tunic over her head, but didn't bother with trousers.

Lane studied her long, bare legs. Plenty of men had complimented her on them and she wondered what Damien's reaction would be when she walked in. She smiled, a little heat in her cheeks.

Lane had spent some time with men, of course, but never anything serious. Most found her mother too intimidating and she was often busy on a diplomatic assignment. Some found her success hard to take, but she hadn't gotten to be one of the kingdom's top diplomats by worrying about some man's disapproval. Ultimately the only man she had to please wore the crown.

Damien didn't strike her as the type to be intimidated by a successful woman, or anything else for that matter. His door opened then thumped shut. He'd been up and gone out already? She took a deep breath and let it out slow. Was she really considering getting involved with a sorcerer? She didn't even know if Damien liked her. Considering how she'd treated him for most of the trip it wouldn't surprise her if he couldn't stand her.

Well, all she could do was apologize and tell him how she felt. If he rejected her she couldn't blame him.

Lane knocked once on the connecting door and pushed it open. Her jaw dropped. Damien was halfway across the room, an unconscious girl over one shoulder and a basket in the opposite hand.

He stopped and looked over at her, a sheepish smile on his face. He held out the basket. "I brought breakfast."

A million questions whirled in Lane's head, but she couldn't force a single one past her lips. She took the basket from him and Damien continued on to the wardrobe. The doors opened at his approach and he set the girl gently inside before closing them.

He rolled his shoulders and turned back toward her. All Lane could manage was to stare dumbly at him, the unopened basket still in her hand.

He took the basket back and sat on his bed. When he opened it the mouthwatering aroma of bread and bacon wafted out. Her stomach groaned and jolted her out of her stupor.

"Why did you carry an unconscious girl into your bedroom?"

A golden table appeared in front of Damien and he spread the contents of the basket out on it. "She's the one that tried to poison you yesterday."

Lane sat beside him. "What happened?"

Damien told her about his adventure this morning. "So when the hellfire ward went off and the guard's charred brains leaked out his nose the girl fainted. She saw me use sorcery and tried to kill you once already, so I decided to take her into custody. I put a block in her brain that'll keep her out for a day or so. The real question is, what do you want to do now?"

Lane's head spun. This was too much for her. She was a diplomat and she'd dealt with some tricky situations over the last three years, but murder and warlocks were beyond her comfort zone. Way beyond. Damien just looked at her while he ate a bacon sandwich.

"Is the warlock in the area?" she asked.

He swallowed and took a drink from a skin of ale. "I doubt it. I would have sensed a powerful, corrupt soul force if it was within a few miles. Do you still want to go to the meeting?"

She nibbled on a piece of bacon and frowned. "Do you think they're in on it? Trying to kill me, I mean."

"I don't know. I don't know a lot of things. The guard's brain melted before he could tell me anything useful. It's risky if you go, but their reactions will tell you a lot about how involved they are. I disintegrated the guard's body so no one will know he's dead. Since the girl is missing too, I hope the others will think they ran off together."

Lane finished her bacon and started peeling an orange, the mindless task occupying her hands while she thought. How did this mission become so complicated? First the thugs in Allentown, then the poison, a dead guard and unconscious servant, not to mention the fact that she feared she was falling for her bodyguard. She wanted to throw her hands up and scream.

"If you wanted orange juice I could have squeezed some for you."

Lane stared at him, uncomprehending. What was he talking about? She followed his gaze down to her hands. She'd crushed the orange to pulp without noticing the sticky juice running down her finger into a golden cup.

Damien smiled, stood, and walked over to the bedside stand. He poured water, soaked a cloth, and wrung it out. Lane accepted the proffered cloth and cleaned her sticky fingers.

"Thanks."

"Sure. This'll all work out. If you want to go through with the meeting I can wrap you in a shield of invisible soul force. The barons could beat on you with a sledgehammer and you wouldn't break a nail. As long as you don't eat or drink anything you'll be fine."

Some of the tension oozed out of her. Damien's reassurance set her mind at ease. "Let's do it."

Chapter 35

Two hours later found Damien standing in a little room with nine other guys. No chairs had been provided, no food or drinks either. When he and Lane arrived several of the guards had tensed, but they made no overt moves. Lane went right through a second door to join the barons. He'd caught a glimpse of a large table surrounded by leather chairs before the door closed.

Lane had guts going in there, even with his shield protecting her. He respected that. She'd gotten a lot friendlier since Allentown. Damien didn't know who'd been more surprised when she walked in on him carrying the girl. He'd almost dropped her when he saw Lane standing there in just her tunic, her legs bare from mid-thigh. Maybe it was her way of making up for walking in on him when he was washing up.

A little smile curled his lip. He appreciated the gesture.

"Want to let us in on the joke?" Sloan had made his way across the empty room to stand beside Damien.

"No. Say, aren't we a man short?" Damien looked around as though trying to spot the dead guard.

Sloan grimaced. "Dade was sweet on one of the serving girls. Looks like they ran off."

Damien nodded. “Not very professional.”

“No. What about your charge? Did she sleep well?”

Damien shrugged, trying to appear nonchalant. “She didn’t complain. That’s all I care about.”

“I hear you. I swear Trasker is always bitching about something. The room’s too hot or too cold. The food doesn’t suit him. You’d think I was the man’s valet instead of his bodyguard.”

Sloan was trying to act natural, but the question about Lane and the fact that Dade shouted for him made a lie of the act. With a supreme act of willpower Damien restrained himself from blasting Sloan to ash. “I’ve never been assigned to guard a nobleman. From the sounds of it I don’t want to either.”

“Ha! You got that right, kid. The sooner this meeting ends and I can dump the old fart off on his own people the better.”

The meeting went on for three hours before they broke for lunch. No poison was included with the food and an hour after the meal they went back to it. Damien tried to stay sharp, but damn it was boring standing around the empty little room. After his initial chat with Sloan none of the other guards approached him.

Finally, late in the evening, an exhausted Lane staggered out of the meeting room. “We’re done, and I’m beat. Let’s go.”

Damien escorted her back to their rooms. Neither of them spoke until he raised a sound barrier. “How’d it go?”

She sighed and slumped down on the edge of his bed. “We chased our tails for eight hours. They argued minor, meaningless points to death. None of them seemed to have come to a consensus about what they actually want the king to do. It’s like they don’t want a deal at all.”

“Did they seemed surprised to see you?”

“No. If any of them knew about the poison they’re excellent actors.”

Damien frowned and paced around the room. What in heaven’s name was going on here? “How did you leave it with the barons?”

“We’re going to try again tomorrow afternoon. I frankly can’t see much point, but I’ll do my best given the alternative.”

The alternative wasn’t what she imagined, but he’d give her one more day before he carried out his orders.

Chapter 36

A hand clamped over Lane's mouth. She struggled and tried to scream for Damien. Warm breath on her ear then Damien's voice, barely a whisper. "Relax, it's me. Someone's trying to pick the lock to my room."

Lane's racing heart slowed and she stopped fighting. Damien's hand slipped off her mouth. "What do we do?"

"You don't do anything. I'm going to let them in and capture them. Maybe I can get something before their brains melt."

In the pitch-black room Lane's sense of hearing seemed heightened. She imagined she could hear the scraping of the lock pick in Damien's door. A faint click sounded and a dim light showed under the connecting door.

She held her breath. What was happening?

The sound of tearing cloth then angry shouts. Damien uncovered her glow lamp. Lane winced and squinted her eyes at the bright light. When her vision cleared she found Damien, fully dressed, sitting beside her on the bed.

He grinned. "We caught three little fish. Shall we go see what they have to say for themselves?"

"I have to get dressed."

He nodded. "I'll go check things out. Don't worry, I won't start the questioning until you're ready."

Damien left and Lane rolled out of bed. She took several deep breaths, trying to bring herself under control. When she fantasized about having Damien visit her room this wasn't what she had in mind. Lane shook out yesterday's tunic and pants and slipped into them. She groped around under the bed for her boots then pulled them on. She didn't bother washing up.

She opened the connecting door and found Damien standing over three golden cocoons laying on his bed. He turned her way and smiled. "Ready?"

Lane crossed the room and stood beside him. "Ready."

The energy covering the three men's heads vanished and they started yelling. Lane winced at the noise, but Damien just watched them, cold and indifferent. A minute passed before they finally gave up and fell silent.

"As you've no doubt realized, no one is coming to your rescue," Damien said. "I'm going to ask you some questions. You're going to answer me honestly. If you don't, I'll make you scream until your throats bleed."

The captive men went pale and Lane knew how they felt. Damien threatened them in such a matter-of-fact way it sent a chill down her spine. She didn't think he was just saying it for effect either.

Damien pointed at the first man and he flinched. "Let's start with you. Who sent you to kill Lane?"

The prisoner opened his mouth but nothing came out. Damien shook his head. "I've blocked the portion of your brain that controls lies. You'll either speak the truth or you won't speak at all. Who sent you?"

The captive man clenched his jaw and remained silent.

Damien sighed and turned to her. "Did you know a sorcerer can directly stimulate the pain receptors in a person's brain, causing them extreme agony without resorting to cutting or breaking bones? I've never done it, but it looked simple enough. Of course, if I use too much power the subject's head might explode, but we have spares and I'm sure I'll get it right before I kill all of them."

Lane stared in growing horror at Damien. Why was he telling her all this? The last thing she wanted to know was how a sorcerer could best torture people. When one of the prisoners whimpered Damien winked at her. Lane released the breath she hadn't known she was holding. He was just playing, trying to convince them to talk without hurting them.

Damien turned his attention back to the prisoners. "So who wants to go first?"

"Wait!" the center man said. "Sloan sent us. He's in charge of the guards."

"Shut up!" the right-hand prisoner said. The cocoon wrapped his head up and he fell silent.

"Keep talking," Damien said.

"Sloan said if the king's envoy was killed while visiting one of the barons' keeps the barons wouldn't be able to back out. Since the poison didn't work he sent us. We were going to kill you first then the girl."

Lane blanched at the casual way the prisoner said he was sent to kill her. Like it was no big deal. Maybe to him it wasn't.

"Who are you people?" Damien asked. "You're obviously not kingdom men."

"The Bandit King sent us to keep an eye on the barons. Our master feared they lacked the spine to uphold the bargain they struck."

"What bargain?"

"I don't know the details. Our master offered them something in exchange for leaving the kingdom and swearing allegiance to him."

The bindings expanded to cover all the prisoners and Damien turned to Lane. "What do you make of that?"

She shook her head. Lane didn't know what to make of it. She now understood why they hadn't made much effort at negotiating. The barons didn't want a deal. They wanted her to give up and leave. "I don't know and I can't imagine what the bandits might have to offer the barons. I wasn't under the impression they had a single ruler. Everything I've read says the bandits work in small groups that fight with each other as much as they raid us."

"That was my understanding as well. Perhaps the warlock that put the hellfire wards in their heads is this Bandit King. That, at least, would make some sort of sense."

"I suppose. What are we going to do now?" Lane knew she was in charge of this mission, but it had become clear to her that she was in way over her head.

"First, I have to tell you something. Your mother didn't just send me to protect you. My secondary mission was to eliminate the barons if they proved unwilling to see reason."

Anger flashed through Lane. Had her mother believed her incapable of resolving this matter or did she know about the bandits and used Lane as a way for Damien to get close to his targets without drawing undue attention? Either way she should have trusted Lane enough to tell her.

"When were you planning on telling me?" Lane thought she managed to keep the resentment out of her voice.

"My instructions were not to tell you until absolutely necessary. If the negotiations went well you were to never know about my mission. That was the result we were all hoping for."

"You should have told me." Lane failed to keep the heat out of her voice.

Damien shook his head. "Not my decision. The archmage thought this was the way to handle things. It's hardly the place of a first-year sorcerer seven months out of the tower to question her."

Damien had a point, she knew that, but Lane needed someone to be angry with and Damien was here. "So what now? Are you going to go kill the barons?"

"I suppose I could, but I'm curious about what the Bandit King offered them that would make them betray their country. Once I hear their answer I'll decide whether to kill them for treason or not."

"What about them?" Lane jerked a thumb toward the cocooned assassins.

"The bindings will hold them for a day or two. Once I understand what's happening I can either leave them for the barons to deal with or execute them along with the traitors."

Lane stared in horror at him. "Just like that?"

Damien nodded, seeming untroubled. "They're murderers. As an agent of the king I'm well within my authority to execute them."

She remembered what he said as they left Allentown, about the ability to kill without hesitation or regret. Lane had thought he meant in battle, but now she realized it extended beyond that. She couldn't comprehend his way of thinking. Damien didn't seem to take any pleasure in killing, but he wasn't shy about it either. It seemed a part of his life, as ordinary as cleaning his teeth or shaving and as unworthy of comment.

The bound men floated off the top of the bed and flew under it, like bags being put under the bed for storage.

"Let's go talk to the barons," Damien said.

Lane couldn't manage more than a mute nod.

Chapter 37

Damien left the bound men under his bed and turned to Lane. "I'll turn us invisible. Stay close and keep quiet."

"What about the guards?"

"They won't be a problem."

Lane favored him with that horrified look again. You'd think he'd said he was going to drown kittens or something. Was she really so worried about a bunch of killers? How many people had these bandits murdered over the years? Yet she was looking at him like he was the bad guy.

Damien scanned the hall outside and found the way clear. He wrapped them in invisibility and they slipped out into the hall. The barons' chambers were in another section of the keep. With each step the hard soles of Lane's boots clicked on the stone floor. No way they'd be able to sneak up on the guards at this rate.

He stopped and Lane asked, "What's wrong?"

"Your boots are making too much noise." He held out his hand. "Hang on."

She gripped his hand and Damien conjured a floating disk under them. Lane stumbled, but he caught her. When she'd settled in Damien willed the disk down the hall. They made no more noise than a whisper of wind.

This late at night even the servants slept, allowing Damien to zoom along the halls at a good clip. Several twists and turns later found them at the end of a long hall that branched left and right. Ten doors lined the far wall and a guard stood in front of each one. They reminded Damien more of jailers than protectors.

He turned left and drifted to the last door. None of the guards reacted when they ghosted past. Damien studied the men in passing and soon realized they weren't the same group he'd seen guarding the barons during the day. Those men were probably sleeping. That worked out well for Damien as none of the night guards were warlords.

Damien wrapped the last guard in an invisible binding. The unfortunate young man couldn't even twitch without Damien's permission. He looked a little stiff, but unless one of the others came to talk to him he should pass inspection.

With the guard bound and helpless, Damien conjured a screen between them and the remaining guards so they could work without fear of being spotted. Lane gave the door a tug and shook her head. Locked.

That was no problem. A dark blob of energy the size of his finger appeared in the air and slid into the keyhole. Damien concentrated, shaping the key to the lock then twisting it. The tumblers snapped into place and they slipped through the open door.

Inside, the baron's room was pitch dark. Damien wrapped the room in a sound barrier then conjured a small light. Despite being in another section of the keep, the bedroom looked almost the same as Damien's, though the bed was a little bigger and had four posters. There was also a small fireplace for really cold nights.

A snoring heap of blubber lay sprawled on the bed, thankfully wearing a silk sleeping robe. Damien crossed his arms and stared at the man. "Which one is this?"

Lane grimaced. "Baron Marris. I thought you were going to kill the guard."

"Why?"

"You said—"

"I said the guards wouldn't be a problem, you assumed the rest."

She managed a weak smile. "I suppose I did. What now?"

"Now we wake the disloyal turd and see what he has to say for himself."

Damien conjured a needle and stuck the baron in his giant ass. The man yelped and sat up. He spotted Damien and Lane and glowered. "How dare you enter my—"

Damien silenced him with a soul force gag. "Baron, we know about your deal with the Bandit King. You're going to provide me with details then I'll decide if I should kill you or not. What did he offer you that made you betray your country?"

Damien removed the invisible gag so the now-trembling man could answer.

"Please. We didn't have a choice. They took our families, my wife, my son, and two daughters. He said if I did what they wanted everyone would be returned. I ne—"

The baron choked on whatever lie he was about to tell. The bit about his family, at least, was true. If the bandits had taken the barons' families it explained a lot.

"Trasker told me they left their wives and children at home because of the tension with the kingdom," Lane said. "And I bought it."

"No reason you shouldn't have. Under the circumstances it made a reasonable enough explanation. The real question is how did they grab the families, and where are they now? How about it, Baron? And don't try to lie to me again."

Marris cleared his throat. "I don't know where my family is and I don't know who took them. I saw a man, at least I assume he was a man, with pale skin, and black lines running under his skin like overfull veins. His eyes were crimson pits. He came to my castle, landed right in the courtyard. My guards tried to stop him, but he swatted them away like insects. We tried everything—swords, axes, arrows—but nothing fazed him. He wrapped my family in a black bubble and said unless I did what he wanted I'd never see them in one piece again."

"What, exactly, did he want?" Lane asked.

"He told me to leave the kingdom and swear allegiance to him. I said I needed to talk to the others and he gave us until our annual meeting to decide. My family has been gone for three months."

"That's too simple," Lane said. "The kidnapper had to know the king wouldn't just let you leave the kingdom."

"Unless the king was dead." The assassination attempt was starting to make more sense to Damien now. "If the assassin had succeeded it would have taken Karrie and her mother months to solidify their authority. By then who knows how many bandits might have crossed the border or how much damage they might have done."

Lane stared at him, her eyes wide.

"Didn't your mother tell you about the assassination attempt?"

Lane shook her head. "Apparently a couple of things slipped Mother's mind when she briefed me about this mission. What now?"

"We need to talk to the rest of the barons and see if we can learn anything else. Where's Trasker?"

Marris chewed his lip. "The opposite end of the hall. Please, don't let the guards know I talked. If word gets to the Bandit King my family's dead."

"How are we going to sneak past the guards to see the other barons?" Lane asked.

"I thought we'd take the direct route."

Damien pointed at the connecting wall and a golden beam lanced out from his finger. He sliced a disk out of the wall, pulled it out, and leaned it beside the hole. "See, no problem."

Damien and Lane visited the next eight barons and received almost identical stories. Their families had been taken and unless they did what they were told they'd be killed.

Before he approached the last wall Damien turned to Lane. "What do you think Trasker will have to say? He's the one that was supposed to have hired the assassin."

"If he was willing to leave the kingdom to keep his family safe I see no reason he wouldn't hire an assassin if so ordered."

"I suppose. Well, he can tell us himself in a second."

Damien sliced through the wall just as he had all the others. Trasker lay sleeping in his oversized bed. Lane was starting toward him when shouts sounded from out in the hall. Sounded like someone was raising the alarm. Damien poured power into the sound barrier changing it into a solid wall. That would keep the barons safe.

The door to Trasker's room burst open and a pair of guards charged in, their swords drawn. Damien wrapped them in golden cocoons. The guards fell to the floor, completely immobilized.

The baron sat up, sputtering. "What's going on here?"

Damien gagged him with a band of soul force. The baron mumbled unintelligibly and pawed at his mouth.

When no more enemies presented themselves Damien walked to the door and poked his head out. The hall was empty. Where'd the other guards go? Even the one he bound had disappeared.

Chapter 38

Damien raced back through the barons' rooms. Everyone was huddled in their beds just as he left them, all except Marris. The fat tub of goo was gone. He must have been the one that alerted the guards. The question was why. Damien couldn't imagine, but he hoped some of his prisoners could tell him.

He rejoined Lane in Trasker's room. The baron sat on the edge of his bed holding his head in his hands, a heavy dressing gown around his shoulders. "Marris is gone," Damien said.

Trasker looked up. "Of course he is. Marris belonged to the bandits long before this most recent assault. We could never prove anything, but we all suspected he allowed the bandits to slip across the border in exchange for a cut of their loot and a promise not to raid in his territory."

"It didn't occur to you to mention this to someone in the capital?" Lane sounded as outraged as Damien felt.

"We had no proof!" Trasker ground his teeth. "Without something solid it would have been an empty accusation. Marris would have brushed it off as nothing but envy on our part."

The man had a point, Damien had to concede that. Still, if the barons had at least mentioned their suspicions, agents of the crown could have kept an eye on Marris and tried to find proof.

The other barons gathered in the opening Damien had cut in the wall to listen in.

"Did you hire the assassin that tried to murder the king?" Damien asked.

"Yes." Trasker's head slumped into his hands again. "If I hadn't done it someone else would have. That pale monster threatened to send me my daughter's left foot if I refused."

"I don't suppose you know where your family is?" Damien asked.

Trasker gave a mute shake of his head.

"Marris might know," one of the barons in the other room said. "Or Sloan, the head guard."

Damien gestured and one of the bound guards floated upright. A quick search revealed the hellfire ward in the same place as the men that broke into their room. He neutralized the ward and caused the cocoon around the bandit's head to vanish, revealing a terrified face.

"Where did Marris and the rest run off to?" Damien asked.

The bandit opened his mouth, but no sound emerged when he tried to lie. Damien conjured a pair of blades and set them spinning a few feet from the man's head. "You'd better tell me or I'm going to slice your face off."

The bandit trembled. "South, half a day or so's ride there's a farm where we stashed horses and supplies, just in case. That's where they'll go before they head for the badlands."

"Thank you." Damien flung the man up against the wall. His head bounced off the stone with a dull thud and he slumped to the ground.

Damien turned to Lane. "I need to go after them. If you don't feel safe with the barons I can barricade you in your room until I return."

Lane looked at the huddled, frightened men. "I'll be okay here. Go."

Damien ran out the door, pausing long enough to seal the barrier and pour enough power into it to make it last until he got back or a day passed. He'd swing by the suite he shared with Lane and renew the binding on the three would-be assassins and the servant girl. Lane would be safe enough as long as she could handle the barons. Judging from the looks on their faces they wouldn't give her any trouble.

For their sakes they'd better not.

Chapter 39

The sun was just peeking over the horizon as Damien flew south, low over the trees, in the hopes of catching the bandits by surprise. He wasn't optimistic. Sloan struck him as a clever man and he'd have to know Damien would be pursuing them. After leaving Lane and the barons Damien had run to the castle's stables and found them empty.

A short ways ahead, the shingled roof of an old, weathered gray barn jutted up out of a clearing. That had to be the place. He hadn't seen another sign of life since leaving the castle.

Damien strengthened his shield before he landed in a dusty yard fifty paces from the barn. Tracks covered the ground as far as he could see, leading to the barn. This was the place all right. To his left the burned-out husk of a farm house jutted out of its root cellar. Whatever had happened, it looked like it was a long time ago.

Amplifying his voice with soul force, Damien shouted. "Come out of there and I might let you live."

Metal squeaked on metal as the barn door slid open. That had gone better than Damien hoped.

Ka-chunk!

A ballista bolt hurled out of the open door. He barely registered it before the iron-tipped bolt hammered into his chest. Damien flew back across the clearing, bounced twice when the bolt lost momentum, and skidded to a stop against the trunk of a twisted old oak.

He groaned and sat up, head spinning. Dizzy, but uninjured, Damien clambered to his feet and touched his chest. The bolt hadn't penetrated his shield. Thank heaven for that.

He turned his furious gaze on the barn. In the dim light figures rushed around, cranking the winch, carrying another bolt over and sliding it into the slot.

Damien frowned and leapt into the air. He flew five hundred feet straight up, hovered a moment, and then accelerated toward the barn roof. Dry timbers shattered when he struck. Splinters the size of daggers bounced off his shield. He hit the dirt floor and flooded the barn with white light.

Eight men surrounded him, one warlord and the rest regular warriors, squinting against the glare. The ballista rested on a swivel mount in the back of a wagon. The operator wrestled the heavy siege weapon around to point it at Damien. He managed to turn the ballista halfway before a blast of raw soul force obliterated both man and weapon.

Six of the survivors charged him, waving a mixture of swords and axes. Lances of golden energy pierced the bandits from every direction. Weaklings. They'd have been better off surrendering. The men collapsed and the lances' energy returned to Damien.

He turned to find the last man a foot from him, his iron-studded mace streaking for Damien's head. The mace bounced off his shield.

The bandit warlord's eyes went wide. Damien wrapped him from the neck down in soul force bindings.

He'd done it enough times now that removing the hellfire ward and putting the truth barrier in place took only a moment. Damien crossed his arms and glared. "Where are Sloan and Marris?"

The bandit's jaw clenched and he looked away. Damien conjured a golden blade and used it to force his prisoner to look at him.

Since he had just one prisoner Damien didn't dare try any of the fancy interrogation techniques he'd learned. "Talk or bleed."

"Go to hell, sorcerer."

Damien shook his head. Why were they all so stubborn? He drove his conjured blade into the bandit's shoulder. It sliced through the man's weak iron-skin technique like it was nothing. The bandit growled and clenched his teeth against the pain.

"You'll have to do better than that if you want to break me."

Damien caused needles to grow from the blade in every direction.

The bandit screamed as the needles burrowed into flesh and bone. After a couple of seconds Damien stopped them. "It only gets worse from here. Those needles take a long time to burrow to your heart."

His prisoner panted and tried to swallow. He didn't talk.

Damien shrugged. "Have it your way."

"Wait! They rode south, back to base. Marris is going to have the prisoners killed."

That was no surprise. "Where is this base?"

"Across the border. Twenty miles south and a little east. You can't miss it, it's the only building in the area."

"Tell me more about your base."

"Can't you take this thing out of my arm?"

Damien made the needles grow another inch, prompting a shout of pain. "The base."

The bandit snarled. "It's an old stone fortress built into a rock formation. The bosses found it years ago, before my time, cleared out the scruffs, and moved in."

Damien raised an eyebrow. "Scruffs?"

"Big, ugly lizards, with frills around their necks. We call 'em scruffs. Three hundred of us live there, though most of the time it's just forty or fifty. There's dungeons on the lowest level. That's where they took the women and kids."

"What about the Bandit King?"

"That freak, him and his muscle. He showed up one day, maybe six months ago, and says we all work for him. That got a laugh. The way he killed the old chief didn't. You're an amateur compared to him. He made us all watch. When he finally finished he announced again that we all worked for him. No one argued. He hung around for a couple months then flew off. We haven't seen him since."

"Who's in charge now?"

"Sloan and Janson handle the day-to-day stuff. That big armored bastard comes by once in a while to make sure we're doing what we're supposed to. Like we'd be stupid enough to do anything else."

Damien nodded. He had a pretty good handle on things now. "Thank you. You've been very helpful."

He sliced the bandit's head off with a conjured blade. Now he had to catch Sloan and Marris before they could warn the others their plan had failed.

Chapter 40

Damien floated far above the ground, searching for signs of movement. Dealing with the bandits at the farm had taken less than an hour so the rest couldn't be too far ahead of him. If Sloan and Marris kept to the forest he might miss them, but a mile or so from the border the thick hardwood gave way to scrub and eventually a mix of sand and gravel. He'd have no trouble spotting them when they emerged. The bandit he'd questioned told him everything he needed to know in order to rescue the hostages so there was no need to capture either the baron or Sloan.

Lane's disapproving face appeared in his mind's eye. No, she wouldn't like it if he killed them out of hand. Contrariwise he felt like both men had earned a death sentence. As a high-ranking bandit Sloan had no doubt done many horrible things and Marris was a traitor to his country and his people. Damien considered that the worse crime.

He caught movement through a gap in the branches. Damien dove toward the opening, flashing through the leaves and shattering branches. On the ground he found two horses racing away, their saddles empty.

Damn it!

No way Marris was running for it. Either they had extra horses or—

Something heavy landed on Damien's back, driving him to the ground. A dagger pounded his ribs, trying with no success to penetrate his shield. More annoyed than hurt Damien sent spikes of soul force out his shield and into whoever was on top of him.

The rain of blows stopped and he shrugged off his attacker. Halfway to his feet someone kicked him in the back of the head. He dropped back into the dirt. Snarling, Damien conjured a whirlwind of blades around his body. Bits of his attacker spattered him.

Satisfied that he wouldn't be attacked again, Damien clambered to his feet. Eight bandits surrounded him, with Sloan in the center, a curved blade dripping black flames in his right hand. The weapon's corruption made Damien nauseous.

Eager to end the fight Damien sent his barrier of blades flying toward the bandits. Most of them fell, pierced repeatedly. Sloan blurred and his horrific weapon sliced every golden blade that came close out of the air before it hit.

Damien grimaced. He was in for a fight now.

He sent more power to his shield an instant before Sloan appeared a couple feet away. His sword snaked toward Damien's face at warlord speed. The tip skipped off Damien's shield. Even though it didn't penetrate, Damien's skin burned under his barrier where the corrupt blade had touched it.

Sloan recovered from his failed attack in half a heartbeat. The blade darted back in for another try.

Damien expanded his shield, pushing it out from his skin. Once again the corrupt blade skipped off. It sickened Damien, but didn't burn him.

Like a tornado of steel Sloan slashed over and over again. His sword couldn't break through, but every blow drained a little of Damien's power. It wouldn't happen fast, but eventually Sloan would wear him down.

He couldn't let that happen.

Damien sent soul force into the ground. It burrowed under his shield and sprang up around Sloan's ankles. Tentacles of golden energy wrapped around the bandit's legs. Thorns shot out, piercing Sloan to the bone and locking him in place.

Sloan ripped his right sleeve back, revealing a black tattoo of a horned skull. He dragged his thumbnail across the skull. Blood welled and burst into dark flames.

The flames surged across Sloan's body, burning the thorns and tentacles away and healing his wounds. The bandit threw his head back and howled like an animal.

Damien leapt for the sky. He needed to put some space between them. Sloan wouldn't be able to channel that much corrupt soul force very long. The smart move was to wear him down from a distance, then when Sloan collapsed, finish him.

Sloan must have known it too. He leapt twenty feet up, kicked off a small maple with enough force to shatter the trunk, and arced over to an old oak. His boots landed on a gnarly branch. He kicked off again, sailing straight toward Damien.

Damien powered higher. There was no way a warlord, even augmented with demonic soul force, could leap as high as Damien could fly.

The burning sword swung toward Damien. Black flames streaked up. Damien dodged the first burst, but the stream twisted like a serpent.

Damien drew more power. Somehow he put enough energy between him and the flames that they didn't consume him. They did drive him down into the ground with enough force that his body embedded six inches into the forest floor.

Sloan landed fifty paces away, panting. Veins had burst in his face and black blood dripped to the dirt, sizzling where it hit. He couldn't keep this up much longer and Damien still had half his power left.

A quarter of Damien's soul force went into a pair of golden griffins. The constructs rushed at Sloan. Gleaming claws slashed and curved beaks snapped.

With insane speed even Jen would have envied, Sloan blocked every attack and somehow found openings to carve chunks out of the griffins. Another vein burst in the bandit's forehead. Blood ran down his face, but it didn't seem to faze him. Damien fired an energy blast. If he could score a hit or even distract the warlord the griffins would tear him to shreds.

If someone asked, Damien would have had no way to describe how Sloan twisted his body to avoid the blast. Bones weren't supposed to bend like that. However he managed it, the golden blast brushed past Sloan's chest with a fraction of an inch to spare.

Sloan turned his twisting dodge into a pivot that brought the edge of his burning sword across the neck of a griffin. The construct's head fell away and vanished, though that accomplished nothing beyond removing one of the beaks Sloan had to dodge.

When the bandit turned his attention to the more-intact griffin Damien sent a surge of power into the damaged construct. Ten blades of energy sprang from its severed neck to plunge at Sloan.

He dodged and deflected, but couldn't avoid them all. Two swords scored deep slashes on his back and chest. Dark fire dripped from the wounds. The injured bandit gasped for breath. His sword wavered.

The griffins lunged. With a final effort Sloan cut them in half with a single stroke of his corrupt blade. Three quarters of the way through the second griffin, the steel shattered. Sloan collapsed under the dissolving beasts.

Damien eased over to the dying bandit, cautious of any potential deception. When he stood over the unmoving bandit it became clear Sloan had nothing left. Thick, black blood covered him from his hairline to his waist. He stared up at Damien.

"I lost." Sloan coughed up blood and spat to one side.

Damien nodded. "You put up a good fight."

The bandit laughed, his voice hoarse and bitter. "Not good enough. My master promised the demon fire would defeat any opponent."

"Did he tell you it would burn away your life as well?"

"So what. Wining is all that matters. If you're going to die, better to send your enemies to hell before you."

Damien shook his head. It isn't winning if everyone died. "Where's Marris?"

"Dead. I gutted the pig and left him on the side of the path. He was slowing us down."

So much corrupt energy swirled around Sloan's head Damien couldn't tell if he was lying or not. The part about slowing them down was certainly true.

"Finish me, boy. At least allow me the dignity of dying by the hand of my enemy rather than being consumed by these black flames."

Damien raised a hand and drew deeply from his rapidly refilling core. He didn't do it for the dignity of the fallen bandit or anything else so ridiculous. The corruption needed to be cleansed to eliminate the possibility of Sloan rising again as some undead horror that might threaten the area.

Golden flames roared from the air in front of Damien's palm. Sloan's body disintegrated in an instant and his shattered sword followed a few seconds later. Damien incinerated everything in the vicinity of Sloan's body then hunted down every drop of black blood on the ground and burned those away too.

He didn't stop until every trace of corruption was gone. Exhausted, but nowhere near finished, Damien turned his gaze southeast.

Chapter 41

Damien allowed himself an hour's rest after the battle with Sloan. He wished he'd taken the time to bring his writing supplies so he could let his master know what had happened. He settled for tearing a relatively clean strip of cloth out of one of the dead bandits' tunics. He conjured a pen and dipped it in the corpse's fresh blood. A gruesome way to write, but Damien had limited options. He sent the message on its way and stood up.

Most of his power had returned and he figured the rest would regenerate during the short flight south. He leapt in the air and moved along at a modest pace. Below him the hardwood forest gradually gave way to patchy, twisted evergreens. Soon enough the vegetation went away altogether, save for the occasional clump of scraggly grass. Hot, dry wind struck his face.

The badlands spread out before him in shades of brown, gray, and dull orange. Towering mesas dotted the otherwise featureless desert. One of them must house the bandits' fortress. Damien assumed from the directions the dead bandit had provided that the first mesa he came to flying southeast would be the target.

He wrapped himself in invisibility and flew toward the stone tower. The trip only took five minutes and he soon found himself hovering fifty feet off the ground facing a massive wood-and-iron double door. A well-worn path led up to the gates. It looked like they received regular visitors. Higher up on the rock face narrow slits looked out over the approach. Damien peeked inside and found every third one had a lookout. They all seemed alert and their bows well oiled and in good condition. These men resembled real soldiers rather than scruffy bandits.

Damien landed a short distance away behind some boulders and wracked his brain trying to think how he could get the women and children out in one piece. He could blast the place to pieces easily enough, but at the first sign of trouble the hostages would be killed. That wouldn't do at all.

A little ways to his left, movement caught Damien's eye. A narrow head covered in tan fur popped up out of a hole, looked around, and vanished again. A second later the little guy popped up from another hole twenty feet from the first. Damien grinned. The prisoners were underground. A tunnel would be the perfect way to slip them out.

He tipped an invisible salute to the critter that inspired him and flew away. Damien would need a hidden place to dig. The terrain was so open the lookouts would notice at once if he just started flinging dirt around. He circled the mesa, hoping to spot something not too far from the fortress. On the back side a clump of trees grew maybe a mile away. That could work.

Damien slipped through the palm fronds and landed beside a small pit filled with water. He scanned it and found the water pure. There was probably an aquifer deep underground that bubbled up in this little oasis. The bandits must have tapped it as well. They couldn't survive out here without a good source of water.

Now that he had a starting point Damien needed to find out exactly where the prisoners were. It'd be a hell of a thing to discover he tunneled into a storage room instead of the dungeon. He sat with his back to a palm tree, conjured a spy bug, and connected it to a viewing rectangle.

When he was satisfied with the link Damien sent the spy buzzing toward the fortress. The tiny wasp flew through an unwatched arrow slit and flitted down a long, empty corridor. He needed to find stairs. The corridor ended at an intersection and Damien guided the bug left, deeper into the fortress. Halfway down the hall he reached a loose-fitting door. The bug crawled underneath and went down a set of steps to a massive open chamber filled with benches and tables. There had to be enough seats for five hundred people. At the far end of the chamber a pair of guards stood at attention beside a closed door.

That looked promising. The bug slipped through a gap in the frame and flew down another set of stairs. At the bottom was a circular depression filled with water. Now he was getting somewhere. This had to be the bottom floor. Now where was the dungeon?

Two archways led out of the well chamber. Damien had good luck with left before so he tried it again. The spy bug flew into a chamber filled with sacks, crates, and joints of meat hanging from the ceiling. A pantry, great. So much for lucky left.

A short ways through the opposite arch was a locked door with a small barred window. That was more like it. Wherever there were bars the dungeon couldn't be far off. The bug flew through the bars into a hall with cages on either side. Filthy, gaunt women and children filled the cells. Once-fine clothes were torn and caked with dirt. The women held on to the little ones, trying to offer what comfort they could.

Four men sat around a rickety table, passing a bottle and playing cards. This must be where they stuck the lazy guards. Lucky for Damien, less lucky for the guards.

The spy flew to a bare section of wall and fused with it, changing color to blend in. Now Damien had a target, he just needed to hit it.

Chapter 42

Damien drew a quarter of his power and conjured a digger. Nothing fancy, a crude body with massive arms ending in long claws. The construct burrowed down at an angle, flinging dirt behind it as it went. Once it dug a ways down, golden buckets formed to drag the dirt out of the tunnel followed by regular arches for support. Damien frowned as his constructs worked. This was taking a lot more power than he expected.

When the digger reached a depth Damien sensed was even with his marker he sent it straight toward the fortress. His constructs worked tirelessly, scraping away rock and dirt and spreading it out behind him. Foot by foot, hour by hour the tunnel grew, until sixteen hours later the digger reached solid rock.

Damien touched the stone and sensed his marker on the other side. By some miracle he'd ended up exactly where he wanted to be. He reabsorbed the digger and buckets and settled in to sleep. Damien had been awake for thirty-six hours straight and used up a good portion of his soul force. Five hours of sleep would clear his foggy head and regenerate his lost power. Though he was eager to free the prisoners as soon as possible, rushing into it in his condition would most likely end with all of them getting killed.

A hint of sunlight glinted at the far end of his tunnel when he woke. His core had fully regenerated and all he lacked was a hot breakfast to be at his peak. Not feeling optimistic about a hot meal Damien reconnected with his spy bug and had it shift back into insect shape.

A different set of guards appeared on the viewing rectangle. They sat at the table eating bowls of heaven only knew what. Damien pointed at the wall and used a lance of golden energy to slice a disk out of the stone. He pushed it in and the instant the guards came into view spears of light pierced them with barely a sound.

Damien strode through the opening into the dungeon. The stink almost knocked him over. Women crowded the bars of the cells. He held a finger to his lips and they obliged him by staying silent. Two slices opened the locked cells. Damien motioned them out and toward the tunnel. Some walked, others limped, and two of the kids had to be carried out. For his part Damien watched the door to the dungeon and eased over to the table.

Up close the contents of the bowls turned out to be sausage gravy. Damien conjured a spoon and devoured the contents of two bowls before the last prisoner entered the tunnel. He followed along behind and ten minutes later everyone stood in the oasis taking turns drinking from the well.

An older woman with sunken cheeks, dark, matted hair, and haunted eyes approached him. “You’re a kingdom sorcerer.”

“Yes, ma’am. Whose wife are you?”

“I’m Baroness Trasker. May I assume my husband sent you?”

“No, ma’am. The king sent me to deal with what he assumed were traitorous barons.” The energy from the tunnel supports ran out, causing it to collapse. Damien winced at the noise. “I only learned your location and situation a day ago. I assumed rescuing you would end the traitorous baron situation. Rescued hostages are a much better result than executed nobles.”

“Heaven’s blessing on you, boy. I don’t know how much longer we would have lasted in that pit.”

“My pleasure, ma’am. When everyone’s had a drink I’ll fly us out of here.”

Chapter 43

Exhausted, sunburned, drenched in sweat, Baron Marris clung to the back of his trembling black gelding. The horse was on its last legs, but the fortress was in sight, close enough that he could make out the heavy, closed gate. The beast only had to last a little longer.

Yesterday—was it yesterday or the day before? Marris had lost track of time. Some time ago at any rate, Sloan had told him to ride ahead. The bandit leader said he'd stay behind, deal with the boy sorcerer, and catch up. Marris had seen nothing of the other man since.

Who would have guessed a sixteen-year-old brat and that skinny bitch of a diplomat could have so completely ruined his plans? He'd sacrificed everything to see the warlock's plans through. Not that his shrew of a wife and the two screaming brats were a huge loss, nevertheless he expected to get something for their lives. Right now he'd take a cold pitcher of wine and a rare steak.

His mount stopped and shuddered. Marris freed his foot from the stirrup and fell off its back just before the beast collapsed. He squinted into the predawn gloom. Maybe a quarter mile to go. The baron staggered to his feet. He could make it.

Marris pounded on the heavy doors. The lookouts had to have seen him. They were just letting him stew for a few minutes, to show him what they thought of him. He knew a power play when he saw one. They'd all learn soon enough who was the master's favorite.

A dull boom sounded from behind the doors a moment before they creaked open, just enough for him to slip inside. Blessedly cool air washed over Marris. A pair of rough men in soiled leathers with swords strapped to their backs pushed the doors closed and replaced the heavy bar.

Marris snapped his fingers. "Food and drink, now."

The men shared a look and led him deeper into the bleak fortress. The baron trudged along behind them, head hanging, sweat pouring off his back. He wouldn't give the bandits the satisfaction of collapsing. With grim determination Marris put one foot in front of the other until at last they reached the massive dining hall. Twenty people sat huddled together, heads down as they ate whatever passed for food in this place.

Marris turned to his guides. "Food. Drink. Now."

He plopped down on the nearest bench and sighed. The hard wood felt as fine as the softest chair in his castle. The two bandits shuffled toward the kitchen to fetch his meal. Not the most enthusiastic servants, but under the circumstances he'd take it. Maris laid his head on the table and shut his eyes.

A minute later a bowl of some white glop, a pair of biscuits and a chipped ceramic cup of water clattered on the table in front of him. He looked at his servant and raised an eyebrow. "What is this rubbish and where is your partner?"

"Breakfast. Mick went to fetch the master." So saying the unnamed bandit left him to his unappetizing meal.

Marris grimaced, but his empty stomach overruled his squeamishness. He dunked the biscuit in whatever the gravy was and popped it in his mouth. Surprised and pleased to find the mess edible Marris tucked in with a will. He'd nearly finished emptying the bowl and was considering who he could send for seconds when the clank of a heavy tread drew his attention.

A massive figure in black armor strode toward him, a horned skull engraved on his breastplate, the hilt of a sword jutting up by his shoulder. Marris's lip curled. The warlock's flunky, terrific. He'd hoped to find the master himself in residence, but wasn't shocked that he was absent. The armored figure removed his demonic helm revealing the surprisingly human face underneath.

"What are you doing here?" the flunky asked.

"Watch your tone or the master will hear of it."

The knight glowered down at Marris. "If you don't have a good reason for abandoning your task the master will let me peel the skin from your body to make a new pair of gloves. Now speak!"

"Our business with the barons has failed. The king's agents forced us to flee and I assume killed all the others."

"Someone killed Sloan?"

"I assume so since he never caught up to me. The point is I can't return to the kingdom now. I'll be assuming command here. You're welcome to serve as my subordinate."

A thump followed by a vibration that ran through the floor cut short any reply the flunky might have made. He mashed his helm back over his head and stalked toward the rear exit. Curious, Marris heaved his bulk up and followed along behind.

They reached the dungeon and Marris stared at the empty cells. All the prisoners had vanished. Four dead guards lay on the floor and piles of dirt covered the stone near the back wall. "What happened?"

The flunky rounded on him. "Someone dug a tunnel into the dungeon and freed my prisoners. Any idea who might have done that?"

Marris thought of the boy sorcerer. "I have a fair idea. One of the king's agents was a sorcerer. He pursued us and I suspect defeated Sloan and the others. Someone must have talked."

The flunky roared at the ceiling, pulled his sword, and rammed it through Marris's stomach. Pain became his whole world.

"If you can't return to the kingdom, what good are you?"

The last thing Marris saw was a black boot descending toward his face.

Chapter 44

Marris's skull crunched most satisfyingly under Mikhail's boot heel. Fat, useless worm. The master had made a grave error entrusting the incompetent baron with even the tiniest portion of this great task. Mikhail, no, Sir Darkness, had rectified that error.

Sir Darkness wiped the brains off his boot and stalked back up the stairs. Perhaps it would be best not to mention that the master had made an error in judgment with the baron. Sometimes the great warlock could be touchy about such comments. If he asked, Sir Darkness would simply say the baron had outlived his usefulness. Perhaps the escape of the prisoners could be pinned on him as well. The dead couldn't defend themselves after all.

At the top of the steps one of his minions waited, head bowed, showing the proper respect. "My lord, what is the trouble?"

"The prisoners have escaped."

"I'll organize search teams at once."

"No! I will deal with the prisoners and whoever took them myself. Keep everyone inside. It will be safer."

"As you command, my lord."

The Black Knight smiled behind his mask. That was the way he should be spoken to at all times. If his family had shown him such respect they might still be alive. But probably not. His father at least had to die in order for Sir Darkness to be born and rise to his current height. The rest were nothing but anchors holding him down. Better to cut them away so he could soar.

He reached the stables at the rear of the fortress. Horses snorted and whinnied in fear at his approach. Stupid beasts. Did they not realize what an honor it was to be chosen as the mount of Sir Darkness?

He dragged the first horse he came to out of its stall. The beast tried to resist, but it was no match for the strength granted him by his armor. When they reached the open center of the stable Sir Darkness poured corruption into the terrified horse. Its brown hair turned black and its eyes became flaming pits. The horse stopped fighting as the demonic power took control of it, bending the animal to his will and shaping it into an appropriate mount for Sir Darkness.

When the process was finished he grabbed a handful of its mane and swung up onto the horse's back. At the far end of the stables a hidden door let them out into the desert. The moment they left the fortress his mount leapt into the air. Mikhail sensed many life forces a short distance away at one of the oases that dotted the badlands. His prisoners were there. He would either reclaim them or send their souls to hell.

Chapter 45

Damien watched as the Baroness Trasker took her turn drinking from the little well. Somehow the woman managed to make drinking out of her cupped hands look dignified. When she straightened he asked, "Everyone ready?"

They all indicated they were.

"Then gather around."

The women and kids moved to join him. Some of the little ones had fallen asleep and their mothers carried them. He couldn't remember ever seeing such a bedraggled collection of people in his life.

A chill went through him and Damien looked up. A dark figure was riding across the sky on the back of a horse so dark it appeared to absorb the light. He narrowed his eyes and focused on the imposing figure. The horse was a seething mass of demonic energy, but nothing compared to the armor. A black cable of dark energy connected the rider to his mount.

Damien had read about men like him. They were called Black Knights. One step removed from actual warlocks, a Black Knight was a warrior who had formed a contract with a demon. The demon provided power to the knight. In exchange, at the moment of his death, the demon would consume the knight's soul thus increasing the demon's own power. His demon was bound to the ornate armor, much as Lizzy was bound to his father's sword.

Was this the same Black Knight the archmage mentioned in her account of Jen's adventure in Port Valcane? He hoped so. One of the monsters was bad enough.

Some of the children started whimpering and their mothers tried to calm them. Success seemed unlikely. The kids were feeling the effects of the Black Knight's corrupt aura.

"What is that thing?" the Baroness Trasker asked, disgust dripping from her voice. "That creature has been our captor these many weeks. Since the other one disappeared."

"He's trouble. Keep everyone together. It'll be easier for me to protect you that way."

"Won't we make an easier target, gathered all in one place?"

Damien really didn't want to argue with the woman, but the baroness wasn't used to taking orders. "Together or spread out, without my shield he'll kill you all in a second. Please, keep everyone together."

She pressed her lips in a thin line.

Please don't argue.

The Black Knight was getting closer by the second.

Please, please, don't argue.

"Very well, young man."

Thank heaven.

"I'll keep everyone together while you deal with that, I hesitate to call him a man, that thing."

The knight drew power from his armor and a ball of hellfire came screaming toward the oasis. Damien conjured a giant hand and swatted it aside.

The ball exploded a safe distance away. Wind mixed with corruption blew through the oasis. The children started crying and several of the women threw up. The Baroness Trasker never faltered. She guided the last two people into a tight group.

Damien conjured an invisible shield over them, investing a quarter of his power to be sure they'd stay safe. He hated going into battle with such a disadvantage, but anything less would leave the ladies and their little ones exposed.

He shot into the air and met the monstrous man a hundred yards from the oasis. Anxious to confirm his identity Damien asked, "Mikhail Santen?"

A hollow snarl came from inside the helm. "Don't call me that. Mikhail died when he sacrificed his father to gain the power of a demon. Sir Darkness was born in that moment."

"Sir Darkness? What a stupid name. Couldn't you have come up with something a little less idiotic?"

Mikhail drew his sword and leveled it at Damien. He drew power from the demon and sent a stream of fire roaring toward Damien.

Damien dodged easily enough, but like Sloan's attack earlier the fire twisted and pursued him.

This time Damien was ready. He spun away, conjured a golden sword, and severed the stream of fire from the demon's power. The hellfire behind him flared and vanished.

It worked, excellent. He fired a pair of golden blasts at Mikhail's chest.

The Black Knight didn't bother trying to dodge or deflect. The blasts hit his breastplate and fizzled. "Is that the best you can do?"

Damien frowned. He hadn't put much power into the blast, but he'd hoped to at least dent the armor.

Mikhail leveled the sword again. This time he drew a huge amount of demonic energy. "Burn away to nothing, worm."

A river of hellfire poured from the tip of Mikhail's sword. More power than the demon Damien killed had possessed in its whole body screamed toward him.

Damien drew deep from his core and raised a shield. He angled it to deflect the blast rather than take it full on.

Black fire hit golden shield. Cracks spread all over in his construct as the corrupt power ate away at it. Damien drew more power and repaired the damage.

Still the river of flames came on, no end in sight.

Damien poured more power into his shield, his vast reserve of soul force draining in a hurry. He had to hold on. If he failed, twenty-four women and children would stand defenseless before this monster of a man.

When only a small fraction of his power remained, the river dried up. Damien reabsorbed the meager energy remaining in his shield. Before him Mikhail's sword trembled in his hand. He'd used the bulk of his power with that attack.

Maybe Damien had a chance.

"Impossible!" Mikhail screamed in nearly inarticulate rage. "That should have reduced a worm like you to nothing."

Damien shrugged and began conjuring a pair of invisible swords behind Mikhail. If he could keep the idiot merchant distracted maybe he could take him by surprise. "It was an impressive attack from a halfwit greengrocer. I didn't think you could manage it."

"Greengrocer!" Mikhail shrieked.

That hit a nerve.

"I am Sir Darkness, right hand to the mightiest warlock in the land, Connor Blackman."

Blackman! This fool worked for the missing sorcerer? That must be who opened the hell gate in Port Valcane and gave Mikhail his demon armor. He probably put the hellfire wards in the bandits' heads too. No way this clown had the skill to do such fine conjuring.

Damien needed to end this and report back. The archmage had to know Connor Blackman had become a warlock and was behind the attack on the barons.

Damien's invisible swords struck Mikhail in the back. Armor screamed in protest as the soul force blades cut it open. Black fire burst from the rent in Mikhail's armor, shattering Damien's swords before they could pierce flesh.

The demon horse's mouth hung open and with Damien's enhanced sight it was clear the idiot had drained the beast almost dry. If Mikhail had possessed a fraction of Sloan's skill combined with the demon's raw power... Best not to think about it.

"You've proven a formidable opponent." Mikhail turned his gaze to the former prisoners huddling under his shield. "I wonder if the other worms will prove as durable."

Damien raced for the ground at full speed. Hellfire spewed from Mikhail's sword. A stream of soul force shot from Damien's hand, striking and reinforcing his barrier.

Black flames hit a moment later. Palm trees withered and turned to ash. The dirt blackened as the dark flames consumed every shred of life in them.

When the onslaught ended, his shield, cracked and wavering, still stood. The people inside remained unharmed.

Damien needed to end this. Now.

He absorbed and reshaped the shield into a focused blast, augmenting it with most of his remaining power. The golden lightning bolt streaked up at Mikhail.

It struck the side of the demon horse's head, burning off an ear and exposing its skull. An instant later it struck Mikhail in the shoulder. His armor gave way before the assault.

Mikhail roared in pain.

An armor-covered left arm came crashing to earth.

Damien crafted the last of his power into a crackling javelin and held it ready to throw.

The Black Knight snarled at him. "This is your lucky day, worm. We'll finish our battle another time."

Mikhail kicked the demon horse in the ribs and flew north, back into the kingdom. Damien waited until he was well out of sight before he collapsed to his knees. The javelin vanished when he absorbed the energy to refill a tiny portion of his depleted core.

As first missions went this one was turning out to be a doozie.

A gentle hand settled on his shoulder. Damien looked up into the concerned eyes of the Baroness Trasker.

"Are you all right?" she asked.

Damien sighed. He needed to rest and burn away the corrupted arm and armor Mikhail left behind before he flew the baronesses and their children home. "Sure. Just give me a few minutes to catch my breath and I'll get you people out of here."

Chapter 46

Lane squinted into the bright noon sky. On either side of her the nine barons did the same. Five minutes ago one of the guards, a loyal one, they'd left on watch had come running into the dining hall shouting about something in the sky flying their way from out of the badlands. Everyone had rushed into the courtyard then up on the southern wall. Either Damien was returning or he'd failed and the Bandit King was coming to exact his revenge for the barons' failure to live up to their agreement.

When the object got close enough Lane recognized it as a golden sphere. It had to be Damien. A warlock's power would be darker. Some of the tension went out of her. He'd survived. When one day passed, then another, she'd feared the worst for her young bodyguard.

The sphere passed over the wall and Lane realized it was bigger than she'd thought. It settled in the courtyard and vanished. Dirty women and children in torn clothes surrounded a slumped-over Damien. She joined the barons as they rushed down the stairs to seek out wives and children. Most of the normally stoic men wept openly as they gathered loved ones in their arms.

Damien straightened, caught her eye, and grinned. He was pale and had dark circles under his eyes. An ugly red burn decorated his cheek, but other than that he looked intact.

"The barons give you any trouble?" Damien asked.

Lane choked back a sob. He was worried about her. This young man she hardly knew, who'd just gone through hell if his face could be believed. She hugged him and he patted her back.

After a moment she let him go. "They behaved like gentlemen. Once their minders fled they had no more reason to be hostile. They threw the assassins, along with the servant in your wardrobe, in the dungeon before the bindings wore off. I think they were waiting to see if you succeeded in rescuing their families before they hung all four."

Damien nodded, seeming neither shocked nor surprised at the self-serving ploy. "What about their complaints against the kingdom?"

"They were pretexts to do what the Bandit King wanted. We had a meeting after your barrier vanished and they explained everything. With their families returned I don't think we'll have any more trouble."

"I hope you're right, but the king will have to make some changes down here all the same. The barons are too vulnerable to blackmail. I doubt His Majesty will leave them in charge of border security after this debacle."

Lane saw his point, but feared any drastic change would raise the prickly nobles' hackles. She wanted to ask what he thought the king would do, but the barons and their families had turned their attention to Damien. Everyone wanted to shake his hand and several of the wives and children hugged him with tears in their eyes.

Damien bore it all with a disconcerted look that made Lane smile. When the last of the hugs had been distributed Baron Trasker and his wife moved to the fore. As the oldest of the barons he often seemed to take the lead. Did that annoy the others or had they gotten used to it?

"I don't know how we can thank you for saving our families. It seems a miracle you returned everyone alive. Anything within our power to grant you, just ask."

"Which one of you is in charge of Allentown?" Damien asked.

That seemed to surprise the barons as much as it did Lane. Baron Kannon moved to stand beside Trasker. "Allentown is within my lands. Is there some problem?"

"The Lord Mayor is corrupt and I intend to remove him on my way back to the capital. I suggest you think of a replacement, one less susceptible to bribes and underage girls."

Kannon stiffened at Damien's cold tone. Lane would have to give him lessons in diplomacy on the trip home.

"Is the Lord Mayor's removal the reward you desire for saving our families? He's my cousin and it will be difficult to convince him to renounce his position, but I can manage it."

Damien's expression turned hard. "I require no reward for doing my duty, nor do I require your assistance or permission to remove the Lord Mayor. Eliminating corrupt officials is one of the responsibilities of a kingdom sorcerer. If I find the accusations against him true his head will decorate a flag pole at his residence before dark tonight."

Baron Kannon stalked off, muttering to himself. Lane debated going over to try and soothe him, but decided it wasn't worth the effort. If he knew about his cousin's actions he was lucky Damien decided to only punish the mayor himself.

"Are you ready?" Damien asked.

"What about horses? The bandits stole or drove off every mount in the stable."

He smiled at that. "I think it's safe to assume everyone knows I'm a sorcerer. How about I just fly us home?"

Lane looked away. She'd never been comfortable trusting a sorcerer to keep her from falling to earth. It seemed like such a precarious, unnatural thing, to fly without wings.

When she thought about flying with Damien she felt no doubts about his ability to keep her safe. If she were honest with herself the only real reason she hesitated was because the trip would only take two days and then they'd be home and go their separate ways. She found the idea left a hollow feeling in her chest.

"Flying would be okay, I guess. I started packing yesterday, more to keep busy than anything."

Damien nodded. "Then let's finish packing and get out of here."

Chapter 47

Damien stuffed his last tunic in his rucksack and slung his sword over his shoulder. Drawers opened and closed on Lane's side. It didn't surprise him that he finished first; Lane had three times as much stuff as him.

Someone knocked on his door. Damien was surprised to find Baroness Trasker on the other side. She'd washed up and found some clean clothes. She wasn't a beautiful woman. The lines of her face, the way she carried herself, everything was too harsh.

Damien bowed. "Ma'am?"

"Before you leave I wanted to thank you once more for what you did, both on my own behalf and for the others. Are you certain there's nothing we can do to reward you for your heroic actions?"

"There is one thing, Baroness. You and the other ladies can keep an eye on your husbands. Be their conscience, keep them on the proper path as good kingdom men. I don't want the king to have to send me back here looking for traitors. Your husbands love you. I could see it in their reactions when you got back safe. Keep them on the right path and I'll consider that reward enough."

The baroness pursed her lips. "You don't trust them?"

"The border's a long ways from the capital. They don't have anyone keeping an eye on them, though that may change after this incident. The temptation to cheat will always be there. Look at Marris. It won't end any better for the others if they make a similar decision."

"Rest assured all the ladies watch over their husbands, though Baroness Kannon mainly watches to make sure he doesn't pester the female servants too much. There's nothing else?"

"I am curious about something. I saw no sign of Marris's family."

"They're dead. The pig actually bragged about it. He liked to say if we didn't behave we'd join them soon enough." The baroness nodded and glided away down the hall, a slight limp the only sign of injury from her time in captivity.

Damien shut the hall door and frowned, trying to remember exactly what Marris had said when they spoke in his room. The baron had never actually said his family was alive. He'd said in one piece and like the inexperienced fool he was Damien assumed the rest. He wouldn't make that mistake again.

Lane opened the door connecting their rooms, three stuffed bags sitting on the floor behind her. "I thought I heard voices."

"Baroness Trasker stopped by to offer me one more bribe. I don't know what she hopes to accomplish beyond getting her hooks into me."

"Maybe she's genuinely grateful."

Damien raised an eyebrow at that. Nobles were seldom genuine and even less often grateful.

Lane shrugged and smiled. "I'm sure she had a good reason."

"On that, at least, we're in agreement." Damien conjured a box around her luggage and they set out for the courtyard. They passed a pair of servants who both curtsied. The barons and their families made no appearance which was fine with Damien. He'd probably offended them with his little speech to Kannon.

"Not much of a send off," Lane said.

"Disappointed?"

"Not especially. How will we be traveling?"

"Do you have a preference? I remember you mentioning a gold dragon."

She blushed a little at that. "I was being sarcastic. Perhaps something a little less ostentations."

Damien conjured a black horse with a double saddle. "How's this?"

"Much better."

Damien climbed up into the front saddle and reached back to help Lane up behind him. Remembering his first flight with Master Shen, Damien conjured a belt around Lane's waist to hold her in place. "Ready?"

"Ready."

The horse galloped into the air, Lane's luggage box right behind. She yelped and grabbed Damien around his chest. Damien grinned, but kept his face turned away so she wouldn't see.

They flew for a minute or two before she finally let go. Behind him Lane gasped.

"It's amazing. I've never seen the world from this high before."

Surprised, Damien asked, "Didn't you ever fly with your mother?"

"She offered to take me, but I wouldn't go. I was angry, a lot, when I was younger."

"So you naturally became a diplomat."

"The position got me away from sorcerers and the capital which helped with the anger. When we get back I need to talk to Mom, tell her I'm sorry for being so difficult."

Damien reached back and patted her knee. "I don't know your mother very well yet, but she was adamant that I keep you safe. Difficult or not I think she loves you very much."

Behind him Lane sniffed and a moment later her head pressed against his back. Damien suspected when they reached the capital many hugs and tears would be shared. He envied Lane the chance to get closer to her mother. He wished he had a similar chance with his father. Maybe if he tried harder to talk to Dad they could find some way to set aside the anger of the past few years.

A twenty-minute flight brought them to Allentown. Damien brought the conjured mount down a little ways out of town and transformed the box carrying their luggage into a mule. Now if anyone saw them they'd look like regular travelers, more or less.

"What now?" Lane asked.

Damien guided the construct toward the town gates. "Now I deal with the Lord Mayor, we head over to the Golden Stag for twelve hours' sleep, and in the morning we fly home."

Chapter 48

Damien and Lane walked through the afternoon shadows up the long path to the front door of the Lord Mayor's residence. He'd suggested Lane remain at the inn while he handled the mayor, but she insisted on joining him. Just to be safe he wrapped her in an invisible shield. Damien didn't expect any real trouble, but after everything they'd been through these last eleven weeks he'd hate for anything to happen to her now that they'd almost reached the end.

A pair of guards holding spears stood beside the pale wood doors. They looked young, older than Damien, but still young. They probably received the assignment straight out of training. They crossed their spears to bar his way. "The Lord Mayor isn't seeing anyone else today," the older guard said. "You'll have to come back tomorrow."

"I'm here to remove the mayor from office." Damien drew on his soul force and caused his shield to crackle. "I know his crimes. Stand aside or be judged with him."

"Please, sir, we have sisters. If we let you through we lose his protection. They may be taken. The Lord Mayor is a man of great appetites."

Damien crossed his arms and scowled. "So you serve this pig to protect your own families while others less fortunate have their daughters kidnapped and given over to his tender mercies. You dare call yourselves men of the kingdom? I should kill you both for your cowardice. Now get out of my sight before I change my mind."

Spears clattered to the ground and the guards fled back down the path. How had they even made it through training? Damien didn't know what sort of training the regular army required of its cadets, but if those two were representative they needed to improve their standards.

"Would you have killed them if they didn't run?" Lane asked.

"Of course not. They were only doing what they believed necessary to protect their families. Still, if they'd had the courage to run a spear through the mayor's guts when he came out this door some morning it would have saved a lot of people a great deal of trouble. I guess that's why the crown keeps people like me around."

Damien yanked the heavy iron door handle. It was barred from the inside. A golden blade made short work of that. The bar clattered to the floor and the doors swung open. Inside waited a grand foyer. Paintings, all of them erotic and explicit, decorated the walls and a pair of nude statues stood beside a sweeping staircase leading to the second floor. No guards waited inside the door. Either the mayor trusted the two outside combined with the bar to ensure his privacy or the guards were stationed elsewhere.

Damien glanced at Lane who was gaping at the artwork. "If you were a pig with grotesque appetites where would you be late in the afternoon?"

At the same moment they both said, "Bedroom."

Damien didn't know the layout of the place, but he figured the bedroom would be above. They went upstairs. The halls were lined with red carpet and more paintings like the ones below decorated the walls. If anything the ones on the second floor were more explicit and violent than the ones downstairs.

"I think I'm going to be sick." Lane stared at a painting of two little girls tied up, naked, getting spanked by masked men.

"Try not to look at them."

At the end of the hall a muffled thump sounded above them followed by a soft sob. Damien pointed at the ceiling and a cutting beam shot out. He sliced a disk out of the ceiling and let it fall to the floor. Staring down at them, his mouth partway open, was a fat, naked man with a scruff of gray hair around the base of his skull. He held a small, thin knife in his hand

Damien and Lane flew up into a bedroom-cum-torture chamber. One girl, she looked about Karrie's age, was tied to some sort of restraining device, her back covered in fresh welts, Damien guessed from the cat o' nine tails on the floor beside her. A second girl, younger yet, lay bound on the bed. She bled from three shallow cuts on her bare stomach.

"Guards!" the naked man bellowed.

The door burst open and four men with drawn swords rushed through. Fifty golden lances pierced the guards from every conceivable direction. Lane went to the bleeding girl and tore strips out of the bedding to make bandages.

"What do you think you're doing?" the fat man asked. "Do you know who I am?"

"You are a dead man," Damien said. "The only question I have is: are you the Lord Mayor?"

"I am." The fat man drew himself up to his less-than-impressive height. "Baron Kannon is my cousin and when he hears of this outrage he'll have your head."

"I've already informed him of your removal and advised him to find a replacement who's less corrupt."

The mayor lunged at Damien, striking him with the little knife. The blade bent in half when it struck Damien's shield. The mayor whimpered and held up the ruined weapon. "Please. I have gold, jewels. Please, take anything, everything, just let me go."

A golden band formed around the mayor's neck and Damien squeezed, choking off his pleas. Damien drew power, maybe a little too much power, and blasted the wall. It exploded out, reduced to little more than splinters. Damien hurled the mayor out the hole with way more force than necessary. His body exploded when it hit the ground.

Damien turned away from the hole and found Lane had bound the girl's wounds and dressed her in a thin shift. "Is she okay?"

"Physically she'll be fine. The cuts weren't deep." Lane stroked the trembling girl's hair. "Mentally I have no idea."

Damien went over to the second girl and cut her down. She latched on to him and cried. Damien held her and looked over her head for something he could dress her in. He spotted a dirty shift lying discarded in the corner. A tendril of soul force brought it to him and he got enough space between him and the girl to slip it over her head.

"Is he dead?" the girl asked.

"Yes. You're safe now."

"I want to see."

Damien winced when he thought of the mess he'd made out of the mayor. "It isn't pretty."

"Nothing about him was pretty. I want to see."

Damien guided her over to the hole in the wall. The girl stared for a long minute then spit on him. Damien couldn't help smiling. She had spirit. "Are there any others?"

"I'll show you."

In the next room three more girls, all of an age with the first two, sat huddled in an iron cage. None of them wore more than a stained shift. The girl spoke to them while Damien opened the cage. Once they had all the girls free he and Lane took them home. Long after dark they returned to the inn.

He walked with Lane to her room. They paused outside. "I never imagined it would have been that bad," Lane said.

"Me neither, but you know, this might be the best day I've had in my short career. I don't think I've ever done anything as satisfying as helping those girls. I hope they're okay."

"I think they will be, thanks to you." She kissed him. "Good night."

Damien touched his lips and stared at the closed door. What was that about?

Chapter 49

Karrie stalked towards the royal quarters. Servants hastened to move out of her way. Damien had been gone for almost two months and she'd considered and rejected half a dozen plans to convince him to agree to marry her. The problem she kept running into was none of them would work if he didn't fall in love with her and Damien had made it clear that while he did like her that was as far as it went.

Daddy should be done with court by now and back in their rooms for his noon meal. Her only hope was to convince him to force Damien to marry her. She knew he thought Damien would be a good match for her so it shouldn't be too hard to convince him.

Karrie pushed the door open and found her father seated at the dining room table, a plate of pasta in white sauce in front of him. He smiled when she entered.

"Hello, sweetheart. Will you join me?"

She'd get fat if she ate like her father, but she did sit beside him. "I need to talk to you."

"Of course. What's on your mind?"

She couldn't think of any way to say it other than to just say it. "I want you to order Damien to marry me."

He sucked in a breath along with his sip of wine. When the coughing subsided he asked, "What?"

"I know you think he'd be a good match for me. I spoke to him about it before he left on his mission, but he didn't seem interested. You could order him to do it, for the good of the kingdom."

"I don't think you've thought this through, Karrie. I have considerable power, but I can't command men's hearts. I think too much of Damien to force him into something like this, not to mention commanding someone to marry against their will is the sort of thing that could lead to a conclave."

Karrie shook her head. "I hardly think the generals and high sorcerers care enough about the fate of one man to consider removing you from the throne."

"No." Her father ran his hand through his hair. "But it is the sort of capricious use of power that they watch for. If I do it once I might do it again, for something bigger. Since our ancestors went from being imperial governors of a colony to kings of an independent country we've had a responsibility to rule for the good of all the people and not use the powers we've been given irresponsibly. The conclave system was set up to prevent any king from becoming a tyrant."

Karrie sighed. She'd learned all that from her tutors. "What's the point of being king if you can't do what you want?"

He smiled. "The point is to be a good steward and see that you leave the kingdom stronger, safer, and happier than your predecessor. Maybe you should forget about Damien and find another boy."

Karrie ground her teeth. She didn't want another boy, she wanted Damien. If her father couldn't help her maybe her mother could. She kissed his cheek. "Thanks, Daddy. Do you know where Mom is?"

"In her sewing room, I think. Oh, I forgot to tell you. I spoke to the archmage this morning. Damien should be home today, any time now in fact."

She brightened. If Damien was home she could start working on him again. She forgot about talking to her mother and jogged out to watch the front gate.

Karrie found an unused guest bedroom overlooking the courtyard, dragged a chair beside the window and settled in to watch. She had a bit of good luck. Less than an hour after she sat down a black horse flew over the wall and landed in the courtyard. Damien sat in the front saddle and Lane sat behind him, her arms around his chest in a way Karrie didn't like at all.

Damien swung down and reached back to help Lane dismount. They walked toward the castle together. Damien put his hand on her back in a far-too-familiar way. Daddy never should have sent him on a mission with Lane. The woman was too pretty and even if she didn't like sorcerers in general she seemed to like Damien well enough.

Karrie's lip curled into a snarl and she slammed her fist on the arm of her chair. If Lane had her hooks in him, how could Karrie dig them out? Mom would know. She rushed back to their quarters. Daddy had finished his meal and returned to his duties. Karrie hurried to the back of the suite and into her mother's sewing room.

Her mother sat in the sun, a delicate bit of needlework in her lap. "Karrie?"

"Damien's back. I think he's fallen for Lane Thorn. They looked way too friendly walking together."

"Hmm. That's a surprise. Everyone knows Lane hates sorcerers. Well, Damien is a handsome boy, so I can see where she might make an exception."

"Mom!"

"I'm sorry, sweetheart. I suppose you're planning to go to war with her?"

"I'm not going to let Lane have Damien. He's mine. What do we do?"

"You need to make him think he's going to lose you. Jealousy can be a powerful motivator for men. It's how I convinced your father."

"I'm not sure Damien would feel jealous if I went with someone else."

"It would have to be the right person. I made some quiet inquiries at The Tower. There are two people that might have the desired effect on Damien. His best friend John Kord and Sigurd Iceborn whom he fought a duel with his first day."

"Sig's an ass, but John is handsome enough. It might not be so bad spending time with him."

"Good choice. Nothing like seeing your best friend getting the attention of a girl you thought was interested in you. John is stationed with his father in the north. Perhaps we could arrange for him to come south. We could say you need a personal healer. That would give you a perfect excuse to spend time with him."

Karrie rubbed her hands together. She'd make Damien so jealous his head would spin. "How soon can he arrive?"

Chapter 50

Damien sat in a conjured chair outside the archmage's office while Lane gave her report. He suspected they'd have a good deal more than business to talk about so he made his seat more comfortable than usual. It was just as well his master's office was so far off the beaten path; it saved him many odd looks as he lounged in an overstuffed chair in the middle of the hall. Pleased as he was at having solved the border issue without having to kill any of the barons, Damien's mission had raised as many questions as it answered. The office door opened and Lane came out, her eyes and nose red.

"Did you have a good talk?" Damien stood up and absorbed his construct.

"Very good." Lane hugged him and kissed his cheek. "Thank you."

"For what?"

"For showing me what a brat, and worse, hypocrite, I'd been. I judged sorcerers for their power at the same time I hated being judged for my lack of power. Well, for now on I judge people as people, no more no less."

"I'm glad I could help. I'm sure it'll make you an even better diplomat."

"More than that, it'll make me a better person. Maybe I'll see you around."

"I'd like that." Damien smiled as she walked down the hall. When Lane had gone he rapped on the open door and stuck his head in. The archmage was wiping her eyes with a handkerchief. "Master?"

"Come in. Close the door."

Damien did as she said, taking his place in front of her desk, hands clasped behind his back. He felt her sound barrier fall into place.

"For heaven's sake, Damien, sit down. You don't need to stand like a man waiting for news of his execution every time you report in. Lane tells me you did good work, though she was a little vague on the details of what happened in the badlands."

Damien settled into an empty chair, still uncomfortable sitting in the presence of his superior. "I wasn't certain how much I should tell her. I figured I'd let you fill her in on any details she might need."

"Good decision. Why don't you just start at the beginning."

Damien did as she said. It took a good half an hour to complete his report and she never stopped him once. When he reached their arrival at the royal castle Damien said, "That's what happened. Mikhail Santen escaped and I'm sure many bandits still inhabit the fortress, but the families are safe, for the moment anyway."

The archmage shook her head. "Connor Blackman, who would have thought. We knew that boy was trouble, but to become a warlock and threaten the kingdom... I wouldn't have believed it. We need to find him, and Mikhail too."

"Yes, Master. The kingdom is a big place. Where should we start looking?"

"The Tower. Some of Connor's yearmates might have some insight into his habits. He must be in the wild lands. We could hardly miss a crimson-eyed warlock wandering around civilization."

"Judging from Mikhail's armor the Cult of the Horned One is involved somehow. I wonder if Connor summoned the demon I killed and opened the hell gate Jen found."

"I wouldn't be the least bit surprised." The archmage steepled her fingers, tapping the index fingers together as she thought. "In fact it wouldn't surprise me if he either took over the old cult or created a new one from scratch. On a more straight-forward note, good work dealing with the mayor of Allentown. I don't know how he operated without our notice for so long. I need to speak to Banlon about sending more sorcerers to patrol the little southern towns."

"Banlon?" Damien didn't recognize the name.

"Sorry, High Sorcerer Banlon, Master of the South. He's too interested in his research and it takes away from his more mundane duties. I never figured out why he stood for High Sorcerer at the last gathering."

Damien had no interest in politics. "What should I tell the king? I'm sure he'll want me to have dinner with him now that I'm back."

"I'll give him a full report, but if he asks hold nothing back. We have no secrets from the king." The archmage groaned to her feet and Damien leapt up to join her. "I knew I was right to make you my agent. This mission just solidifies it. On a personal note, I don't know what happened between you and Lane, but you brought home a different person. Wherever you buried her anger I'm glad to see it gone. For that gift I thank you, not as your master, but as a mother glad to see her daughter happy."

"She's a wonderful woman and I'm glad I got to spend some time with her. Is there anything else, Master?"

"No, take a few days, rest, relax. When you're ready come see me. I'm sure I'll have no shortage of missions for you."

Chapter 51

Mikhail hurt everywhere, but nowhere so much as his shoulder. His shoulder where an arm should have hung. Instead, his arm lay on the ground back in the badlands. All thanks to that puny worm. The boy had ruined everything. The horse under him shuddered. The beast had almost reached its limit. The animals could only bear the demonic energy so long before it burned them out. He'd have to land soon or risk falling to the mountains below.

Not that it mattered. Below him the entrance to his master's base was only half a mile away. The stupid animal could last that far anyway. A minute later Mikhail spotted the shadowed cave mouth. He urged the horse down.

It landed in a patch of snow, shuddered again, and collapsed. Mikhail held out his hand and absorbed the demonic energy he'd used to transform his mount. When the last of the power drained away from the horse, all that remained was a rotted corpse. He'd need a new mount. Mikhail rotated his damaged shoulder. He'd need a new arm as well, assuming the master didn't kill him.

Mikhail shook his head. Master Blackman wouldn't dispose of him so lightly. He was the master's strong right hand, well strong left hand anyway.

The tunnel had no lights burning anywhere, but to Mikhail's demon eyes the path was clear. He followed the rough passage for fifty paces, ignoring several side passages. With each step the master's power grew stronger. The warlock was probably brooding in his library again. He should get out more. It wasn't healthy to sit in the dark and think too much.

Mikhail barged into the library. The master sat on his black chair at the far end, turning his amulet over and over. Mikhail walked past the shelves and their demonic artifacts. The creepy things never did fascinate him like they did Morana.

He went down on one knee in front of the warlock. "Master."

Master Blackman looked up from his amulet. "What happened to you?"

"I was defeated, Master." The words almost stuck in his throat. He wanted to make excuses, but the master wouldn't accept them. "A sorcerer bested me and freed the prisoners."

"Took your arm as well." The master's cold voice was indifferent to Mikhail's suffering. "Tell me about this sorcerer."

"He wasn't much more than a boy, but he was strong and he fought well. Can you fix my arm, Master?"

"Morana warned me you weren't suitable for the task of being my knight. She said you were vain, weak, and stupid. Perhaps I should have listened. But you were so enthusiastic. You practically tripped over yourself in your rush to murder your father and take your place at my side. Now your incompetence has ruined my plans for our southern front."

Mikhail winced to hear his master lay out his many failings. To hear that Morana had tried to convince the master not to accept his service didn't surprise him. The bitch had always been jealous of him. "If you fix my arm I can make everything right. The women and children won't be difficult to reclaim."

"You truly are an idiot. General Taos will be on alert and the archmage will have sent more sorcerers to protect the border. No, that avenue is closed to us." Master Blackman rose up off his throne and walked through the shelves. He finally stopped and plucked a long, black, desiccated arm off a shelf. "Come here."

Mikhail stood and rushed over to his master's side.

"Don't move."

The master touched the stump of the arm to his shoulder. Black fire burst from the appendage. Pain such as Mikhail had never imagined screamed through his body as the flames fused the new arm to his shoulder.

When the pain died down Mikhail flexed the fingers of his new hand. They worked well and felt stronger than the one he lost. That it was an ugly, black, scale-covered thing seemed a small price. "Thank you, Master."

"Best be careful, Mikhail, I have no more spares."

"Yes, Master. What shall I do now?" He desperately wanted a new task to prove his worth.

"You will stay here and guard our base while I'm gone. You would have led the fight on the southern border, but that option is now gone."

"Please, Master, take me with you. Morana can—"

"Morana has her own work to do. Unlike you, she's never failed me. My own task is too important to have you getting in my way. I doubt anyone will stumble on this place, but if the wrong people should show up you will kill them. Surely you can manage that simple task."

The master's contempt clawed at Mikhail. He wanted nothing so much as to prove he was worthy to join the master when he ascended to true power. "No one will get past me, Master."

"Remember, only kill the wrong people. If some of our allies should show up I don't want to find their bodies bleeding on the stone. Everyone has their part to play if the plan is to succeed despite your failure. If you fail me again I'll have your own arm strangle you. Understand?"

"Yes, Master. I won't fail."

"Good. A new world is waiting for us, Mikhail. If you wish to see it you must prove your worth. Otherwise you burn with the rest of the garbage."

Author Notes

And so we reach the end of volume one. I hope you've enjoyed reading it as much as I enjoyed writing it. If you'd like to get a free story telling more about how Lizzy went from flesh and blood demon to sword spirit please sign up for my newsletter at signup.jamesewisher.com. I promise no spam, I hate it too. Just a monthly newsletter and, if anything interesting, like a new release, happens between letters, I'll let you know. I end this note by thanking you very much for reading my story and with the hope that you'll join me for volume two.

James E. Wisher

About the Author

James E. Wisher is a writer of science fiction and fantasy novels. He's been writing since high school and reading everything he could get his hands on for as long as he can remember. This is his seventh novel.

Made in the USA
San Bernardino, CA
14 February 2017